Praise for Keri Arthur

**Nominated for the *Romantic Times*
2007 Reviewers' Choice Award for
Career Achievement in Urban Fantasy**

**Winner of the *Romantic Times*
2008 Reviewers' Choice Award for
Career Achievement in Urban Fantasy**

"Keri Arthur's imagination and energy infuse everything she writes with zest."　　—CHARLAINE HARRIS

Praise for *Full Moon Rising*

"Keri Arthur skillfully mixes her suspenseful plot with heady romance in her thoroughly enjoyable alternate reality Melbourne. Sexy vampires, randy werewolves, and unabashed, unapologetic, joyful sex—you've gotta love it. Smart, sexy, and well-conceived."

—KIM HARRISON

"*Full Moon Rising* is unabashedly and joyfully sexual in its portrayal of werewolves in heat....Arthur never fails to deliver, keeping the fires stoked, the cliffs high, and the emotions dancing on a razor's edge in this edgy, hormone-filled mystery....A shocking and sensual read, so keep the ice handy." —*The Celebrity Café*

"Keri Arthur is one of the best supernatural romance writers in the world."　　—HARRIET KLAUSNER

D1040349

Praise for *Kissing Sin*

"Strong world-building, vivid personalities and the distinctive cultures of each of the various paranormal strains combine for a rich narrative, and Arthur's descriptive prose adds texture and menace."
—*Publishers Weekly*

"The second book in this paranormal guardian series is just as phenomenal as the first. . . . I am addicted!!"
—*Fresh Fiction*

"Riley Jenson returns with a vengeance in Keri Arthur's *Kissing Sin*. . . . The sex is hot and intense, but it doesn't detract at all from this fast-paced story."
—*Romance Reviews Today*

"Arthur's world building skills are absolutely superb and I recommend this story to any reader who enjoys tales of the paranormal." —*Coffee Time Romance*

"Fast paced and filled with deliciously sexy characters, readers will find *Kissing Sin* a fantastic urban fantasy with a hot serving of romance that continues to sizzle long after the last page is read." —*Darque Reviews*

"*Kissing Sin* will captivate readers from page one with its kick-ass heroine's struggle to do what's right without losing herself. . . . Keri Arthur's unique characters and the imaginative world she's created will make this series one that readers won't want to miss."

—*A Romance Review*

Praise for *Tempting Evil*

"Riley Jenson is kick-ass . . . genuinely tough and strong, but still vulnerable enough to make her interesting. . . . Arthur is not derivative of early [Laurell K.] Hamilton—far from it—but the intensity of her writing and the complexity of her heroine and her stories are reminiscent."

—*All About Romance*

"This paranormal romance series gets better and better with each new book. . . . An exciting adventure that delivers all you need for a fabulous read—sexy shapeshifters, hot vampires, wild uncontrollable sex and the slightest hint of a love that's meant to be forever."

—*Fresh Fiction*

"An amazingly awesome book that completely blew me away. Ms. Arthur's world building skills are absolutely second to none. . . . I simply must have more please, as soon as humanly possible. Five cups."

—*Coffee Time Romance*

"Pure sexy action adventure . . . If you like your erotic scenes hot, fast, and frequent, your heroine sassy, sexy, and tough, and your stories packed with hard-hitting action in a vividly realized fantasy world, then *Tempting Evil* and its companion novels could be just what you're looking for."　　　　　　　　　　　*—SF Revu*

"Keri Arthur's Riley Jenson series just keeps getting better and better and is sure to call to fans of other authors with kick-ass heroines such as Christine Feehan and Laurell K. Hamilton. I have become a steadfast fan of this marvelous series and I am greatly looking forward to finding out what is next in store for this fascinating and strong character."*—A Romance Review*

Praise for *Dangerous Games*

Finalist for the 2008 Fantasm Award for Best Urban Fantasy Romance

"*Dangerous Games* is by far one of the best books I have ever read. . . . The storyline is so exciting I did not realize I was literally sitting on the edge of my chair seat. . . . With this series, Ms. Arthur has a real winner on her hands. Five cups."　　　　*—Coffee Time Romance*

"The depths of emotion, the tense plot, and the conflict of powerful driving forces inside the heroine made for [an] absorbing read."　　　　　*—SF Revu*

"This series is phenomenal! *Dangerous Games* is an incredibly original and devastatingly sexy story. It keeps you spellbound and mesmerized on every page. Absolutely perfect!!"　　　　　　*—Fresh Fiction*

Praise for *Embraced by Darkness*

"Takes on a much more mature tone, at least when it comes to Riley and her men . . . Add to that plenty of action and intrigue, and readers will definitely want to be *Embraced by Darkness.*"

—*Romance Reviews Today*

"Reminiscent of Laurell K. Hamilton back when her books had mysteries to solve, Arthur's characters inhabit a dark sexy world of the paranormal."

—*Parkersburg News and Sentinel*

"Packed with fast-paced action, paranormal intrigue and passion at every turn, *Embraced by Darkness* is a steamy addition to this thrilling series."

—MediaBoulevard.com

"I love this series."　　　　　　—*All About Romance*

Praise for *The Darkest Kiss*

"The paranormal Australia that Arthur concocts works perfectly, and the plot speeds along at a breakneck pace. Riley fans won't be disappointed."

—*Publishers Weekly*

Destiny Kills

**2008 *Romantic Times* Reviewers' Choice
Nominee for Best Contemporary
Paranormal Romance**

By Keri Arthur

Beneath a Rising Moon

BENEATH
a
RISING MOON

KERI ARTHUR

DELL
NEW YORK

Beneath a Rising Moon is a work of fiction. Names, characters, places, and incidents either are the product of the author's imagination or are used fictitiously. Any resemblance to actual persons, living or dead, events, or locales is entirely coincidental.

A Dell Mass Market

Copyright © 2003, 2012 by Keri Arthur

Excerpt from *Beneath a Darkening Moon* by Keri Arthur copyright © 2012 by Keri Arthur

Published in the United States by Dell, an imprint of The Random House Publishing Group, a division of Random House, Inc., New York.

Originally published in different form in paperback in the United States by ImaJinn Books, Hickory Corners, MI, in 2003.

DELL is a registered trademark of Random House, Inc., and the colophon is a trademark of Random House, Inc.

ISBN 978-0-440-24649-7

This book contains an excerpt from the forthcoming novel *Beneath a Darkening Moon* by Keri Arthur. This excerpt has been set for this edition only and may not reflect the final content of the forthcoming edition.

Cover design: Lynn Andreozzi
Cover illustration: Juliana Kolesova

Printed in the United States of America

www.bantamdell.com

9 8 7 6 5 4 3 2 1

Dell mass market edition: August 2012

AUTHOR'S NOTE

THE RIPPLE CREEK werewolves differ from the werewolves of Riley Jenson's world. While many similarities exist—such as soul mates and swearing your love to the moon—there are just as many differences. These books were the start of my journey into the werewolf realm, and it was these books that gave life to the world that became Riley Jenson's.

I hope you enjoy them!

Chapter One

THE MUSIC SWIRLED through the darkness, its beat rich and seductive. Night cloaked the ballroom—a mantle challenged only by the occasional flicker of a torch burning high on the rough-hewn stone walls. On the dance floor, couples swayed to the music, their bodies so close they almost seemed to be one. Heat and sweat mingled with the growing odor of lust and need—scents that stirred her senses, made her hunger.

Neva Grant looked uneasily over her shoulder. Though the moon was masked beneath the clouds that crowded the night sky, she could feel its presence. Feel its power.

The full moon was too close. She shouldn't be here. She shouldn't be doing this when the wildness within was so close to the surface.

But she'd made her promises, and she intended to see them through—no matter what the cost.

She let her gaze roam the dance floor again. Somewhere down there, a killer lurked. A man who was using this secluded, exotic retreat as his own private hunting ground.

A man she had every intention of finding. And slaying.

She raised her glass and finished the last of her wine. The alcohol slithered warmth through her body, and perspiration beaded her skin. Hunger rose, flashing white-hot through her veins. She closed her eyes and took a deep breath.

Not tonight. Please, not tonight.

But the pulsing need suggested it was already too late for such prayers. The wildness had woken. It would not remain leashed for long.

Maybe she shouldn't even bother trying. The killer seemed to be choosing the more adventurous of this wanton crowd. Unleashing the wildness might be the quickest way of attracting his attention.

Bile rose up her throat and she swallowed heavily. While she had no real choice about what she had to do tonight, she wasn't about to give the wolf within free rein. She wasn't like any of the hunters who danced on the floor below. Her world was one of sunshine and restraint, of trying to live normally.

These people rejoiced in the night and the power of the moon. They came to this mansion for the freedom and the safety it offered, seeking to sate the moon-spun lust surging through their veins. That was why most of the men were naked, and why most of the women wore little more than wisps of material that covered everything yet left nothing to the imagination. Only their faces were concealed. Once the moon's spell had faded and daylight returned, they would return to their packs, picking up their lives where they'd left off, not knowing the faces of any of those they'd chosen to mate with.

Unlike her pack, these wolves were free spirits, exhilarated by the thrill of the chase, by the excitement of capture and possession. The belief in one mate, one life partner, had never touched these dark halls.

But for her promise, she would not be here tonight.

She put aside her glass, then adjusted her ornate mask and made her way down the stairs. The deeper shadows that lined the walls were filled with hunters in various stages of mating. She forced her gaze away even though the wildness within yearned to watch. Hungered to join them.

Her stomach turned again. God, she hated this place. Hated everything it represented. Given the choice, she'd rather burn the Sinclair estate to the ground than be walking its halls. She wasn't a prude; far from it. She'd given in to the power of the moon more than once herself. But if it wasn't for this place, if it wasn't for the wanton and careless behavior of its guests, her twin sister would not now be lying in the hospital, so close to death.

Tears stung her eyes, and she took a deep breath. *Don't think. Just do.*

She moved onto the dance floor, inching her way past the slowly dancing couples. Her pulse throbbed in time to the music's heavy beat, and the deep-down ache grew stronger.

She clenched her fists and made her way toward the rear exit. She'd spent most of her adult life fighting the worst of her desires, and she would not give in now. Not even here in this place of dark freedom.

And yet, at the same time, she knew she'd do whatever she had to—even unleashing the wildness—if it led her to the man who had attacked her twin.

She'd studied the files in Savannah's office before she'd come down here this evening. The killer had struck three times—each time near dawn and just beyond the boundaries of the Sinclair mansion. The victims were always alone, though forensics had, not surprisingly, found evidence to suggest each victim had taken more than half a dozen lovers the night of their deaths. Savannah and the other werewolf rangers who patrolled the Ripple Creek Reservation—which was the mountain homeland of the four Colorado wolf packs—believed that the killer was shadowing his victims as they left the mansion, and attacking once they were clear. But they had no proof of this—nothing more than scents and suspicions. And neither of those were admissible in court, be it human or werewolf.

Savannah had been following one such scent when she'd been attacked by a silver wolf. Only the fact that she'd been in wolf form herself had saved her. The winter coat of their tribe was thick, and the silver wolf had been unable to gain a true grip around her sister's throat. But even so, her wounds were multiple and life threatening.

And Neva had shared the last, terrifying moments of her twin's horror. While she never wanted to go through something like that again, in the end it was the link between them that had saved Savannah. Her sister had siphoned Neva's stronger psychic abilities and used them to finally fend off her attacker.

Neva closed her eyes and took a deep breath. Even now, her sister's pain edged Neva's consciousness. When she'd left home this evening, the doctors still weren't sure if Savannah would survive. Even *she* couldn't say with any degree of certainty. Savannah was hanging on by the slenderest of threads, and it wouldn't take much to snatch that lifeline away.

Which was why Neva had touched her twin's unresponsive mind and made a silent vow: she'd hunt down the killer and finish what her sister had started if Savannah found the strength to live.

It may have been foolish, but it was better than sitting at home, waiting for the worst.

But unlike Savannah, she was no ranger. Far from it. She had no idea how to load a weapon, let alone shoot, and she only had a wolf's natural skills when it came to tracking. But she was still far from defenseless. Like most of the wolves of her tribe, she rated high in telepathy, but she was also almost off the scale empathically. The two abilities combined could be a deadly weapon if one knew how to use them properly—as the wolf who'd attacked Savannah had learned.

So far, Neva had kept her shields up tonight. Skimming the minds of hunters when the moon bloomed was far too dangerous and would attract the kind of sexual interest she was trying to avoid. Besides, she might just alert the killer she was here, seeking him.

The rangers believed it was probably one of the Sinclairs behind the killings, but they were a large and closemouthed pack and had yet to provide the rangers with any real help. And while the Sinclairs were all silver wolves, like the one who had attacked her sister, they did not have a monopoly on the color. Even in her own pack, which were primarily golden-coated, silver could be found.

No, she'd never find the killer roaming the outskirts

of the Sinclair stronghold. It was doubtful if even the rangers could. It had to be done from within. And there was only one way she could achieve that. Goose bumps skated across her skin, and she sent a silent prayer to the moon for strength.

She'd spent a good part of the day studying the Sinclair lineage. The wolf she'd chosen to seduce was the pack leader's third son. By all accounts, he was the wildest of them all, but he was the only one who'd been away from home when the first two murders had occurred. So he was safe—or as safe as any of the Sinclairs could be.

She'd also spent time studying the mansion's floor plans before coming here, and she had talked to Betise, a regular customer at her family's diner. Though barely thirty-six, Betise had been attending moon dances at the mansion for a good twenty years and knew the place almost as well as the Sinclairs themselves. It had been Betise who told her that Duncan Sinclair rarely joined the dance before midnight, and that before then he could usually be found close to his rooms on the west side of the mansion.

Of course, he'd been away for ten years, and anybody—even the wildest of the wild—could change in that amount of time. But for her sister's sake she had to hope that wasn't the case.

She hurried out the rear doors. The night breeze stirred her flimsy skirt. Its touch was cool against the fever-kissed skin of her thighs. She glanced skyward again, judging the time by the position of a moon she could feel, not see. Close to midnight. She had to hurry. She tugged the delicate material clear of her bare feet and ran to the back of the mansion.

A cherub-filled fountain came into sight. She slowed, scanning the windows until she found his. Her heart was beating so fast it felt as if it would tear free of her chest, and she knew the cause was fear, not exertion. She'd never done anything like this before. She didn't know if she even had what it took to attract, let alone hold, a wolf with Duncan Sinclair's experience.

But she had to try. It was the safest way to gain full access to the mansion.

She could smell only one wolf in the rooms above, and there were no others in the immediate area. So Betise's information had been accurate. If she pulled this off, Neva was going to keep the woman supplied with free coffee for the next year.

She walked over to the fountain and stripped off the flimsy excuse for a gown. Then she stepped into the icy water, avoiding the most vigorous of the water-spewing cherubs as she turned her attention to his window.

Everything she'd learned about Duncan Sinclair suggested he liked a chase and preferred his mates to be sexually adventurous. While she could never claim to be that, she was a wolf, and the moon was high. And Betise had offered more than a few tips.

But she couldn't exactly send out a blatant invitation to the man. The rules of the moon dance said no names, so she had to be a little more devious. The Sinclairs were the only other wolf pack who were strong telepaths, so she just had to make it seem he was catching her thoughts.

Lord, I ache tonight.

She kept her mind voice breathy, wistful. For several tense seconds, nothing happened, then his presence stirred and he walked across to the windows. She dipped her fingers into the water and wet her neck, letting the cool droplets dribble between her breasts.

Hunger surged through the night—a force so strong it almost knocked her over. His need for the dance was high. Very high. The thought churned her stomach, but she was here now and would not back away.

She let her gaze roam the windows until she saw him. If his shadow was to be believed, he was big. Bigger than she'd expected. She cupped another handful of water, sipping it quickly to ease the dryness in her throat.

Why do you ache? The moon is high and the night free.

His mind voice was rich and husky, and stirred her senses with longing. She clenched her fists. She had to remain in control. She couldn't let the wildness free.

Perhaps I am choosy.

You can be choosy as many times as you like on a night such as this. Amusement swam across her senses, warm and sensual.

Perhaps I long for a more careful seduction once the initial fire has passed.

His silhouette stirred. She caught the brief glimpse of a muscular arm before the shadows closed in again. *A difficult request when the moon rides high.*

So it would seem. She arched her back, stretching her arms skyward. The emotive swirl of his thoughts became a wall of heat. He wanted her, of that she was certain. Whether he would take her was unclear. He hadn't yet moved from his dark hideaway.

Perhaps I should go home. The moon, it seems, offers me no comfort tonight.

He hesitated. *Perhaps we should talk further on the matter.*

The bait had been taken. Now to snare him fully. But the elation that ran through her was tempered by the knowledge that true victory would mean spending the rest of the week in this man's bed. But it was a small price to pay when her sister's life hung in the balance.

She considered him a moment longer, not wanting to seem too eager. *You are little more than a shadow to me. I cannot discuss possibilities with someone I cannot see.*

The French window opened and he stepped out onto the balcony. Her heart slammed into the wall of her chest, then it seemed to drop somewhere to the vicinity of her toes.

He was tall, close to six feet, if not over, his build quietly powerful but lean like an athlete's. His hair was dark and long, full of unruly waves that brushed his shoulders. His face was that of a dark angel's— beautiful and yet somehow sinister. And while it may have been true that the eyes were the window of the soul, this man's were shuttered and black. There was nothing to be read in his expression—or the lack of it. If not for the hunger that burned between them, she would have thought him uninterested.

Do you like what you see?

She gave a disinterested shrug. *Looks are not the measure of the man.* Even though *this* man's looks were stirring her in ways no man's ever had before.

A wise statement for one so young.

She raised her eyebrows, a smile teasing her lips. *And that is a very condescending statement from one likewise so young.*

Amusement touched his sensual mouth. He crossed his arms and continued to regard her in that oddly disturbing manner of his.

I have squeezed many years of living into this young body, believe me.

So his reputation had suggested. Had she any other choice, she would have stayed far away from this particular wolf and his wild, hungry ways. But he was the only Sinclair the rangers did not have under suspicion and, therefore, her safest route into the Sinclair stronghold.

Ah. Then perhaps you have little interest in one less well traveled. She picked up her gown and pulled it on. The sheer material clung to her damp breasts and caressed her aching nipples. Again his need swam around her, leaving her breathless.

I did not say that.

No. She hesitated and stepped from the water, then raised her gaze challengingly to his. *I intend to leave. But if you can find me before I depart these grounds, we shall indeed . . . talk . . . more on this matter.*

She turned around and walked away, not looking back. Yet his gaze burned into her back as surely as his hunger sent a fever blistering across her skin. He would come for her, she was certain of that.

Now all she had to do was pray she could hold his attention for more than just one night.

•

Duncan Sinclair moved through the crowd, silent as a shadow. Unnoticed, unseen. The music pounded through his veins—a heavy, throbbing beat that matched his need.

He'd had no intention of joining the dance tonight. He'd wanted nothing more than to complete his task and leave as quickly as possible. But his intentions had flown out the window the minute he heard the wanton, wistful thoughts of that woman.

He let his gaze roam the darkness. There was still a wealth of unclaimed flesh ready for the taking, but most of the women were longtime participants of the dance, as jaded as the night itself.

Not so the wolf who'd played in the fountain outside his rooms. There was a freshness about her, a vibrancy, which suggested she was new to the mansion and the dance.

She was here somewhere. He could sense her. She was a teasing hint of sunshine in the darkness, a caress of warm shyness that taunted the outer edges of his mind.

He wanted her. God, how he wanted her.

He continued on through the crowd and made his way out the rear doors. The night breeze riffled cool fingers through his hair, but it failed to ease the fever pulsing through his body.

She was close. The musky scent of the female stirred the air, mixed with the gentle tang of jasmine. He walked through the stand of aspens that divided this section of the house from the main gardens, his strides long. If she was indeed leaving, she would have to depart through one of three gates. The gate closest to his room lay behind the summerhouse. He made his way past the grand old pavilion, but her scent didn't linger there. She hadn't come this far yet.

He backtracked to the summerhouse and there he found her. Stopping in the shadow-filled pavilion, he once again drank in the sight of her. She was small and delicately built—not what he usually chased, that was for sure. Her hair was a silky wave that brushed her hips, and a deep gold in color. She still wore the mansion's gown, and the gossamer material hid little. He hungrily surveyed the lean length of her—from the proud thrust of her breasts to the dark gold triangle of hair between her thighs, then down the long length of her legs to her toes and back up again.

Her mask was heavily ornate and hid most of her features. But even from where he stood, he could see her eyes. They were the green of a newborn leaf, rich and exotic.

The heat in his loins became an ache that almost consumed him. He had to have her. Now.

He moved out of the shadows. Uncertainty flickered in her beautiful eyes, then she came toward him. Her gaze boldly traveled the length of his body, seeming to linger on the hard evidence of his excitement before finally rising again to his face. Her nipples were puckered, straining against the gossamer gown—evidence of the desire he could clearly smell.

She entered the pavilion and stopped in front of him. The musky scent of her desire grew stronger, fueling his already-raging need. But he wasn't the only one aching with the night and the moon.

"So you found me."

Her voice was huskier than before, but still as

smooth as silk, as rich as velvet. Despite the heat that surged between them, her gaze was cool. Wary.

"Yes."

He touched her cheek, running his fingers down to the warm fullness of her lips. She trembled under his caress but didn't back away.

"So you wish to discuss the matter further?" she asked.

"No. What I wish is to dance with you."

The words were little more than a formality. She'd all but consented to his advances back there in the fountain.

Panic flitted through her eyes, making him wonder just *how* new she was to the mansion and its ways. Certainly he'd never seen her here before, but then he'd been away for nearly ten years.

She swallowed convulsively. "Indeed?"

He moved his hand down the long line of her neck. Her pulse was a wild flutter under his fingertips. "Indeed."

"And what of my desire for a more lingering seduction once the initial fire has gone?"

He let his hand drift down to her breasts and gently rubbed one nipple through the film of her dress. She shivered, her lips parting a little, as if she couldn't suck in enough air.

"I think that could be arranged."

She closed her eyes briefly. "One night holds no interest for me this phase."

"But you have not yet sampled the goods and cannot say whether one night or more will be enough." He leaned close, his mouth capturing hers, gently demanding.

For the briefest of moments, she froze, her lips hard and unyielding under his. Then she sighed and seemed to melt toward him, deepening the kiss, opening her mouth, letting him explore more fully.

Heat shivered through his soul, and the urgency increased tenfold. He wanted her as he'd wanted no other in his life, and the effort of holding back—of not taking her right then and there—had every muscle trembling.

But she had yet to say yes. Until she did, he couldn't take her fully. There were rules—even here in this mansion that some called a den of debauchery.

He slid his hand down her waist and found the slit in her skirt, touched the silk of her thigh and worked upward. He cupped the triangle of her curls, then gently delved into her moist heat.

Her moan shuddered through him, testing his strength, his will. He delved deeper, sliding through her slickness, until her muscles pulsed around one finger, then two. She pressed against him, riding his hand with increasing urgency. Her skin was feverish, flushed with desire and need.

A need he understood only too well.

She grabbed his shoulders, fingers trembling, nails digging deep.

"By the moon." Her voice was little more than a fractured whisper. "Please . . ."

Her plea raged across his senses, almost destroying his control. Yet at the same time, an oddly primeval sense of power surged through him. She was his for the taking, whether she'd admitted it or not.

He stroked harder, faster. Her body shuddered against his, her skin glossy with perspiration. He kissed her ear, ran his tongue down the long line of her neck. She tasted of honey, desire, and sunshine—and he knew then she was a wolf who played in the daylight more often than in moonlight. They lived in two different worlds—but right then he didn't care. She'd stepped into his realm, and he intended to take every advantage of it.

He took a nipple into his mouth, sucking hard through the gossamer material. Her shuddering reached a crescendo, and her cry of pleasure sang through the night. He knew he could take her higher, deeper, than what she'd already tasted.

He slid his fingers free of her and began undoing the ties of her gown. Her eyes, darkened by a mix of pleasure and surprise, flew open.

"Dance with me." The ancient, formal words of binding slipped hastily off his tongue, his voice little more than a hoarse whisper. "Let your body join with mine and rejoice in the power of the divine light."

He slid the gown from her shoulders and let it fall to the ground. Her skin was pale gold silk and glowed softly in the darkness. Her breathing was quick and sharp, every intake seeming to shudder through her body.

He pushed her back until she was trapped against the wall of the pavilion. The heat of her washed across his senses, and the wild beat of her heart was a siren's song that fueled his urgency to greater heights. It was all he could do to simply stand there, his body pressed hard against hers, seeking and yet not entering.

"This night," he continued raggedly, "and the remaining nights of this phase."

An odd mix of apprehension and elation ran through her eyes. She took a deep breath, then released it in a shudder. "This night," she whispered, "and the remaining nights."

Mine. With savage exaltation he surged into her, groaning in bliss as her muscles contracted against him. God, was there a sweeter sensation on this earth? He slid his hands down her hips and cupped her buttocks. "Wrap your legs around me."

His demand was little more than a growl, but she seemed to understand him. Her legs wrapped around his waist and her arms slipped around his neck. His movements became hard and fast, hot flesh slapping against hot flesh. There was nothing gentle about this mating. There couldn't be, not with the heat of the moon riding them both so fiercely. Gentleness would come later, once the initial urgency had gone.

He claimed her mouth, kissing her ferociously. Passionately. Their tongues dueled, explored, the rhythm echoing the thrusting of his hips.

The red tide rose, becoming a wall of pleasure he could not deny. His movements quickened. Deepened. Her gasps reached a second crescendo, and her cries echoed across the silence as her body bucked against his. And he came—a hot, torrential release whose force tore a shout from his lips.

He couldn't say how long they stood there like that, bodies locked together, the night air gradually cooling their fever-kissed skin. It could have been minutes, or it could have been hours.

It could have lasted an eternity and he wouldn't have cared.

He breathed in the scent of her—the sweet flowery

tang of jasmine mingled with the more evocative musk of femininity and sex. He couldn't remember a time when he'd felt more satisfied, more fulfilled. And yet there was so much more to come. This delicate beauty had agreed to be his not only tonight but for the remainder of the week. They had the time to explore each other more fully. It was a thought that sent a jolt of primitive pleasure coursing through his veins.

He kissed the pulse point in her neck. Felt the still erratic flutter under his lips.

"Do you have a name?"

It was a question he had no right to ask. No names, no faces. Those were the rules set by his ancestors long ago—rules he'd abided by until now. But if she was new to this place, she might not be aware of them. There was something about this woman that intrigued him in a way no other had, and he had no intention of simply letting her walk away in the morning without some means of finding her should she decide not to return. Not after he'd sampled the delights she had to offer.

Tension crept through her limbs. She was still trembling, but he couldn't say whether its cause was his closeness or something else.

"Neva." Her breath whispered past his ear, a heated touch that stirred barely sated embers. "Yours?"

"Duncan."

She unwrapped her legs from his waist and he carefully lowered her to the ground. Though her gaze met his without a qualm, the rush of color through her pale cheeks suggested she was not as bold as she was making out.

She tucked silken wisps of gold behind her ears. "Do you come here often?"

"Not recently." Not since he'd left this place ten years ago in an effort to find something more—something sweeter and longer-lasting than the random empty pleasures that still filled the Sinclair mansion. "You?"

"My first time." Reluctance filled her voice, and the red bloom in her cheeks grew. "I wasn't sure if I was doing the right thing or not."

He was glad she'd taken the chance. Glad it was he who'd heard her wistful thoughts. He touched a hand to her cheek. "And now?"

A smile teased her lips. "I'm more uncertain than ever."

"Then I shall endeavor to prove your decision was no mistake." He leaned forward, needing to taste her again.

Her eyes widened slightly and her uncertainty surged, crowding his mind. Despite her promises, she still wasn't sure about him. Not that it really mattered now. While it was a female's right to pick and choose as she pleased, once she had said yes to mating, the male had the right to enforce it. And he would do so, if that's what it took to keep her by his side these next few nights.

Her mouth was warm and sweet under his, and as the kiss deepened, the moon's heat began to burn through his veins again. But this time, he would pleasure her more fully.

A howl sang through the night—the cry of a wolf in trouble. But not just any wolf. His brother.

What? He broke off the kiss and stepped back. The

night was silent for several seconds, then the howl came again. A long, demanding note.

René was either out of range or simply too angry to hear any mind contact.

"Trouble?" She rubbed her arms, her eyes haunted, sad.

He touched a hand to her cheek and wondered what she sensed. Even though he could feel only anger, the golden wolves were the more powerful telepaths. She was probably picking up a lot more than him. But she wasn't from his tribe, and he had no right—and no wish—to involve her in any way in his problems.

"I'm afraid so. Will you wait here or would you prefer to go to my rooms?"

She hesitated, and again her reluctance washed around him. She didn't want to face the moon-hungry pack again, and of that he was fiercely glad. He wasn't in the mood to fight tonight, though he would if another tried to usurp his claim on her.

"Here," she responded at last.

He touched her lips, outlining their kiss-swollen sweetness. "Then I won't be long."

She nodded, her gaze searching his, green depths filled with uncertain wariness. "Be careful."

He raised an eyebrow, but again restrained the urge to ask what she sensed and called instead to the wildness within him. His body became liquid, flowing from one shape to another, then he was on all fours and running through the trees.

He found René just outside the main gates. And at his brother's feet lay the mangled, bloody remains of what once had been a woman.

Chapter Two

THE MINUTE HE left, Neva slid down the wall, shuddering, hugging her knees close to her chest and taking deep, careful breaths. But it didn't help the churning in her stomach. Didn't help the deep sense of loathing coursing through her.

Everything she'd believed in, everything she'd been taught, had slipped away under the raging of the moon and the smooth skill of his hands. And he'd proven her as wanton as any of those in the hall below, despite the high ideals she'd spouted half her life.

A sob tore up from her throat, followed quickly by a rush of bile. She scrambled to her feet and raced out to the nearest tree, where she lost what little she'd eaten for dinner.

When there was nothing left to lose, she made her way back to the pavilion and sat on the steps.

Moons, what was she going to do?

She closed her eyes and leaned her head against the wall. It wouldn't have been so bad if the whole episode had been nothing more than a quick, heated mating in which there'd been little pleasure. That was all she'd been expecting, and something she could have survived. But this man's touch was like no other. His caresses sang across her skin, his kisses seared her mind. And his scent invaded every pore, claiming her just as surely as his body had.

Lord, even thinking about him made her ache. And it was *that* fact, more than anything, that frightened her most.

Duncan Sinclair was the wildest of the wild. His ferocious appetite for women and sex was renowned—a fact she'd been well aware of when she had set out to seduce him. But she simply hadn't expected her own intense reaction to the man. Her cheeks flamed as she remembered the way she pressed against his hand, wanting, seeking so much more than just his fingers. She'd howled in pleasure when he'd thrust into her, for the moon's sake. *Howled.* She, who'd once sworn to give no wolf the satisfaction of her cries until she met the one destined to be her life mate.

And Duncan wasn't that. He could never be that. By all accounts, the longest he'd ever stayed with a mate was one phase of the moon—which was the second major reason she'd chosen him. A phase gave her enough time to hunt down a killer before escaping.

But after one, all too brief, dance, she very much suspected she wouldn't *want* to leave after only a week of his caresses. A chill ran down her spine. What if she became so addicted to the fever of his touch that she came back, night after night, hungering for something he would no longer give? What if she became just another rabid seeker of pleasure like so many others in the hall below?

She took a deep breath and tried to calm her thoughts. One night of pleasure—or two or three—would not make her a slave of the moon. She was stronger than that. It was stupid to believe that the touch of *any* man could destroy her beliefs in such a short time, no matter how good that touch was. Her fear, her uncertainty—it was little more than the shock of discovering that she was as capable of yielding to the wanton fever of the moon as anyone else here tonight.

It didn't *mean* anything. Not unless she let her fear and humiliation override common sense.

She'd come here to do one thing—to find and destroy the man who had attacked her sister. As long as she kept that goal uppermost in her mind, she could survive anything.

Even Duncan's touch.

She pushed to her feet, retrieving her gown and quickly donning it. Though it hid little, it at least offered the illusion of coverage. Better than running around naked—especially if she came across another hunter in the forest.

That howl had come from near the main gate, and it had been filled with anguish and anger. She couldn't risk using telepathy to find out what was going on, simply because skimming the mind of a hunter like Duncan was dangerous when she had secrets of her own to keep. She turned and followed his scent through the trees.

Something bad had happened, and she had every intention of finding out what.

•

Duncan shifted shape and came to a halt three feet from the bloody corpse. The victim was on her back near a melting drift of snow, a look of horror etched on what remained of her face. Her throat had been torn out, and chunks of flesh were missing from her shoulders and exposed breasts. Her skirt was rucked up, and her panties torn—visible evidence of the violation he could almost smell.

"Moons, René, what in hell have you done?" As much as he tried to keep his voice even, a hint of revulsion still crept through.

René glanced up sharply. His face was a mottled red, the vein in his neck visibly throbbing. "Do you think I'm such a savage that I'd do this? By the moon's light—" He thrust a hand through his dark hair. "I like it rough, true, but not like this. Never like *this*."

"Then why the hell are you here?" Duncan squatted on his heels, studying the bloody rents in the woman's pale skin. The width between the bottom and top jaws suggested her attacker was a smaller than normal wolf. Certainly smaller than René, at any rate.

"I was looking for her. We were supposed to dance after midnight. She didn't appear, so I came searching."

"Did you see or smell any other wolf close by?" Blood still oozed from the wounds, its smell sharp and metallic. She hadn't been dead that long. His brother couldn't have missed the killer by more than a few minutes.

He studied the ground around them, but there were no footprints apart from their own. In fact, there was little in the way of leaf matter, either. Someone had swept away the evidence, probably with a tree branch.

But that didn't explain why there was no scent on the air beyond that of this woman and his brother.

René shook his head. "I heard nothing, saw nothing—other than you and some pretty little hunter over near the pavilion." A mirthless smile touched his mouth. "I thought you had no intention of participating in the dance this time."

He hadn't. The only reason he was at the mansion at all was at the request of their sire, who knew the Sinclairs were under suspicion and who'd wanted someone he could trust to investigate these killings. Someone within the family who knew the system but had no true loyalties to the police or justice. Duncan had certainly seen the inside of more than his share of jail cells in his youth, so he guessed it was fair to presume he knew how the justice system worked.

He shrugged. At the very least, Neva's presence would maintain his wild reputation and stop suspicions being focused in the wrong direction. "She made an offer too good to refuse."

René snorted softly. "It certainly looked like it."

Silver flashed in the short grass to the left of the victim's head. Duncan shifted slightly, gaze narrowing. It was a hair, short and bristly.

"What color wolf was the victim?"

He felt rather than saw his brother's frown. "From the red pack. Why?"

"Then her attacker is silver—unless you were in hunter form when you came here."

"No, but you were."

"I shifted before I reached the body. I doubt this is from my coat."

"So it was one of our own?" Shock cracked his brother's deep voice.

"The hair would suggest so."

"It could be a plant."

"It could be." Though he very much doubted it. The rangers already knew it was a silver wolf behind these attacks. Planting one hair didn't make any sense—even though other clues that implicated his pack had been left at each of the other crime scenes.

René cleared his throat. "Do you know that this is the fourth attack in as many weeks?"

"Yes." Duncan rose and studied the trees around them. There were three trails from the gate, but all of them led to Ripple Creek. Had the killer continued on to town, or had he simply turned back around and rejoined the dance? There were plenty of fountains inside the grounds where a bloody wolf might wash—though if he were one of their own, slipping unseen into the mansion was a simple matter. Every Sinclair in the pack knew the locations of the secret passages—and there was one near every gate.

"You'd better get the rangers out here. I'll update the old man."

René grunted. "Damn horrible way to end the night's dance."

Duncan raised an eyebrow. "That's the first time anything has stopped you from enjoying the moon fever."

"Yeah, but this is the first time I've seen one of my chosen mates dead." René shrugged. "But then, I don't have the tasty morsel waiting for me that you do."

A tasty morsel whose delights Duncan could not

enjoy again for a while yet. He had every intention of being here when the rangers arrived. "Go call the cops. I'll tend to my morsel."

René stepped around the body and clapped a hand on Duncan's shoulder. "Don't take long. I want you to back up my story, or the rangers are likely to throw my ass in jail. They're desperate for a quick arrest on this one."

"Even the rangers can't convict without evidence." Though he'd known one or two in his time who were certainly willing to concoct it.

He returned through the gates and headed for the pavilion. Jasmine stirred the air, and he stopped abruptly, his gaze roaming the trees. She'd been here.

Listening. Watching.

Why?

He remembered the fear in her eyes, the uncertainty. Remembered thinking she was not the usual type of woman found at these dances.

Something clenched deep in his gut. Disappointment, perhaps. Certainly anger.

He was being played.

Someone obviously suspected why he was here. And what better way to keep an eye on him than to offer something even his jaded tastes could not resist? Neva was alluring, sensual, a wolf in the full peak of her sexual prowess, and yet oddly, almost innocently, unaware of that fact.

And he'd taken the bait without thought. Moons, what a fool.

Anger surged through him. Still, it was a game that worked both ways, now that he was aware of it. Over the next couple of days, he could push their union to the extreme and wait for her to reach the breaking point. She *would* break; of that he was certain. Their one brief mating had confirmed that while she wasn't innocent, she was certainly inexperienced. Sooner or later, she'd go running back to whoever was behind this, desperate to end the charade. And once she did, he'd have a suspect to follow.

He took a deep, calming breath, then continued on through the trees.

She was waiting near the pavilion steps, but her welcoming smile faded as he approached. He swallowed his anger, knowing he had to be careful. The Sinclairs might be strong telepaths, but in this regard the golden pack far outstripped them. He couldn't give her the slightest hint that he knew her game—not yet. Not until he'd made her desperate enough to run back to the person behind all this.

And he had to admit, he was rather looking forward to the task. René was right—she was an extremely tasty morsel. He wondered what she was being paid to seduce him. It had better be a lot, because she was certainly going to earn it over the next few days.

"Problems?" Her voice faltered and fear touched her gaze as she backed away a step.

Okay, perhaps he wasn't controlling his anger as well as he thought. "I'm afraid so."

He caught her arm, stopping her retreat and pulling her close. Her body molded against his, her flesh trembling, flushed with heat. The musky scent of her desire spun around him, fueling the ache in his loins.

They'd certainly chosen their bait well. Even knowing what she was, he still wanted her more than he'd wanted any other wolf in his life.

He cupped a hand to her cheek, holding her gaze as his lips claimed hers. There was nothing gentle in this kiss. It was filled with the ferocity that burned through his body—a hungry, angry possession that took everything she was willing to give, and more.

Her eyes widened and her fear deepened, until it was something he could almost taste. Yet at the same time, the scent of her arousal intensified. She wanted him, even if she feared him.

He touched her, caressed her—made her burn with need. When he thrust deep, she moaned in pleasure, but this was a mating that had nothing to do with pleasure and everything to do with anger and betrayal. It was hard and fast—a union in which he took but did not give.

When he'd finished, he stepped back. She stared at him, her chest heaving, her lips swollen and red, body still flushed and quivering with unfulfilled desires. But it was the anger, the reproach, in her eyes that cut the deepest.

"Wait for me here," he said curtly and walked away.

Neva clenched her fists and stared at his retreating back. It took all her willpower not to pick up the fallen tree branch near her feet and throw it at his stiff, uncaring spine. In the space of ten minutes, he'd gone from a warm and generous lover to a detached, unfeeling machine. A man who cared for nothing but his own needs.

And she wasn't sure why.

Nor could she read his thoughts or taste his emotions to find out why. It was as if a wall stood between them—a wall so high and wide that she half-suspected even *he* had lost touch with his feelings.

Up until now, she'd met only a couple of wolves whose minds she couldn't read easily—although even then, she could still share telepathic conversations with them if they allowed it. Generally it was a blessing more than a problem, simply because it gave a break from the constant need to filter out the thoughts of others. But Duncan Sinclair was no safe haven, and she had a bad, *bad* feeling she needed to know exactly what was going on in that man's mind.

She rubbed her arms, but it did little to ease the chill racing across her skin. To think, only a few moments ago she'd been worried about hungering for his touch so badly that she'd want to remain in this den of darkness. What a fool's thought *that* had turned out to be.

She wasn't about to wait here for more of the same. She may have agreed to be his for the remainder of the moon phase, but with the discovery of a fourth victim, this place would soon be crawling with rangers. It was better she leave now before anyone recognized her. The last thing she wanted was one of the rangers reporting her presence to her parents. *That* would cause a scene of gargantuan proportions.

And they certainly wouldn't understand her reasons for coming here. They were old school, and believed the dance should be delayed until you'd found your one, true mate.

But as much as she wanted to go home right now,

she couldn't. Not until she'd taken a closer look at that body. It was doubtful the rangers would let her go unescorted into Savannah's office a second time.

She resolutely turned and made her way back to the gate.

The stench of death almost overpowered her. She took a deep breath, trying to control her stomach's churning. Her twin faced this type of thing regularly. Surely *she* could do it once.

She bit her lip and moved closer, stepping in old footsteps so her own wouldn't show. This death was the very image of the photos she'd studied in Savannah's files—right down to the bite marks on the woman's shoulders and breasts. But it was the damage to the women's faces that Savannah had questioned. Why such destruction? None of the victims had been beauties, just pleasant-looking. Ordinary. None of them were even similar in any way. They all had different-colored hair, eyes, and facial structures. All belonged to different packs. Yet the man behind this went to great pains to render their faces almost unrecognizable. It certainly suggested there was some sort of connection—but if Savannah's notes were anything to go by, the rangers had no idea what. And if the Sinclairs knew, they certainly weren't telling.

Neva's gaze slipped down, stopping at the rucked-up dress and torn panties. Her stomach churned, and she fought the sudden urge to run. Lord, it was all too easy to imagine the horror, the fear . . . She swallowed heavily. The visual evidence might indicate rape, but the coroner's report on the last three victims certainly didn't. All victims had had numerous partners during the night, but there was nothing to indicate forced sex. Which Savannah had again questioned. Why was the killer depicting rape if he wasn't actually violating them? It was a puzzle to which there were no answers—as yet.

Neva raised her nose, tasting the air. Beneath the scent of death lay a myriad of other aromas. Pine and balsam were heavily entwined with the rich bouquet of snowbound loam. Beyond that, a lingering caress of warm spices and freshly cut wood stirred her pulse. Duncan's scent. His brother, who'd been here longer, left a warm touch of muskiness. Beneath that was blood, sharp and metallic. And something else—a scent she couldn't pin down, but one that seemed vaguely familiar.

She frowned and carefully walked back to the nearest path, keeping to the stones as she studied the ground. No footprints here. Nothing to indicate anyone had moved past here recently. Only that nebulous scent. Of course the murderer could have kept to the stones like she had, but that didn't explain the fact that there were only two sets of prints near the body. There should have been three.

She studied the path for several moments, weighing her need for answers with her desire to flee, then sighed. Closing her eyes, she reached for the wildness. It came in a rush of power that blurred her senses and numbed the pain as it reshaped and changed her body.

Then it was gone, and she padded through the trees on four legs rather than two. The scent led her halfway down the mountain before it disappeared. She sniffed both air and ground, trying to find it again, then noted a flash of silver caught in the branch of a small aspen just off the path. Hair from a silver coat. Paw prints flirted with a slight drift of snow beyond that, then disappeared again. The scent no longer lingered. She nosed about a bit more but knew it was worthless.

Then she glanced over her shoulder, contemplating going back for her clothes, but there were voices up at the top now. Maybe the rangers were here. Maybe Duncan and his brother had returned. Either way, she had to get going. The scent of jasmine would linger, and that could lead to trouble if she wasn't careful. Besides, nothing she'd left in the mansion could be traced back to her. Jasmine was a strong scent, which was exactly why she'd chosen it. Very few noses would be able to track her true scent through the clothes she'd left up there.

She moved back to the trail and continued down until she hit the stream, then followed that upwind. The water was icy against her paws, but unless she did this, they would trace her too easily.

As she continued padding through the water, she reached out, briefly touching her sister's thoughts. No response. No change. She sighed. At least some good had come out of the night. She'd achieved her aim—she had breached the inner circle of the mansion and attached herself successfully to Duncan. Nor did she have to worry about hungering for his touch. For whatever reason, he'd become as unfeeling and as unresponsive as she could ever want.

So why did she feel such a deep sense of loss?

Moon madness, surely. She ducked into a small waterfall, washing the scent of jasmine from her coat, then continued home.

•

Two hours later, Duncan made his way through the mansion. The arrival of the rangers had put an end to the dance, and there were few people occupying the shadows in the hall. But they would be back tomorrow night. They always were.

He took the stairs two at a time and tried to ignore his vague sense of disgust. He'd taken part in more than his fair share of dances—was still taking part in them, in fact—so he had no right to judge the others.

Or were his own actions behind that vague, unsettling emotion?

Damn it, she'd come here with the sole purpose of seducing him—he was certain of that, if nothing else. He owed her no right to pleasure. And if anything, her willingness to take whatever he dished out without comment proved her guilt. He hadn't acted in the spirit of the dance, and she'd every right to be furious.

But she hadn't said anything. Why? Because she was being paid to stay by his side. Because she would do whatever it took to remain there.

Yet while he had no regrets about his actions, the reproach in her green eyes haunted him. He'd never been like René. He didn't like rough tactics, found no thrill in fear. Yet tonight he'd tasted both and *had* enjoyed it.

And it was something he would have to continue. He couldn't play the gentle, caring lover with this woman—not if he wanted to stop these murders and get away from this place sooner rather than later. He would have to push her, and keep pushing her, until she could take no more.

He stopped at the door at the end of the hall and rapped his knuckles on the wood. A gruff voice bid him to enter. He walked inside and slammed the door shut.

Zeke stood near the window, tall, broad, and straight of spine, despite having seen more than a century pass him by. He turned as Duncan entered, one steel-gray eyebrow raised in query. "I would gather from your entrance that the meeting with the rangers did not go well?"

Duncan walked over to the bar and poured himself a drink. "Quite the opposite. René's not a suspect, and they found skin and blood under the woman's fingernails which they believe might belong to the killer."

"It was Mariata who was killed, wasn't it?"

Duncan nodded, then downed his drink in one swift gulp. The liquid burned its way down his gullet and sat like a weight in his gut.

"Mariata liked pain—and liked inflicting it. I wouldn't be surprised if they find the flesh of more than one wolf under her nails."

Duncan cast a sharp glance his father's way. "You danced with her? Tonight?"

Zeke sighed and turned around. Scratches marred his shoulder blades. "I may be old, but the fever still burns through my veins. She and I are familiar partners."

Just what he needed to hear—especially with the rangers insisting on checking all family members for wounds. He poured himself another drink. "Did you dance with any of the other victims?"

"No."

"And my brothers?"

"The first was one of Tye's regular mates, and the third was one of Kane's."

Tye was the oldest of the four of them, and Kane the youngest. René was born between him and Tye. He took another drink and felt the anger begin to slip away. He knew alcohol offered no real solutions, but right now it drowned the vague sense of self-loathing. And of that he was glad.

"So someone's targeting your lovers, and those of your get."

"So it would seem."

"Any idea why? You haven't pissed off any females or their families lately, have you?"

His father's smile was wistful. "My wild days are behind me, I'm afraid. I'm more staid than many of my mates would wish."

But not *too* staid, if those marks were anything to go by. "Have you told anyone I'm here to investigate the murders?"

Zeke shook his head. "No. News spreads fast in a tribe of this size, and I didn't want to risk warning the killer—if indeed it is someone from our immediate pack."

"Then you'd better get the rooms swept for bugs, because someone knows."

"I did—yesterday." Zeke hesitated, dark eyes touched with concern. "And why would you think that?"

"Because I've been set up with a mate, and I think she's intending to keep a very close eye on me."

Zeke moved to the bar and poured himself a drink. "So what are you going to do?"

Duncan shrugged. "Nothing."

"I could take her off your hands. Keep her locked away and occupied."

The thought of his father going anywhere near Neva made his blood boil. She was his to deal with, and *no one* was going to touch her except him.

"I'll take care of her." Despite his best efforts to remain calm, the hint of steel was evident in his voice.

"Just be wary of the bait, Son. It might just turn around and trap you."

"I know what I'm doing."

Zeke leaned a shoulder against the wall and regarded him with amusement. "So, what are you going to do with her—besides the obvious?"

"I'm going to force her to stay here for the next five days." He took another drink of whiskey. "Then I'll push her, and keep pushing her, until she runs back to whoever it was that set her on me."

"The sort of wolf who's willing to profit from the dance is not one who would easily break."

"This one's new. She'll break." And hopefully soon. He had no taste for the game he was about to play.

"And in the meantime?"

He raised his hand, refusing his father's offer to top off his drink. "I'll start talking to people. See what I can dig up." If this was some sort of revenge killing aimed at his brothers, then someone, somewhere, *had* to know why. As his father had said, a tribe this size held no real secrets. "Did anything unusual happen before the first murder?"

"Not that I can remember. Of course, it's hard to keep a finger on every pulse."

Duncan snorted softly. The day his father didn't know exactly what was going on would be the day death claimed him. And the fact that he truly had no idea *why* these murders were happening only made them all the more mystifying. "You've talked to my brothers?"

"As have you. I daresay the responses were the same."

They were; he'd surreptitiously listened in. René's shields were not as strong as they should be. "Will you be able to get a copy of the autopsy report? We'll see if Mariata's varies any from the previous three."

Zeke nodded. "You do realize you might also be in their sights?"

"If that were the case, why put a watch on me? The mere fact that they have suggests I'm not a target."

Zeke snorted softly. "Even the craziest wolf alive would consider you dangerous. Maybe they simply want to keep an eye on you until they decide to kill you."

A smile touched Duncan's lips. "And here I was thinking I've calmed down since my wild days."

"You have," his father said. "But it makes no difference, because what you do now, you do with a clear head."

Duncan thought of Neva, of the reproach in her beautiful eyes. "I do what I have to," he said, with a trace of bitterness.

"I know. And that's precisely *why* you're considered so dangerous by just about everyone who knows you."

Duncan finished the last of his whiskey, but it did little to erase the sour taste in his mouth. "So when do you think you'll be able to get your hands on that autopsy report?"

Zeke shrugged. "Tomorrow afternoon at the earliest. I don't want to push my source too hard."

"Then I'll be back tomorrow afternoon."

Duncan strode from the room and made his way through the shadow-filled house. And when he reached the pavilion, he wasn't surprised to discover Neva gone.

Chapter Three

NEVA ROSE WITH the dawn and took a long, hot, scented bath, hoping to erase any trace of Duncan that might linger on her skin. But she couldn't erase the throbbing in her body so easily, or the needy ache that flicked fire through her veins. She wouldn't be surprised if his ears were burning right now, because she'd cursed him long and loud during the night as she'd tossed and turned, trying to sleep.

And yet she knew relief would not come tonight. Not if their second mating was any indication of his intentions.

But that was exactly what she'd wanted—a quick, passionless rutting, easily forgotten once this phase of the moon was over. She could hardly complain, now that she'd gotten her wish. And she probably wouldn't if he hadn't first given her a glimpse of how truly extraordinary their mating could be.

She closed her eyes and pushed him from her thoughts. His pack belonged to the night, and that's where all thought of him should remain. She would not let him wreck her days as well.

Besides, she had far more important people to worry about.

She reached out, carefully touching her sister's thoughts. Though there was no response, the sensation of death hovering close had fled. And pictures were beginning to unroll through the darkness of her sister's mind, like fractured images of a violent movie viewed through a broken projector. Relief surged, and tears blurred Neva's vision. Savannah was going to live, and consciousness wasn't that far away.

Which was good. She couldn't bear this endless silence. Didn't know if she'd want to go on without having Sav's warm, cheerful presence in her mind.

She dressed, swept her hair into a ponytail, then clattered down the stairs to grab a quick breakfast of toast and coffee. Then she snagged her leather jacket from the arm of the chair and made her way outside.

The day had dawned crisp and clear, but the smell of rain was in the air. The weather could change quickly up here in the mountains, especially in the early days of spring, and it had caught many a tourist by surprise. Not that Ripple Creek was anywhere near as popular with humans as nearby Aspen—but then, most of the wolf packs who lived here didn't want it to be.

Her pack was the exception. Her father even headed the Bring Ripple Creek into the Twenty-first Century Committee. Or the Future's Committee, as they sometimes called themselves.

A smile touched her lips, but just as quickly faded. She'd have to watch her step around her parents today, or the shit really would hit the fan.

She thrust her hands into her coat pockets and made

her way toward the diner. Her parents lived above it—as had she, until her mother's incessant nagging that she find a mate and settle down had grown beyond the joke it had originally started out as.

Sav certainly didn't receive half the flack she got—but then, Sav had what her mother considered a worthwhile career. She, on the other hand, was simply another waitress in the diner. Which was a job she actually enjoyed doing and had no intentions of leaving.

A bell chimed softly as she pushed open the door. The rich aroma of omelettes and coffee filled the air, stirring her hunger even though she'd already eaten.

"Morning, Cub," her father, Levon, called from the kitchen.

She snagged an apron from under the counter, tying it around her waist as she pushed through the double swing-doors into the kitchen.

"Morning, old one." She dropped a kiss on his leathery cheek.

He swatted her with his spatula, green eyes twinkling. "Enough with the 'old,' thank you very much."

She grinned and pulled herself up on the nearest counter. "Where's Mom?"

"Still at the hospital."

"No word from the doctors on Savannah's progress?"

His mask of cheerfulness slipped a little and he sighed, thrusting a hand through his thinning blond hair. "They said her vital signs were getting stronger. It's just a matter of waiting now."

"Her thoughts are stronger, Dad. I don't think consciousness is that far off."

He lightly squeezed her arm. "Thanks. I'll tell your mother that."

"Need anything done here before I start setting tables?"

"I did it all last night. I couldn't sleep. You want an omelette?"

When she nodded, he slapped one onto a nearby plate and began making another. She shifted her leg and grabbed a knife and fork from the cutlery drawer underneath the counter, then dug in.

They ate in silence. When they'd both finished, she collected the dishes, throwing them into the dishwasher before pouring them both a coffee.

"Your mother wants to know if you'll come for dinner tonight," he said.

She stared at him for a second, her heart feeling like it was about to race out of her chest. "Is this a request or a demand?"

He grimaced. "You know your mother."

A demand, then. By the moon's light, what on earth was she going to do now? "I—" She hesitated, but knew it was better to tell a half-truth than a straight-out lie. "I was planning to go out later, but I can come over if dinner is early enough."

He nodded and raised an eyebrow—curious, but not overly so. "Going anywhere in particular?"

She shrugged nonchalantly. "They're rescreening *Charade* at the Playbox. I thought I might catch that." She'd actually caught it two nights ago, but he didn't know that.

Her dad snorted. "How many times will that make it?"

She grinned. "Only fourteen."

He shook his head. "You're never going to catch a mate if you keep spending your time down at that old movie theater, lusting after ancient actors."

"Well, until I meet a man with Cary Grant's looks, charm, and style, that's exactly what I intend to keep on doing."

"We're never going to get grandkiddies, that's for sure," he muttered. He slapped her leg, amusement dancing in his eyes. "Go set the tables before I'm inclined to lecture on the virtues of finding a good man."

Grin widening, she slipped off the counter, planted another kiss on his cheek, and headed off to work.

The morning rush came and went. Arianne, a fellow waitress and longtime friend, swept in at eleven, all color and energy and smiles.

"Such a wonderful day," she all but trilled, shucking off her coat and grabbing an apron.

"Got lucky last night, did we?" Neva commented dryly.

Ari grinned. "No, but I'm intending to tonight. Hooked myself a fine specimen last night."

"And you didn't dance? Good grief, girl, are you sick?"

"Nope. He was with another mate at the time, and it's not polite to steal."

"Since when has that stopped you?"

Amusement twinkled in Ari's dark-green eyes. "Since his mate was twice my size."

Neva snorted softly. "Good enough reason, I suppose."

"Generally. You filled the saltshakers yet?"

Neva shook her head, and the two of them got to

work. Lunch was busier than normal, thanks to the rising influx of fly-fishermen wanting to take advantage of the early warmth. At one, when there was a brief slowdown, Neva grabbed a soda and leaned wearily against the counter. Lack of sleep was beginning to tell. Thank God it was Monday and the diner was closed tonight.

Then she remembered what she had to do, and a shiver ran down her spine.

Ari joined her near the fridge, leaning her forehead against the cool glass. "Man, I'm hot."

Neva raised an eyebrow. "Can't wait for tonight, huh?"

Mischief danced in Ari's eyes. "Well, now that you mention it . . ." She hesitated as the doorbell chimed. "Maybe we should put the 'Closed' sign up. Otherwise, I don't think we're going to get out of here today."

Neva smiled as she glanced toward the door—and felt her smile freeze on her face. It wasn't just any old customer who'd entered. It was Duncan Sinclair.

Ari's soft gasp of admiration seemed a hundred miles away. Neva could only stare at him, her mind whirling with a thousand different thoughts and fears.

What on earth was he doing here? Was it just chance that brought him here or something more?

He adjusted a small brown-wrapped box tucked beneath his arm and took off his dark glasses, his gaze skating across the crowded room. No, she thought, knees weak, it wasn't chance, but something more sinister.

"Now, there's a honey I wouldn't mind wrapping

my legs around," Ari whispered. "Moons, what a delicious bod."

He certainly had that, Neva thought with a chill. She'd thought him dangerously handsome last night, but now, when he was wearing dark jeans that hugged his legs with such thigh-defining tightness, and a black sweater that seemed to show every ripple of muscle, the impression of a dark angel was doubled. Tripled.

His gaze collided with hers, and something trembled deep inside—but whether in fear or anticipation, she wasn't sure.

Which of the free tables are yours? His mind voice was brusque, unemotional. A tight beam only the two of them could hear—thankfully, given that her dad was next door in the kitchen.

The booth second from the end. She kept her tones as clipped as his.

"God," Ari continued. "Hope he chooses one of my booths."

"I thought you had a date tonight," she said, hoping Ari was too intent on drooling over Duncan to notice the slight tremor in her voice.

"Are you crazy? If that honey gives me the slightest indication of interest, I'll be a puddle at his feet."

Neva watched him stride to the booth, and she had to admit, if only to herself, that if he'd shown the slightest bit of interest in *her,* she would have puddled right alongside Ari.

But he wouldn't. She knew that without a doubt. Whatever his reasons for coming here, it had nothing to do with interest or pleasure—at least, not for her, anyway.

So why the hell *was* he here? She'd promised him the nights, not the days. What was he up to? And why did she feel with such sick certainty that his appearance here boded ill?

He slipped into the booth she'd indicated, and Ari sighed. "Typical. The best-looking man I've ever seen walks in here and he sits at one of *your* tables." She hesitated, visibly brightening. "Can we swap?"

Neva wished they could have, but there was something in his ebony gaze that suggested retribution if she tried. "Sorry. No can do."

"That's right, be greedy. Keep the hunk all to yourself."

"And you wouldn't?"

"Beside the point." Ari waved a dismissing hand and slapped a menu into her hands. "Go get him, tiger."

Neva took a quick drink of soda, then made her way around the counter and toward him. He watched her every step, his dark gaze as impassive as his thoughts. By the time she'd reached the halfway point, her stomach was tumbling worse than a clothes dryer, and she was seriously regretting her quick drink of soda.

"Care for a menu?" she asked, forcing a cheerful smile to her lips.

I think we both know what I came here for. He took the menu from her trembling hands and casually opened it.

It felt like he'd clubbed her in the stomach. She stared at him for a second, knuckles white as she gripped her notepad for dear life. *What the hell are you talking about?* Aloud, she said, "The specials today are spicy chicken burgers with fries or a salad, and minestrone soup with a small platter of home-made bread."

I told you to wait for me last night.

So? You also said you'd take the time to pleasure me more fully, and that didn't exactly happen, now did it?

Though there was not the slightest flicker in his shuttered eyes, she knew her barb had hit home. His anger boiled around her—a distant touch of thunder only she could hear.

You agreed to mate with me. You had no right to leave. He studied the menu for a moment, then ordered the chicken burger and fries.

And you have no right to come here chasing me. "Would you like a coffee with that?"

I have every right. "Black, thanks. With the meal, not before."

She wrote it down, mouth dry. *What do you mean?*

It's one of the more obscure rules of the dance. If a female who has agreed to a mating does not fulfill her promises, then the male has every right to pursue her and make her. He hesitated, his gaze snaring hers with deadly intent. *No matter where she might be.*

Oh God. She took a deep breath and released it slowly. Surely he wouldn't. Not here in the diner. Even he couldn't be that wild, that uncaring. But as she returned his gaze, a tremor of fear began deep inside. She may have studied this man, but she didn't know him. Didn't have a clue as to what he was capable of doing.

I agreed to the nights. I intend to uphold that bargain.

Not last night you didn't.

We mated. If you could call what happened between them the second time mating.

You ran. I was far from finished, believe me.

The trembling was beginning to work its way down her legs. Her knees felt fluid. She desperately wanted to tell him that *she* was finished, that she'd had enough of his stupid dance and magnificent but uncaring body. But she couldn't. She was snared by the very net she'd thrown, and she had no choice now.

But she had a horrible suspicion she'd better find Savannah's attacker fast, before this man destroyed her.

Tell me what you want. Aloud, she added, "Anything else with that, sir?"

His smile was slow and sexy and sizzled heat across every nerve ending. "Oh yes," he said softly. "But we'll discuss that a little later." *When the diner isn't as full.*

She flipped closed her notebook and all but ran back to the counter, where she stood, back to him, taking deep breaths as she tried to control the shaking. She couldn't go into the kitchen like this. Her dad would know something was wrong and be out here in an instant, searching for the troublemaker.

Ari came around the counter. "He has that sort of effect on me, too," she said, voice sympathetic. "And I haven't even been anywhere near him."

"I'll be fine once I catch my breath," Neva said. Which certainly wasn't a lie.

"So what does he smell like?"

"Like a warm whiskey on a cold night," she said without thinking.

Ari chuckled softly. "You have got the hots for him bad, don't you? Shame your old man is next door. You could've dragged our sexy stranger into the storeroom and had a quick dance with him."

That was certainly a possibility, if the heated promise in his eyes was anything to go by.

"Of course you'd have to dust yourself off with bicarb afterward," Ari continued blithely.

Neva blinked and looked at her. "What?"

"Bicarb absorbs smells."

"Yeah. So?"

"So you don't want your straitlaced parents knowing you've actually gone out and enjoyed yourself, do you?" Ari winked saucily. "It works beautifully, believe me. I've been doing it for years."

Neva laughed softly and pushed away from the counter. "You're incorrigible."

"But a hell of a lot more satisfied than you'll ever be if you don't start pulling your act into the twenty-first century." She waved a hand toward the kitchen. "Your dad may be the head of the Future's Committee, but *both* your parents still act like they were brought up in the fifteenth century."

"That's easy for you to say," Neva said dryly. "You don't have to live with their fifteenth-century ideals."

"Neither do you. You moved out two years ago, remember?"

Moving out was easy. Ignoring the twenty-six years spent under their roof, absorbing their influences and ideals, was not. She wasn't even sure she *wanted* to ignore them.

"I'm trying, Ari, believe me."

"Not hard enough if you let that delicious stranger slip through your fingers."

Neva forced a smile and walked into the kitchen, handing her dad Duncan's order. Eight minutes later, when it was ready, she grabbed the plate and his coffee, took a deep breath, and walked over.

"Here you go," she said, placing his plate in front of him.

"Thank you." He let his hand slide across hers as he reached for his cutlery.

It felt like flame caressing her skin and she jumped. The coffee cup she still held tumbled sideways, splashing hot dark liquid all over both the table and him.

"Oh God, I'm sorry," she said, horrified. "Are you all right? Are you burned?"

His expression suggested he didn't believe the sincerity of her words. "No. Just clean everything up, and it'll be fine."

She pulled the towel from the side of her apron and mopped up the worst of the spill. Ari tossed her another towel, and she finished the job. Luckily, the burger had somehow avoided getting drenched. She didn't fancy going back into the kitchen right now. "What about your parcel?" She flicked her cloth in the direction of the brown-wrapped box.

"It's fine," he said softly. "But you did still miss a bit."

She frowned. "No, I didn't—" Her voice faded as he shifted, revealing the dots of coffee on his sweater and the crotch of his pants.

Surely you can't expect me— The thought froze as she met his gaze. He could. And he did.

She took another deep breath, then quickly dabbed

the stains from his sweater and jeans. And couldn't help noticing—or feeling—the huge bulge of his excitement.

An odd slither of feminine satisfaction ran through her. At least he couldn't deny his interest in her when the evidence of it was so clearly visible.

"Will there be anything else?" she asked, voice a little more breathy than she would have liked.

His smile smoked her insides. "Not right now."

She nodded and retreated to the other side of the diner.

"Impressive move," Ari whispered in admiration. "I'll have to remember that one."

Her smile felt tight. Ari wasn't likely to believe it had been an accident any more than Duncan had.

The time dragged by. He finished his meal and sipped his coffee, which she kept topped up. Everything she did, everywhere she went, she could feel his gaze on her—a heated caress that promised far more than it would probably deliver.

By three, with the crowd thinning out, she was close to nervous exhaustion. Her dad came out of the kitchen, folding down the collar of the jacket he now wore over his uniform. "I'm heading over to pick your mother up at the hospital. You coming?"

She shook her head. She didn't need to go into that sterile place to see her twin. She could see her anytime she liked by simply opening her thoughts. And she would know a lot sooner than any damn doctor when Sav had woken.

"Your mother thinks you should."

"I hate hospitals, you know that." They were too full of pain, too full of misery and hurt, and it overwhelmed even the strongest of her shields. "Savannah will understand, believe me."

"Your mother won't."

"Mom doesn't run my life anymore." Though she certainly tried. Neva had images of being sixty and still crossing swords with her disapproving parent. "I'll finish up here and close once the last of our customers leave."

He nodded. "And don't forget dinner."

As if she dared.

"Now's your chance," Ari whispered the minute Neva's dad walked out the door. "Go chat with that delicious man."

There were three customers still in the diner, and Ari herself. If Neva was going to confront Duncan, she'd rather do it when they were alone. "I don't know."

"Oh for moon's sake, he's been watching you all afternoon. What have you got to lose?"

Nothing but my sanity, she thought. And what remained of her self-esteem. But she took her apron off, grabbed the coffee pot and a cup for herself, then walked across to his booth.

"Sit," he said, voice soft but holding no inflection.

She slid into his booth and poured herself a coffee. She didn't refill his, but simply shoved the coffeepot his way. A tight smile touched his full lips.

"No longer the charming host, I see."

"I'm on a break. What do you want?" Her voice held an edge.

"You," he all but drawled. "Why else would I be here?"

Something in the tone of his voice sent a tingle of

anticipation crawling across her skin. Which was ridiculous when the only pleasure he seemed to care about was his own.

"Well, we do make the best burgers in town."

Amusement touched his obsidian gaze—a warmth so fleeting she wondered if she'd imagined it. "But they're not as tasty as the morsel I had last night."

Her cheeks flamed in memory, and she dragged her gaze from his. It was far safer to stare at her coffee than into his soulless eyes. "Tell me what you want," she repeated.

He crossed his arms and leaned forward. "Look at me," he demanded.

Almost against her will, her gaze rose to his. How could a man with a face so beautiful be so totally devoid of anything resembling humanity?

"My pack is having a fancy-dress dance tonight, separate from the main one. You will accompany me, and you will wear the outfit I have in this box."

She stared at him, her stomach churning. "I won't be shared. I don't care what your sordid dance rules say, but you *can't* demand that of me."

Amusement touched his lips, but again held little warmth. "Have no fear, little wolf. You are mine, and only mine, for the remainder of the week."

Relief slithered through her, though it was hardly much comfort knowing she had to submit to his uncaring touch for the next five days. Even if that was what she had planned.

She looked at the box, hating to think what sort of outfit he'd chosen for her. Probably a hooker's, if his recent treatment was anything to go by. "What if the outfit doesn't fit?"

"Try it on. If it doesn't fit, I'll exchange it."

"I'll take it into the back room and try it now, if you'd like." She started to rise, but he clamped a hand on her arm, stopping her. His fingers burned against the chill of her skin, searing deep.

"No. Later, when your friend and customers have left."

She sat back down, her gaze locked with his. And knew, with sickening certainty, that he intended to take what he'd missed out on last night. Right here in this diner, when her parents lived right upstairs.

"Don't." Her voice held a note of pleading, but she didn't care. "Please, not here."

He raised an eyebrow. "Do you deny it is my right?"

Damn it, I promised you the nights, not the days. You can't make me do this.

Oh, but I can. His mind voice was silky.

Her throat was drier than the Sahara. She licked her lips, wishing she could pick up her coffee and throw it in his face. But she couldn't, simply because her hands were shaking so much most of it would be spilled over the table long before she tossed it at him. "What do you mean?"

He reached across the table, capturing her hand, turning it palm side up. His thumb stroked her wrist, a gentle, almost possessive caress that sent shivers of desire skating across her skin. God, she hated that he could do this to her—and so damn easily.

"When you participate in certain sports, you should always make sure you understand the rules before you start to play."

"Meaning?"

"Remember what I asked, and how you replied, before our first mating?"

The first, and probably only, time of magic between them—and one she wasn't likely to forget, especially over the next few days. "Yeah. So?"

"So those words were actually an ancient spell of binding. They allow me to enforce my will on you."

A cold chill ran down her spine. "You're kidding."

He raised an eyebrow. "Am I? Shall we test the theory right now?"

"No." Her voice was little more than a breathy whisper of horror. "Not here."

His smile was mirthless. "Reach up with your left hand and undo the top button of your uniform."

Energy slithered across her skin, then became a noose that slipped around her mind and pulled tight. She fought the compulsion with every ounce of strength she had, but still her hand rose, her fingers trembling as they touched the button.

"Damn you to hell," she muttered, tears springing to her eyes. But she couldn't let him get away with this, no matter what he did to her afterward. She wasn't defenseless, and it was about time he realized that.

So she channeled her fear and humiliation into a thin lance of energy and flung it back at him. She might be restricted to just hearing his thoughts rather than having full access to his mind, but that didn't mean her empathic abilities would suffer the same constraint.

It hit him with enough force to throw him back in the seat. His gaze went wide, eyes filled for the briefest of moments by the echo of everything she was feeling. Then his shields slammed home.

"What the hell was that?"

"A taste of what you'll get if you try to use the binding on me. You'll pay for my submissiveness, let me tell you."

He studied her for a moment, then smiled. It held very little warmth. "Thank you for warning me. I'll be sure to stop you from using your gifts before I issue any orders from now on."

She wanted to smack him. She clenched her fists, but rose and walked away instead. This was her doing, her mess. What sort of fool was she to believe she could enter into any sort of sexual game with a man like Duncan Sinclair and come away unscathed?

"So?" Ari whispered, clearing the table as the last of the customers walked out. "How did it go?"

She forced a smile. "I'll tell you tomorrow. For now, consider yourself rushed out the door."

"Now *that* sounds promising." Ari dropped a kiss on Neva's cheek, then picked up her bag and coat. "I want details. Lots of details. And remember the bicarb."

Once she'd left, Neva headed into the kitchen, checking to ensure that everything was turned off, then walked around the building, locking the doors and windows. The diner's front door was the last one she locked.

"Don't," he said softly when she reached for the blind.

He made it an order, and she had little choice but to obey. She took a deep breath, but it did little to ease the trembling inside. The only trouble was, she knew it wasn't all fear. The full moon was closer tonight, and the wildness was raging to be free. She clenched her fists and turned around.

Without the lights on, the diner was filled with dusky shadows. Evening came early here in the mountains, and she was glad of that. At least it meant if anyone did walk by, there'd be less chance of them seeing what was happening inside.

Her gaze met his and, for the briefest moment, amusement flashed in the dark depths of his eyes. Then it was gone, locked behind the shutters.

"Come over here," he said, his voice as seductive as the kiss of silk against skin.

She forced her reluctant feet forward. He'd shifted from the booth to a table, turning his chair sideways and stretching his long legs out in front of him. The small parcel was still sitting on the booth's seat.

"Undress."

He could have been asking her to clear the table for all the emotion he showed. She stared at him but knew she had no real choice. Sure, she could make him pay, but his shields were almost as strong as hers. Now that she'd so stupidly warned him, they'd undoubtedly remain up and would take most of the brunt of an empathic attack. Her gift was a weapon best used when a victim's mind was wide open and unaware.

And she'd much rather be embarrassed of her own free will than be forced into it. And in the end, no matter how she fought him, he *would* force her.

She slipped off her shoes and slowly began undoing the buttons on the front of her dress. Hunger slipped warm and bright between them, caressing her mind.

She threw her dress on the other seat, followed quickly by her panties and bra.

His gaze all but devoured her, and pinpricks of desire skidded across her skin. Her nipples puckered, as if in anticipation of his touch, and the longing he'd left unquenched last night stirred anew.

"What now?" she said, crossing her arms.

He leaned forward, gripped her elbows, and pulled her forward. "Straddle me."

She did. He was as hard as she was achy, and she couldn't help the fleeting wish that he were as naked as she.

He raised a hand, skimming his knuckles down her neck and between her breasts. Goose bumps scurried across her skin, and her heart hammered so loudly its beat seemed to echo through the silence.

His hand slipped around her waist, then rested against her back, pressing heat into her spine as he gently pushed her forward. His tongue skimmed her skin, sending a delicious shiver of anticipation through her body. He outlined a breast with that liquid touch, circling it, gradually working his way inward. He teased the outer edges of that dark circle, but never touched the aching, sensitive center.

Sweat skittered across her skin, and every muscle quivered. Ached. His whisper-soft touch moved to her other breast, and by the time he'd finished circling its center, she thought she was going to die of frustration.

He moved on, tasting her collarbone, her neck. He kissed her ear, her cheek, before finally claiming her mouth. It was a long, slow possession that left her gasping for breath.

His kiss eventually made its way down her neck, and when his mouth closed around one aching nipple, she groaned at the sweet delight of it. He sucked hard, sending glorious waves of pleasure lapping across her skin, then claimed her other nipple, repeating the process and leaving her moaning.

"What are you doing for dinner?" he whispered, his breath searing her skin as he kissed her throat.

She blinked at the unexpected question. "Eating with my parents." The slither of unease surfaced again. "Why?"

"Don't you think they should meet the man you're spending the next five days with?"

She stared at him, her throat so dry it ached. "What do you mean?"

"I mean that I want you by my side, and in my bed, night and day."

Horror slid through her. She tried to push away, tried to stand, but his hand held her securely in place. "You can't. I won't." And yet, deep down, she had to acknowledge that this was the chance she'd been looking for. It would offer her the freedom, night *and* day, that she needed to roam the mansion, talk to the people within the pack—and hunt down the killer.

But the cost would be her parents' respect. Was that too high a price to pay?

Then she remembered the torn and bloodied remains of the woman who'd been killed last night. Remembered the way her sister had looked, swathed in bandages, so small and frail and pale against the antiseptic brightness of the hospital. She relived the horror of the moment she'd shared with her twin when the wolf had attacked her.

Was the cost too high? She couldn't honestly say.

"You have no right to demand this."

He raised an eyebrow—a gesture that was both eloquent and arrogant. "No right, but certainly the will."

"You must know my parents are old school." Desperation touched her voice, but right then she didn't care. "They don't believe in the dance or in mating for pleasure. Something like this will kill them."

He still caressed her, sending tremors of longing rolling through her. It was as if she were a well-tuned instrument designed only for his touch. And as much as she wanted to, she couldn't suppress her desire.

"Would you rather I wait until dark, walk into that dinner of yours, and demand you uphold your promise to mate with me right there and then?"

Her stomach clenched tight, and for a moment she thought she was going to throw up. "You wouldn't." But even as she said it, she knew he would. He was the wildest of the wild, and seemed eager to live up to his reputation—no matter what that might do to her.

And she had no one to blame but herself.

She licked her lips, searched desperately for an argument that might work. "I have to work here during the day."

"You've never taken a vacation? Hasn't anyone ever filled in for you?"

"That's beside the point."

"No, it's not. I want you, and I shall have you. I will play the charming suitor if you wish, but you will leave with me after dinner, and you will stay with me for the next five days."

She stared at him helplessly. Part of her *did* want

this—and not just because of her promise to Savannah. His touch affected her like no other, and she hungered for all he had to give. She was a wolf, after all, with a wolf's desires and urges—however repressed she might wish them to remain.

"Why?"

"Because I find myself craving more time with you."

But his tone was nonchalant, and that casualness hurt her—though she had no idea why. What else did she really expect from the man? This coldness was the very reason she'd chosen him.

"After that second excuse for a mating last night? I find that hard to believe."

He shrugged again. "I've an extremely high sex drive. Sometimes it will not allow me to pleasure my partner first."

"Some might call that selfishness."

"Some do. So what's your answer?"

She bit her lip, studying him—even though, in the end, she had no real choice. No matter what she did now, she was going to lose.

Lord, how she wished she'd never started down this crazy path. She wished she'd simply sat back and let the rangers do their job. But she hadn't, and it was too late for regrets now.

"Only if you play the part of a suitor. At least give my parents the illusion you really do care for me."

He brushed a kiss across her lips. "How much of a suitor do you want me to be?" His touch moved down to her moistness and probed gently. She bit her lip and fought the desire to press into his caress. "A newfound friend or a lover?"

"Friend," she said, her voice little more than a throaty whisper. And hated herself for wanting him so.

"Done." He placed both his hands on her waist and set her onto her feet. "You'd better get dressed, then, in case your parents get back early."

She stared at him, aching, trembling, and totally unable to believe he'd done it to her again.

"You're a bastard, you know that?"

"I've been called a lot worse in my life." The shutters were tight shut behind his eyes, and his face was impassive. If it wasn't for the rather obvious bulge in his pants, she would have thought him totally unaffected by their little session.

Moons, how she wished she could read this man—look beyond the wall he'd raised so effectively and see, or feel, what he was really thinking.

"I'll wait for you out back, if you'd like. Don't forget to bring your costume along when you come out."

He walked away, stride long and oh so casual. And once again, she had to resist the urge to throw something at his stiff, arrogant back.

Chapter Four

DUNCAN THRUST THE door open and stalked across the yard, breathing deeply of the sweet night air. It had taken a supreme effort of will to get up and walk away from the warmth and hunger in Neva's eyes. He would have liked nothing more than to give in to the desire that burned them both, but he couldn't. Not if he wanted to crack her defenses and discover who she worked for.

The quickest way to do that was to keep her off balance. To play the caring lover one moment and the cold, uncaring bastard the next—something many of his past lovers would probably say wasn't much of a stretch.

He stopped at the wire fence designating the end of the property and stared almost blindly into the forest beyond.

She'd been easy to find, and that had surprised him. All he'd had to do was ask a passerby in the main street where he might find Neva. That she was the daughter of Levon Grant, the wolf who'd spent much of his lifetime opposing all things Sinclair, surprised him even more.

And it would be interesting to see Levon's reaction tonight. It might tell him a whole lot about Neva and what was really going on.

At least he'd be able to sate his lust over the next few days. The thought sent a surge of heat through his veins. She might be working for whoever was behind these killings, but he still wanted her. And it wasn't just the sex. He wanted to see her warm smile, wanted to hear the rich music of her laugh.

Foolish, perhaps, but it was a desire he could not deny—not when he'd spent all afternoon watching her. The way she'd interacted with the diner's customers and her friend had only increased his fascination. She was nothing like any of the women he'd known up until now, projecting such an alluring mix of heated sexuality and sweet innocence.

So what did she want so badly that she was willing to sacrifice her self-esteem and destroy her reputation? He knew how strict families from the golden pack could be, and he was well aware of Levon's views when it came to the dance and mates. And while she'd obviously flirted with the dance in the years since puberty, she certainly wasn't a regular participant. Her innocence, her shyness about the sexual act, told him that.

So was she doing it for money, or something else? Maybe that was another direction in which he could push. If he could discover more about her wants and needs, he might just uncover a thread or two about their killer.

The door swung open behind him. He schooled his features into blankness and turned to face her. She no longer wore the diner's uniform but faded jeans and a soft white sweater that rolled around her neck and emphasized the fullness of her breasts. The ache in his groin increased tenfold, and he had to wonder how he was going to get through the next few hours without giving in to the need to touch her.

She stopped several feet away, face impassive but contempt obvious in her eyes. She threw the small box at his chest. He caught it instinctively.

"I won't wear that disgusting outfit anywhere!"

He raised an eyebrow. "You were wearing a whole lot less last night, were you not?"

Heat crept across her cheeks. "Yes, but the night was dark, and most of the others were wearing nothing at all."

"So?"

"So chaps and a whip are not my idea of a costume, and I refuse to wear them."

"I can compel you."

She crossed her arms and regarded him stonily. "You can try."

He glanced down to hide his slight smile. So there were limits beyond which even she would not step for her employer, and of that he was fiercely glad.

"Then what will you wear?"

"Does this dance have a theme, or is it just a costume party?"

"The theme is fantasies." And he was certainly having some erotic ones right now—with and without the cashmere sweater that hugged the taut peaks of her breasts so tantalizingly.

She regarded him for a second, then shook her head. "What is the fascination you Sinclairs have with all things sexual? There's more to life than just mating, you know."

"Is there?" he drawled. "It's a shame I've never met anyone who's tempted me to discover that."

His implied insult had her cheeks flaming again. "Is there any particular reason you're being such an arrogant bastard, or does it just come naturally?"

"You know the reputation of the Sinclairs. You judge."

She snorted softly, then looked over her shoulder as lights swept across the darkness and the sound of a car engine drew close. "Here come my parents," she said, meeting his gaze again. "Remember your promise."

"If you remember yours."

She swallowed, the pulse at her neck running faster than a startled deer. "Friends," she warned, stepping forward and twining her fingers through his. "Not lovers."

Though he nodded, he had no intention of following her rules. By the end of the night, there would be no doubt in her parents' minds as to why he was whisking her away for four days. Nor would they have any doubt of her willingness.

One more crack in her shields. One more push closer to that edge.

On the surface, dinner was a friendly, casual affair. Neva's parents played the charming hosts and Duncan played the suave, likable guest. But underneath, tension slithered. In her mother's case, it was simply annoyance that she'd been given no warning and had no time to prepare a proper welcome for the man she already considered a prospective son-in-law. Her father was harder to read. Like Neva, he had his shields fully up, so no one could tell what he was thinking. But his emotions leaked, regardless, and it was obvious he was well aware of Duncan's reputation. His distaste and anger were an emotive swirl that singed her senses.

She didn't eat much. Couldn't, given the churning in her stomach. Yet its cause wasn't only nerves, but Duncan's very closeness. Her mom had insisted they sit together, and every time he moved, his arm brushed hers, sending desire coursing through her. His actions last night and again in the diner had worked her into a feverish state, and her body responded to his every touch with needy, excited anticipation.

And she was positive it was deliberate. Heat burned every pore, but there was nothing she could do to cure or retreat from the situation.

"Why don't you and Duncan head into the living room?" her mother suggested, rising from the table once the meal was finished. "We'll bring in the coffee after we clean up."

Neva nodded and, without looking at Duncan, rose and led the way into the other room. Once out of immediate earshot of her parents, she swung around and faced him.

"Stop it," she said fiercely, clenching her fists and glaring up at him.

"Stop what?" He continued to advance on her.

She swallowed and backed away from the almost liquid desire so evident in his eyes.

"Stop playing this game. We're friends, nothing more. Remember?"

A cold smile teased his lips. He kept advancing, and she continued to back away.

"We're not friends, but we *are* definitely lovers. What is so wrong with letting your parents see that?"

Her back hit the wall and he stopped. She stared up at him, hating him and yet wanting him.

"We're not lovers. I doubt you even know the meaning of the damn word. We danced, that's all."

He slid his hand under her sweater, his fingers so cool compared to her fevered skin. She tried to step aside, but he pressed his hard body against hers, overwhelming her senses with his masculine odor, burning her mind with the flames of his hunger. His gaze all but devoured her as he leaned closer still.

"Don't." Her voice held very little force.

"Don't what?" His warm breath stroked her lips and sent a tingle of anticipation down her spine. "You want me to kiss you, Neva. Say it."

"No."

His cold smile became almost teasing. If it wasn't for the hardness in his eyes, it might have tugged at her heart. But he was still playing games, still playing her, for whatever sick reason.

He leaned closer still, and his lips brushed hers as he spoke. "One day you will, you know."

A tremor ran through her. He was right; she *did* want his kiss. She wanted him. Footsteps echoed down the hall. Her mother, coming closer. She thrust a hand between them and tried to push him away. It was about as effective as a fly pushing a boulder.

"Not until I get my kiss."

"Damn you to—"

The rest of her words were lost as his mouth took possession of hers. Had it been a harsh, demanding kiss, she might have been able to fight him. But it wasn't. It was a tender and gentle caress that promised things he would never deliver.

The footsteps stopped, then her mother cleared her throat. Heat flamed Neva's cheeks and she thrust both hands between them, but he would not be moved or hurried.

She could only thank the moon it was her mother. Her father would probably have demanded a wedding right there and then—and, given Duncan's eccentric, unpredictable behavior since they'd met, she wouldn't have put it past him to agree. If he was intent on ruining her life, that would certainly be the ultimate act of bastardy.

He dropped a second kiss on her nose, then stepped away, his fingers twining through hers. "Sorry, Mrs. Grant. Didn't mean to get carried away."

Her mother tittered like a teenager. "Please, call me Nancy. And it's all right. I'm not so old that I can't remember what young love is like."

Young love. The words made her feel ill. If she and Duncan shared anything, it was an undeniably strong sexual attraction. Once the moon had passed its zenith, that would fade, leaving nothing but dislike.

He pulled her down onto the sofa beside him and wrapped an arm around her shoulders. His long, strong fingers brushed the top of her breast and sent slithers of anticipation across her skin.

Don't you dare, she warned heatedly.

Dare what? This? His thumb pushed across one

aching nipple, and she jumped as if stung. *Or this?* He brushed sweet kisses down her neck. *Or—*

Enough! She pulled away, her cheeks so hot she was sure they were glowing. Thankfully, her mother had been too busy pouring coffee to see what he was doing.

You are not a teenager, Neva. Stop worrying about what your parents are thinking and start enjoying yourself a little.

Ari had said the same thing this afternoon—but neither of them had to live with the fallout of such actions. *I have to return to this life once the moon phase is over. You could at least be considerate enough to leave me something to return home to.* She lifted her gaze to his. *Or is my total destruction truly your aim over these next four days?*

Her words shook him. Though there was no slip in the mask that shuttered his face and eyes, she sensed the quick thrust of surprise. And, beneath it, a slither of loathing.

It was that emotion, more than anything, that alarmed her. What had she ever done to this man that some small part of him loathed her? And how could he still want her so badly if he did?

"So, what are your plans?" her mom said, handing them both a cup of coffee before sitting down. "And why haven't we met before now?"

"I work with the Eagle County search-and-rescue team. It's hard to get back here with any sort of regularity." He shrugged.

She wondered if he was telling the truth. She hoped he was, because her dad would undoubtedly check.

But then, this was all going to go to hell eventually anyway, so it didn't really matter.

And she certainly couldn't picture him as the type willing to risk his life rescuing others.

"Doesn't Mike Maher work search-and-rescue in that district?" Her dad walked into the room and leaned a shoulder against the wall, regarding Duncan with angry eyes.

"Mike Maher retired eighteen months ago. Dave Richards is in charge now. I'm his assistant."

It was hard to tell if her dad bought the story or not, as his expression and the tight blanket of anger that surrounded him hadn't changed. "So how did you two meet?"

Playbox, she told him quickly.

He glanced at her, an odd smile touching his lips. "We met at the Playbox. I was there watching *To Catch a Thief* three months ago and literally ran into her. She wasn't too pleased about getting a lap full of popcorn, let me tell you."

Her mother laughed, and Neva relaxed just a little. At least someone had bought the lie.

"And here I was," her mom said, "telling her only last week she'd never meet a nice man if she kept spending all that time watching old—"

"So, what is it you've come here for?" Her dad ignored her mother's reproachful look and continued to glare at Duncan.

Duncan hesitated and glanced at Neva. Just for a moment, indecision touched his eyes. Then the shutters flashed back up, and her stomach began to churn painfully.

"There's an awards dinner this Saturday I have to

attend. I've asked Neva to come back with me tonight and attend the dinner with me on Saturday."

Her dad didn't move, didn't blink. "And just where would she be staying?"

"With me."

She closed her eyes. Yup, the shit had just hit the fan.

Her mom laughed nervously. "In her own room, of course."

"No," Duncan breathed softly.

You couldn't even leave me that glimmer of respect, could you? She looked at him bitterly. *Just what in hell have I done to you to deserve this sort of treatment?*

You're a smart woman. You figure it out. His thoughts were as angry as hers. *I'm sure it won't be that hard.*

She stared at him. What on earth was he talking about? They'd never met before last night and, realistically, she was the only one who had the right to be angry. He was the one who had taken without giving. Who was still taking.

You could have said we were staying in separate rooms. It wouldn't have hurt.

I could have said we were going to the mansion and the dance tonight, too. Don't push, Neva.

Don't push? What a laugh. Pushing was *all* he was doing. She closed her eyes, took a deep breath, then turned to face the storm brewing on the other side of the room. It was a storm that would probably have happened eventually, but one she hadn't been prepared to face tonight. And certainly not with this man at her side.

"I absolutely forbid it," her mother said, voice flat.

"You can't forbid anything anymore," Neva replied. "I grew up a long time ago, Mother. Accept that fact and stop trying to control my life." Her words held a touch of bitterness that surprised them both.

Duncan squeezed her hand as if in encouragement. She wanted to rip her fingers free of his and smack him in the mouth, but she didn't, simply because she needed this charade to continue if she was to have any hope of her parents ever speaking to her again. Lord, if they found out her true destination was the dance at the mansion . . .

"And what of your sister?" her dad asked softly.

She raised her gaze to his. "She'll understand." But she wouldn't. Not this. But at least she'd be close enough to see Savannah, or talk to her telepathically when she *did* wake. "You're in charge of the Future's Committee, Dad. Like it or not, this is part of that future. It's not a sin to enjoy yourself before marriage." And, as Ari was prone to saying, who bought a car without test driving it?

Not that she was buying *anything* but four days of misery and frustration.

Her dad didn't say anything; he just walked out of the room. And that hurt deeper than anything she could have ever imagined. She blinked back the sting of tears and glanced at her mom.

"Please understand—"

"The only thing I understand," her mother cut in sharply, "is that you've decided to turn your back on everything we've taught you over the years." She thrust to her feet—a thin, disapproving figure. "I think you'd both better leave."

Neva stared at her for a moment, wondering if it was possible to hate anyone as much as she did Duncan right at that moment. Then she rose, gathered her handbag and that stupid parcel, and left. Duncan followed her out.

The night air hit like a slap across the face. She took a deep breath, but the shuddering had begun and wouldn't stop.

She leaned her back against the wall of the diner, closed her eyes, hugged her arms across her body, and silently cried. For the loss of her parents' respect. For her own stupidity in ever thinking she could calmly waltz into the Sinclair mansion and come away unscathed.

For the fact that she still wanted Duncan more than she'd wanted any other man in her life, no matter how much she hated him.

The moon certainly had a lot to answer for.

He stopped in front of her, a warm but forbidding presence. She didn't look at him, didn't say anything to him. Nothing she said seemed to make one bit of difference to whatever his agenda was anyway, so why bother?

"Neva—" he began eventually, voice soft but still emotionless.

Just for a moment, she had the distinct impression he was controlling himself very tightly, but it was an impression that made no sense at all. Maybe her psychic senses were as rattled as the rest of her.

"Don't," she said, voice harsh. "You've made it

very clear you have no respect for me and no respect for the way I'm trying to live my life."

"It's a little hard for me to show any respect when you show so little damn respect for yourself," he all but exploded.

His fury charged the air between them. She scrubbed the tears away with the sleeve of her sweater, then opened her eyes. He stood three feet away, a barely visible shadow against the blanket of night—a man with the face of an angel and the heart of a devil.

Though his stance appeared casual, the hands he had thrust into his pockets appeared clenched. It was the only visible sign of the angry tension she could almost taste.

"I had my reasons for attending the dance last night—" she began.

"Of that I have no doubt."

She clenched her fists. "How dare you judge me, when your own actions over the last twenty-four hours are no more worthy of respect than mine!"

"I have my reasons," he echoed, voice bitter.

"And what makes you think those reasons are any more noble than mine?"

"So why *did* you join the dance last night? If your reasons are so damn honorable, you have nothing to fear in telling me, have you?"

She was tempted, so very tempted, to tell him. But if he was treating her like this now, what would he do when he discovered she'd deliberately set out to seduce him? That she'd only intended to use him to gain entry into the mansion?

"You're destroying my life," she said softly, "and all I've done to you is agree to share a dance for the length of this moon cycle. Does that equation seem at all equal to you?"

She didn't wait for his answer. She just pushed herself from the wall and walked away.

Duncan took a deep breath and released it slowly. He let her walk away—a slender, angry, and very hurt shadow. It felt as if someone had reached into his chest and squeezed his heart tight. He could barely breathe under the crushing weight of her pain.

Of course, she was right. What he was doing to her wasn't entirely fair. Did the crime of spying on him merit the punishment of destroying her life? Hardly.

And what if she didn't know the reasons behind the assignment? What if she'd been spun some tale that made her believe she was doing the right thing? Given his wild past, any lie would be more than half-credible to those who didn't know him—and no one in Ripple Creek could truly say that they knew him these days. Not even his own family.

He took another deep, calming breath and thrust the uncertainty away. He needed to find this killer. Fast. He needed to get away from the mansion and its environs, and get back to the real world of his new life. A life he'd spent the past ten years building.

The problem was, he had no real clues as to the killer's identity, and four women had already lost their lives. If destroying Neva emotionally was the fastest way to find and stop this killer, then he had no real choice in the matter. Neva could rebuild her life. The women whose blood had been shed under the moon couldn't.

But these next four days were going to be hell. He might possess her physically, but by the time he'd finished with her, she would truly despise him. And he had a suspicion he might live to regret that.

But that would just be another item on an already too-long list, he thought bitterly.

Neva threw the parcel into the trash can, then stormed into her house and went straight to the cabinet that held the few bottles of alcohol she possessed. She poured herself a large glass of whiskey and drank it in one long gulp.

The liquid burned all the way down, settling like a weight in her agitated stomach. And though it gave her a heady rush, it certainly didn't make her feel any better about herself, or about the situation she'd so stupidly put herself into.

I got what I deserved for sticking my tail in places it had no right to be, she thought bitterly. And yet, at the same time, she very much suspected she'd have reacted the same way even if she *had* known what would happen. Savannah was her twin; she couldn't just sit around and do nothing. Besides, she had no doubt Savannah would have reacted the exact same way—though she probably would have picked a better method of entry into the mansion than the moon dance. It was just the quickest and easiest way . . . or so Neva had thought.

She sighed and rubbed her temples. What was done was done. Maybe once all this was over, she could try to talk to her parents. Explain. Or maybe Savannah would. She'd undoubtedly disappointed them; she understood that. But deep down, she was still the child they'd raised.

She walked into the kitchen and reached for the telephone, dialing Ari's cell.

"Y'ello," her friend said almost immediately.

"Sorry to interfere with your date, but I have a favor to ask."

"Hey, no probs. Honey buns has gone to the bar to get us a drink. What's the favor?"

Ari's exuberant tone made Neva smile. At least *she* was enjoying herself tonight. "Do you know anyone who'd be interested in working at the diner? I need a fill-in for the next few days."

"Wow, that coffee-spilling trick really worked, didn't it?"

If only. "Yeah, it worked."

"Cool." Ari hesitated. "You told the folks yet?"

"Yeah." Tears stung her eyes and she blinked them away. The deed had been done, and there was nothing she could do, or say, to take back the hurt. She could only hope they'd see past this sometime in the future. "The 'Sound of Silence' is the only tune I'll be hearing from them for a while."

Ari snorted. "They'll get over it. And you've played the dutiful daughter for long enough. Go screw that beautiful man's brains out and enjoy yourself for a change."

"That's the plan." And somewhere deep down, some small part of her half-wished it was. But she had a feeling the frustration of the last twelve hours would continue.

"So, where is he taking you?" Ari asked. "Somewhere wild and wicked, I hope."

If she told Ari just how wild and wicked, her friend would faint. Ari enjoyed the dance as much as the next wolf, but even she refused to go as far as those at the mansion.

"He has some awards dinner on Saturday." It was better to continue the lie, especially since Ari would more than likely give her dad a piece of her mind at the diner tomorrow. Her friend didn't believe in holding back thoughts or feelings, and she'd clashed with Levon more than once over the years. "I'm staying with him until then."

"An awards dinner? That sounds boring."

"But *he's* not." And wasn't that the truth!

"Woo-hoo!" Ari's excited bellow echoed down the line, and Neva winced and pulled the phone away from her ear as Ari continued. "So the deed has been done. Was he good?"

"A master." At manipulating. At ruining her relationship with her parents for no justifiable reason. At leaving her so totally frustrated she thought she'd burst.

At giving her a glimpse of the stars, then snatching it away again.

And the fact that her mind placed the most emphasis on those last two only proved how rattled she was.

"Then I expect to see you in a week with the biggest smile on your face. *And* I'll want details."

"Only if you buy the coffee. I may not have a job when I get back."

"They can't fire you. Who else would they find to work the sort of hours you do for such crap pay?"

She had a point. "So, back to the original question—do you know anyone who could fill in at such short notice?"

"Yeah, my nieces. They've been looking for part-time work, so between the two of them they could probably cover all your shifts."

"Perfect. I'll talk to you next week."

"Take care of yourself, sweetie," Ari trilled and disconnected.

Neva placed the phone back on the receiver and stood staring out at the dark expanse of her back garden. Duncan hadn't followed her into the house yet, and while she had no doubt he would soon appear, she was extremely glad for the space.

She closed her eyes and reached for the warmth of her sister's mind, as she had in the past when in trouble. But there was no response other than a slight stirring in the cloud of memories. Consciousness was drawing closer, but it could be several days yet before it came.

She bit her lip and resolutely turned away from the window, making her way upstairs to her bedroom. She packed a bag with enough clothes to last four days, then studied her wardrobe for something to wear to his stupid costume party tonight. She flicked through her dresses and eventually pulled out the elegant black number she'd bought two years ago when she and Ari had gone on a somewhat drunken shopping spree in Denver.

It was form-fitting, plunging past her breasts in the front and to the base of her spine at the back. The skirt was full and swirled around her toes, but the four panels were split right up to the top of her thighs so that, when she walked, she flashed a lot of leg. The hem of the skirt was beaded, the tiny drops forming gentle flames that shimmered like the real thing with every movement.

Match it with that stupid mask she'd worn last night and she might just pass as a she-devil. Which was only fitting, given her partner.

She found a matching pair of heels, then took the lot downstairs. Duncan still hadn't appeared, and hope flickered briefly. Maybe he'd given up his whole sordid game—whatever it was. Maybe he was so overcome by remorse that he'd decided to just walk away.

And maybe tomorrow the earth would stop spinning.

She rubbed her forehead. A large glass of whiskey on top of an agitated and practically empty stomach had not been one of her better ideas. She stretched out on the sofa and closed her eyes. The temporary darkness felt like heaven to her aching head.

She wouldn't sleep; she'd just close her eyes and rest a little.

Duncan glanced at his watch as he followed Neva's scent toward what he presumed was the front door of her house. It was nearly eight. He'd spent almost an hour on the phone, covering his one lie should Neva's parents call to check. Once Dave, his boss and good friend, had known the reasons behind Duncan's lie, he'd had no hesitation in playing along. He'd even offered use of his contacts in the sheriff's department. And Duncan had no doubt he'd need them before this week was out.

He took the steps two at a time and knocked lightly on the front door. There was no answer, though he knew she was home. The warm scent of citrus swirled around him—a warmer, more alluring scent than jasmine, and one that suited her better. Heat surged through his body, though after this afternoon's efforts, it certainly didn't take much to get him aroused.

He twisted the handle and the door opened. Light shone softly in the kitchen, and a small suitcase waited near the door, along with a pair of shoes and a long black dress.

"Neva?"

He walked into the living room and found her on the sofa, fast asleep. He squatted beside her and gently brushed the dark gold strands of hair from her face. She stirred slightly, murmuring something he couldn't quite catch.

Her delicate features had a drawn look to them, and the smudges beneath her eyes were as dark as bruises. She'd obviously gotten as little sleep as he last night.

He trailed his fingers down her cheek to the full lips he ached to kiss, then on past the long line of her neck to the round fullness of her breasts. The cashmere sweater was soft under his fingertips, her nipples hard.

He rose. His family's costume dance didn't start until midnight, so they didn't have to leave just yet. He walked out of the living room and headed up the stairs.

Her bedroom was like her—soft, feminine, and golden. The bed was big, crowded with brightly colored cushions and cheerful bears. He swept them aside and pulled back the comforter and sheet. Then he went back down the stairs.

She hadn't moved. He took a deep breath, then gently pulled off her shoes, then her jeans and panties. The sweater he left. He had too many fantasies about caressing her in that sweater to take it off right now.

He tucked his hands under her body, then carefully lifted her. She snuggled into his chest, her skin so cool compared to his, then sighed softly. It was then he smelled the alcohol on her breath.

Given how little she'd eaten this evening, it was probably that, more than anything, that had made her fall asleep. And would certainly explain why she hadn't woken, spitting fire, when he'd stripped her.

He carried her up the stairs and placed her in her bed. For a moment, he simply stood there, his gaze lingering hungrily on her breasts under the cashmere sweater before moving on, past the flat plane of her stomach to the golden triangle of soft curls, remembering the way her long legs had wrapped around his waist as he thrust so very deep. He almost came just thinking about it.

He quickly stripped and climbed in beside her. She wouldn't be happy to find him there. This was her sanctuary—the one place no woman wanted to find a man unless he was invited. But he had no intention of leaving, or letting her leave, until he'd finished what he'd started this afternoon in the diner.

He wrapped an arm around her waist, pulled her close, and waited for her to wake.

•

The dream was one of pleasure.

Neva lay wrapped in the darkness, part of her covered but part of her exposed and so ready for invasion. And she was invaded. By hands. By tongue. By body. She writhed and moaned, her skin on fire, every muscle screaming for release. The stroking continued. Outside. Inside. It took her higher and higher, until the need was so strong she couldn't even breathe. Then she came with such powerful force she screamed to the moon. It was a sound echoed by her dream lover.

And she woke to discover it was no dream.

To discover the gentle invasion had not yet stopped.

"That was but a beginning," Duncan whispered in her ear. His tongue gently explored her lobe, and she shuddered under the assault.

She opened her eyes and realized she was home. In bed. *Her* bed.

Anger surged. He had no right to be here. "What the hell are you doing?"

He shifted his weight off her, then moved his hand down her stomach and gently pressed past her damp curls. She shifted, trying to escape his touch, yet unable to deny the sweet pleasure of it.

"What does it feel like I'm doing?" His voice was lazy, amused.

Her gaze flew to his. His dark eyes were filled with enough heat to start a forest fire—and that was certainly the impact it had on her. "Seducing me in my own bed."

"That's correct."

"You have no right." She hesitated, eyes widening as his mouth drew close.

"I have every right," he murmured, breath warm across her lips. "And every intention."

His kiss was a honeyed affirmation of his words, a gentle possession she could not escape, didn't really want to escape. The moon was high, and given this afternoon's and last night's frustrations, she so very desperately needed his touch. Needed him. Though she would never have admitted as much.

His mouth moved on, trailing fiery kisses down her neck to her breasts. She still wore her sweater, but he didn't seem to care. His teeth encased a nipple, biting lightly. She squirmed, trying to deny pleasure as he sucked and nipped one aching nub, then the other. As the gentle assault continued, she gave in to the urge to touch him, and ran her hands down the muscled plane of his stomach to stroke the still-hard length of him. He shuddered, thrusting into her touch, and an oddly primitive sense of power ran through her. Whatever else he might think or feel about her, he couldn't deny his need for her.

A small comfort that was better than nothing, she supposed.

She continued to explore as he explored—by taste, by touch. Heat rose, shimmering between them, warming the night, warming them, until his touch pushed her into a place where only sensation existed. The air was hot and thick and almost impossible to breathe. Every inch of her quivered under the relentless assault of his fingers and tongue. Then the convulsions began, the power of them curling through her body like a tidal wave.

It was a wave that became even more glorious as he thrust inside her again. She groaned and wrapped her legs around him, forcing him deeper still, until it felt as if the rigid heat of him was claiming every inch.

Her climax hit, stealing her breath, stealing her sanity, sweeping her into a world that was sheer, unadulterated bliss. A heartbeat later he went rigid against her, the power of his release tearing a groan from his throat. He held her for one last thrust, then his lips sought hers, and his kiss was a lingering taste of passion.

In that one moment, all the fears that had plagued her the first time they'd made love returned in a rush. Because this time he hadn't only let her glimpse the stars, he'd well and truly taken her past them.

Worse still, there was something in the way he touched her that she'd never felt before, and it scared her. Because no matter how powerful the dance, it would never mean anything to a man like Duncan Sinclair. He was a lone wolf—a man who lived for momentary pleasure, who searched for nothing beyond it. And he'd certainly proven time and again over the last twenty-four hours that he cared nothing for *her*.

And the mere fact that she was even thinking something like that, after the abominable way he'd treated her, showed just how dangerous the next four days were going to be.

He rolled off her and onto his back, one arm flung across his forehead as he stared up at the ceiling. He might have been alone for all the notice he seemed to take of her. The night air caressed her rapidly cooling skin, but it had little to do with the shiver that ran down her spine.

"You'd better get dressed," he said. "We have to be back at the mansion by twelve."

His voice was flat, unemotional. She certainly wouldn't have thought they'd just shared a mind-blowing dance only moments before.

"Right," she said, keeping her voice as flat as his. "I'll just go take a shower."

"Don't."

She stared at him. He didn't look at her, didn't acknowledge her, but just continued to gaze at the ceiling. And it was beginning to grate. "Why not?"

"Because I want everyone to smell my scent on you. I want them to know you're mine, and mine alone."

Relief slithered through her. At least he was keeping one promise. "I can't see how having a shower will affect that."

"It's the dance, and the moon rides high. They must know I have claimed you tonight, or there will be challenges."

Her stomach began to churn. What in the hell type of dance was he taking her to? "What do you mean?"

"What I said. Tonight is my pack's get-together. Some bring mates. Others bring dancers to be shared. If you don't have my scent on you, you'll be considered the latter rather than the former."

The implications of that swirled through her and settled like a weight in her stomach. "So it's an orgy?"

He finally glanced at her, and amusement sparked briefly in his eyes before it was quenched. "The whole moon dance is an orgy."

She supposed it was—at least where the Sinclairs were concerned. "Can I at least clean up a little?"

"If you hurry." He hesitated, and a mirthless smile

touched his full lips. "Wouldn't want to miss any of the fun, now, would we?"

She wondered yet again just what she'd gotten herself into. How in hell was she going to get through the rest of *this* night, let alone the next four?

Chapter Five

DUNCAN STOPPED AT the top of the stairs and let his gaze roam across the lust-filled darkness. This ballroom was far smaller than the main one, but no one here really cared. Tonight was for the main pack to come together and rejoice in the freedom of the moon. And if there was ever a time to discover discontent, it was tonight, when the heat of the moon and the whispering magic entwined through the music to make blood boil and tongues loosen.

Neva edged closer to him. Her hand was tense in his and he could smell her fear as clearly as he could taste the seductive aroma of her femininity. And while he could certainly understand her desire not to be here, right now he had no choice. Not only was it a perfect night to catch nearly the whole pack in one place, it also provided yet another opportunity to push her that little bit further.

He spied his father and two of his brothers near the buffet table. He swept his gaze around the room again and saw René enjoying the delights of a statuesque blonde he vaguely recognized. He smiled grimly. His brother certainly wasn't bothering to mourn the loss of a mate. But then, why would he? In the heated rush of the moon, she'd been just another face. Just another body to sate his lust on. René might have momentarily mourned her loss, but in the end he didn't truly care. There were plenty of willing replacements to be found in the Sinclair mansion.

A fact Duncan knew entirely too well. And it was one of the reasons he'd left.

The only trouble was, he wasn't sure anymore if there was anything better out there. Not for him, anyway.

He led the way down the steps and into the crowd. The heavy beat of the music throbbed through his veins, and the air was thick with the rich aroma of sex.

He glanced at Neva. Though the mask covered half her face, he could still see the glow of color in her cheeks. She kept her gaze firmly fixed ahead, but the smell of her arousal stung the air. She might be from the golden tribe, but she was still a wolf, and she could no more ignore the scents and sounds of those around her than he could.

His gaze slipped from her face to her body. She looked absolutely stunning in the barely there black dress, and every step she took revealed tantalizing flashes of warm, golden skin. Her hair was a river flowing down her back, swaying like golden silk with every movement, drawing the eye to the perfection of her rear. He wasn't the only one who hungered for her. It was a feeling that followed them as they made their way through the crowded room—a sensation she would feel more acutely than he could.

And while he knew his proprietary hold on her ensured no one would approach her, she didn't. Left alone, the fear so evident in her pretty eyes would rise, and maybe—just maybe—she'd run to whoever had employed her to watch him.

He reached the far wall and found space enough to press her back into the shadows.

Trepidation flicked through her eyes. "What now? You ravage me in front of your packmates to show what a big man you are?"

If he'd had the time, yes, most definitely. He ran his hand down the long line of her neck, noting the wild flutter of her pulse under his fingertips. It wasn't fear, just as the widening of her pupils wasn't fear. Underneath the strictness of her upbringing, there was a wild wolf desperate to be free. And if what they'd shared so far was any indication of what was to come, he certainly wouldn't mind being her mate when that wildness finally exploded.

He leaned close, letting his lips brush hers as he said, "Is that what you want me to do?"

Her breath caught, then caressed his mouth with quick warmth. He let his hand drift down to her breasts and gently rubbed one firm nipple through the silk of her dress. She shivered, her lips parting, her breathing rapid.

He pressed himself closer so that it seemed every inch of their bodies was molded together. He could feel her trembling, feel the heat radiating off her skin. The musky scent of her desire spun around him, the wild beat of her heart resonating through every fiber of his being.

"Tell me what you want," he murmured and brushed another kiss across her lips.

"Food," she all but gasped

He grinned and pushed away. "Then food you shall have."

Surprise flitted through her eyes. Good—because the more he kept her off balance, the more likely it was that she'd make a mistake.

"Wait for me here. I have to go talk to my father, then I'll bring you back something to eat."

"Why can't I come with you?"

"Because I have pack business to discuss, and you're not of my pack. Wait here." Then he turned and walked away from her.

Neva crossed her arms and watched his muscular back disappear into the crowd. The urge to run after him was fierce, but she fought it. As much as she didn't want to be left alone in this place, it at least provided an opportunity to do some investigating. She swept her gaze across the room. There was a feel to the air she didn't like—a feeling that went beyond wanting, beyond lust. One that was almost angry.

But it was a feeling she couldn't pinpoint to one person or group. Not yet, anyway.

The ballroom was smaller than the one she'd seen last night, but just as dark. There was no dance floor, just couples moving through the shadows—some talking, some making love, some doing both.

Most of the women wore outlandish costumes, and the men leather pants that left little to the imagination. Chaps and a whip seemed almost tame in comparison to some of the attire, but she was still glad she'd refused to wear them. There'd been enough hunger aimed her way as Duncan had led her across the room as it was.

A small band occupied the far corner of the room, and their music was a caress of sound that raced through her veins—a sensual and erotic melody designed for one thing only: seduction.

She shook her head. The Sinclairs were certainly a hedonistic lot, but surely that was no justification for killing their mates. Especially when the women involved weren't even of the Sinclair tribe.

She blinked at the thought. Was that a clue? Could the killer be going after only those who *weren't* of the Sinclair pack?

It was certainly a possibility. Maybe the hatred she could feel in this room tonight wasn't aimed so much at the Sinclairs but at the outsiders among them. Of which she was one.

She rubbed her arms, her gaze seeking Duncan. He stood near the buffet table with three other men. Given the similarities of their features, it wasn't much of a guess to say two were his brothers and the other his father. And it was easy to see where the sons got their looks. Even though his hair had gone silver, the Sinclair pack leader was a picture of male perfection.

And, from all reports, the sons had learned their wild ways from their father. While all four had been born to one woman, Zeke Sinclair never committed himself to her, preferring to cast his charms more widely during the moon dance.

Her gaze slipped to Duncan. Would he chase other wolves during this moon phase? While sanity suggested it might be good if he did, some small part of her reacted almost angrily at the thought.

Which was totally insane. She'd come here for one reason only—to catch a murderer. What Duncan did or said during the next few days didn't really matter, particularly as he'd made it so clear he was only after one thing from her. At least if he was with other mates, she'd have more time to investigate. Which is exactly what she should be doing right now.

Tearing her gaze away from him, she scanned the room again. She saw a mask that was familiar, and surprise rippled through her. Betise hadn't mentioned that she'd be attending the dance this week, and Neva wasn't sure whether to be happy about seeing her or not. While Betise was a regular customer at the diner, she very rarely spoke to anyone but Neva and Ari. The chance of Betise mentioning Neva's presence at the mansion was slim.

Even so, she briefly thought about retreating to the shadows and keeping out of sight. But if anyone would know the secrets of this place, it would be Betise. She'd certainly proven a valuable source of information so far.

The blond wolf was dressed in what looked like a dozen gauzy veils, and every movement revealed glimpses of flesh. She was talking to the man Neva had seen Duncan with last night. Even as Neva watched, the man made a chopping motion with his hand, then walked away. What Neva could see of Betise's expression was savage, to say the least.

If that look was anything to go by, it probably wasn't the best time to be asking Betise about the Sinclairs. But right now, Neva had little choice. She might not get a second chance.

She took a deep breath, then headed back into the

crowd. The sensual beat of the music was accompanied by sighs of pleasure and the slap of flesh against flesh. Revulsion stirred, yet the fever rose in her blood, and the deep-down ache Duncan had started only minutes ago became fiercer. *She* might hate this sort of wanton, exhibitionist behavior, but the wildness within hungered to join in. Hungered to become part of this lusty, sweating crowd.

She definitely *wasn't* that different from any of those here tonight, no matter what her parents might have taught her over the years. High ideals meant little in the heat of the moon, it seemed.

She finally broke free of the crowd and saw Betise heading for a side exit. She followed, breathing deeply the crisp night air before she called out to the other wolf.

Betise swung around, and surprise flitted across her hard features as she took off her mask. "Neva. I didn't expect to find you here tonight."

Neva shrugged and stopped several feet away from the other woman. "If I had any choice, I wouldn't be." Though perhaps *sense* would have been a better word to use than *choice*.

Betise frowned. "Why not?"

"Apparently I agreed to some form of ancient binding without even realizing it, and now I'm stuck here for the remainder of this moon phase."

Betise's pale eyebrows rose. "Who did a moon binding with you?"

"Duncan. What a bitch, huh?"

"I guess it is if you don't want it." The slight edge in Betise's voice suggested a binding was something she certainly wouldn't have minded.

"Well, I don't, believe me."

Betise smiled, but it never reached her silvery green eyes, and the thick sensation of envy briefly stung the air. "Being bonded to Duncan the rest of this phase should be a pretty amazing experience."

Amazing was certainly one way to describe what they'd shared so far. *Harrowing* was another. So was *life-destroying*. And it was all self-inflicted. No one had forced her into this situation. She'd stepped into it with her eyes wide open.

She raised an eyebrow. "I take it you've danced with Duncan?"

"In times past." Betise waved a hand toward the distant fountain. "I need to cool down. You want to walk with me?"

Neva nodded and fell into step beside the older wolf. "When was this?" She kept her voice carefully neutral, even though she was desperate to know.

The moon and this place were making her insane, for sure.

"Before he left for Denver. He and I had something of an on-again, off-again relationship in the last year he was here." Betise sighed again. "I honestly thought he'd ask me to do the moon ceremony. I know he wanted to start a family."

Surprise, and something else, something she couldn't even begin to explain, twisted deep inside Neva. The moon ceremony was a life-bonding ritual that was performed the night of the full moon—and one that was only ever performed between soul mates. But if Betise and Duncan were soul mates, why was he with her rather than Betise? "We are talking about Duncan Sinclair here, right? You know, the wildest of the wild, the man you said no woman would ever tame."

Her smile was bitter. "Why do you think I'm so sure no woman could tame him? He couldn't even commit to his soul mate."

Neva frowned, for the first time wishing she could read Betise's mind. Although she really had no doubt Betise was telling the truth—the pain in her eyes was indication enough of that. "So what happened?"

"I don't know. He disappeared for several weeks, then ended up in jail down in Denver. By the time I got down there, he'd been released and I lost track of him again."

"And you never tried to find him?" If *her* soul mate had disappeared, she would have moved heaven and earth to find him again.

Betise's glance was dark. "Of course I did. But by the time I did, a couple of years had passed, and he wanted nothing more to do with me. I still don't know why."

Doubt stirred through Neva. That made no sense— not if they were soul mates. "You've talked to him recently?"

"No." Betise hesitated. "But I might try this phase, if you don't mind."

"Go ahead," she said. Even though the insane part of her *did* mind. Very much.

The older wolf stopped next to the three-tiered fountain and scooped up a handful of water. She took a sip, then splashed the remainder across her breasts. "How's your sister?" she asked, after a moment.

Neva was startled. The news of Savannah's attack had been suppressed, with the hospital staff under clear orders to say nothing. She suspected the attack on her sister had made the rangers all the more determined to track this killer down themselves, because normally murders were investigated by off-reservation forces—like the State Police or the FBI—depending on who or what the victims were. But of course Betise would know, since she worked at the hospital.

"Slowly recovering. I think she'll probably wake up in the next day or so," Neva responded.

Betise nodded. "Do the rangers have any idea who attacked her?"

Memories rose—quick snapshots of slender shoulders, long legs, sharp teeth. Teeth that had torn so very deep. Neva shuddered and forced them away. She didn't want to relive Savannah's assault. Not ever.

She shrugged. "They're not telling us a lot at the moment."

"That's got to be upsetting for your father." Betise hesitated, then added, "I'm surprised you decided to come to the mansion when your sister is so ill in the hospital."

Neva scooped up some cool water, sipping at it slowly as she tried to think of a plausible way to answer the question. "The day before she was attacked, Sav and I were discussing the things we wanted to do before we die." She hesitated. "I guess her accident brought home just how close death really is, and how little I've done with my life."

"And a moon dance was on top of your list of things to experience?"

Right alongside sprouting wings and flying to the moon. "Yeah, but one night, not five."

Betise chuckled. "At least you're with Duncan. He's one of the best lovers you'll find here at the mansion."

But only when he wanted to be, Neva thought sourly. She forced a smile. "Sounds like you've had a dance or two with a few of the Sinclairs."

Betise's smile was almost wistful. "You could say that."

"And that gorgeous specimen I saw you dancing with a few minutes ago?"

The older wolf's smile faded and her face became hard again. "That was René, one of Duncan's older brothers."

"I take it things aren't going well between you?" And why was she dancing with René if Duncan was her soul mate? None of this was making any sense, and it only made her wish again she could read the other woman's mind. Her body language might suggest no lies, but for some indefinable reason, Neva suspected the whole truth was not being revealed.

"No." Betise's reply was short. Sharp. "He's just as bad as the rest of them. They all make promises in the heat of the moment, but never—" She bit off the words and took a deep breath. "Sorry. I shouldn't go on about it."

Neva wished she would. She had a feeling she'd learn a whole lot more that way. "I totally understand, believe me. Duncan hasn't exactly been a picture of politeness in the day I've known him."

Betise grunted softly. "It's a wonder someone isn't killing Zeke's get rather than just their lovers."

Bingo, Neva thought. Nothing in any of Savannah's reports had indicated the victims had been anything more than casual dancers. She ducked her gaze away, taking another sip of water as she tried to calm her racing heart. "So it's their mates being targeted?"

Betise hesitated. "So rumor has it."

At least it gave her a lead she could follow. While she couldn't risk talking to Duncan's brothers, she could certainly track down their mates and talk to them. "Did you know any of them?"

Betise shook her head. "Though I may have met them here. The masks make it difficult to say."

Neither of them seemed to have had any trouble recognizing each other, even with the masks on. "Aren't you worried that you might be in danger?"

The older wolf's smile was bleak. "No. From what I've heard, the victims were more permanent mates rather than casual dancers."

"So why haven't you gone to the rangers with this information?"

"With little more than a rumor? I doubt it would be appreciated—by the rangers or the Sinclairs."

The Sinclairs might not appreciate it, but the rangers certainly would. Right now, they were desperate for the slightest scrap of information that could lead them toward the killer.

"So make an anonymous phone call."

"Not from the mansion. The phones are tapped."

Thanks for the warning, Neva thought. "Who by?"

"It was done years ago, apparently."

"Why?"

"Because the Sinclairs don't trust anyone but blood, and there are always people out to implicate them in some scandal or another."

Her father being one of them, Neva thought. Although he, at least, had always been straightforward when it came to his battles with the Sinclairs.

Betise glanced skyward and stepped away from the fountain. "I have another dance to attend. You here all phase?"

"Unfortunately."

Something flashed in Betise's pale eyes. Annoyance—or envy, perhaps. "Then I'll see you tomorrow night." And she spun away and walked toward the row of aspens and red-trunk pines.

Neva took another sip of water, then glanced at the ballroom. As much as she didn't want to go back in there, she needed to find out who danced with each of the Sinclair brothers. She couldn't risk asking anyone and raising suspicions, which left her with only one option—watching them. And on a night like this, and in a place like this, that wasn't going to be an easy task.

Duncan glanced at the side exit for the umpteenth time. Neva had left a few minutes ago, and if she didn't return very soon, he was going after her. Though he really doubted that she'd risk meeting her employer right now, he couldn't take the chance she wasn't.

"Any progress?" Zeke asked softly.

Duncan shook his head, switching his gaze from the door to René as his brother began talking to a pretty redhead. "Did you manage to get a copy of the autopsy report?"

"My source doesn't want to risk being seen, and so won't be coming until after four."

By which time, only a few diehards would be left at the dance. "Who's that redhead René's with?"

Zeke hesitated. "Rozin, I think her name is. Why? Fancy her yourself, do you?"

Duncan gave his father a wry smile. "Hardly. I've got my hands full with our little spy."

Zeke's dark eyes gleamed with amusement. "Wolves from the golden tribe can be surprisingly wanton once they shuck the restraints."

Neva hadn't thrown off her restraints yet, but the wildness within was certainly beginning to show. "Is Rozin one of René's regulars?"

Zeke frowned. "Not that I know of, though he's certainly been with her a few times this phase. Why?"

Duncan swept his gaze around the room, looking for his other brothers. "What about Tye and Kane?"

"Kane's got two regulars left alive, and Tye one."

"If the killer is targeting your sons' lovers, it might be wise to have someone watching over those women. The last thing we need right now is another death."

Zeke nodded. "I arranged it this afternoon."

"Then I hope they're discreet. You know how Tye feels about being observed."

"A fact the first guard I'd placed on his mate discovered a little too quickly. The second is keeping a more sensible distance."

Zeke's voice was dry, and Duncan smiled. "And well out of the range of Tye's fists, I gather."

"Exactly." Zeke paused, then added, "The rangers want to fingerprint the five of us."

"So they've finally found a print?"

"They took it off the last victim's skirt, apparently."

"If she was here the whole night, that print could belong to anyone."

"It was a blood print, and evidently it matches the blood type they've found under the previous victims' nails."

"The previous reports said the blood they'd found was A-positive. None of us are."

"The rangers don't know that."

Duncan glanced back at the door. Still no sign of Neva. "It might be best if we cooperate with them on this. Maybe when they realize it's not one of us, they'll start looking for the real killer."

Zeke smiled. "You really think that?"

"No." Because the last time *he'd* cooperated with the police, he'd ended up in jail. "I'll drop by the ranger office tomorrow and make arrangements."

"Do that. And come to my suite about five. We'll see if Mariata's autopsy report varies any from the other three." Zeke hesitated, his smile widening. "If you dare spend the time away from your pretty spy, that is."

Duncan grinned. "With what I intend to do to her over the next couple of hours, she'll undoubtedly be in a deep and exhausted sleep come five A.M." He clapped his father on the arm, then headed for the door.

Neva had barely taken three steps when Duncan appeared in the doorway. The moonlight gleamed off his skin and caressed his face, making him appear more like a dark angel than ever. His obsidian eyes were almost otherworldly.

And so hot. So hungry.

Her throat went dry and she stopped. His gaze swept down her body, and he might as well have been caressing her with his hand, because every inch of her responded with heated delight.

"What happened to the plate of food I requested?" Her voice came out little more than a husky whisper, and his eyes gleamed in response.

"The buffet has been sitting there for a while. I thought something fresher would be better."

"A burger would be good right now."

His slow smile made her stomach flip-flop. "I had something more substantial in mind."

She let her gaze roam down the firm planes of his body until she came to the very visible evidence of his arousal under his jeans.

"So I can see," she murmured—and even as she said it, she wondered where her mind was. Playing games with this man was *not* a good idea. Not when his need blanketed the air, making it difficult to even breathe. Not when desire skated across her skin and it felt like her heart was going to race out of her chest. And she knew it wasn't the moon's influence, but the man himself. *She* might hate him, but the wolf within wanted him. Badly.

But she didn't dare give that part of herself freedom. Not here, and definitely not with Duncan. Once the murderer was caught and this moon phase was over, she had fences to mend and a life to get back to. A life *he* had practically destroyed.

"Why don't we take this discussion somewhere a little warmer?" His voice was soft and sexy enough to melt stone.

She nodded mutely. He touched a hand to her back, searing heat past her spine. A tremor ran through her. What was it about this man that got to her so badly? Surely it was more than just his experience and skill when it came to lovemaking. Lord, she might be new to the mansion and its environs, but she *wasn't* new to the dance itself. She'd had several mates over the years since puberty, but none of them had ever affected her this deeply. This quickly.

There again, none of them had the reputation that Duncan had, either.

He led her along the path and past several doors. The swirl of music from the ballroom gradually died, and the only sound to be heard was the soft crunch of gravel under their shoes. The moon caressed the night with its silver light, and the heat of it raced through her veins, seeming to pool where his fingers pressed so lightly, so tenderly, against her back.

He guided her through an arch, then opened a door and ushered her inside. Though the room was dark, her night sight was wolf-keen. They were in what looked like a commercial kitchen, filled with stainless-steel appliances and countertops.

"We're raiding the kitchen?" she asked, amused.

"Can you think of a better place to get fresh food?"

"I guess not."

There were no seats, so she pulled herself onto a countertop and caught the loaf of bread he tossed her. He turned on a small light near the stove, then continued on to the refrigerator, pulling out a plate of cold meats and a platter of fruit. Which was exactly what she'd wanted five minutes ago, but definitely not what she wanted right now. The thought sent a shiver across her skin. Being with this man, in this place, was dangerous. It made her hunger for things that just weren't safe. Or sane.

He placed the two platters on the table, then met her gaze. His dark eyes were shuttered, his face shadowed. If not for the hunger that burned through the night, she might have thought him immune to the moon fever and her.

So why was he even with her? Especially when Betise was at the mansion? It didn't make sense—particularly given the loathing she'd sensed in him earlier. Or was there more to the story than what Betise had said? Did Duncan celebrate the rising of the moon with casual partners because he had no other choice? Had she turned away from him rather than he from her?

She didn't know, and she suspected he wouldn't tell her if she asked.

He pressed her knees open then stepped between her legs and pulled her close. Her breasts were sandwiched against his chest, and she could feel the wild thumping of his heart. Could feel the heat radiating off his skin, surrounding her in a furnace that was all desire.

"Anything else you want?"

His breath caressed her lips, and a tremor ran through her. "A knife to cut the bread would be good."

"And a soda?"

She nodded. She couldn't do anything else because her voice seemed to have fled.

His mouth brushed hers—a tingling, tantalizing

promise of what was to come—then he stepped back and returned to the refrigerator. "Ice?"

Again she nodded. Within seconds, he was back with two drinks and a bread knife. He cut several slices of bread, offering one to her as he slid the meat platter closer. She made herself a sandwich and ate it, her skin tingling with awareness as his gaze did a slow tour of her body.

She finished her drink and put the glass down on the counter. The remaining ice clinked softly, a sound that seemed to reverberate in the tense, overheated silence.

Or maybe it was just she who was overheated.

He stepped closer again. She instinctively inched back. A smile touched his sensual lips and he reached out, gently running his fingers down her neck and across her shoulder, displacing the thin strap of her dress as he continued down her arm.

She swallowed, but it didn't seem to help the dryness in her throat. Didn't seem to help the dizzy trip of her pulse. He was far too close. All she could smell was the earthy spice of him; all she could feel were the whisper of his breath and the caress of his hand on her skin. And all she wanted was to feel him inside.

It was crazy. Totally and utterly crazy. For no good reason, this man had forever altered her relationship with her parents. And while that might have happened eventually, it was a change she hadn't been prepared to deal with just yet. Especially when the man by her side was Duncan—a wolf so totally opposite to everything she wanted in a mate.

But the moon was burning through her veins, and at this particular moment she didn't care who he was or what he'd done. In all the years since puberty, she'd never felt anything this strong—and that in itself was a scary thought. But maybe it was nothing more than a combination of the moon and being in the presence of a wolf well versed in the art of seduction.

His fingers slipped back up her arm and across to her other shoulder. The second strap slid down her arm, and her breath caught as her dress shimmied to her waist. His gaze met hers, and in those dark depths she saw a desire so intense it made her squirm.

"You feel hot," he murmured, leaning forward to brush the line of her neck with feather-soft kisses.

She closed her eyes, enjoying the sensation. "It's warm in the kitchen."

"Very warm. Perhaps we should try to cool you down a little."

The glass clinked again, and she opened her eyes. "Ice is not a good idea."

A smile teased his lips. "Really?" He ran his hand up her arm, the cube of ice trapped in his palm. The momentary chill of the ice was quickly lost to the heat of his touch, and the overall sensation was incredibly arousing.

His hand reached her chest, then moved down. She tensed, her breath catching in her throat. The cube skimmed one breast, then the other, and she gasped, jerking back from his touch. He chuckled, then his mouth enclosed one nipple, and she forgot the chill, forgot everything, and simply enjoyed as he sucked and nipped.

Then, when she was all but squirming with need, he continued on—past her breasts, down toward her stomach. The ice had become little more than droplets of water running past the heat of his fingers, quickly soaked up by the folds of her dress. But the silky material provided no barrier to his hand, and as his fingers slid into her moist heat, she groaned and leaned back, giving him greater access.

"You want me, little wolf. Say it."

"No." It was obvious that she wanted him, but she was never going to admit it. Because if she admitted *that*, then she'd have to admit just how intensely he affected her. And that was one pleasure she refused to give him.

"What harm is there in admitting you have needs like everyone else?"

He continued to slide a finger through her moistness, every stroke providing just the right amount of pressure. Ripples of pleasure radiated across her body.

"Great harm," she somehow managed to croak, "when the man who asks seems intent on destroying my life."

"Freedom always has its price." He leaned forward, nuzzling her ear, nipping lightly at her earlobe, all the while continuing his gentle, insistent stroking, driving her insane with need.

"I didn't come here to find freedom." Did she say the words out loud or merely in her mind?

His tongue skimmed her skin, trailing fire down to her breasts. When he flicked one aching nipple with that rough moistness, she shuddered and thrust toward him, wanting to feel more than just his tongue on her breasts. He chuckled softly and captured them in both hands, lightly pushing them together. His gaze held hers as he ran his tongue from one aching nub to the other. She shuddered and shifted, not sure how much more sweet torment she could take.

"What did you come here to find, then?" he said softly.

You, she thought. Only he'd turned out to be a whole lot more dangerous than she'd ever imagined. "Not this."

"Then what?" He lightly nipped one nipple, then the other, and sweat prickled across her skin. Her heart was hammering so loudly its cadence seemed to fill the silence, and every muscle in her body was quivering. Aching. For him.

"I was just curious. Nothing more. I never meant for this to happen."

"You're lying, little wolf."

And the fact that he sensed it scared her, because it meant he was reading her far better than she was reading him.

"I'm not lying," she said, almost desperately.

He released her breasts, and his fingers slipped into her moistness again. She gasped, arching into his touch.

"You *will* tell me the truth, you know. And before this night is over."

She shook her head. His steady stroking was taking her higher and higher, until the need for him was so strong her whole body was shaking and she could barely even breathe.

The sound of a zipper being pulled down was almost lost in the frantic beating of her heart. Anticipation raced through her.

He pulled her closer, but nowhere near close enough. The quivering tip of him pressed against her moist heat, but went no farther. His hands slid to her rear, cupping her lightly. The effort of control had him trembling, and despite the fog of pleasure, she half-wondered what, exactly, he thought she was up to.

Perhaps she should tell him why she was here. But if she did, she had no doubt he'd expel her from the mansion. These murders fell under the category of pack business, and he'd already made it perfectly clear he had no intention of letting outsiders get involved in such matters—and that included not only her, but the police as well.

And then she'd have destroyed her life for no damn reason at all. At least by withholding the truth a little bit longer, she had a chance of discovering something— anything—that might give her a clue as to the murderer's identity.

She'd made her promise and she intended to stick to it. Though in many ways, she had no other choice now.

His hands tightened on her rump, pulling her forward. His hardness slipped inside a little more, and it felt so good she moaned.

"Tell me what you seek, Neva." His words were harsh, his breathing heavy. He was punishing himself no less than her.

She shook her head and knew she had to end this before the need for release overwhelmed common sense and loosened her tongue. She wrapped her legs around his waist and pulled herself forward, taking him deep inside.

He groaned and began to move, his strokes quickly becoming fierce, hungry thrusts that shook her entire body. The sweet pressure built and built until it felt as if she would explode with sheer pleasure.

Then she did.

"Oh Moons, *yes*!" Her body bucked wildly against his. He came with her, his roar echoing across the silence, his body slamming hers so hard the whole countertop seemed to shake.

He caught her lips, kissing her fiercely as their orgasms ebbed and sanity returned. She opened her eyes and stared into his. For the briefest of moments, the shutters were open, and in those black depths she saw compassion and surprise and warmth. It was almost easy to believe they were lovers who actually cared for each other; then the shutters slammed back home and the cold stranger returned.

But before either of them could say anything, a scream rent the silence.

The scream of a woman in pain.

Chapter Six

FOR A HEARTBEAT, Duncan couldn't react. He was too lost in the warm aftermath of loving Neva to really register what he was hearing.

Until the scream came again. The voice sounded vaguely familiar, yet it brought no immediate images to mind. He stepped back from Neva and wondered who in hell was playing it a little too rough. He hoped it wasn't René. "Stay here," he said, fastening his jeans.

"No." She slipped off the counter and fixed her dress.

"Neva—"

"No," she repeated, her expression determined as her gaze met his. "I know the voice—I was talking to her just before we came here. I may be able to help."

He frowned. Given her reluctance to let anyone know she was at the mansion, it was surprising that she'd risk talking to anyone. "Who?"

"Betise."

She gave him a strange look as she said the name, and he wondered why. The voice might have sounded familiar, but the name certainly wasn't. And while he had no desire to drag her into any pack business, she was right about one thing. If there was a hysterical female to deal with, she could be of some assistance. He had no doubt this was nothing more than a wolf playing the dance a little too hard, simply because it broke the well-established pattern set by the murderer. Then another scream sounded, and he grabbed her hand as they raced out the door.

The night air was glacial against his lust-heated skin, and the wind had sharpened. Overhead, the moon was lost behind a covering of thick, dark clouds. There would be a storm by morning. Part of him hoped it was one of those early-spring monsters Ripple Creek was renowned for. At the very least, it would keep everyone indoors and the rangers away a bit longer, giving him the chance to find and deal with the monster behind the murders.

They raced past the row of aspens and pines and across the well-manicured lawn, heading toward the pavilion where he'd first danced with Neva. He didn't hear anyone else speeding through the night, neither ahead nor behind them—thanks, undoubtedly, to the wind blowing the sound of the wolf's screams away from the ballrooms. Which was good. Right now, the last thing they needed was an audience, and they certainly didn't need any more rumors circulating around Ripple Creek.

The sound of soft sobbing broke through the night. He couldn't smell the presence of another male, only a female. She was a hint of musk and lemon on the icy wind—an odd, almost unpleasant aroma, and one that stirred a few memories. He'd danced with a wolf who'd smelled like that, though it was a long time ago, back in the hellion days of his youth.

The old pavilion came into sight, and he slowed. Neva wrenched her hand from his, but he caught her again before she could run ahead.

"If this *is* another attack by the murderer," he said, before she could speak, "then racing blindly into the situation might well destroy any clues."

Not that he really thought there'd be any to find. Even this close, he couldn't sense the presence of another wolf. Only the female—and as they walked closer, it became obvious she'd danced many times this night. The scent of many males stung her skin, and that in itself *did* match the previous attacks.

They found her sitting on the pavilion's floor, huddled next to a seat and wrapped in shadows. She was willowy and blond, reminding him of the wolf he'd seen his brother dancing with when he and Neva had first walked into the ballroom.

She looked up. There were tears in her eyes, and the hard planes of her face were gouged and bloody. The arms she had wrapped around her drawn-up knees were littered with gouges. Wounds made by claws, not teeth.

Neva made a strangled sound, then tore herself free of his grasp and went to the older wolf, kneeling down beside her.

"By the moon's light, Betise, what happened?"

"I was supposed to meet someone here, but he was late." The older wolf's voice was little more than a broken whisper, and yet it grated against his nerves. Though he couldn't say why—and it certainly wasn't all that unpleasant.

"Another wolf came out of the shadows . . . and he . . . he . . ."

If another male had been here, why couldn't he smell him? "Where did he go?" he asked, voice clipped.

The look Neva gave him was dark. "Does it matter right now? Why don't you give Betise some comfort—"

The older wolf placed a hand on Neva's arm, silencing her. "The last I saw of him, he was heading for the main gates."

"Stay here, both of you."

He spun and shifted shape, running swiftly for the main gate. The air was fresh and cold, the wind stronger. He might have thought it possible that the weather had blown away all aroma of the attacker except for the fact that the tang of balsam still rode the air, as did the flowery scent of several females who'd passed through the gates recently.

Betise had obviously been attacked, but by whom? And if the attacker hadn't retreated this way, where had he gone? Was Betise lying to protect him, or had she been too confused and terrified to truly notice which way her attacker had fled?

He suspected it was the former, though why he felt this, he had no idea. But he'd learned long ago to trust his instincts. Over the years, they'd gotten him out of more trouble than he could remember.

Neva glanced up as he entered the pavilion again, the rich and exotic mint of her eyes making the older wolf's seem almost silver in comparison.

"Do you have a doctor in this place?"

The scorn evident in the word *place* more than emphasized her thoughts about the mansion, which only confirmed his suspicion that she was here to watch *him*, not dance.

"Yes." He squatted down beside her. The sunshiny scent of her spun around him, thankfully overwhelming the other wolf's unpleasant, very used, smell. He couldn't really remember dancing with her, and it was only the familiarity of her scent that told him he had. Looking at her now, he had to wonder what had attracted him. Beyond her hair, there was nothing even remotely pretty about her, though that probably wouldn't have mattered when he was younger. The combination of alcohol and a willing bit of tail was all he'd been interested in for more years than he cared to remember.

"Can you describe the wolf who attacked you?"

She shuddered. "He was average-sized, and silver-coated."

So was the murderer, he thought, but that in itself wasn't much of a link. There were plenty of average-sized silver wolves in the mansion—a whole pack of them, in fact.

"And you didn't recognize him?"

Betise shook her head, but something flickered in her pale eyes and he knew she was lying. Was she trying to protect her attacker, or did she have other motives? He intended to find out—and maybe he could use Neva's apparent friendship with this wolf to do that.

"Duncan, enough." Neva's voice was sharp. "She needs medical attention."

She did, though he suspected her wounds were not as bad as they looked. "Can you walk?"

Neva's expression got darker. "Of course she can't. Carry her, for moon's sake."

The *last* thing he wanted was this wolf's scent on him again. He frowned and suddenly wished he could remember what had happened between them all those years ago. At the very least, he could then warn René to be wary of her—something he might do anyway.

"Her legs aren't injured from what I can see," he said coldly. "I'll go find the doctor. You help her to the study. She knows where it is."

"Bastard," he heard Neva mutter as he walked away.

He smiled grimly. He was all that and more—and would continue to be that way for as long as this murderer was on the loose.

He strode past the rows of wind-tossed aspen and pine. As he got closer to the ballroom, the music began to seep through his blood again, and need rose. He ignored it, but he wondered if that was going to be at all possible on the coming nights.

He might have practiced restraint over the last ten years, but coming back to the mansion seemed to have loosened the control he had over his old habits. Part of him ached to celebrate the rising of the moon as he had in years past—to drink himself senseless and lose himself in the pleasure of a female's body, over and over and over. Only right now, it wasn't any female he hungered for, but one with dark-golden hair and leaf-green eyes.

It was a need that was more than a little worrying. If she wasn't in jail by the time this was all over, then she'd certainly hate him more than she already did. It would be the mother of all ironies if, for the first time in his life, he'd actually found a woman he wanted to spend more than one moon dance with and she couldn't even stand the sight of him.

Though undoubtedly fate would probably think it a fitting retribution for his youthful unthinking and uncaring behavior.

He walked into the ballroom, and the heat and the smell of sex hit him like a punch to the gut. He took a deep breath, half-thinking of grabbing the nearest free female to mate with, if only to ease the sharpness of the moon-spun pain. But he resisted the temptation and swept his gaze across the rutting, sweating crowd. His father and Tye were nowhere to be seen, but René and Kane were both still here. A second later, he saw the doctor heading out another side exit.

He pushed through the crowd. The associated scents and sounds of lovemaking flushed heat across his skin, and even though he'd made love to Neva less than ten minutes ago, he wanted her again, with a fierceness that made it difficult to concentrate.

His father's warning ran through his mind. He would indeed have to watch the bait, or he really could end up getting hooked.

He caught the doctor heading for the stairs leading to the wing housing staff and guest rooms.

"Hey, Duncan," Martin said with a smile. "Long time no see."

"Certainly has been." In his heyday, Martin had been responsible for the delivery of most of the Sinclair pups, but failing health and the odd, often long, hours of obstetrics had forced him to retire just before Duncan had left, ten years ago. These days, he did little more than ensure that all male wolves attending the dance received the injection that kept their fertility under control. Wolves might only be fertile during the week running up to the full moon, but given the number of partners many had, Ripple Creek would quickly be overrun with pups if he didn't.

And while the presence of werewolves might be tolerated in the human world, human tolerance only went so far. Ripple Creek had survived where many other reservations had failed simply because they kept their numbers under tight control and didn't push the boundaries.

"I need you to do me a favor, Doc," Duncan said.

The old wolf raised a bushy white eyebrow. "What?"

"A woman's been attacked in the pavilion and needs some medical attention."

"Is she badly off? If so, it might be better if she heads to the hospital—"

"Mainly scratches on her arms and face." He hesitated, then added on impulse, "But on the off chance they're not just scratches, see if you can grab a blood sample from the wounds so we can test for saliva, and perhaps see if you can get a scraping of whatever's under her nails."

"A tall order." Martin paused, dark eyes worried. "Is this attack linked to the recent murders?"

"I honestly don't know. She's alive, for one thing, and she's been scratched rather than bitten. But it's better to be safe than sorry."

"So you're not calling the rangers?"

"I can't see the point, but if she wants to, we will." Though he very much doubted she would.

Martin nodded. "And what do you want me to do with these samples?"

He hesitated. His boss, Dave, had offered the use of his contacts, and it was possible those contacts included someone in the police labs. "Keep them secure until I can arrange for them to be tested."

"I'll just go get my medical kit. Where is she now?"

"I've put her in the study."

The old wolf nodded. "Then I'll meet you there."

Duncan spun on his heel and headed for the study. Once the doc arrived, he'd have to keep Neva out of the way just so she didn't see Martin taking samples. If Betise *had* been attacked by the killer, then the last thing he wanted was Neva reporting back to whoever had set her on him.

Both women jumped when he thrust open the study door. Neva stood, her expression hostile. But her gaze slithered down his body, and awareness flashed between them. An awareness which her clenched fists suggested she was resisting.

"Where's the doctor?" she demanded.

"On his way." He glanced at Betise. The older wolf was lying back on the sofa, eyes closed and breathing even, but he could feel the tension in her. The anger. "We've danced, haven't we?"

The smile that tugged her thin lips was bitter. "Yes," she said, not opening her eyes. "We have."

"I don't remember."

Neva gasped softly, her mental voice harsh. *Do you really enjoy being such a callous bastard?*

Neva's thoughts were acrid and filled with anger. Obviously, she knew a whole lot more than he remembered. He looked at her. *It's nothing more than the truth.*

He'd had so many women since his first moon dance, how could he possibly be expected to remember his time with every one? That he recalled this wolf's scent was a miracle.

She said you were a semiregular item for nearly a year. Surely that in itself would be momentous enough for a womanizer like yourself to recall.

He'd never been with *any* wolf longer than the period of one moon dance. Had never wanted to be, especially in his youth. *If she told you that, she lied.*

Uncertainty flicked through her glorious eyes. *Or you're lying, for whatever sordid reason you might have.*

I may be many things, but a liar isn't one of them. He hesitated, then added harshly. *Shame you can't say the same thing, isn't it?*

She blushed, but she held his gaze almost defiantly. *I haven't lied to you.*

She was lying now. *Then tell me why you came to the mansion.*

To try the moon dance.

And?

I'm regretting every damn minute of it.

That, at least, was a truth, and one he *did* regret. *It's a shame you've got four more nights to go, little wolf. Rest assured, I aim to enjoy every one of them.*

Bastard, she said again.

He smiled grimly and switched his gaze back to Betise. "When, exactly, did we meet?" Not that he really cared. He was just puzzled as to why she'd bother lying.

"You were twenty-two."

Which was a year before he'd left to go to Denver, where he'd ended up in jail while the police sorted out the mess of his accident. While it hadn't been one of his more sober years, he was sure he'd remember having a semipermanent mate. He'd never been like his brothers in that respect. He'd never made promises to the women he mated with. Even back in his hellion days, he'd been honest enough to admit he was after nothing more than a brief interlude, and those he was with always knew that. So why this woman believed *he'd* believe they'd been together for more than one moon dance was beyond him. Unless she thought he'd been so drunk he wouldn't remember.

Even so, what would it gain her?

"And we were together how long?"

She hesitated. "Nearly the whole year."

No way. He couldn't stand this woman's scent. Maybe drunk he wouldn't have cared so much, but even so, they couldn't have been together an entire year without him at least remembering some part of it. He'd never been *that* drunk. And he *could* recall most of the year—just not her part of it, which again implied she was lying.

"Sorry, but I have no memory of you or our time together."

Moons, you're such a cold—

Yeah, he cut in, oddly annoyed at Neva's insistence at believing her friend rather than him. *I know what I am. What I don't know yet is what* you *are.*

The door behind him opened, then Martin stepped inside. "Ah. Nasty wounds you have there, young lady."

Betise's smile held the first true hint of warmth Duncan had seen, but it did little to wipe the hardness from her face.

"I don't think I can be called young anymore."

Martin smiled as he placed his medical bag on the table and opened it up. Duncan noted the small, empty vials inside. "Compared to me, you're little more than a pup."

Duncan glanced at Neva. "Why don't you and I move out onto the balcony while the doctor looks after Betise?" He made it an order, using the power of the moon bond to ensure her obedience.

Her eyes flashed and her fists clenched, but she had no option other than to obey. She spun and all but stomped out the French doors.

He followed her. She didn't go far, stopping to the left of the doorway. She crossed her arms and glared at him. *You'd better keep those shields of yours well up, because the minute you lower them, you'll pay.*

Then he'd better make sure he did something worthy of the pain she planned to inflict. He continued to advance on her. Her face went pale and she held out a hand, pressing it against his chest. "Don't."

He stopped, took her hand from his chest, and lightly kissed her fingers. "Don't what?"

"You know what." Her soft voice was a mix of breathlessness and scorn. "We can't, not with Betise this close."

"I don't particularly care about Betise. I never have."

"Even if you weren't as close as she's saying, she obviously cares for you. You could take that into consideration." Her gaze searched his, the green depths an odd mix of uncertainty and outrage. "But I guess you really haven't got a heart in that chest of yours, have you?"

"I certainly haven't discovered one yet. Take off your dress."

Anger ran around him. "No." She wrenched her hand from his and crossed her arms.

He raised an eyebrow and reached for the power of the moon again. She swore softly and vehemently, and amusement swam through him. "And I thought the golden tribe were such gentle souls."

"We are, generally. Must be the company I've been keeping of late." She threw her dress on the ground, then crossed her arms again.

The moon caressed her golden skin, and her nipples were taut with cold and arousal. He was as hard as hell and wanted nothing more than to take her right there and then. But that's exactly what she expected him to do, so it was the one thing he wouldn't do.

He reached out, gently running a finger across her breasts. She trembled under his touch, swallowing heavily. Hate and desire warred in the emotive swirl that briefly surrounded them both.

"How well do you know Betise?"

Surprise flickered briefly in her eyes. "She's a regular customer at the diner. She's been coming there for years."

"Uncross your arms." He made it an order and she bit her lip, her knuckles whitening as she battled the command. It was a battle she had no hope of winning.

"So it's a casual thing, not true friendship?" he added, running his finger to the center of one breast and slowly circling the engorged point. Goose bumps flitted across her skin, and the smell of her arousal was rich and sweet on the strengthening wind.

"Yes," she said, voice breathy, eyes angry.

"Why aren't you afraid that she'll report your presence here to your parents?"

She snorted softly. "Betise hates my parents. They're against the moon dance, against everything the mansion stands for."

Which made Neva's decision to come here all the more suspicious. "But what about other friends? Wouldn't she mention it to them?"

Neva hesitated, and fear flickered through her eyes. "Maybe."

"Then why didn't you avoid her?"

"Maybe I was just desperate to see a friendly face."

He shifted his touch to her other breast. She trembled, her skin flushed and hot under his fingertips. "And maybe you had some information for her to pass on."

She frowned. "I have no idea what you're talking about."

He sensed no lie in her words. Whatever the reason for Neva being here, Betise wasn't a part of it. He reached for the moon power again, then said, *The next time you meet Betise, I want you to question her about her attacker, and I want you to report every word back to me, and only me.*

And by using the moon power, he'd ensure she couldn't go running back to her employer with any information Betise might give her.

Her eyes practically spat fire. He smiled and slid his

hand down her stomach. "Yeah," he said softly. "I'm a bastard."

He gently delved into the golden triangle of curls. Lord, she was so hot, so moist. He probed deeper, sliding through her slickness, until her muscles pulsed around one finger, then two. Her whole body quivered, and the smell of her need stung his senses, testing his strength, his will. He wanted it every bit as badly, but right now the need to push her into revealing what she knew and who employed her to watch him was stronger than the need to dance with her.

Though he wasn't entirely sure it would remain that way.

He kept stroking her until her skin was flushed with heat and the fine sweat of desire, and the tremors in her body indicated she was close to the edge.

At that moment, he withdrew his touch and stepped away.

Heat climbed into her cheeks. "Why are you doing this to me?"

His smile was tight. In many respects, he was punishing himself as much as her. "Anticipation is half the pleasure."

"Believe me, it's not."

"Perhaps we should see?"

She studied him warily—an aching, golden angel he desperately wanted to lose himself in.

"What do you mean?"

"Go up to my room and climb into bed." He gave her the directions. "You'll wait there until I return, and go nowhere else until then."

He made it a command, and she swore again. Her eyes narrowed slightly, and he hastily raised his shields to full. Even so, the trickle of fury that got through nearly blasted his mind. She wasn't kidding when she said he'd have to watch himself. With that sort of power, she'd probably fry his brain.

"That could get awfully damn messy if I have to go pee," she muttered eventually.

"You can go to the bathroom. Nowhere else."

"Isn't *that* goddamn generous of you."

"Go," he ordered. "Now."

She picked up her dress and stomped down the stairs. He watched her until she'd fled around the corner, and fought the desire to go after her. Right now, he had more important matters to tend to. Satisfying his lust could wait.

He went back into the study. Martin glanced up and gave a small nod, and Duncan relaxed a little. He looked at Betise. As he'd guessed, her wounds were not as serious as they'd looked.

"Are you staying for the remainder of the night's dance or going home?"

"Going home." She arched an eyebrow, and her voice became little more than a husky whisper as she added, "Are you offering to escort me?"

He hesitated, but knew in reality he had little choice. Not if she *had* been attacked by the murderer. "Yes."

A smile touched her thin lips, and the smell of her desire stirred the room—but not him. Neva's scent clung to him, and it was her he wanted, not this well-used dancer who claimed to have some sort of past with him.

Her gaze switched to Martin. "Thanks, Doc."

The old wolf nodded. "You're most welcome. Duncan, I'll talk to you later about that other matter."

He nodded. Betise raised an eyebrow as she climbed off the sofa. "Other matter?"

"Pack business," he said flatly. "Are you changing before you leave?"

Her fingers toyed with the gauzy material of her gown, drawing his gaze down her body. She was very shapely, but these days it took more than just a well endowed body to catch his interest—though Neva had captured him with little more than a wistful thought.

"I can't see the point," she said huskily. "Not when I plan to come back tomorrow night."

"Fine. Let's go." He pressed his fingers to her back and ushered her out the door. Once outside, he dropped his hand and ensured there was plenty of distance between them.

She noticed. "I won't bite," she said softly. "Not unless you want me to."

He didn't even glance at her. There was nothing about this wolf that attracted him, and nothing he wanted from her. Which was odd, given the hunger that boiled through his blood.

"I don't want you." He kept his voice harsh and flat, to leave her in no doubt as to his feelings, and he felt rather than saw her gaze slide down his body. It was a touch of heat that left him itchy.

"Your body suggests otherwise," she said.

They walked past the pavilion, heading for the main gate, and he briefly wished Ripple Creek was a little closer. He had no desire to be in this wolf's company any longer than necessary. "My body does little more than react to the power of the moon. Believe me, it's not you I want."

"Neva!"

She practically spat the word, and he frowned. "Neva is nothing more than another dancer I'm spending time with this moon cycle, and she certainly has nothing to do with my lack of desire for you."

They passed through the main gates and headed for the trees. He paused, allowing her to go first down the narrow path.

"You *have* changed over the years, haven't you?" she growled. "There was a time when the opposite was true."

"You and I both know we did little more than share one dance," he bit back. "And I'd like to know what you hope to gain by stating otherwise."

She glanced back at him, pale eyes gleaming with fury. "We shared more than one dance."

They hadn't. He was more positive of that than ever. But why was she so adamant that they had? "Either way, it doesn't matter. The past is something I have no wish to relive."

She snorted. "You're as bad as your bastard brother."

He smiled grimly. "Which one? I have three."

"*All* of them. You all make promises in the heat of moon passion, but when the sanity of the sun returns, you renege."

He very much doubted that *any* of his brothers had made any promises, particularly to this wolf. They enjoyed their freedom and the dance far too much. And it was unusual for all four of them to have mated with the same dancer. Their tastes in women were quite different. Still, at least it was one thing he could check.

"So you're not exactly sorry that the Sinclairs are in trouble at the moment?"

"Oh, I'm sorry, all right—sorry the murderer is taking out innocent dancers instead of you lying pack of bastards."

He smiled grimly. Must be his night for being called a bastard. They walked through the remainder of the trees in silence, and the lights of Ripple Creek eventually came into sight. The town was quiet, which didn't surprise him, given the somewhat puritanical hold the golden tribe had on the place. Those who truly wanted to celebrate the glory of the moon did so in private, or at the mansion.

Betise lived in a small, somewhat run-down house on the outskirts of town. He walked her to the front gate, then stopped.

She swung around. "You're not coming in?"

The heat was back in her eyes, the smell of her arousal thick and heavy on the air. Yet two minutes ago, she'd been wishing him dead.

"I have no desire for you," he repeated.

She caught his arm and stepped close, wantonly pressing her body against his. "A wolf with experience can give you far more pleasure than an uptight bit of fluff like Neva."

Anger surged through him. Neva was more wolf than this bitch would ever be. He grabbed her shoulders and pushed her backward, none too gently. "Go inside and lock your door. And if I hear you've spread word of Neva's presence at the mansion, I'll ensure you never attend another moon dance." And to a wolf so hooked on the pleasures of the moon, that was a threat worse than death.

Her pale eyes glittered silver in the night, and for an instant it seemed sanity had fled their depths and all that was left was hate.

"Bastard," she muttered.

"So people inform me."

She spun and walked away, but halfway up the path, she hesitated and looked over her shoulder.

"There's something you should know. Three weeks ago, Levon Grant pulled me aside in the diner and began asking questions about who was dancing with whom up at the mansion."

Shock rippled through him. Neva's father had been asking about the mansion? Why? While it was patently obvious Levon Grant hated the dance, he wasn't the sort of man who'd go behind their back to do something about it.

But maybe Duncan was wrong. Maybe Levon had just been waiting for the right opportunity to take matters into his own hands.

Yet if that were the case, why was Neva at the mansion? Would a wolf so set against the mansion's moon dance force his daughter to join them?

Given what he'd seen of the man, he doubted it. And yet he couldn't say for certain, and that was worrying. Maybe he was being played more than he realized.

"You'd better watch what you do over the next couple of days, wolf." Betise's cold words seemed to echo his thoughts. "It might just turn out that you're dancing with the murderer's not-so-sweet accomplice."

Chapter Seven

DUNCAN RAPPED HIS knuckles against the wooden door leading into his father's suite, then entered without being asked. Zeke wasn't in the main room, but he could hear soft voices in the bedroom. He strode over to the bar and poured himself a large bourbon. A habit he'd have to watch, he realized. The last thing he wanted was a return to the bad old days.

He leaned against the bar and listened to the murmurs of conversation in the other room. While he couldn't hear many words, one thing was obvious. His father's source was female, not male.

A cold breeze whistled around his ankles, indicating the French doors had been opened. Two seconds later his father entered the room, wearing little more than a black silk robe.

"No wonder you didn't want me appearing before five," Duncan noted dryly. "You knew you'd be busy paying off the messenger."

Zeke smiled, but didn't refute the accusation. He poured himself a drink, then slapped a folder on the bar. "There's the report. There don't seem to be any variances from the other attacks."

"Did they find any more hairs?"

"Other than that one you saw, no. But one hair is all they need to place a suspect at the scene."

"If they had a suspect."

"They've asked for hair samples from all us. You care to make a bet about the DNA matching one of us?"

Duncan had no doubt that it would. Whoever was behind this had so far been doing a thorough job of implicating them, if only by circumstantial evidence. Zeke paused and took a drink. "My source did drop one interesting nugget that's not in the reports."

"What?"

"While the coroner's report couldn't confirm whether sexual penetration had occurred during the attack, the rangers themselves believe none of the women were raped. They believe it's only being made to look like they were."

If that were the case, the murderer was damn good at make-believe. "Why would anyone want to do that?"

"You might as well ask me why the murderer is targeting these women," Zeke replied dryly. "When we know why, we'll find our killer."

Duncan glanced down at his drink for a moment. "What do you know about a wolf named Betise?"

His father's lip curled. "She's a dance addict and has been well used over the years. I've never danced with her, but I believe René and Kane both have. And you." Zeke hesitated, dark eyes glinting with sudden amusement. "But then, you did have a reputation to live up to."

Duncan grimaced. There was no use regretting his

past, and there was certainly nothing he could do to change it. "She was claiming tonight that we were an item for nearly a year."

Zeke snorted. "Even at your drunkest, you had more sense than that."

"That's what I figured." He took a drink, then said, "She was attacked tonight."

"By the murderer?"

"I don't know. She claimed it was a silver wolf, and scratches on her arms certainly attest to the fact it *was* a wolf."

"But you don't believe her?"

"I don't disbelieve her, either. She *was* attacked."

"But?"

"But if it was the murderer, then he's breaking his set pattern. It happened in the pavilion, not near the gates. She was waiting for another dancer, not leaving the mansion. And there were no signs of bites on her breasts or neck. She had scratches on her face and her arms, but neither were very deep. I doubt they'll even scar."

Zeke's expression was thoughtful. "It is always possible the murderer has changed his pattern. There are no set rules governing that sort of thing, you know."

"I know. But he's been so careful up to this moment. Why would he risk attacking a wolf who was obviously waiting for someone? It just doesn't ring true."

"Maybe he thought he had no other chance."

"Maybe." Duncan picked up the bottle and half-filled his glass. "I asked Martin to take some samples from her wounds and from under her nails. I thought I could use Dave's contacts to get them tested."

"I'll get them tested. It'll be quicker and easier."

Duncan nodded. The sooner they knew whether Betise's attack was linked to the murderer, the better. "What do you think about Levon Grant?"

Zeke snorted. "Why would I even bother thinking about him?"

"Betise told me tonight that he'd been questioning her about the mansion and the dancers. From what she said, it happened just before the first attack."

His father frowned. "Levon might hate the dance, but he would not do anything underhanded or illegal to stop it."

"Neva's his daughter."

"Then he surely doesn't know she's here, because if he did, he'd be here dragging her away by the scruff of the neck. "

Which is exactly what Duncan had thought. Yet the itchy feeling that Neva was up to something still remained. And if she *was* here at her father's request, she wasn't going to admit it. He could force the information out of her, of course, but to do so would tell her he was on to her, and if she ran, he doubted it would be back to the person behind her presence here.

He downed the rest of his drink. It only fueled the fire already burning in his veins. "Even so, I think it's worth digging around for information on Levon. Maybe his turn-the-other-cheek attitude is little more than a front."

"Maybe." Zeke's expression was doubtful. "So what are you going to do about Neva?"

"Keep pushing her. I'm sure she's here for a reason, and I'm just as sure she'll run very soon."

"Might be worth doing a check on her, as well. Although, be careful—her sister is the head ranger, and I doubt she'd take it too kindly if she discovered you were running a check on Neva."

"Neva's sister is in charge of the investigation?" Then why the hell was Neva even here? Or was the sister the force behind this little charade? Was it, perhaps, a means of getting evidence against them, any damn way they could?

Zeke shook his head. "She was, but she seems to have disappeared. Which is odd, really. She's normally pretty hands-on when it comes to investigating crimes on the reservation."

Duncan put his empty glass on the bar. "I'm also going to run a check on the murdered women. See if there was any link between them, other than the mansion."

"I imagine the rangers would have already done that."

Duncan's smile was grim. "They have to stick within the boundaries of the law to gather their information. I don't."

"True."

He glanced at the clock. "Time to go do a little more pushing. If I find anything, I'll let you know."

He spun and walked out. His rooms were in the far wing and a long way away from the main halls and the dancers. As much as he'd enjoyed the dance over the years, he enjoyed his solitude more. He always had.

He wound his way through the dark hallways. He

couldn't smell anyone in the rooms he passed, but he wasn't surprised. This wing was part of the old section and hadn't yet been fitted with central heating. He doubted it ever would be. As big as the pack was, the mansion was bigger—a rambling network of rooms and halls that had once been filled to the brim with laughing pups, but never would be again. Not these days. All the packs had to be watchful about birth control. Human law forbade any pack growing beyond a certain size. Werewolves and shapeshifters may finally have been acknowledged in the eyes of the law, but lawmakers the world over still feared the consequences of allowing them to breed unchecked.

As if they could ever compete with human birth rates, he thought sourly.

In the silence of the long halls, the wind seemed to howl, battering at the roof and windows. In the chill sharpness of the air, he could smell snow. A Ripple Creek Special was definitely headed their way.

He walked into his suite. The air here was almost icy, thanks in part to the row of French doors lining the outer wall. He closed the drapes, then walked over to the fireplace and stoked the fire to life. If it was this cold now, they'd certainly need its warmth by dawn.

When the fire blazed, he headed into the bedroom. Neva was sound asleep in his bed and he stopped, caught by her sheer beauty. Her long hair was a river of gold that swept across her pillow. And in sleep, she looked so angelic, so innocent, it was hard to believe she could be anything else.

But she was here for a reason, and until he discovered that reason, he had no choice but to keep on pushing her.

And it was certainly a task part of him *did* enjoy. Maybe he was more like René than he cared to admit.

He stripped and climbed into bed. She stirred, murmuring something he couldn't quite catch before turning away from him. He spooned behind her, pressing himself against the warmth of her skin and the richness of her scent. Her very closeness had the heat surging through his veins, and he wanted her so badly it was painful. Their lovemaking tonight would be hard and fast. It couldn't be anything else when the fever burned so fiercely through his veins, and it was what he needed to do to keep on pushing her.

He slid a hand down her belly to the triangle of hair between her thighs. She was still so gloriously wet with need, even though a couple of hours had slipped by since he'd touched her. She shifted under his caress, pressing back against him. It was a sleepy invitation he was more than ready to accept. He slid deep inside her, groaning at the sheer glory of it. She felt so good, so hot and firm.

He knew the instant she woke. Though she didn't move, a sound that was part pleasure, part surprise, and part anger whispered from her lips. He wrapped an arm around her waist, holding her still as he continued to thrust inside her. With the urgency of the moon driving him so hard, there was nothing gentle about it now. He claimed every inch of her, delving so deep her taut muscles quivered against the entire length of him.

The red tide rose, becoming a wall of pleasure he could not deny. He came—a hot, torrential release whose force tore a shout from his lips and sent his body rigid.

But the moon and he weren't finished yet. Not by a long shot. He withdrew and tugged her around to face him. Her eyes flashed with anger, but before she could say anything, he claimed her lips. He kissed her, caressed her, licked every inch of her, until her scent and her taste were imprinted on every fiber of his being, inside and out. Then he loved her.

And continued to make love to her through the rest of the night and well into dawn.

A constant rattling woke Neva many hours later. She groaned and flung the thick comforter off her face, then squinted in the general direction of the noise. Though the clock on the bedside table said it was nearly eleven, the day beyond the rattling French doors was dark and filled with a swirling whiteness. She blinked, but the image didn't seem to get any clearer.

It was a blizzard, she realized. And while Ripple Creek had a reputation for wild spring storms, this one seemed worse than most.

But maybe that was a good thing. Maybe it would keep the killer away and the dancers safe for one more night. Surely not even the most ardent dancer would risk weather like this.

She yawned and rolled onto her back. Duncan wasn't in bed with her, and she had no idea when he'd left. But if the lack of warmth on his side of the silk sheets was anything to go by, he'd been gone for a while.

Heat flushed her cheeks, and she closed her eyes. She had no idea what to think about their recent lovemaking. He'd been harsh and uncaring one moment, taking what he wanted and giving nothing in return. Then he'd become so generous, so caring and thoughtful, that she all but melted for him. He'd pushed her through such a gamut of emotions in such a few short hours that she felt burned out—physically *and* emotionally.

She still didn't know how she felt about him, other than that he confused her, totally and utterly. She should hate him—every sane, rational cell in her body knew that. But she wasn't sure that she did—and yet she wasn't sure that she liked him, either.

And the fact she was so uncertain frightened her.

As did the jealousy that had risen when she'd smelled Betise on his skin last night. For the briefest of moments, she'd wanted to rip out the throat of the older wolf, a territorial emotion she had no right to, and no true desire for. Not when it came to someone like Duncan—a loner who was after nothing more than enjoyment.

And in truth, she shouldn't have been surprised that he'd enjoyed himself with Betise before coming back to her. The only *truly* surprising thing was the fact that he'd come back to her at all.

She rubbed a hand across her brow. Her head ached, but it was probably nothing more than lack of sleep. She'd had little more than three hours overall, and given what had happened over the last few nights, it was nowhere near enough. Not that she was likely to catch up on any more sleep over her remaining days here; Duncan had certainly made that perfectly clear this morning.

A tremor ran through her, and she wasn't sure if it was excitement or trepidation. Or maybe both. What she needed right now was someone sane to talk to. Someone like Savannah. And while her sister would probably go ballistic when she realized what Neva was doing, she was the only one who *would* understand. After all, Sav had done some pretty damn crazy things herself in the past.

She reached out with her thoughts. Warmth sparked briefly through the fog of memories in her sister's mind, then faded. Consciousness was close, but not yet close enough. Neva sighed. She was briefly tempted to call Ari, but she knew her friend would probably tell her to forget about feelings and just enjoy the dancing. Though Ari would have a fit if she realized Neva was at the mansion, rather than tucked away safe and sound in boring old Eagle.

Sighing again, she thrust the comforter aside and climbed out of bed. The chill hit her immediately and, shivering, she grabbed Duncan's robe off the end of the bed. The black silk whispered sensually across her skin, and desire rippled through her as the scent of spice and forest enveloped her. Why was she so attuned to his scent and his touch? Or was it simply a matter of her inexperience being totally overwhelmed by a man whose skills at the dance were almost legendary?

Frowning, she thrust the question aside and headed out to the sitting room, wincing slightly at the ache in her muscles. No one had ever told her dancing could be so . . . active. But then, no one had ever told her it could be so frustrating one moment and totally amazing the next. And the scattering of mates she'd had before Duncan certainly hadn't prepared her to be played by a master.

She stoked the fire with more wood, then padded back through the bedroom and into the bathroom, only to discover someone had very recently drawn her a bath. Two towels had been placed on a chair at the end of the big old claw-foot tub, along with shampoo and soap. She picked up the bar of soap and sniffed it lightly. The faint scent of citrus teased her nostrils. Her favorite. She wondered how he'd known, given she'd been wearing jasmine when they'd first met. Then she remembered he'd been in her house. And in her bed.

Heat flushed through her again. Even thinking about the man made her want him. The moon, she thought, had a lot to answer for. And yet there seemed more than just the moon fever between them—which, in itself, was crazy, because it could never be anything more if Betise were to be believed. But now she wasn't entirely sure that she could be.

Damn it, she didn't even know if she *liked* the man. And why in hell was she even worrying about it? Once this moon phase was over, she'd never see him again. Which is exactly what she'd wanted—what she'd planned—from the very beginning.

Only she wasn't so sure it was what she wanted now.

Crazy. She was definitely going crazy.

She stripped off the robe and climbed into the bath, sighing with pleasure as she eased into the hot water. She soaked in the sweet-smelling tub until the water began to cool, then climbed out. Grabbing the two towels, she wrapped one around her hair and used the other to dry herself. Then she padded into the bedroom to grab some fresh clothes from her bag.

She was sitting on the bed, brushing her hair, when the sensation hit her. Heat flashed white hot across her skin and fear clawed at her, making it next to impossible to breathe. There'd only been one other time in her life when she'd felt something like this, like someone had reached into her chest and attempted to pull out her heart. It had happened when she was eight years old and Savannah had been about to get caught in an avalanche. The link between them had saved Sav's life back then. Maybe it was about to save it again.

She reached for her sister, but the response was still the same. Neva thrust to her feet. Blizzard or not, she had to get down to the hospital. *Now.*

She shoved on her shoes and ran to the French doors. She couldn't chance going through the halls and running into Duncan. He'd undoubtedly try to stop her, and he'd definitely want an explanation— something she had no time for. She'd have to leap from the balcony and hope the snow was deep enough to cushion her.

The wind ripped the doors from her hands, smashing them back against the walls. Snow swirled in, thick, fast, and frigid. Shivering, she battled the storm to the balcony's edge. The world beyond was a sheet of white. She couldn't see the ground, let alone the trees. She climbed over the rail, hanging by her fingertips for several seconds as the wind battered her sideways, then let go.

She hit the ground with a grunt, falling backward into a thick snowdrift. Wild flurries of white danced around her, quickly coating her body. She rolled onto her hands and knees and called to the wolf within.

It came in a rush of power, and she leapt forward on all fours. But the snow was thick and soft under her pads, forcing her to bound rather than run, and the fear swelled. She was running out of time. And so was Savannah.

She surged through the main gates and down into the trees. The snow here was lighter, allowing her to pick up speed. But the wind tore at her coat, and it felt like the icy air was invading every pore. Not even the thick winter coat of a wolf provided much protection against a storm like this.

She couldn't yet see the lights of Ripple Creek, and normally they would have been visible by now. The fierceness of the storm was whiting everything out. She leapt the stream and raced on, her heart slamming against her rib cage and her tongue lolling as she battled for breath.

The minute she came out of the protection of the trees, the wind hurled her sideways. She tumbled downhill, gathering momentum until she smashed into a tree. She yelped, and pain rose in a red tide through her body.

Neva?

The tremulous voice cut through the pain, blanketing her mind, and joy swept through her. *Sav, I'm coming.*

She scrambled to her feet and, ignoring the ache in her ribs, ran on. The smell of wood smoke and humanity stung the freezing air. She was close to Ripple Creek, even if she couldn't yet see it.

There's someone here.

Oh God. *Who?*

Confusion swirled through the link between them. Savannah was holding on to consciousness by the slenderest of margins, and if she slipped away, she'd die. Of that, Neva was certain.

I don't . . . Her voice faded away.

Savannah!

Here. But her reply was soft. Distant.

Neva raced down Main Street, suddenly glad for the storm. At least she didn't have to worry about traffic. *What do you smell? Tell me.*

Age. Death. Antiseptic.

Sav didn't realize she was in the hospital, obviously. *Look beyond that.*

Sour milk.

Sour milk? What on earth did that mean? *Give me more, Savannah. You're a wolf and a ranger. Use your skills, damn it.*

The link was silent for a long moment. Neva raced left onto South King Street and saw the warm glow of lights through the icy whiteness. She wasn't that far away now.

I remember that smell. It belonged to the wolf who attacked me.

Fear flashed though her, spreading like fire through her body, lending her feet greater speed. *He's in the hospital with you?*

Not in the room. Sav hesitated. *But close.*

Can you see him?

No. Can't see anything. Bandages.

Neva felt like cursing. The severity of the wounds on her sister's face had forced many painstaking hours of microsurgery, and most of Savannah's face and neck had been bandaged.

Listen, then. What do you hear?

Footsteps. Coming closer.

She was never going to get there in time. *Feel for the buzzer, Savannah. Call the nurse.*

It might be *the nurse.*

Not if she smells the same as the wolf who attacked you. None of the nurses in the hospital smell like sour milk.

Neva changed shape as she raced through the hospital's main entrance. An almost overwhelming tide of emotion hit her—not Savannah's, not hers, just the misery and pain of countless hospital patients, past and present, lingering in the air. She slammed up her shields, but the emotive swirl still seeped past, making her ache. And her parents wondered why she refused to come to the hospital much.

She continued on toward the stairs, knowing she couldn't afford to wait for the elevator. Not when the killer was in the hospital and going after Savannah. Nurses shouted after her, telling her to slow down, telling her visiting hours weren't for another two hours. But she ignored them and took the stairs two at a time.

She crashed through the door to the third-floor corridor and raced down the hall. There were nurses running ahead of her, and fear surged. Both hers and Savannah's.

Surely the murderer couldn't have gotten to her sister. Sav was still listed as critical, and no one but immediate family was allowed in the room. Down at the far end of the hall, the exit door slowly closed. Was it the killer retreating or someone else?

The nurses are here. He's not. Savannah's mind voice was stronger. *He's left. Don't give chase.*

Like hell she wouldn't. She was not only going to go after him, but she was going to kill the bastard. Going to grab his mind and fry his brain with emotion.

No! Savannah's horror stung her mind.

He has to be stopped, Neva said grimly.

He has to face the weight of the courts.

Neva snorted. *Yeah, right. With good behavior he'd be out in ten or less. That's not enough punishment for what he's done.*

I'm a ranger, Neva. I can't condone vigilante behavior, and I certainly can't let you do this.

I made promises to the moon—

I don't care! You can't do this. I won't let you!

Right now you can't stop me.

If you want to do something, follow his trail. But nothing else. Promise me!

Neva hesitated under the weight of her sister's fury.

Promise not to kill him! Sav all but yelled.

Neva winced and sighed. While she so desperately wanted to avenge Savannah, she also knew her sister was right.

All right. I promise. She slid to a stop outside her sister's room. There were two nurses inside, and Savannah was waving her hand weakly at them and trying to get up.

Are you all right? Neva asked.

Yes.

Then lie down and be still.

Damn it, you can't do this—

Sister, you have no idea what I can and can't do. Believe me. Up until a few days ago, even *she* hadn't been aware of the extremes she'd go to in order to protect those she loved.

Savannah's sigh was a warm breeze through Neva's mind. *Just make sure you don't get too close.*

Neva's smile was grim. She didn't have to get close to use her empathic abilities. All she had to do was find him. And she'd keep her promises—both of them. The killer would experience the pain he'd inflicted on Savannah and the others, but she wouldn't kill him.

And part of her was extremely glad of that fact.

She pushed open the exit door. Footsteps rattled down the steps below her, and the smell of sour milk stung the air. She leaned over the railing, briefly catching sight of a lone figure with black hair wearing a white coat—the sort of coat doctors wore. Then the door below opened and he was gone. She raced down the stairs and flung open the lobby door.

There was no white-jacketed male to be seen anywhere. She sniffed the air and followed the scent toward the exit. The doors swished open, and the chill of the storm swept in. She shivered and headed out, even though there was no hope of finding a scent in this sort of weather. She did find the coat in the trash can near the entrance and saw a trail of footsteps leading away. She followed for a little while, but they were quickly obliterated by the storm.

Cursing, shivering, she headed back to the hospital to talk to her sister.

•

Duncan leaned back in the chair and rubbed his eyes as the words on the computer screen began to blur. He'd only been sitting here for a couple of hours, but he'd had little more than an hour's sleep in the last twenty-four, and probably three or four in the last forty-eight. He had to be getting old. Once upon a time, he could have gone four or five days on that amount of sleep.

The phone beside the computer rang. He swiveled the chair and rested his feet on the edge of the desk as he picked up the receiver.

"Duncan Sinclair," he said, stifling a yawn.

"Lance here. Got those search results you wanted."

Lance Wilton was a computer geek he'd met in jail. Lance was a hacker extraordinaire, but he'd liked to drink a little too much and had very few qualms about driving while intoxicated. He'd ended up almost killing someone and, in the end, had landed in prison for five years.

"That was quick work."

"Hey, you saved my life by getting me this dream of a job. It's the least I can do."

Duncan smiled. Lance's dream job was developing software for Tye's small but profitable company. Being stuck in front of a computer screen for long hours was not a job Duncan would have considered a dream—he'd always been a wolf who preferred the freedom to roam.

"Did you come up with any connections among the four victims?"

"Other than the fact that they all lived in Ripple Creek and were regular attendees of the dance, no."

"And what about Levon Grant? Anything interesting on him?"

"He's squeaky clean. No police record, never even had a parking ticket. School records show he was an average student who didn't quite live up to the potential he showed. He apparently hated sports, but loved debating. He never did drugs or alcohol, and he was an outspoken advocate of saving oneself for marriage."

The word *boring* came to mind, but then, most of the wolves from the golden tribe tended to be. It was only the current generation who were starting to break the leash and embrace life—and the dance. Though some, like Neva, were doing so more reluctantly than others.

"What about Nancy Grant?"

"Ah, now there's a totally different proposition."

Duncan raised an eyebrow. Holier-than-thou Nancy had a past? "Why?"

"Nancy was born and raised on the Bitterroot Reservation over in Idaho. She was a straight-A student until she fell in with the wrong crowd and as a sixteen-year-old was part of a pack that raided the Sinclair stronghold over there and burned it to the ground."

Though he'd been too young to remember that happening, he could recall reading about it some years back. Thirteen people had died that night, and many more were injured. "Was she charged?"

"No. Word is, her father slipped a lot of cash to the right people and a blind eye was turned. She was sent to relatives in Ripple Creek, and that's how she met Levon."

"Anything since then?"

"Quiet as a mouse."

Did that mean her involvement with the raid had merely been a one-time prank that had gone horribly wrong, or did the anger that had led to the raid still simmer deep inside? "Did you find any connection between Nancy and the four murdered women?"

"None, but you'd probably uncover more by talking to her relatives."

Probably. Only he very much doubted whether her relatives would give him the time of day right now. Which left him with Neva—and she certainly wasn't going to tell him anything willingly. "Nothing else on either of them?"

"Nothing you wouldn't already know."

He hesitated. "You want to check into the Bitterroot raid a bit more? See if you can get names and perhaps trace what has happened to those who *were* charged?" It was always possible one or two of the others had recently gathered in Ripple Creek and old prejudices had flared. It was certainly a link worth exploring.

"Sure. I'll get back to you."

"Thanks for your help, Lance."

"No prob."

Duncan hung up, then glanced across at the window as the glass rattled. The Ripple Creek Special had well and truly hit. They'd only get the diehards at the dance tonight.

He looked at the computer screen again, then grimaced and reluctantly continued his search. He'd spent most of his time this morning going through the online news. Something must have triggered the start of these murders three weeks ago, and if it was at all newsworthy, it might be mentioned in one of the papers somewhere. A long shot, but one worth trying. He had very little else to try right now—at least until his father got the test results back from the samples Martin had taken from Betise. Talking to his brothers again had provided nothing new in the way of clues.

He worked his way through the remainder of last week's news reports and was just about to give up when he caught sight of a small photo that looked horribly familiar. Something clenched in his gut as he enlarged the image.

Neva, in a ranger's uniform.

Impossible. There was no way on this Earth she was a ranger.

He glanced down at the name under the caption. Savannah Grant. Neva's sister—twin sister, if this photo was anything to go by. And now that he knew, he could see the slight differences. Neva's mouth was slightly lusher, the look in her eyes less analytical, her hair a shade lighter.

He quickly read the accompanying article, which was little more than a report about the murders and Savannah stating she was doing everything possible to solve the crimes.

So why had she suddenly disappeared?

Was that the reason Neva was here? Had something happened to her sister? Was someone using Savannah to force Neva into the current situation? It was certainly more than possible.

If that *were* the case, then—while his suspicions

about her might have been right—she'd had very little choice in the matter. And it made what he'd done to her all the more unforgivable.

And if someone *had* kidnapped Savannah, then that surely crossed Nancy Grant's name off the suspect list—or would, if he actually had a list of suspects. She might be against the dance, but there was no way she'd attack her own daughter. Not from what he'd seen of her, anyway.

Which led him to another question—why would the kidnapper want Neva here? Was she really just a means of keeping tabs on his investigation? After all, while few people had been told his reason for being here, there were no doubt many who could guess. His arrival home just after the first two murders would be fuel enough for the gossip mills.

He rose, and headed for his room. The wind whistled icily around his ankles as he entered the older section of the mansion, and he frowned. It felt like there was a door open somewhere. These halls were normally cold, but not *this* cold. Or windy.

He opened the door to his suite only to be greeted by a snowstorm. He cursed loudly and made his way into the bedroom, from which the storm seemed to be blowing. Neva wasn't there, and the French doors were open wide. He swore again and walked out onto the snowbound balcony. She was gone—and if the depth of snow inside the bedroom was any indicator, she'd left at least an hour ago. He swept his gaze across the swirling whiteness and knew something serious must have happened for her to brave a storm like this. And that something undoubtedly involved her twin. If she was willing to risk her reputation and her relationship with her parents for her sister, this storm certainly wouldn't provide much of a challenge.

He spun and walked back into the bedroom, closing the French doors behind him. He swept a disparaging glance around at the mess, then picked up the phone and called his father.

"I'm going to Ripple Creek," he said the minute Zeke answered. "I may or may not be back tonight, depending on what the storm does."

"Why?" His father didn't sound surprised—but then, he'd raised four sons who all walked the wild side of life. Maybe nothing they did surprised him any longer.

"Neva's gone."

"Well, you were expecting her to run. Looks like you've achieved your aim."

"I don't think she's running from me," he said. "What if Neva's sister didn't back off the case? What if she was actually kidnapped?"

"Well, that would put a somewhat different spin on Neva's reasons for being here. And it would also explain the rangers' desperation to solve this case." He paused. "However, it doesn't explain why someone is so intent on implicating us."

And if they could find the answer to that particular question, they'd no doubt have a clearer idea of who the damn murderer was. "A friend of mine came through with some interesting information." He quickly filled his father in on everything Lance had said.

"Detrek's the head of the Sinclair pack over in Bitterroot, and an old friend of mine. I'll give him a call and see what he remembers of that night. I doubt Nancy Grant would be involved, though. She wouldn't endanger her own daughters."

"No, but maybe someone else from the Bitterroot burning *is*."

"It's possible. Some wolves have very long memories." Zeke hesitated. "I'm posting security at all the entrances tonight. I know the storm will deter some dancers, but I'm not risking another death. The guards will remain in place until after the full moon."

"Good idea." Anything that made life difficult for the murderer was worth trying. "Give me a call on my cell phone if you get the results back from the samples we took from Betise."

"Will do. Just be careful out in that storm."

"I will." He hung up, then stripped the sodden comforter and sheets off the bed and shoved them down the laundry chute. He cleared the snow and relit the fire to help dry the rest of the room, then grabbed his jacket and headed out to find Neva.

Neva wrapped her hand around Savannah's warm fingers. She'd been allowed to stay with her sister a little longer, though it was against the doctor's recommendation and only at Sav's insistence.

"We called the rangers," Neva said softly. "Once they get here, make sure you arrange for twenty-four-hour protection."

"Don't start trying to tell me how to do my job." Sav's voice was little more than a harsh whisper, but Neva had never heard a sweeter sound. "And why are your hands like ice?"

"I ran through a snowstorm to get here, and I got both wet and cold when I chased the killer back outside."

"You should go home and change before you catch a chill."

"Right now, catching a chill is the least of my worries."

Sav's curiosity swam around her. "Where in hell were you, anyway? It felt farther away than either the diner or your place."

She hesitated, but there was really no hiding the truth. Sav would have to know sooner or later, and right now Neva needed help from someone who knew what they were doing. Someone who could possibly see the clues she was missing. She took a deep breath, then said, "I've been continuing your investigations."

With Sav's face still bandaged, Neva couldn't see her reaction. But she could feel it, and right now her sister was annoyed . . . and more than a little apprehensive.

"What do you mean?"

"I mean I raided your office and read the files." She hesitated again, then added, "And I've been up at the mansion."

That sense of apprehension increased. "Doing what?"

Celebrating the moon with an incredible man I can't quite hate. She cleared her throat and hoped like hell her sister didn't catch the thought. She still had her shields up, but between the two of them that often didn't matter. "Your files suggested the Sinclairs were high on your list of suspects. So I've been talking to them."

"*We* can't get them to talk to us. How would you be able to?"

She didn't suspect, Neva thought. Or didn't imagine. But before she could answer, a babble of voices rose from out in the corridor. Angry voices, male and female. One was altogether too familiar—as was the scent that touched the air. Neva closed her eyes and silently swore. The last thing she needed right now was for Duncan to make an appearance.

Footsteps echoed—a sharp tattoo that spoke of anger. A nurse came into the room, face flushed and blue eyes irate.

"Sorry, Miss Grant," she said, her gaze seeking Neva's. "But there's a man outside who claims to be your mate and demands to be let in the room."

Savannah's shock stung the air. Neva took a deep breath and slowly released it. So much for keeping her tryst with Duncan a closely guarded secret. And given who her father was, the whole damn town would know tomorrow. "Let him in."

The nurse spun and marched back out. Savannah's grip on Neva's hand grew fierce.

"By the moon's light, Neva, what in hell have you done?"

Chapter Eight

WHAT HADN'T SHE done? Especially in the last forty-eight hours? Heat flushed Neva's cheeks, and she was suddenly glad her sister's face was still bandaged.

"I told you, I was up at the mansion."

"But to join the moon dance?" Sav's voice was incredulous. "Even *I'm* not that foolhardy."

"I told you I was going to find the bastard and make him pay for what he did!"

Sav took a deep breath and slowly released it. "Who did you use to gain entry?"

"Duncan. He's the only one you didn't have under suspicion."

"And the wildest. He's spent time in jail."

"A few days, for some drunk-driving-related offenses."

"He's a repeat offender. And a fool."

Neva had no doubt Duncan would probably be the first to admit it, then wondered why in hell she was tempted to rise to his defense. Duncan certainly didn't seem to care what anyone thought about him, so why should she?

Sav was silent for a moment, and the sharp rap of approaching boot heels seemed to echo as loudly as Neva's heart. She wasn't sure if it was trepidation or merely the excitement of being close to him again.

"I can understand why you did it," Sav said quietly, "because I know if anyone hurt you, I'd do whatever it took to bring them in. But Moons, you'd better hope Mom and Dad don't find out."

Neva smiled grimly. "They know about Duncan. They just don't know I'm up at the mansion."

"Oh God—" Sav cut the rest of her words off as Duncan entered the room.

Neva met his gaze. His dark eyes were still shuttered, his face impassive. It was impossible to even guess what he was thinking right now. He stepped toward them, and suddenly the room didn't seem big enough. Nor did it contain enough air.

"Did you have to tell the nurse you were my mate?" she snapped, annoyed by both his presence at the hospital and her continuing reaction to him. The moon wasn't even *out* at the moment, so why was she still feeling a buzz of excitement?

He raised an eyebrow. "It's the truth, is it not?"

His rich voice was neutral and gave no clue as to his thoughts. "Only for this phase."

He shrugged. "Why didn't you tell me about your sister?"

She wondered how he'd found out. Betise, perhaps? "Would you have allowed me entry into the mansion if I had?"

"No."

"Then that's your answer."

He studied her for a moment, then switched his gaze to Savannah. "Are you going to introduce us?"

She did. Savannah didn't offer him her hand, just turned her bandaged face in his direction. Imprinting his smell, Neva knew. Feeling his thoughts. She wondered if Sav would have more luck than she had.

No. Sav's mind voice sounded tired. *But I like the smell of him.*

So did Neva. His smell and his taste and his touch. She just didn't know if she liked the *man*.

"Why are you here, Sinclair?" Savannah asked, voice getting hoarser. "The dance is tonight. You have no right to the days as well."

"In this case, I do."

Moons, Neva, you didn't agree to a bonding, did you?

I'm afraid so. It seemed logical at the time.

And now?

I'm discovering I'm a little wilder in nature than I ever thought.

The warmth of Savannah's smile ran around her. *That's something we all discover, sooner or later.*

"Would you two mind keeping the conversation to conventional methods?" Duncan said. "Because there are several things we need to discuss."

"Like what?" Neva and Savannah said in unison.

A small smile touched his sensual lips and just as quickly fled. "Like why you believe the killer is one of the Sinclairs and not one of the dancers."

"If in fact the Sinclairs *were* suspects, do you really think I'd discuss the case with you?"

"Given that I hold your sister's reputation in my hands," he bit back, "you might want to."

"Bastard," Neva said, truly, *truly* hating him at that particular moment. But she suspected it wouldn't last anywhere near long enough.

"I could have you arrested for a threat like that," Savannah said.

"You could. Or you and I could start cooperating and try to find this killer." His gaze hardened, and Neva hadn't thought that was even possible. "What evidence do you have that suggests the killer is a Sinclair?"

"The reputation of the Sinclairs, the location, the silver hairs—"

Duncan snorted. "The Sinclairs aren't the only silver wolves around. That coloring is found in many other packs as well."

"Yeah, but it *is* the predominant color in the Ripple Creek Sinclairs."

"In all the years the Sinclairs have run the moon dance, there's never been a death. Until now. It's not one of us."

"And, of course, I can trust the word of a felon," Savannah snapped hoarsely.

He didn't react in any way. Not physically, nor emotionally. Maybe he'd been expecting such a reaction from Savannah, who was, after all, an officer of the law. "If you won't trust the word of a felon, then it's not much use offering what I know, is it?" He glanced at Neva, obsidian eyes slightly narrowed. "You and I need to talk. I'll wait outside for you."

He walked from the room and Savannah puffed out a breath. "If that man looks half as sexy as he sounds . . . wow!"

Wow seemed nowhere near adequate when it came

to describing Duncan. He was a man with a wild past—a man with the face of an angel and a body designed to corrupt the virtuous. A man who could be both incredibly generous and utterly selfish when it came to lovemaking. But above all else, he was a man who held the world at a careful distance. She very much doubted if anyone actually knew the real Duncan Sinclair.

Certainly not anyone here in Ripple Creek, anyway. And maybe not even the man himself.

"You should talk to him about this case. I've got a feeling you're both on the same side here."

"I know. But we'll do it on my terms, not his." Savannah's voice was little more than a raw whisper.

Neva switched to telepathy. *Bit hard to do it on your terms—or even your turf—when you're stuck here in the hospital.*

I'll be out in a couple of days.

Your stitches won't even be out in a couple of days.

I don't care about the stitches. I care about catching this killer.

And you have deputies who are more than capable. Use them. Stop trying to do everything by yourself.

This from the wolf who decided to sidestep the official investigation and undertake her own?

Sav's mind voice was dry, and Neva grinned. *I think it's a case of do as I say, not as I do.*

The nurse stuck her head around the corner. "Time's up," she said. "The doctor wants Savannah to rest a little before your parents get here."

Neva nodded and rose. *I'll keep in contact.*

Make sure you do. And I want to know everything

that man says, especially if it's anything related to the case.

Neva hesitated. *You know he can use the bonding to forbid me to mention anything?*

He can't forbid what's a natural part of you. He can't forbid the telepathy we share. Savannah hesitated, and her thoughts became somewhat grim. *Believe me, I know.*

Neva raised an eyebrow. *I sense a story I haven't been told.*

Savannah waved a hand. *Old history.*

But not forgotten, from the sound of it.

Let's just say I know a little about being used and leave it at that.

Would you leave it at that?

Sav's smile was a flutter of warmth through her mind. *I guess not. I'll tell you when I'm feeling stronger.*

Neva hesitated, then said, *I've found out a few interesting snippets of information I have to tell you myself. But later.*

Tonight. Savannah's thoughts were becoming sleepy.

Neva leaned forward and placed a kiss on her sister's nose, then released her hand and walked out. Duncan leaned against the wall, his arms crossed and his face impassive. With his damp black hair, the black leather jacket straining across the width of his shoulders, and dark jeans clinging to his lean but powerful legs, he looked sinister and yet so sinfully delicious that desire curled through her. He looked every inch the dark angel—a man who walked the line between good and bad, and who didn't seem to give a damn what anyone thought.

And she realized then it didn't even matter what *she* thought of him, because no matter how good it sometimes seemed between them, in the end it was only physical. It never could and never would be anything more than that. All he wanted out of a mate was a few days of pleasure. He didn't believe in love or life mates and certainly wasn't the type to settle down. And she wanted all those things. She always had.

She stopped and crossed her arms. "Do you want to go back to the mansion to talk?"

He shook his head. "The storm is getting more severe. Your place would be better."

She didn't want this man in her house. Didn't want his scent on the air or memories of him to linger once this moon phase was over and he was history. She glanced out the window, studying the blanketing whiteness for a moment. A motel room really wasn't a good option, though, especially in a town this size. If her parents were determined to find her, they would. All they'd have to do is follow the gossip.

"Let's go," she said, not bothering to look back as she stalked toward the exit.

He didn't say anything as they walked down the stairs, but as they headed toward the exit, he took off his coat and offered it to her. She glanced at it, then at him, and wished she knew what was going on behind those shuttered eyes.

"I'm all right, thanks."

"You're so cold your lips are practically blue," he snapped. "Take the damn coat."

She glanced down at the coat he held out, then shifted shape and raced out into the storm. Maybe she was being stupid, but right then she didn't want to be bound to Duncan any more than she already was—even when it came to something as simple as accepting the offer of a coat. She might be obliged to mate with him for the entirety of this moon phase, but she wasn't about to lean on him. Not in *any* way. She'd chosen him as a means to an end, nothing more—though whether he'd let her continue her investigations now that he knew who she was, she didn't know. But undoubtedly she soon would.

Her teeth were chattering by the time she reached her house. She flicked on the lights and the heating, then moved into the kitchen to fill up the coffeepot.

"I'm going for a shower," she said, flicking the switch. "Alone."

But when she turned to face him, all thought of showering immediately fled before the desire so evident in his dark eyes. Her heart began to beat in double time, and she knew it had nothing to do with fear. Freezing cold or not, she wanted this man with a fierceness that was almost scary. As was the fact that she'd never felt anything like this before. But then, she'd never been with a wolf as wild as Duncan before. Her previous mates had been sensible—the sort of wolves her parents would have approved of.

She stood her ground and he stopped, leaving only inches between them. The heat of him melted the ice from her skin, and the wave of his anger and passion burned in her mind. She might have her shields at full strength, but right now she was feeling this man's emotions all too clearly.

"Tell me one thing." His voice was soft. Emotionless. But his dark gaze held hers with an intensity that curled her toes. "Is Savannah the only reason you're at the mansion?"

She nodded, wishing he'd touch her. Hoping he wouldn't. Crazy, that's what she was.

"You joined the dance for no other reason than to hunt down her attacker?"

Again she nodded. With the emotive soup of passion and need and hunger swirling around her, she could do little else.

"And no one else knew of your decision?"

She couldn't help a derisive snort. "Not until you announced to the whole damn hospital ward that I was your mate."

Something flickered in his eyes. What, she wasn't sure, though she doubted it was regret. This man didn't seem to regret anything he did.

He ran the back of his fingers down her cheek, his gentle touch sending a shiver of longing through every fiber of her being. Then he dropped his hand and stepped back.

"Go have your shower."

She stared at him for a moment, wondering what sort of game he was playing now. Or was it merely an extension of the same one? His behavior over the last day certainly suggested he enjoyed stirring her to the brink of climax, then pulling back, and while she was nowhere near that point at the moment, his closeness had her so hot it wouldn't take much to reach it.

"Go," he said when she didn't move. "I'll rustle up something to eat."

She went, though in truth, it was really the last thing she wanted to do. By the time she'd showered and changed, the aroma of the fish and fries she kept in the freezer for emergencies wafted through the air. Her stomach rumbled a reminder that she hadn't eaten breakfast, and she hurriedly dried and brushed her hair before padding barefoot down the stairs.

Stopping in the doorway, she watched him pull the baking tray from the oven and plate up the meal. He'd taken off his coat and rolled up his sleeves, and he looked so completely at home in her kitchen that something stirred in her heart. He glanced up, his dark gaze catching hers and seeming to delve deep into her soul. The intensity that flared between them went beyond the natural heat of moon-spun lust. It was deeper, stronger. But just how deep or strong was something she had no intention of finding out. Such exploration could only lead to disaster with this man.

"That smells good," she said, breaking the moment and refusing to contemplate what that moment actually was.

He picked up the two plates and brought them over to the table. "Living on my own for so long has taught me to cook, but I'm afraid there really wasn't that much else in this house I'd call edible. Eat up, while it's still hot."

It was hard to imagine Duncan being on his own for *any* length of time. You don't acquire the kind of reputation he had living like a hermit. She sat down on the opposite side of the table from him, picked up the knife and fork, and quickly discovered just how hungry she was. They ate in silence, and when they'd both finished, he carried the plates over to the sink and poured them both a mug of coffee.

"So," he said, sitting down once again. "You want

to explain why you and your sister are so convinced that the killer is hiding in the Sinclair mansion?"

"You want to explain why you think he isn't?"

His smile was grim. "I know my family. They're many things, but they're not killers."

She raised an eyebrow. "Even you?"

He met her gaze squarely, and though his face was expressionless, his exasperation and anger stirred around her. "Even me."

She leaned back in her chair and contemplated him over the rim of her coffee cup. "Then why did you go to jail?"

"You mean you haven't already gotten all the details from your sister?"

"She's only just woken, so I haven't had time." Besides, she wanted to know just how willing he was to be honest with her now that he knew what she wanted—and why she was at the mansion. "But I do know it was drunk-driving-related. Did you kill someone?"

"No. And I didn't spend a lot of time in jail—just enough for the police to find the evidence that backed my story."

"'Not a lot of time' could be anything from a month to a year, depending on your point of view," she said dryly.

He didn't react, though the anger touching the air increased. In some regards, that surprised her. After all, he didn't seem to care what anyone else thought, so why did it matter what she thought?

"In this case, it was only a couple of days while the police checked my story, and only because I couldn't make bail. A man who suspected I was having an affair with his wife cut the brake lines, and I couldn't stop the car. Luckily for us both, the driver of the car I crashed into wasn't seriously hurt."

"But you *were* drunk at the time."

"Like most wolves, I have a high tolerance for alcohol. I was nowhere near drunk, but I *was* just past the legal limit."

Until lawmakers decided how to deal with the different metabolisms of humans, werewolves, and shapeshifters, they all had to cope with the laws as they were. And it didn't matter if the legal limit meant nowhere near intoxicated for a wolf. The law was the law, and they had to live with it.

"So you got a fine and did community service?"

"Yes."

"So why is it that Savannah thinks you're a felon?"

"Because it's not the first time I've landed in jail for being drunk—though the other times I wasn't driving."

"So you were a fool thrice over?"

"Yes."

"And were you having an affair with the guy's wife?"

"They were separated."

"So the answer is yes."

He shrugged and didn't answer, his dark gaze as impassive as his thoughts. If not for the mix of exasperation, anger, and hunger that burned between them, she would have thought him totally disinterested in both her reaction and *her*.

"Have you seen her since you got out of jail?"

"A fool I might be, but an idiot I'm not. I got the hell out of Denver the minute I could."

"And you've been with search-and-rescue ever since?"

"Basically."

"And sober?"

"Definitely. I have no intention of ever going back to jail. Being locked up for a couple of days was long enough for me to realize that being locked up for longer would kill me." He regarded her for a moment, then said, "Satisfied I'm willing to tell the truth?"

It would be easy enough to check out everything he'd told her, though she really didn't doubt he was telling the truth. "Can I ask one more question?"

He raised an eyebrow. "What?"

"Why did you leave Ripple Creek, and why did you come back?"

"Why I left is none of your damn business, and you've already guessed why I'm back."

She sipped her coffee and made a mental note to ask Savannah to do some digging into his background—if she hadn't already. "So you *are* here to investigate the murders for your pack?"

He crossed his arms and leaned forward on the table. Hunger slipped between them, caressing her skin with its heat, stirring her mind with its fervor. The deep-down ache increased, and she squirmed, trying to ignore the sensation. She might as well try to ignore the rising of the moon. "Yes. And now, are you willing to offer the same sort of honesty?"

She hesitated. "Yes."

"Then tell me why the rangers suspect it is one of the Sinclairs behind the killings."

She took a deep breath and slowly released it. Savannah wasn't going to be happy with her for doing this, but instinct suggested she had to trust him. And right now, instinct was the only thing she *did* trust. She certainly wasn't about to trust common sense, which was currently suggesting she leap this table and dance herself senseless with this beautiful but cold-hearted man.

"They haven't got anything concrete, and certainly nothing that would be admissible in a court of law."

His dark eyes watched her intently. Hungrily. "But?"

"They found scent trails near two of the three victims that led back into the mansion, and they've identified them as belonging to Kane and Tye."

"Considering they were the ones who found the bodies, that's logical. They undoubtedly found René's scent near the fourth victim, as well as mine."

And probably hers, though it had been well covered by the scent of jasmine—she'd have to remember to tell her sister who was responsible for that particular scent. Otherwise the rangers might waste precious time chasing a dead end.

"They also found several hairs on the first and third victims."

He nodded. "From a silver coat."

"No. These were human. Or at least from a shifter in human form."

"Really? That wasn't mentioned in the reports I read."

She gave him a long look. "I wouldn't confess to something like that. Not unless you want me to report it to my sister."

He reached across the table, capturing her hand,

turning it palm up. His thumb stroked her wrist, a gentle, almost possessive caress that sent shivers of desire skating across her already overheated skin. "You won't tell on me, will you?"

It was teasingly said, but the power that slipped between them ensured she'd obey. She tried wrenching her hand from his, but he held on tight.

"You could have just asked. You didn't have to use the moon bond."

"Didn't I?" The smile that touched his sensual lips was short-lived. "Considering the lengths you've gone to track down your sister's attacker, I think I'll continue to play it safe."

"So you're asking me to trust you, but you're not willing to offer the same in return?" Annoyance bit through her tone, and he smiled.

"If it came down to a choice, you'd take your sister's side every time."

He was still stroking her wrist, and it was beginning to do weird things to her breathing. "Naturally. She's family, and I love her."

"Exactly. While I—" He hesitated, his gaze seeming to deepen. "Mean absolutely nothing to you."

"As little as I do to you." But as her gaze got lost in the obsidian depths of his eyes, she had to wonder if either of them was being entirely honest.

"And these hairs they found—are they matching or different?"

Right then, she didn't particularly care. His fingers had slipped up her arm and were caressing the inside of her elbow. It felt so damn good that desire trembled through her. "Matching," she somehow managed to say.

"Black hair? Is that why they've asked us all for hair samples?"

"I presume so. I've only read the preliminary reports." His fingers slipped farther up her arm, and the back of his hand brushed against her breast. Her nipples ached to feel his touch, pressing almost painfully against the restrictions of her bra. She swallowed and said, "But your pack *are* the only wolves who are black-haired when in human form."

"Is there any chance of getting back into your sister's office and reading the rest of the report?"

His touch retreated back down to her wrist, and she almost groaned in disappointment. "We have about as much chance of that as we have of this storm stopping by nightfall."

"Then ask your sister."

"My sister is still listed as critical. She won't be looking at anything for a while yet." Which wasn't exactly the truth. Knowing Savannah, by tomorrow morning she'd be demanding full reports on everything that had happened since she'd been attacked.

"And that's the only evidence the rangers have that it's a Sinclair? Hairs they haven't yet found a DNA match for?"

"I know they've taken samples from the black-haired humans in town, just to be sure, but they've come up blank." She hesitated. "But you tell me. You seem to have better access to the files than I did."

His sudden smile was warm and sexy and all too fleeting. "There's not much evidence to point to one of us, is there?"

"Well, no. But who else could it be?"

He leaned back in his chair, the shutters well and

truly in place. It made her uneasy, though why, she had no idea. It wasn't as if she'd been able to read much in his expression anyway.

"Someone who disagrees with the dance, perhaps?" he drawled softly.

The uneasy feeling increased. She eyed him for a moment, then said, "Half the golden pack doesn't like the idea of the dance, myself included. Are you trying to imply some sort of conspiracy is occurring?"

"Is it any more implausible than one of the Sinclairs being the murderer?"

"Yeah. My pack are strong telepaths. A secret *that* big would not stay a secret for long."

He raised a dark eyebrow. "The fact that you're all strong telepaths also means you all have strong shields, doesn't it?" When she nodded reluctantly, he continued. "So why is it implausible?"

"Because my pack aren't murderers."

"And the Sinclairs are?"

She wished he'd get to the point—if he had one. "Well, you Sinclairs do have a rather wild reputation you're not afraid to live up to."

"There's a difference between being wild and being a murderer."

"From what I've heard, a lot of the Sinclair pack walk the edge."

"Still, walking the edge doesn't make us killers."

"No." She hesitated, then put her coffee cup on the table and crossed her arms. "So, who do you suspect?"

He studied her for a moment, face impassive, dark eyes hard. The air around her practically buzzed with tension—both his and hers.

"Your mother was born on the Bitterroot Reservation over in Idaho, wasn't she?"

It felt like he'd punched her. Her breath left in a whoosh of air, and for several seconds, she couldn't even breathe. Couldn't do anything more than look at him in horror.

"Did you know," he continued mercilessly, "that as a sixteen-year-old she took part in a raid of the Sinclair stronghold over there and burned it to the ground?"

"*No.*"

"Yes." His voice was monotone. Relentless. "Thirteen people died that night, and many more were injured. Your mother was never charged because her old man paid off the right people."

She slapped her palms on the table and thrust upright. "Get out!"

His smile was grim. "She's done it once, Neva. She could easily do it again."

"I said, get out!" Her voice shook with the force of the fury rolling through her.

"A good investigator considers all options."

"My mother is *not* an option. Now get the hell out of my house."

He didn't move. Didn't even blink. He might have been made of stone. She was certain his heart was.

"Then perhaps you should consider your father," he said, his rich voice as cold as the storm outside. "Did you know he'd been questioning Betise about who was dancing with whom up at the mansion?"

She'd been questioning Betise—and the older wolf had certainly never mentioned her father doing the same. And she would have, if only because Betise hated Neva's father almost as much as he hated her. It was doubtful whether one would give the other the time of day. "I said, get out. And I meant it."

"Your days and nights are mine, little wolf. I'm not going anywhere."

"You're a . . ." Words failed her. Somehow, *bastard* just didn't seem strong enough.

His smile contained little warmth. "So you keep saying."

She hit him. Not physically, but emotionally. Hit him with all the anger and humiliation and pain that had built up over the past couple of days. Although his shields were up, the force of her emotive blow still leached all color from his face and thrust him backward, off the chair and onto the floor.

"It's not a nice feeling, is it?" His voice was little more than a hoarse whisper, and beads of sweat dribbled down his face. "Having your family treated as suspects?"

She met his soulless gaze and realized then what he'd been doing—making her feel what he and his family were feeling.

Even so, to accuse her mother . . .

She took a deep breath and released it slowly, then let the power slip away and slumped back on the chair, covering her face with her hands. After a few seconds, he climbed slowly to his feet. She could feel the heat of his gaze on her, but she refused to look up.

"I'll be back at dusk," he said softly. "And I will claim what I am owed."

His words made her tremble, but it was a reaction that had nothing to do with fear.

And that, she thought, as his footsteps retreated to

the door, was a major problem. He could push her buttons as easily as he breathed. He didn't even have to touch her. All he had to do was look at her.

Cold air swirled around her as the back door opened and closed. Shivering a little, she dropped her hands, surprised to find that he really had left. Given the heat that had been flaring between them, she'd expected the conversation to end in bed.

Had half-wanted it to.

She rose and walked over to the coffeepot. How could she want a man she hated?

Easy. She didn't really hate him. She never had.

She closed her eyes at the thought, but knew it was a truth she had to acknowledge. Despite everything he'd done, she *didn't* hate him. In fact, she rather liked him—at least when he wasn't being such an arrogant idiot.

But what good did such an admission do? It wasn't as if anything could develop between them. It was one moon dance, nothing more. She'd known that going in, and he'd certainly emphasized it more than a few times since.

But that deep-down crazy part of her wanted more.

She sighed softly and wondered what the hell she was going to do. Because the one thing she'd feared the most after their very first mating was beginning to happen. She didn't want to let him go at the end of this moon cycle. Didn't want to walk away. Didn't want *him* to walk away. She just wanted to explore the possibilities that might lie beyond the heat that flared between them.

Which was stupid thinking. Especially when his soul mate didn't live all that far away.

She bit her lip and glanced at the clock. Betise had recently moved from the run-down house owned by her mother's pack into a small apartment just off Main Street to be closer to work. She had no idea whether or not Betise had been scheduled to work her nursing shift at the hospital today, but if she *hadn't*, then it might be her one chance to find her alone and ask her some questions—the ones she wanted to ask, and the ones Duncan had ordered her to ask.

Chapter Nine

Duncan shivered and pulled up his jacket collar as he headed across town to Neeson Jones's place; the force of the wind pushed him along so hard he was almost running. The old wolf had only recently retired as editor in chief of the *Ripple Creek Gazette,* and if there was anyone in this town who'd know all the secrets, it would be him.

Though right now, battling this storm and talking to the old wolf were really the last things he wanted to do. He'd much rather be curled up with Neva in her big old bed, loving her and holding her until the storm died down. But given what he'd done over the last day or so, it was very doubtful that she'd dance with him willingly again. Not during the day, anyway. And he certainly wasn't going to force her. He wasn't *that* callous.

He briefly closed his eyes, remembering her shocked expression, seeing again the hurt and anger shining in her pretty eyes, and swore softly. Part of him had still needed to push, had needed to confirm what he already knew in his heart the moment he'd seen Savannah lying bandaged and bruised in that hospital bed—that Neva had no part in whatever was going on. That in fact—against all common sense, and at incredible cost to herself—she'd agreed to the moon dance simply because she'd wanted to find whoever was behind the attack on her sister, and that he was her safest path into the mansion. Right now, he felt like the bastard she kept calling him.

And that he regretted. Very much.

But he'd set his path, and it was too late to undo the damage now. He just had to be thankful the moon was still rising. If nothing else, he at least had the nights to enjoy.

He sped past houses he couldn't really see, their shapes lost to the white blur of the storm. Neeson lived up on Seventh Street, not far from the building that housed his beloved paper. Duncan wondered why he'd finally decided to retire. Ten years ago, he'd been adamant that he'd die on the job.

When he swung onto Seventh Street the wind hit him broadside, sending him staggering several steps before he caught his balance. The dance was in trouble tonight. It was doubtful if even the most dedicated followers would be willing to battle this storm for the sake of pleasure.

He ran across Neeson's lawn and rang the doorbell. Inside the house, bells chimed an annoying melody that seemed to go on and on. After several minutes, he heard shuffling steps approaching.

"Who is it?"

"Duncan Sinclair. I need to talk to you."

The door opened, revealing the stout, silver-haired figure Duncan remembered. But as he studied the old man's face, he realized there was no life in his eyes.

No spark of recognition. He was blind—a fact confirmed by the white cane clenched in one hand.

"Come in, come in," Neeson said, his nostrils flaring as he opened the door wider. "You want a drink to warm the ice from your bones?"

"Coffee would be good."

Neeson snorted softly as he slammed the door shut. "I can remember a time when you would have sneered at the mere mention of coffee."

"Even the baddest of the bad can alter in ten years," Duncan said dryly.

The old wolf tapped his way down the hall, but once he got to the kitchen, he put the cane down and moved with more assurance. Obviously, he spent most of his time here and didn't have many visitors—or at least not many who used the front door.

"So," Neeson said, picking up the coffeepot and feeling for the mugs. "You didn't come here to talk about old times, as we haven't had many. What do you want?"

"I'm trying to hunt down this killer for my pack." He saw no reason to lie to the old man. Neeson might be blind, and he might be retired, but he probably still knew more about what was going on in this town than anyone else. And his next words confirmed this.

"Thought you might be, considering you swore ten years ago never to set foot in this . . . what did you call it? 'Blighted town'?"

Duncan smiled. "Even I got a little tired of trying to live up to my own reputation."

"You wouldn't have thought it." Neeson slid a chipped mug across the table, then added, "And from what I heard, you took your bad behavior with you."

"Yeah. But cooling my heels in jail for a while had a sobering effect."

"It often does," Neeson said. "And, to repeat the question, what do you want from me?"

"Information about Nancy Grant."

Neeson's rheumy gaze drifted Duncan's away. "You've obviously been digging."

He shrugged, even though he knew the old wolf couldn't see the movement. "I have to start somewhere."

"Nancy Grant isn't what I'd call a starter."

"Why not?"

"Because she was sixteen when the Bitterroot fire happened, and she was fueled up on alcohol and drugs. She's been on the straight and narrow ever since."

"So no rumblings whatsoever about the dance?"

"Nothing more than any of the golden tribe."

"And what about Levon?"

"Doubtful. Besides, both he and Nancy are golden wolves. The killer is silver."

"The evidence points that way, but it could be planted."

"The rangers don't think so."

"If the rangers were so certain, they'd have arrested someone by now." Although it was always possible they were simply waiting to get the hair samples from everyone at the mansion before they made their move. "I'm told Levon was recently asking about the dance and who was partnering whom."

"Then the person who told you was lying."

Interesting. If Betise was lying, he'd have to find out

why—and what she hoped to gain by doing so. "What makes you say that?"

"Because Levon may have tried to stop the dance many a time, but I think he now realizes it's essential—even if he's banned anyone in his pack from participating. I did an interview with him about two years ago. You should read it if you want to get a handle on the man. It's very interesting."

He might indeed dig it out, but only because it might give him more insight into Neva. "Have there been any rumblings about the dance in recent months? Has anyone been trying to close it down?"

"There are always rumblings about closing it down. There always will be. But it never will be shut down, because everyone fears what might happen if it was."

Duncan swallowed some coffee, then asked, "So . . . nothing more than the usual grumbling?"

Neeson hesitated. "There *has* been more than the normal anger directed toward the Sinclairs this past month. Someone is stirring up trouble, but I haven't been able to discover who."

Join the club, Duncan thought. "Where have you been hearing this?"

"Everywhere." Neeson hesitated, then smiled. "People seem to equate blindness with deafness. Some of the things I hear amaze even me."

"And what's the opinion on the street about the murders?"

"That it's one of the Sinclairs. That your games have finally crossed the line."

"And your opinion?"

"That it's all too pat—it just doesn't feel right." His

sudden smile was a touch wistful. "It's just the sort of juicy story I loved when I was at the *Gazette*."

"So who's running it now?"

"Some fancy-pants from Denver. He's as useless as a neutered dog."

Duncan smiled. "If you hear any more interesting rumors, would you mind letting me know?"

"As long as you come back when this is all over and give me a blow-by-blow of how you found the killer."

At least someone outside his family had confidence in him. "Planning to submit a story to the *Gazette*?"

Neeson snorted. "And give that asshole a scoop? No way in hell. I just like knowing outcomes, that's all."

He nodded. It was *that* desire, more than anything, that had made Neeson a great reporter, and an even better chief. "It's a deal."

"Good." Neeson rose and escorted Duncan to the front door. "Where are you off to now?"

"I think I'd better talk to my lying source of information."

"Good idea." He opened the door, and Duncan hurriedly left before the icy touch of the wind stole too much heat from the old man's house.

He rang his father to get Betise's address, then shifted shape and ran through the storm.

Neva hurried up the apartment's front steps and leaned heavily on the buzzer. The air was almost white with snow and every intake of breath just about froze her lungs. The ski mask, like the two coats she was wearing, didn't seem to be doing a whole lot to keep out the chill.

She continued to lean on the buzzer, stomping her feet and cursing the insane urge that had made her venture out in a storm like this. After what seemed forever, a sleepy, disgruntled voice croaked, "Go the fuck away. I'm trying to sleep."

"Betise," she said quickly into the intercom, "it's Neva. I'm sorry for waking you, but I really need to talk to you."

"Neva?" Betise didn't really sound any more awake. "Why the hell are you here?"

"Betise, it's freezing out here. For God's sake, just let me in."

The other woman muttered something, but a moment later the buzzer sounded and the door clicked open. Neva hurried in and slammed it shut behind her. The heat hit her immediately, making her gasp, and she quickly shed some layers before running up the stairs.

"Don't tell me," Betise said dryly, looking and smelling the worse for wear as she opened her door. "You felt an urgent need for some of my famous muffins."

Neva grinned as she took off the last of her coats and shook her hair loose. Betise's muffins were famous for the fact that they were the consistency of concrete and could break toes if you dropped them. But every year she made them for the school fundraising fete, and every year someone bought them. "In weather like this, a paperweight muffin might just be a good thing."

Betise snorted and leaned a hip against the counter.

"So what can I do for you, then?" Though the friendliness had not fled from her voice, there was a touch of wariness in her green eyes.

Probably because she'd been caught in a lie, Neva thought grimly. "Why did you tell Duncan my father was asking you about the dance?"

Betise sighed. "I'm sorry, but Duncan was bothering me, asking me all sorts of questions."

Hostility rose in a wave, and Neva briefly looked away. She had no right to feel proprietary when it came to Duncan, and if anyone should be angry at sharing, it was Betise—*if* she wasn't lying when it came to her relationship with him. And Neva was growing more certain that she probably was. "But why say something like that?" she said, once she was sure her voice was under control.

"Because he's been away for so long and is the only one in town likely to believe such a statement."

That was certainly true. The animosity between her parents and Betise was no secret. Though why her father was so against Betise and not the other dancers who came into their diner was something Neva had never been able to understand—or get an answer to.

But maybe it was time she tried again. She should question her mom, at any rate. They'd know she was here—the hospital staff would surely have mentioned it—and she'd much rather confront them than have them seek her out.

"That still doesn't explain why you'd even make a statement like that in the first place."

Betise made an "I don't know" gesture with her hands. "Neva, as I said, I'm sorry, but it was just the first stupid thing that came to my mind. I didn't really think beyond getting him off my back."

"My father wouldn't pick you up if you fell over in front of him—and vice versa—so why would *that* be the first stupid thing that came into your mind?" She paused, watching the other woman carefully, seeing dislike tightening her eyes. Dislike—for her father, or for her? "Or was that the reason you said it?"

"No other idiot would believe it," she muttered. "So what harm was there in saying it?"

"What harm? He's all but accused my parents of being behind these murders." And although he'd meant it as nothing more than an object lesson, Betise had no need to know that. Neva sat in one of the few chairs and stretched her legs toward the heater vent to warm her feet. The apartment didn't hold much in the way of furniture *or* warmth. But Betise had only been in the apartment since her mom had reclaimed possession of their pack's old house, so most of her stuff was probably still over at her mother's. "My parents may dislike the dance, but they would never resort to murder to stop it."

"Anyone with half a brain would know that," Betise agreed and pushed away from the counter. "Would you like a soda? Or a coffee?"

Neva hesitated. "Just a half cup, to warm my insides before I venture out again. I have to head up to the hospital to see Savannah."

"She's awake?" Betise moved behind the small screens.

"Yes. And itching to get back to work."

"Good for her." There was the sound of liquid

being poured, then Betise asked, "Does she remember what happened?"

"Not really. But I think she just wants to get better and find the killer." Neva hesitated. "Do you mind if I ask you a personal question?"

Betise came back out carrying two white mugs. Though her expression was still friendly, the wariness in the air became almost strong enough to taste. "Sure. Go ahead."

Neva accepted the mug with a nod of thanks. "If you and Duncan are soul mates, why are you still apart?"

Betise didn't answer for several seconds, then grimaced and looked away. "Because I was the only one convinced that we were."

Neva blinked. Of all the answers she'd expected, that wasn't one of them. How could you not know your own soul mate? It was a state that transcended the heart, transcended the mind, and became a linking of spirit. It was something you just knew and couldn't escape—or so her father had always claimed. Never having met her soul mate, Neva couldn't say for certain what it was like. But if Duncan hadn't felt that intense, must-have-you-in-my-life-or-die sensation, then they obviously *weren't* mates. It wasn't something felt by only one person.

Betise was deluding herself.

And the intensity of Neva's relief shook her hands so much her coffee was threatening to spill over the top. She put it down carefully, and said, "Why would he lie about something like that?"

She shrugged. "Duncan's not one to be pinned down, even by a soul mate."

Maybe because he *didn't* feel anything. "Why are you so sure he was lying?"

Betise's smile was touched with sadness. "Because when a bonding is that deep, you can't help knowing everything the other is feeling. It's instinctual."

Neva sipped the coffee and shuddered at its strong, almost bitter taste. It had obviously been sitting in the pot for a while. "Is that why he left?"

Betise hesitated. "Partly, I guess."

"Was there another reason?"

"He was wild, and he had a serious drinking habit. It was a combination that got him into trouble more than once."

If his behavior then was far wilder than it was now, Neva could understand why. He wasn't exactly the caring, sharing type. "So why haven't you tried to pursue him now that he's back?"

Betise snorted softly. "You heard him deny our relationship. What point is there?"

Plenty, if they were *truly* soul mates. For one, it meant Betise could never settle down with another. But maybe that didn't worry her—not as long as she had the moon dance.

Neva drank some more coffee and decided she'd better get to the point of the visit. "How are you doing after the attack?"

Betise shrugged. "I'll heal."

That wasn't what she asked, but she didn't push. "I'm going to report your attack to my sister."

"Please don't. We're not really sure it's linked, and I don't want the rangers fussing over me."

"But if it *is* linked, your attack might hold some clue that could help catch this fiend."

"It's doubtful. I didn't really see much, and to be honest, the rangers annoy me more than your father."

Neva smiled. "Then tell *me,* and I'll pass it on to my sister. That way, if there really is nothing interesting, you won't have the hassle of talking to the rangers."

Betise hesitated, then nodded. "Ask away."

"What did he smell like?"

"Why would that matter? It's not admissible in a court of law."

"Well, no, but it could lead the rangers to our killer."

"I was under the impression they didn't find any scents at the murder scene."

"According to the papers, no. But they did find one at the hospital."

Betise raised an eyebrow. "Hospital?"

Neva couldn't see any point in holding back the information. Betise worked at the hospital anyway and would likely hear through the staff grapevine, even if word didn't get officially out. "We think the killer may have tried to get to Savannah."

"So you were *there?*"

"Yeah. I sensed Savannah was waking and came down."

A smile touched the older wolf's pale lips. "I wondered why Duncan had let you out of his bed. Normally, he keeps his mates occupied day and night."

Heat touched Neva's cheeks. "Yeah, well, he actually didn't know I had slipped away."

Betise considered her for a moment, then said, "My attacker smelled like old sweats."

Not a smell anyone was likely to forget in a hurry,

and not the scent she'd chased in the hospital. It was a strong smell that would not dissipate easily, and while the wind had been strong last night, it had been almost nonexistent during at least two of the other attacks. Surely the rangers would have picked up such an unusual aroma. "And what did he look like?"

Betise shrugged. "As I said, silver. I was too busy defending myself to take much notice."

"No identifying marks? Scars?"

"None that I saw."

"Eye color?"

"Yellow."

Which was the standard eye color of a true wolf, not that of any of the packs that lived in Ripple Creek. Were they dealing with an outsider? Perhaps a wolf that had drifted in from one of the other reservations?

"Was his coat true silver, or was it gray?"

"It wasn't an old wolf. He was young. Virile."

"So he tried to . . . you know?"

Betise looked away, her face suddenly pale. "Thank the moon, you and Duncan were so close. You scared him off."

They'd scared him off—but couldn't smell him? Not even on Betise? Odd. Unless she was lying. Or unless, for some strange reason, she knew her attacker and was protecting him.

Which is exactly what Duncan had thought, even if he hadn't come right out and said it.

"Did you know the other victims?"

Betise raised an eyebrow. "No, but what has that got to do with anything?"

Neva shrugged. "I was just curious. I mean, maybe the Sinclairs aren't the link. Maybe it's the women."

Betise snorted. "If the rangers thought that was a viable line of investigation, I would think they'd be spending less time trying to pin it on the Sinclairs."

Possibly. She stood and handed Betise her half-finished coffee. "To be honest, I don't think the person who attacked you is the same person who attacked the other women."

Betise dumped the coffee remains in the sink, then rinsed the cup. "Why not?"

"Because the rangers aren't sure the murdered women were raped."

"Really? They implied in the papers that they were."

"You can't believe everything you see in print," Neva said dryly. She picked up her coats and ski mask and quickly put them on. "I'm still reporting your attack to Savannah, though—unless you think you want to report it yourself."

Betise's smile was wry. "Given where I was and what I was doing, the rangers aren't going to take it all that seriously."

"*Any* attack is serious. The man who attacked you might just try his luck with someone else." And right now, they certainly didn't need another lunatic running around.

"I very much doubt it."

And with that statement Neva was convinced that Betise knew her attacker. Damn, it would be so handy to be able to read this woman's mind right now! "Thanks for the coffee and the info."

Amusement touched Betise's mouth as she said, "And what about the muffin we mentioned?"

Neva snorted. "I think I'll skip it this time. But thanks for taking the time to see me."

The other woman just shrugged and slammed the door once Neva had left. The sound echoed through the stairwell, chasing Neva's footsteps as she ran down. Once outside, the wind picked her up and almost blew her back into the building. Shivering, she remained under the cover of the entrance for a moment, reaching out with her thoughts. There was little response from Savannah; her sister was asleep. No use going to the hospital just yet.

She glanced up the street. On a normal day, the diner was within easy walking distance. In the midst of a storm, it might as well be in the next county. Or was that cowardice speaking? As much as she knew she had to speak to her parents, she wasn't sure she was ready to do it just yet. But then, would she ever be? She certainly hadn't confronted them before now—and maybe, if Duncan hadn't forced the issue, she never would have. Moving into her own home had been her only attempt to break the leash. And even then, her parents still had too much control over her life—as Ari often commented.

But the attack on Savannah, and being with Duncan these last few days, had forced her to see there was more to life—and more to *her*—than blindly following the path her parents had set.

And while she had no intention of becoming a frequent visitor at the mansion once this moon phase was over, she *was* tempted to explore her wilder side. Not so much sexually, or even emotionally. She just wanted to step beyond the boundaries of her life so far and explore the possibilities. Discover what else might be out there for her. True, she was happy enough working at the diner, but that was a job that would always be waiting. There was a world beyond Ripple Creek to explore. Savannah had taken off years ago on a quest to find herself. Maybe it was past time Neva did, too.

The only trouble was, that deep-down crazy part of her wanted to explore it with Duncan at her side.

She shoved her hands into her pockets and ventured out into the storm. The strength of the wind had, if anything, increased in the last half hour. It was as if nature itself was intent on pushing her back toward the diner rather than home.

She let it blow her along the empty street. The cold began to seep into her bones, despite the multiple layers of clothes, and her limbs felt leaden. What she needed was a good eight hours of solid sleep. Whether she'd get it before the full moon finally rose was another question.

Main Street curved to the right, and the buildings momentarily cut the full force of the wind. She tripped, caught herself before she could fall, then glanced behind her to see what had snagged her foot. There was nothing to see—not even the cracks in the pavement. She shook her head and continued on. Above the howl of the wind came the sound of an engine. She glanced over her shoulder, glimpsing an old blue truck moving slowly along the street. At least she wasn't the only one out. Though she *was* the only one on foot.

She tripped again and cursed softly, smacking her hand against a shopwindow as she tried to steady herself. Her goddamn feet seemed intent on tripping over each other, no matter how hard she tried to lift them. This wasn't good—and it meant she was more tired than she'd thought.

She studied the snowbound street ahead—or what she could see of it. Her house was closer than the diner. Maybe she'd better head home and take a nap. The way she felt, she'd fall asleep long before she got to the diner, and in this storm that would be deadly.

The wind hit her again as she came out of the protection of the buildings to cross the road. She staggered sideways like a drunkard, battling to keep upright against the force of the storm and the sudden weakness in her limbs. Fear slithered through her. It was almost as if the utter cold of the day was leaching all her energy.

She sighed in relief as the next row of shops gave her a brief respite from the wind, but she knew worse was still to come. Her street was the next one over, and to get home, she'd have to walk against the full force of the storm.

She stopped at the last shop, resting a hand on the glass to support herself as she took several deep breaths. Her eyes drooped closed and she forced them open again, blinking rapidly. The slither of fear became stronger. She could so easily fall asleep right here and now. All she had to do was close her eyes.

She had to get home. Fast.

The wind slapped her back the moment she stepped out into it, forcing her several steps rearward. She gritted her teeth, leaned forward, and walked on, but it felt as if she were walking through glue. An icy-cold glue, at that. Every single step was a supreme effort.

Her breath tore at her throat, and the iciness of the air seemed to shred her lungs.

She counted the houses as she passed, needing to keep her mind off the effort it took to walk. And off the need to simply lie down and sleep. Eight houses to go . . . seven . . . A street corner loomed into view. Once she'd crossed it, she was almost there. The thought seemed to rush fresh energy into her limbs, and she stepped out onto the road.

Above the howl of the storm came the roar of an engine. Too late, she became aware of the sullen gleam of headlights rushing toward her.

She yelped and tried to leap away, but the truck clipped her hip and sent her sprawling. She smacked against the ground, saw stars, and for several seconds couldn't seem to breathe.

Then oblivion rushed in, accompanied by the harsh sound of laughter.

Chapter Ten

DUNCAN RAPPED HIS knuckles against the old wooden door. There was movement inside, so he knew someone was home. After a few moments, he heard the approaching scuff of heels against wooden flooring.

"Yes?"

The voice was harsh, elderly. Not Betise, then. "Duncan Sinclair," he said. "I'd like to speak to Betise, if possible."

The door opened. Cool air rushed past him, accompanied by an unpleasant smell that came from both the woman and the house. He resisted the urge to step back into the fresh air of the storm and studied the woman in front of him. She wasn't as elderly as he'd thought, probably in her mid-fifties, and was a tall, angular stick of a woman with harsh yellow hair and gray-green eyes.

She looked him up and down, and an almost disdainful smile touched her thin lips. "You'd be a Sinclair, then?"

"Yes. Duncan Sinclair, as I said." He paused. "And you are . . . ?"

"Iyona, Betise's mother. What do you want with her?"

"I just need to ask her a question."

Iyona snorted. "Yeah, right. The day the Sinclairs just want to talk is the day the moon will stop rising." She sniffed. "She doesn't live here anymore. She's got an apartment in town."

"And yet she came here the other night."

"So the leopard *doesn't* change its spots. Following gals home is the sort of behavior will get you into trouble—if it hasn't already."

"I wasn't following her, I was ensuring she got home after she was attacked," Duncan said, somehow managing to keep his voice even. But between the smell and the insinuations, it was a close thing. "What's her address? I need to talk to her."

"Then you'd better come in. She's on her way over, as it happens."

Good, because he certainly didn't want to be stuck for long in *this* house with its sour, overripe smell. He stepped inside, the sharp rap of his boot heels against the old floorboards echoing in the box-filled hallway.

Iyona slammed the door shut, then shuffled past. "You'd better wait in the living room. I'm cooking sweetbreads, and the smell can get overwhelming if you're not used to it."

That was an understatement if ever he'd heard one. He walked into the room the old woman had indicated and looked around. Like the hall, there were boxes everywhere, piled up on sofas and fighting for space among the old newspapers and magazines scattered everywhere. Obviously, Betise hadn't bothered cleaning up for her mother.

He tossed the papers scattered on the sofa to one side and sat down. The room, like the hallway, was cold. He couldn't hear the breath of forced-air heating, and there wasn't a fire lit in the old hearth. Maybe Iyona didn't feel the cold.

He tapped his fingers against the sofa arm for several minutes, then glanced toward the kitchen. There was no sound of movement. No soft intake of breath. "Have you been in Ripple Creek long?" he asked, wondering if she was still there or had gone somewhere else.

Water flushed and, a moment later, Iyona appeared, shuffling toward the sink to wash her hands. "I only came because my old pack had a house here I could use. Been living with relatives down south until a few weeks ago."

"So you're from the southern packs originally?" Not that he was really interested. He was just making conversation to get his mind off the awful smell.

"Not really," Iyona said. "Shame about the murders happening up your way."

"The rangers will catch whoever is behind them." If *he* didn't get the bastard first.

She glanced at him, amusement glinting in her silvery eyes. "Seems to me the rangers haven't a clue."

Her tone was as amused as her look, and he raised an eyebrow. "You don't seem all that sorry about it."

"The murders?" Iyona snorted softly. "I personally think it should be you Sinclairs being killed, not the fools who choose to dance with you."

Betise had said much the same thing. Maybe it was a speech she'd learned from her mother very early on. But if that was the way she felt, why had she wasted more than half her life attending dances? "You have a problem with my family?"

Her look was scathing. "Yeah. All you Sinclairs are nothing but a pack of lying bastards."

Again, that was something he'd heard Betise say more than once. But then, Neva had called him a bastard more than a few times these last couple of days, and with good reason. He frowned as he thought of her and had to control the sudden urge to get up and find her. He'd promised not to go back until dusk. And if he wanted to undo the mess he'd made of everything and start making amends, he couldn't break that vow.

And the mere fact that he even *wanted* to make amends surprised the hell out of him. She was his for the rest of this moon phase. He could rightfully lose himself in the pleasure of her body until the full moon finally rose and forced them all into wolf shape. But he wanted more than that. He wanted to *know* her. Wanted her to smile at him the way she'd smiled at her friend in the diner.

He wished he'd met her under more normal circumstances, and beyond the time of the rising moon. Maybe then he wouldn't have destroyed any chance he had with her.

At that moment pain flashed, rising from his hip and spreading upward like a flame, until his whole body was encased in agony. Then as quickly as it came the sensation faded, leaving only fear and a cold churning in his gut.

He fought the sudden urge to leave this stinking house. It was crazy. Neva was safe at home. Besides, she had a weapon more formidable than teeth and claws, and could undoubtedly defend herself against most attacks.

Still, he rose and began pacing the small room. "What has my family ever done to you?"

Iyona snorted. "Your lot wrecked my life."

"You've never danced at the mansion." Though he wasn't sure why he was so certain. Iyona was old enough to have been dancing long before he'd ever started.

"There's more than one pack of Sinclairs, isn't there?" she bit back. "You must have bred like damned rabbits in the early years."

Her words sent alarms off somewhere in the back of his mind. He stared at her for a moment, trying to read her thoughts but failing, then asked, "I gather from that statement that you spent some time over at the Bitterroot Reservation?"

The smile that touched her lips sent a chill down his spine. "No, but I wish I had. I would have enjoyed watching you lot burn."

He sensed no lie, and yet he suspected she was doing just that. "If you feel that strongly, then why invite a Sinclair into your home?"

She snorted again. "Because you wanted to see my daughter, and she'd be furious if I sent you away when I knew she was on her way. Seems she has a passion for you lot."

And yet, she'd wished them dead not all that long ago. Or was that merely an aftereffect of exchanging heated words with René? He was definitely going to have to speak to his brother when he got back to the mansion, if only to uncover what sort of game Betise was playing. Especially given the fantasy she had of being a longtime lover of *his*.

Outside the house, a gate slammed shut, then a shadow whisked past the windows. Two seconds later, the back door opened and Betise appeared. Her smile became a look of surprise and quick excitement when her gaze met his.

"Duncan," she said, voice warm. "What a nice—"

"I'm here to ask a question," he said quickly. "Nothing more."

Annoyance and perhaps a flash of anger flitted through her gray-green eyes. She stripped off her coat and gloves and tossed them on the back of the chair. "Let me guess. You discovered my lie. Surprise, surprise."

"Then why bother lying in the first place?"

She shrugged and sat down. "You seemed so enamored of the virginal Neva, I guess it just pissed me off."

Her tone had much the same effect on him as nails down a blackboard. He shoved his hands in his pockets, half-wishing he'd never come. "What does it matter to you if I'm enamored of her? You and I shared one dance, nothing more."

Something flashed in her eyes. Something more than anger. Something almost crazy. She yanked off her boots and tossed them into the corner. "I knew you'd race back and question her. I wish I could have seen her expression."

He wished he *hadn't*. He wished he'd resisted the urge to make her realize what it felt like to have your family accused of everything and anything. "I thought you and Neva were friends."

She glanced at her mother, and the two shared a strange sort of smile. "Acquaintances more than friends," Betise said. "We chat at the diner, but it's nothing deeper."

He was extremely glad of that. He'd hate to think that Neva hung around with someone as unsavory as Betise. "So what did you hope to gain by lying?"

She raised an eyebrow, amusement touching her thin lips. "What do you think?"

"If I had any idea, I wouldn't be asking."

She stared at him for a moment, eyes so bright they were almost otherworldly. "You really don't, do you?"

He glanced at Iyona, saw the same, almost maniacal look in her eyes, and frowned. Something was going on here, something he didn't understand.

"Told you," Iyona said, voice shrill. "They're all no good."

"Seems that way, doesn't it?" Betise's voice was flat, dead, and something in his gut clenched. The house might be cold, but these two could have frozen hell itself.

"Look," he said, meeting Betise's gaze. "You and I shared one dance, nothing more. I have no idea what game you're playing, but if you don't stop your lies, I'll have you banned from the dance."

Iyona snorted. "That's a typical Sinclair response." Her voice was so full of venom he could almost smell it.

He glanced at her. With her thin arms crossed, angular hips resting against the bench and eyes narrowed, she really did remind him of a snake. Neeson might not have any idea who was behind the animosity being directed at his pack, but *he* certainly did. And he had a suspicion he'd better find out why.

He pulled his gaze away from her, concentrating on Betise. "I'm warning you now, stay away from my brothers."

"Who made you pack leader?" she spat. "You can hardly control your own actions, let alone your brothers'."

Which might have been true enough in times past, he supposed, but not nowadays. Control was the one thing he never lost—except, perhaps, when it came to Neva.

But the itchy feeling that something was wrong with Neva not only remained but was growing stronger. He had to go. *Had to.*

"I'm speaking for my father," he said curtly. "Watch your step, or you'll never take another inside the mansion."

"René owes me. I want him to fulfill his promises, nothing more."

"René makes no more promises than I do."

"Not even to the virginal Neva?"

"Not even." Yet the words tasted sour on his lips. If he could have ever made promises with someone, it might have been Neva. "But while we're on the subject of Neva, quit telling her tales about you and me. There *is* no you and me. There never has been."

Her eyes glittered, but he wasn't sure if it was tears or merely the light catching the silver in her eyes. "You lie. Look into your heart, Duncan."

"I have looked into my heart." And up until this moon phase, he'd thought it incapable of any sort of emotional depths.

"Bastard." Her soft voice was filled with hatred.

"So I'm beginning to believe," he muttered and turned, walking out of the house and away from its crazy occupants.

He stopped on the veranda and watched the storm. The snow had eased, but the wind hadn't, and the day was still bitingly cold. Not the sort of day you wanted to be out in.

Not the sort of day you wanted to find yourself unconscious in.

For one second, he froze. Then he swore and dove into the storm, running as if the hounds of hell were after him. He didn't feel the tempest blowing around him. Didn't feel the cold. Didn't even feel the pavement pounding under his feet. All he could feel was an odd sort of numbness, creeping slowly through his body, as if his strength was being sucked away by an unknown force.

Only it wasn't truly unknown. It was Neva, siphoning his strength to bolster hers.

He'd never truly feared before, but he did now. For her.

For them.

Because if she could do *that*, then this thing between them went far deeper than he'd thought—far deeper than just a moon dance.

Wouldn't it be the mother of all ironies if, in a matter of days, he'd managed to destroy the one thing he'd spent the last ten years of his life searching for?

More than eight blocks separated Iyona's house from Neva's. He crossed them in record time, slowing only as he reached her house. He opened the gate, then hesitated, looking at the windblown whiteness to his right. She wasn't home. She was down there somewhere.

He didn't question his certainty. He didn't dare. He only swore again—a growl of sound the wind quickly snatched away—and hurried forward. The sullen gleam of a streetlight became visible, indicating that he was approaching another road. He stopped on the corner, glancing to his left.

And saw her huddled against the curb, looking more like a bundle of snow-covered rags than a woman. His gut twisted, and for a second he couldn't seem to breathe. Then he was beside her, stripping off his gloves and slipping his fingers under her woolen ski mask, feeling for a pulse. It beat beneath his fingers, strong and steady. He checked her ears, then her fingers and her feet. All were well covered. All were warm. Relief slithered through him. Hypothermia didn't appear to have struck yet.

He stripped off his coat, then his sweater, rolling it lengthways and carefully placing it around her neck. As improvised cervical collars went, it wasn't the best, but it was a hell of a lot better than the risk of moving her without it. He carefully turned her over. No blood. That might be good, and it might be bad.

"Neva?" He lightly tapped her cheeks. Her color was good, and he could feel the warmth of her skin through the ski mask.

Her eyes fluttered, and a smile touched her lips. A carefree, easy sort of smile that did strange things to his heart.

Neva?

She giggled, and he raised an eyebrow in surprise. It

sounded for all the world like she was drunk. *Are you okay?*

Okay? No. Perfect? Yes.

Her words made him smile. She *was* perfect, in almost every way imaginable. He picked up his coat and tried to wrap it around her, but she slapped his hands away with a laugh. It was such a carefree sound he almost laughed with her, despite the concern swamping him.

What happened? He managed to avoid her hands and finally wrap the coat around her.

A truck. Clipped me.

She seemed to be moving all right, and he could no longer sense pain in her mind. Still, he'd better get her to the hospital, just to be sure.

No. Take me home. Please.

Her mind speech was a little indistinct, yet he could smell no alcohol on her breath. *You need to go to the hospital. There might be internal injuries.*

No! Her words might be slurred but the alarm in her voice was clear and forceful. *I'm okay. My parents are there. I can't talk to them yet.*

She touched a gloved hand to his cheek, her bright eyes catching his. Her pupils were slightly dilated, but not with desire. He suspected she'd been drugged. But with what? And could he risk not taking her to the hospital when she might have been overdosed?

"Please." Her voice was soft. Imploring. "Just trust me and do as I ask."

He closed his eyes and took a deep breath. He was a fool for even risking a compromise, but he opened his eyes and said, "I'll take you home and look you over. If I think you should go to the hospital, you'll go, okay?"

Her relief slithered through him, flame bright. "Okay."

He picked her up, cradling her close. She rested her cheek against his shoulder and sighed almost contentedly.

"Home, James," she murmured. Her warm breath caressed his neck and breathed life into the embers of desire. Moons, simply holding her felt so good. So damn right.

He kicked open her front gate and hurried up the steps. Her front door was unlocked and he shook his head, unable to believe any woman living alone in this day and age could be so trusting. Even a relatively small town like Ripple Creek had its fair share of creeps.

And she probably saw *him* as one of them.

He pushed the thought away and headed up the stairs to her bedroom. Thankfully, she'd left the heat on, and the house was warm.

"I like your thinking," she said, as he placed her on the bed. "No better way to warm up a cold body than a good bout of sex."

He squatted in front of her and carefully took off her boots, then her woolen socks. Her feet and toes were warm. "You know this for a fact?" he asked, glancing up with a smile.

She sniffed and lifted her nose, her expression haughty but green eyes twinkling. "I have been told," she said in the best impression of snobbery he'd ever heard.

"Extreme physical activity is not good for someone

who might have hypothermia." He rose and un-
wound the makeshift collar, then undid her coat and
discovered another one underneath. No wonder she
was so warm.

"I haven't got hypothermia."

No, thankfully she didn't. He tossed her coats to
one side and started undoing her shirt. "But you have
been hit by a car, and I suspect you've been drugged."
He doubted she'd be in such a playful mood otherwise. Not after what he'd said only an hour or so
earlier.

She touched a finger to his face, running it gently
down to his lips. It was a touch that burned right
down to his soul.

"How about we try some extreme physical activity
right now?" Her voice was low and so damn sexy
that heat shot to his groin.

He ached to do just that. It might still be the afternoon, and the moon might be on the other side of the
world, but right now he wanted her as fiercely as he'd
ever wanted anyone during the moon's rush. But as
much as he wanted her, he didn't want to take advantage of her. Not any more than he already had. Her
shirt joined her coats, followed quickly by her bra.

"See anything you like?" She leaned back, all but
thrusting her wonderful breasts in his face.

Everything. But he resisted the urge to bury his face
in her bountiful flesh and twined his fingers through
hers, gently tugging her onto her feet. "Where did
you go after I left?" He released her, but she swayed
slightly, and he quickly touched a hand to her waist
to steady her.

She wrapped her arms around his neck and gave him a happy sort of smile. "What does it matter?"

He kissed her nose, then began undoing her jeans. "Tell me."

She yawned, then said, "Betise's. Had to ask her some questions, remember?"

He'd forgotten he'd asked her to do that. "I didn't order you to go out in the middle of a snowstorm."

He hooked his thumbs around the waist of her jeans and panties and pushed them down. She stepped free, then flopped back onto the bed, arms and legs akimbo.

"Come here." She sat, then patted the bed beside her.

He again resisted the desire to do just that. "Roll over onto your left side."

She raised her eyebrows and did as he asked. "Planning a little spoon adventure, are we?"

"Maybe." A huge bruise was beginning to appear on her rump, but there were no skin lacerations, and she seemed to be moving her legs without flinching. He carefully checked the rest of her but could find no other signs of injury. "Did you drink anything at Betise's?"

She sighed. "I don't want to talk about her."

"Neither do I, believe me. Did you drink anything?"

"Coffee." She reached up, grabbed his shirt, and dragged him close, green eyes dancing with devilment as they searched his. "Kiss me."

"Love to." And he did. Long and slowly. Tasted her, savored her, until he knew every inch of her mouth as intimately as he knew the rest of her. When he finally broke away, his breathing was harsh, and the desire to take what she was so freely offering pounded through his veins.

"How much coffee?" he asked hoarsely.

She gave him a vixen smile and trailed her fingers down his chest. "Not even half a cup."

If Betise had put something in the coffee, at least Neva hadn't taken all of it. She was probably safe from an overdose, though he'd certainly have to keep an eye on her for the next couple of hours. He flipped back the bedcovers. "Climb inside. I'll make you some hot chocolate."

"I don't want some hot chocolate."

She brushed her fingers up and down the front of his jeans—teasing, but not quite touching, his erection, which seemed to press even more painfully against the restriction of the denim. A shudder ran through him. Right then, he didn't want any hot chocolate, either. He patted the pillow. She sighed and climbed rather gracelessly under the covers.

"Care to join me?"

"Yes, but later." He tucked the blankets around her. "Did Betise say anything of interest?"

Amusement dimpled her cheeks. "She told me you were soul mates. And that you refused to acknowledge it."

Anger flashed through him, warm and bright. He knelt down beside Neva and touched a hand to her cheek. "Betise is not my soul mate. We shared one dance, nothing more." He paused, staring into Neva's beautiful eyes, trying to make her believe him. Trying to make her see. "I have no fear of acknowledging my soul mate."

She giggled. "I know. Betise is delusional. She merely wants what I have."

Relief slithered through him. Neva might not see or understand the reason he and Betise could never be soul mates, but at least she wasn't buying the lie. "What else did she say?"

"That she lied about my dad."

He'd discovered that for himself. "And?"

"She gave me a brief description of the man who attacked her. It's no more than what we already know."

No surprise there. He very much suspected Betise hadn't actually been attacked, but rather had been playing a game in wolf form that got a little too rough for her liking. Why else would she refuse to give them a proper description? She must have seen her attacker—she had scratches on her face.

"Nothing else?"

She shook her head and yawned yet again.

"I'll get the chocolate. You stay here."

Her sigh followed him down the stairs. By the time he'd made them both some hot chocolate and carried the mugs back up the stairs, she was asleep.

He stopped in the middle of the room, his gaze on her face and his heart doing weird things in his chest. He finally acknowledged what he'd known the minute her pain had echoed through him and she'd begun siphoning his strength. This was more than just the power of the moon and the need for the dance. Far more.

He placed both mugs on the bedside table closest to her, then tossed teddy bears off the nearby chair and dragged it closer. Propping his feet on the bed, he picked up a mug and sipped at the drink slowly as he let his gaze rest on her serene, beautiful features.

He hadn't lied to her. He had no fear of acknowledging his soul mate.

What he feared more than anything else in the world was that she would refuse to acknowledge him.

Chapter Eleven

There was a madman in her head. A madman with a big hammer, continually bashing away at her skull. Neva groaned softly and rolled onto her back. Pain flared in her rump and curled up her side.

The truck, she thought. Then she felt the caress of cotton sheets against her skin and realized she was no longer lying in the snow but in bed. Her bed, if the tang of citrus in the air was anything to go by.

She opened her eyes and looked toward the window. It was dark outside, and the storm no longer raged. Snow continued to drift past the glass, the flakes briefly glistening silver as the lamp near the window caught them with its light. She reached out for her watch, wincing slightly as her side protested the movement. It was six o'clock. Four hours had slipped by. Four hours she couldn't remember.

Frowning slightly, she eased herself upright. Duncan had been in her room, but not in her bed. The air carried his warm, woody scent, but it didn't linger on the sheets. Two cups sat on the bedside table. She picked one up, sniffing it lightly. Chocolate. She certainly couldn't remember drinking it.

Her last memory was of the blue truck sideswiping her and sending her sprawling. She frowned, trying to reach past the haze in her mind, sure something important had happened between that point and now. Vague memories of being stripped rolled through the fog in her mind, followed by the flush of remembered passion. Yet they hadn't danced. Of that she was certain.

Neva? Her sister's voice winged into her mind, warm but concerned. *Are you okay?*

I think so. She climbed out of bed, and only realized she was completely naked when the warm air caressed her skin as gently as a lover's sigh. She grabbed her robe and put it on quickly.

What happened this afternoon? I tried contacting you, but it was like you were on another planet.

I'm not sure what happened. I got hit by a truck coming home from Betise's and can't remember much after that. She hesitated at the top of the stairs. Though the hall was dark, light peeked out from under the kitchen door. If the delicious aroma beginning to drift upward was anything to go by, Duncan was cooking dinner.

Savannah's sharp gasp echoed down the mental lines between them, and Neva winced.

Are you okay? Why aren't you in the hospital?

It barely touched me, and I didn't want to go to the emergency room. Not that she could actually remember saying that. *Have you arranged twenty-four-seven protection, like I asked?*

Yes. And we pulled several hairs off that doctor's coat you found in the trash. They match the hair we found at the murder scenes.

Black hair?

Black hair, Savannah confirmed softly.

Neva sighed. According to Savannah, the humans in Ripple Creek had already been tested and ruled out; that left just the Sinclairs. They *were* the only pack in Ripple Creek with black hair when in human form.

Then the murderer was definitely coming after you. So maybe you were closer to something than you'd thought?

Maybe. Savannah's doubt echoed down the line between them. *Tell me about the truck that hit you. I'll have Steve and Ronan look out for it.*

Your deputies have more important things to do. Besides, the storm was a bitch, and the driver probably didn't even see me. Yet she remembered the sound of laughter and wondered if that was true.

He would have felt the bump as the truck hit you.

He didn't hit me that hard. She hesitated. *Have Mom and Dad been in to see you yet?*

Yeah, and Dad's furious. He didn't say anything, but I think he knows you were up at the mansion. I'd avoid him for the next couple of days, give him a chance to cool down.

That would take weeks, not days. Neva rubbed a hand across her eyes and turned around, heading into the bathroom to grab some painkillers. After she'd taken them, she told her sister everything she'd learned over the last couple of days. It didn't take long, because she hadn't really learned that much.

I'll send Ronan over to Betise's place. I wish the damn fool had reported the attack immediately. We might have been able to pull some connecting evi-

dence off her gown. Savannah hesitated. *If you're right about their regular lovers being the targets, we'll have to convince the brothers to give us a list and arrange protection.*

I suspect that's now being handled within the pack.

Probably. And just so you know, we've got a warrant to search the Sinclair mansion, and we'll be requesting hair samples from everyone who currently lives there. So you'd better make sure you stay away tonight and tomorrow.

I can tell you now it wasn't René behind the last attack, and it certainly wasn't Duncan.

I'm not saying it's one of Zeke's get.

No, she wasn't. But she wasn't really considering anyone else, either, and Neva had a suspicion that was playing right into the murderer's game plan—whatever that plan was.

Give me a reason to suspect someone else and I will, Savannah chided. *Right now, I can only work with what I've got.*

Neva could remember a time when Savannah had worked with nothing more than guesswork and intuition, but all that had changed after she'd come home from an extended break five years ago. Neva wondered again what exactly had happened to so completely change her sister's method of policing, but now was not the time to ask.

I hope you're not planning to be up at the mansion, running the whole shebang.

Savannah's mental snort was derisive. *The goddamn doctors won't let me get out of bed. They threatened to tie me down if I tried to leave. I should have the lot of them thrown in jail and see how they like being confined.*

Neva grinned, though she could easily imagine her sister following through with her threat. *You need to rest, Sav. Wait a couple of days, until you're feeling stronger.*

Savannah sighed. *I guess you're the one person I can't lie to.*

Exactly. If I uncover any other information, I'll tell you. In the meantime, catch some sleep. And make sure Steve checks who's coming in and out of the room rather than flirting with that pretty young nurse.

How did you know it was Steve at the door?

Elementary, my dear. You said you'd send Ronan out to Betise's. Bodee is usually home by now, look-ing after the kids, and you can't stand Ike. That leaves Steve.

Ike's got the midnight shift, Savannah grumbled. *I told the nurse if he so much as looks my way to beat him over the head.*

Neva's grin grew. It was a well-known fact that Ike had been lusting after her sister ever since his transfer to Ripple Creek. He was nice, in a boring sort of way, and just the sort of man their parents would approve of. Savannah's method of dealing with his lust was to simply ignore it, but that only seemed to have in-flamed his ardor.

I have no intention of ever mixing business with pleasure again, Savannah said. *And no, I'm not going to explain that statement right now.*

Damn.

The warmth of her sister's smile spun through her.

Remember, don't go near the mansion tonight. I'll talk to you later.

Don't let the bedbugs bite. Or Ike, as the case may be.

Savannah made the mental equivalent of a rude gesture and closed down the link. Still grinning, Neva made her way down the stairs.

Duncan looked around as she entered, and she noted that his gaze was still shuttered. Odd. For some reason, she'd half-expected to see those barriers gone. What on earth had happened between them last night? What couldn't she remember?

"Hope you don't mind fish and fries again." His voice was neutral, almost careful, but his gaze swept down her body—a heated touch that left her tingling all over. "But the shops are closed, thanks to the weather, and you haven't much else in your freezer."

"Because I usually just buy what I need. Saves stuff going bad." She walked over to the drawer to grab some cutlery to set the table. The silk of her gown caressed her skin as enticingly as a kiss, and suddenly she was all too aware of the amount of flesh she was exposing as she walked, and that she wore nothing beneath the robe.

His quick intake of breath suggested he was just as aware of that fact. "And what if this storm doesn't let up?"

"I have chocolate stashed for such emergencies." She set the table, then walked over to the refrigerator. "You have the fine choice of soda, homemade lemonade, or water."

"I'll chance the lemonade."

"A wise choice. The soda's open and probably flat."

She poured them both a drink, then sat as he brought over two plates. She picked up her fork and stabbed one of the fries. "So," she said. "How come you learned to cook?"

"This isn't cooking. This is reheating."

"But you can cook?"

"Yes." He shrugged. "I got bored having steak and eggs every night for dinner, so I bought myself some cookbooks."

"What, no fetching little wolf hanging around to cook for you?"

He studied her, expression totally unreadable. "Occasionally," he said after a moment. "But mostly I was alone."

She picked up her glass and took a sip as she considered him. His mood was restrained—subdued, almost—and yet there was an undercurrent she couldn't quite pin down.

"Why have you been researching the attack on the Bitterroot Sinclairs? Do you really think something that happened over thirty years ago can have any bearing on what is happening now?"

"Honestly? I don't know. But right now I have to consider every avenue, no matter how tenuous or ludicrous the link might be." He hesitated. "How are you feeling this morning?"

She had a suspicion he hadn't asked out of concern for her health, but rather something else. "I've got the mother of all headaches and a sore butt, but other than that I'm fine. Why?"

"Are you up to a little breaking and entering?"

Her heart skipped, then began to race. "Where?"

"Betise's apartment."

Surprise flitted through her. "Why?"

"Because I suspect she slipped some sort of sleeping powder into your coffee yesterday. I want to see if she left the cup lying around."

"She didn't. I handed it back to her half-finished and she rinsed it." Neva frowned. "She may have the mother of all delusions going, but what point would there be in drugging me?"

"The point? Don't know, but you could have died if I hadn't found you so quickly!"

His anger burned her skin and made her throat go dry. Lord, it would be so easy to believe he actually *cared*. Which was ridiculous. He was a lone wolf—a man who enjoyed the dance and wanted nothing more from a relationship. "So how did you find me?"

"I got lucky." He pointed his fork at her barely touched meal. "Now eat, before it gets cold."

She ate, but could only get halfway through the huge plate he'd given her. She pushed the rest of it away and leaned back with a sigh. "Thank you."

He nodded and rose, collecting both dishes and taking them over to the sink. She watched him walk away, admiring the way his faded jeans clung to his butt and wishing she had the courage to actually admit out loud what she really wanted right now. The wolf within might want to be free, but she wasn't. Not yet.

"If she did drop sleeping powder in my drink, it probably came from the hospital. She works there as a nurse, so she has access to all sorts of drugs." She accepted the cup of coffee he handed her, then added, "There's nothing much at Betise's apartment. I think most of her stuff is still at the place her mother's in.

Between work and the moon dance, I don't think she's had much chance to fully move out."

"Then we'll check out her mother's place instead."

She wrapped her fingers around the mug and frowned. "But even if Betise does make it up to the mansion tonight, I doubt her mother will. She's something of a recluse."

"Recluse or not, she might accept a dinner invitation from an old friend."

Neva raised an eyebrow. "I didn't think Iyona had any friends—old or new."

"I called Neeson Jones while you were asleep. According to him, she has two. Neeson's helped me arrange a little get-together at the Blue Nights."

The Blue Nights was the bigger of Ripple Creek's two bars and was usually packed with partygoers when the full moon was rising. "You were lucky to get a table."

"I called in a favor. The owner's an old friend of mine."

She leaned back in her chair and sipped her coffee. His gaze drifted down her body, lingering on the folds of silk covering her breasts. Anticipation tingled across her skin, and the deep-down ache sprang to life.

And all because of a look. It was almost scary just how attuned she was to this man.

"Why do you want to search Iyona's house? What do you hope to find?" She stretched out her legs, her feet touching his. Warmth sprung between them, prickling up her leg.

"I don't know. But something strange is going on with that pair, not the least of which are the lies they've been spreading about me and my family. A clandestine search might uncover a few secrets."

"You don't think Iyona is linked to the murders, do you?" Neva ran her toes up the long, lean length of his foot. She'd never found feet arousing before, but just touching his were doing strange things to her breathing. As was the sexy smile that tugged at his lips, daring her to be bolder.

"At this point, no—though Iyona obviously hates my pack. But it's always possible she does know something."

She slipped her foot up his leg, enjoying the contrast of soft denim and taut muscle under her toes, and half-wishing those powerful legs were between hers. She reached as far as his muscular thigh, but couldn't go any farther without slipping off the chair. "Have you asked her about the Bitterroot incident?"

"Yes."

He reached under the table and began to knead her instep with his thumb. A tremor shot up her leg, jumping her pulse into triple-time.

"She claims she wasn't there," he continued, his rich voice deeper by several notches and as seductive as the moon itself.

She closed her eyes, enjoying the gentle but insistent press of his hand against her skin. "You don't believe her?"

"No."

"I could get Savannah to check it out, if you want."

"I already have a friend checking it out. He should be calling back soon." He wrapped his hand around her foot, his fingers so warm against her flesh it felt like she was being held by hot iron. "Are you ticklish?"

Her eyes flashed open. His grin radiated enough heat to melt the snow drifting outside the kitchen window, and devilment shone in his dark eyes. Her heart did an odd tumble. She had a feeling she was seeing a side of him very few ever did. "No, I'm not." She tried to jerk her foot away, but he held her tight.

"Really?" His ran a finger lightly down the sole of her foot, and she bit her bottom lip, fighting the urge to shriek.

"Really. Now, let go."

"I don't think so."

He flicked a fingernail across her instep and the squeal escaped. She squirmed on the chair, an odd flush of trepidation and desire running through her.

He raised an eyebrow. "For someone who's not ticklish, that sounded suspiciously like a laugh."

"Well, maybe I am a *little* ticklish."

He ran his finger across her foot again. Laughter bubbled through her and broke free. He stopped, his dark eyes a heated mix of desire and amusement.

"Okay," she said breathlessly. "Maybe I'm a *lot* ticklish."

"Just on your foot?" His fingers slid enticingly up her calf, and pinpricks of desire fled across her skin, leaving her hotter than she'd ever thought possible.

"Yes." Her reply was little more than a pant of air.

"You sure about that?"

No. "Yes."

"So you're definitely not ticklish behind your knee?"

His fingers teased her skin as he spoke, and she

couldn't contain her laughter. He stopped again, his grin as delicious as the look in his eyes. "Shall we explore where else you might be ticklish?"

"Not in this lifetime." Grinning, she pulled her leg from his grasp and jumped up from the table, bolting for the stairs.

He caught her in the hall and she laughed, half-heartedly fighting his hold on her. He pressed her back against the wall, his hands on either side of her body, neatly corralling her. His masculine odor filled her senses, and the desire that scorched the air left her breathless and aching.

He leaned close, his gaze all but devouring her. "I never could resist a challenge."

His mouth brushed hers, a tender caress that left her lips tingling—and her wanting more. But before she could react in any way, his hands had slipped to her waist and she was being tickled unmercifully.

She laughed until her knees felt as if they were going to give way and tears were streaming down her face.

"Stop, stop," she begged, between gasps for air.

He did, bracing his hands on either side of her again. "I think we can safely say you're ticklish all over." His grin was boyishly cheeky.

"You think?" she managed to say.

"I think." He leaned a little closer, and his cheeky grin melted into something far more dangerous—and far more luscious. "We can't risk heading out to Betise's for another hour or so. Any idea what we should do until then?"

She hesitated, her pulse zooming, the need to give in to desire warring with the instinct to keep safe and keep her distance—emotionally, if not physically.

"We could go back to the kitchen and finish our coffee." But her voice came out with a betraying huskiness, and the heat singeing the air became a tempest that blasted them both.

His smile faded, but his dark eyes burned bright in the hall's semidarkness. "We could. Or you could tell me what you really want."

She could . . . but she wouldn't. The wolf within might want him with a fierceness she'd never felt before, but she suspected if she openly admitted that, she might also be forced to admit other things. Like how much she *didn't* hate him. Or how she was beginning to fear the thought of him walking away at the end of this moon phase.

"Tell me." He dropped one hand and began undoing the knot at her waist.

A tremor of anticipation ran through her. "No."

"I can taste your desire on the air, little wolf. What harm is there in admitting it?"

"Plenty."

The knot fell away and her gown drifted open. The warm air caressed her even-warmer skin, and her breath caught, then quickened. But he didn't touch her. Instead, he caught the left edge of the gown and gently flicked it back and forth across one erect nipple. The sensation was like nothing she'd ever felt before—erotic, arousing, and torturous.

"Tell me," he said softly.

She swallowed, but it didn't seem to ease the dryness in her throat or the trembling in her belly. "Why do you care? I'm yours for this phase, no matter what I do or don't admit."

"And is that what you want? For me to just take you any time I want? Right here and now?"

She licked her lips and his gaze jumped to her mouth. Pinpricks of sweat danced across her skin. She needed him so badly she ached to scream: *Yes.* But she'd sworn never to admit her needs to this man, and for the sake of sanity—for the sake of her heart— she had to honor that vow.

"Does it really matter what I want?"

"Would you believe me if I said yes?"

"No."

"Why not?" He switched his attentions to her right nipple. She all but moaned at the sweet sensuality of the silk whispering across her skin.

"Because it's just another game. Just another way to destroy me."

His pause was brief, but undeniable. "Would it make any difference if I apologized?"

She briefly closed her eyes. He sounded sincere, and she so desperately wanted to believe that he was. But in the end, it didn't really matter, because he was still leaving once the murderer was caught, and she'd still be left here, alone, to deal with the mess. "An apology won't rectify the damage you've done."

"Perhaps if I explained—"

"Oh, yeah, that'll work." Her voice was sharp with sarcasm. "Tell my dad I went to the moon dance for the sole purpose of seducing you to gain entry into the mansion. That'll surely make everything all right."

He leaned forward, brushing another sweet kiss across her mouth. "I wasn't intending to tell him *that.*"

His warm breath tingled across her lips. She

breathed in as he breathed out, until it seemed as if the spicy taste of him was filling every pore. She swallowed heavily. "I wouldn't tell him anything. If he sees you right now, he's likely to reach for the nearest gun."

He raised a dark eyebrow. "I thought your dad didn't believe in that sort of thing."

"He's a wolf, and I'm his little girl."

"And I'm nothing but trash taking advantage of you." There was a hint of bitterness in his voice that suggested he'd heard that sentiment expressed more than once.

Part of her ached to deny the words—to tell him that he was so much more than his reputation had led her to believe—but she didn't. Salvation and survival resided in silence. He was a lone wolf who didn't want anything more than this moon dance. Except, perhaps, for an admission that she *did* need, just as badly as anyone else at the mansion, despite all the lofty ideals of her pack.

"It doesn't matter what he thinks," she said softly.

"No," he agreed after a moment. "But it matters what you think."

Why? That's what she ached to ask. Especially when he had already admitted he wanted nothing from her but the next few nights. "Right now, I don't want to think." She just needed his touch—on her skin, and deep inside.

"Then tell me what you *do* want," he whispered, bringing them right back to square one.

He stopped teasing her breasts with the silk, but before she could murmur her disappointment, he dipped his head, his tongue circling the dark ring of one nipple, teasing but not touching the oversensitive center.

Every inch of her trembled—ached—with expectation. She closed her eyes and leaned her head back against the wall, enjoying his touch and the sensations storming through her.

"Not that," she said after a moment. Because as much as she was enjoying it, the moon and she both knew that she wanted a whole lot more.

"No?"

The liquid touch left her skin as he shifted his attention to her other breast. This time, he nipped, drawing her nipple deep into his mouth and sucking on it hard. She gasped, her knees almost collapsing at the rush of unexpected pleasure.

"Nor that," she somehow said.

"Then, perhaps . . . *this*?" His tongue teased her skin again as he slowly, tormentingly, worked his way down her belly. Goose bumps scurried across her sweat-beaded skin, and her heart hammered so loudly its beat seemed to echo through the silence.

When his tongue finally delved into her moistness, she moaned and had to fight to keep her knees locked and her body upright. His fingers pressed into her thighs. Trembling, she widened her stance, allowing him greater access. His tongue delved deeper, and pleasure flowed like liquid fire through her veins until her whole body quivered and throbbed to the tune of that gentle yet insistent touch. A touch that quickly created a tide that threatened to overload her senses.

But at the precise moment she needed that touch the most, it left her. She groaned and opened her eyes, wondering what weird, twisted game he was playing now. His gaze caught hers, seeming to delve deep into her soul. The intent, the hunger, so evident in his dark gaze, assured her this was no game, but a carefully controlled seduction. Not only of her senses, but of her mind.

And perhaps, if she wasn't very careful, her heart.

Holding her gaze, he slowly, almost leisurely, stripped off his jeans and shorts and tossed them to one side. He was as hard as she was wet, and the sight of him made her throat go dry. Moons, how she ached to feel that hardness deep inside.

Placing his hands on either side of her again, he leaned forward and claimed her mouth. He tasted of lust, of love, and of her, and it stirred her in ways she had never thought possible. When he finally pulled away, she could barely even breathe, and the throbbing ache was so fierce she thought she'd die.

"Tell me what you want," he said, his voice soft but as fierce as his gaze.

She swallowed, but could no longer deny the need pounding through her veins. "You."

Elation winged through the darkness of his eyes. "How do you want me?"

His touch slid through her slickness and delved deep. She moaned, arching into his hand but wanting so much more.

"Like this?" he asked, his voice little more than a husky growl.

She shook her head, too consumed by the sensations of pleasure shooting through her to do anything more.

"Then perhaps we'll try this." The heat of his flesh, the heaviness of his desire, pressed hard against her, until all she could smell was the spicy mix of man and lust, and all she could feel was the pounding of his heart through her breasts and the pulsing of his need against her belly.

"Tell me what you want, Neva. Admit it."

She could do little else. Not when his gaze was so intense, his body so close, and her need so high. "I want to feel you deep inside."

Her voice was little more than a croak of sound, but a fierce and victorious look shone in his eyes. Then she was in his arms and he was inside of her, thrusting so deep, enveloping her in a heat that was so basic. So pure. So very powerful, and so very, very right.

His mouth found hers again, and their tongues caressed as the pressure built. His powerful body stroked fast and hard into hers, driving her insane with need. She writhed against him, matching his rhythm, matching his urgency. The sweet pressure built until it felt like she would explode.

Then she did, and the force of her climax damn near blew her mind. He came with her, his roar echoing across the silence, sounding as if he was howling her name to the moon. As their orgasms ebbed and sanity returned, he claimed her mouth and kissed her hard.

When he allowed her to breathe again, she opened her eyes and stared into the ebony recesses of his. The shutters were down, and what she thought she saw there scared her. Because what she saw was caring. Deep caring.

But no. That had to be wishful thinking. It couldn't

be anything else, not with a wolf who had once sworn never to share his life or his heart with another.

He kissed her again, soft and lingering. "I think—" He stopped, his gaze hardening as he glanced toward the door.

In that instant, there was a sharp rap against the wood. She jumped, grabbing the edges of her gown and quickly tying them together.

"Who's there?" she called.

"Me. Open up, Neva."

She closed her eyes and took a deep breath. Of all the people she didn't want to see right now, her father had to top the list.

The confrontation she didn't want, and was in no way ready for, was about to happen.

Chapter Twelve

DUNCAN SWORE SOFTLY. Neva's father couldn't have chosen a worse time to come visiting. The smell of lust and sex hung heavily on the air, and Neva's skin still glowed with the aftermath of their lovemaking. It wasn't something either of them could deny, and it would only fuel the old man's anger.

Not that Duncan was worried about himself—just Neva. She loved her parents, and he didn't want the situation to get any messier than it already was. But he had a feeling it would.

Neva whirled and grabbed his jeans and shorts, thrusting them into his hands. *Go into the kitchen and get dressed,* she ordered. *Then sit at the table and make like nothing is happening.*

He gently brushed a sweaty strand of hair from her cheek. *He's not stupid. It's very evident what we've been doing.*

Her eyes flashed at him. *I know, but I don't intend to rub his nose in it.*

Neither did he. Not this time. But he didn't intend to leave her alone to face her father's wrath, either. Especially when that wrath was mostly of *his* making.

He threw on his clothes but didn't retreat, and she made an exasperated sound before moving to turn on the light and open the door.

"So it's true." Though Levon's voice was soft, it was filled with anger. Rich with contempt. "You didn't leave Ripple Creek after all. You lied to me, and you lied to your mother."

Her hurt swirled through Duncan, as bright as a flame. Yet none of it showed in her voice as she said, "Would you have felt any better if I'd told the truth?" She stepped back, opening the door wider. "Are you coming in, or are we going to discuss this on the doorstep for all the neighbors to hear?"

Levon's gaze ran past her, meeting Duncan's. "Oh, I'm coming in all right." He stepped inside and thrust a hand deep into his pocket.

Duncan saw the bulge and knew a weapon was hidden there. And while he had the strength to wrest the gun from the older wolf's grip, he wasn't about to risk it with Neva standing so close. Accidents happened, and he didn't want it happening to her.

So he crossed his arms and leaned against the wall, feigning indifference as she closed the door. "I never figured you for a man of violence, Levon."

She shot him a quick, confused look, then her gaze darted to her father and she made an exasperated sound. "Do you really think he's worth going to jail over?"

Even though Duncan had half-expected her to say something like that, her words still cut. But declarations of caring, after everything he'd done to her, weren't in the cards right now. And maybe they never would be.

"I'd keep that gun in your pocket," he added softly. "Because I know from experience that you wouldn't enjoy jail."

A muscle in the old man's jaw throbbed. "Do you know what they're saying about her in the hospital?"

"Don't talk about me like I'm not here," Neva cut in. "And what does it matter what people are saying about me?"

Levon shot her a furious look. "It matters to me. And it matters to your mother."

"And my feelings and needs don't?"

"You're my daughter," Levon said fiercely, "and I will not have your reputation sullied by a man like . . . *this*."

Neva's expression was an endearing mix of anger and amusement. "Duncan's not the first man I've danced with, Dad, and he probably won't be the last."

"He will be if I have anything to say about it." Levon drew the gun out of his pocket and, with a trembling hand, pointed it at Duncan.

Duncan didn't move. He just tensed, ready to dive away should the older man's finger so much as twitch on the trigger.

Neva swore and stepped between them. "Don't be so damned ridiculous." She hesitated, sniffing the air. "You've been drinking."

Damn it, Neva, Duncan said. *Step out of the line of fire.*

No. He won't shoot me.

That was a risk Duncan wasn't willing to let her take. He reached for the power of the binding. *I order you to step away.*

She shot him a furious look and clenched her fists, her whole body trembling. But she didn't move. Duncan wasn't sure whether to admire her courage or be angry at her stubbornness.

"I'm not drunk," Levon said into the silence

"No, you're just insane. How's threatening Duncan going to help me or my reputation?"

For someone who wanted to avoid this confrontation at all costs, she was doing a fine job of fighting it without help. But he very much suspected this battle had been building for some time now, and that his actions had just made it happen sooner rather than later.

"He leaves." Levon's voice was sharp. "Now. Tonight."

"And as I asked before, how is that supposed to help my reputation?"

"One moon dance is an aberration that will quickly be forgotten, as long as he leaves quickly."

Neva raised an eyebrow. "And if it's not an aberration?"

Levon shot her a furious look. "It is. You deserve far better than a man of his ilk."

"Yeah, right," Neva said, voice flat. "It's not for me you're demanding this, is it? You're here to protect *your* reputation, and *your* image."

Levon glared at her. "I'm not—"

"Aren't you? So why haven't you stopped to ask if this is what I want? Why haven't you bothered to ask how I feel about Duncan? Did you ever stop to consider that this might be more than just a dance?"

Levon's gaze darted between the two of them and his face went pale. Duncan wasn't sure if it was the shock of having his daughter finally standing up to him or the horror of possibly having *him* as a permanent member of the pack.

"You can't be serious," Levon muttered. "Surely you know what sort of reputation—"

"I do. And right now, I don't care."

"But . . . but . . ." Levon stopped and scrubbed a hand across his rough jaw. "You *can't* be serious about a man like him."

She reached out, wrapping a hand around the barrel of the gun and wresting it easily from her father's grip. "Right now, I'm not sure that I am. But I have the right to discover what I do and don't feel. I'm not a teenager anymore, so please don't treat me like one."

"I'm only trying to protect you . . ."

"I know. But right now you're smothering me."

Levon's gaze met Duncan's again, and in the rich green depths he saw both anger and fear. "You deserve better than scum like—"

Even from where he stood, Duncan felt the flash of her fury. "You will not call him scum in *my* house," she said, her voice soft but shaking with anger. "Please go."

"I'm only trying—"

"There's no point in you trying to do anything until you—*and* Mom—are willing to listen to what I have to say. I." She strode past him and opened the door. "Dad, just leave. Please."

"Your sister—"

"—was willing to listen to me and understands what I've done. You and Mom aren't even willing to hear."

"It's just that we're disappointed—"

"Yeah? Well, so am I—in you. Where are all those pretty speeches about tolerance now?" She waved her hand at the open door. "I mean it, Dad. If you want to stay, you'll apologize to Duncan. If not, leave."

Levon turned around and walked to the door. There he hesitated, meeting Neva's gaze for several seconds. "If you do not end this relationship now, I'll—" He hesitated, glancing at Duncan briefly before returning his gaze to Neva, and speaking to her telepathically. Duncan saw her face go pale and found himself clenching his fists again, ready to step in and defend her, even though he had no idea what Levon had just said.

"I mean it, Neva," Levon said out loud.

"I know you do," she replied and slammed the door shut behind her father. It was a sound that echoed through the sudden silence.

She remained where she was, staring at the door and breathing deeply. He wanted to go to her and wrap his arms around her, but he knew she wouldn't appreciate it.

"What did he say to you?"

"Nothing." Her voice was carefully controlled, but he could feel her pain.

"Then why are you so upset?"

"It's pack business," she shot back. "And none of *your* concern."

He took a deep breath, then released it slowly. "Neva, I'm sorry if I caused—"

She rounded on him, green eyes blazing. "If you *ever* try to make me do something against my will again, I'll fry your brains so badly you won't be able to shit without help!"

While he had no doubt she meant what she said, he couldn't help the slight smile tugging at his lips. She was so damned beautiful, even when angry. He let his gaze drift downward, watching the rise and fall of her breasts as she breathed. Watching her nipples peak with renewed awareness. "I was only trying—"

"To control me. The same way my damn parents have been trying to control me. I won't stand it from them anymore, and I certainly won't take it from you."

He pushed away from the wall and walked toward her. "No, what I was going to say was: protect you."

She licked her lips and backed away from him. With the door behind her, she couldn't go far. "Well, how about trusting me instead? The gun wasn't loaded. It never has been."

Her back hit the door and she stopped. Desire widened her pupils, darkened her green eyes, and he was so damned hard for her it was painful.

"You can't know that for certain," he said, reaching again for the silk tie around her waist.

She swallowed heavily. "The firing mechanism is toast. Dad bought that weapon ages ago when there was a rash of break-ins. He figured he could use it to scare intruders away."

And had obviously figured it would scare *him* away, too. Which would have been a fair assumption in his younger years, when all he'd ever wanted was a good time with no strings and no problems. But that wasn't the case with Neva. The tie came loose and the silk fell away, once more revealing her golden curves and luscious triangle of soft hair. A triangle he couldn't wait to lose himself in again. He took the gun from her and dropped it into the pocket of one the coats on the coatrack near the door. "Why didn't you just tell me that?"

"Because I didn't want you taking it off him. He deserved a little more respect than that."

"Even after what he said?" He slid a finger under the silk and skimmed it up to her shoulder, gently dislodging the gown.

She quivered under his touch, her breathing quick, uneven. "Even after. He's still my dad."

He slid his finger across her warm flesh to her other shoulder, sliding the rest of the gown off. It shimmied to the floor, puddling around her feet. Her desire spun around him—a warm, rich scent that stirred his senses and thrummed through his blood.

The moon was rising. And so was his need to bury himself deep inside her.

"You can't," she denied, voice soft, husky. "We have to get to Betise's."

"We have at least half an hour to kill, if not more." He stripped off his clothes, tossing them on the floor next to her gown. "And I intend to spend that time dancing with you."

The pulse at her neck was little more than a wild flutter, her nipples so hard they were like pebbles pressing into his chest. Her gaze searched his for a moment, then a teasing, sensuous smile touched her lips. "How?"

He kissed her sweet mouth, softly, seductively. "What I intend," he whispered, his lips so close to hers he could taste every quick breath, "is to turn you around and spread you against the door, caressing your entire body as I take you from behind until the heat overcomes us and we howl our pleasure to the moon."

Anticipation flared in her eyes, and the scent of her arousal got stronger. She opened her mouth, panting softly, as if she couldn't suck in enough air.

"And then?" Her voice was a husky whisper that damn near exploded his control.

"Then I intend to carry you upstairs and continue with a more leisurely seduction in the shower as we wash the smell of sex and lust from our skins."

"The moon certainly has a strong effect on you Sinclairs, doesn't it?"

It did—but right now it wasn't the moon, it was the woman. "I want you," he whispered against her lips.

"Then take me."

He was only too happy to comply.

Neva shivered and wished she'd taken the time to put on her extra coat. Her breath fogged, hanging on the air, mingling with the silvery snowflakes that danced through the night. Even though the wind had dropped, the night was still bitterly cold.

But, truth be told, it wasn't the night that had caused the ice that seemed to be settling deep inside her belly. It was her father's threat: *I swear to the moon, I will evict you from the pack if you continue your relationship with that man.*

Of course he'd get his wish, because she and Duncan would only last until the end of the moon dance, but it still shook her that he would go to such lengths. She understood the depth of his anger and disappointment, but to cut her off from everyone she knew and loved? How was that fair or just?

She shivered again and rubbed her arms. She could only hope that when all this was over, when Duncan was gone and her father was ready to listen to her, that he'd come to understand her actions, if not forgive them.

But the words she'd said to him tonight she'd meant, and she hoped he understood that, too.

Through the hush of darkness, music throbbed—a bass-heavy beat that stirred her blood almost as much as the man standing in front of her. The Blue Nights was many blocks away from Iyona's house, and Neva half-wished she and Duncan were there now, laughing and drinking with the other patrons. Doing ordinary things, enjoying themselves in ordinary ways. Being an ordinary couple.

Only they weren't a couple, nor ever likely to be one.

She crossed her arms and shifted her weight from one foot to the other. *How long does it take to open a window?*

Though he didn't look around, his amusement spun through her. *I spent time in jail for being drunk, not breaking and entering. Don't expect any speed records here.*

She sighed impatiently and looked around. They were standing in the strip of land that separated the house from the fence, and—thankfully—the house next door had long been abandoned. More houses lined the rear of the two properties, and the warm glow peeking past blinds indicated that most of the occupants were home. They had to be quiet, and they had to be careful.

She wished she were home. In bed. With Duncan.

Her gaze drifted past the snowcapped rooflines to the snow-filled sky. The moon was lost to sight, but she didn't need to see it to know it was rising high. The power of it thrummed through her veins. Made her ache to be touched, to be loved.

But by one man, not many.

She bit her lip and wished she could reach out to Savannah and discuss the confusion of her feelings. But she couldn't—not when they were poised to break into Betise's mother's house. Sister or not, Savannah would send her deputies around to stop them.

There was a soft click, and Duncan sighed in relief. *I'm glad I was never forced to be a thief. It's too damned difficult.*

He opened the window, then cupped his hands. She stepped into them and grabbed the sill, pulling herself through and landing on the floor on the other side in an ungainly heap.

You okay?

Yep. She picked herself up and stepped to one side, dusting off her jeans as she did so.

Duncan quickly joined her. *Looks like we're in a back bedroom.*

You think? She looked around at all the crap piled around them. *It looks more like a storeroom to me.*

Either way, Betise obviously doesn't sleep here. He shrugged and led the way out of the room.

The hallway beyond was shadowed, and the air thick and unpleasant. The doorway to their immediate right led into a mudroom-cum-laundry, and next to that a bathroom. The remaining two doors led into bedrooms.

This is Betise's room, Duncan said, the minute he walked into the first one. *It smells like her.*

It certainly did, she thought. Only it was stronger. More unpleasant. Or maybe that was just the general odor of the house itself, because she'd never before noticed anything this foul when it came to Betise.

She watched him opening drawers for a minute, but most of them were empty. *What are you looking for?*

Don't know, but I'm sure she's up to something. I'm just not sure if it's connected to the attacks. Still, searching through her stuff can't hurt.

It could if any of the rangers happened past. Neva glanced around for a second, then headed over to the student desk tucked into the corner and sat down. The computer was off and turning it on was too much of a risk, especially if they had to get out in a hurry. The last thing they wanted was to leave a brightly shining calling card in the form of a glowing computer screen. So she opened the drawers instead and shuffled through them. There wasn't much beyond the usual stationery items. She leaned back in the chair, staring at shelves that lined the other wall. There were no books—presumably they lay in the boxes sitting to one side of the bookcases—but the shelves still held the usual assortment of childhood items: books, old toys, and, oddly, a hair ball. She blinked. A *black* hair ball.

"My God," she said into the silence.

Duncan looked up. "What?"

"Hair ball. On the shelf." She rose and walked over.

"So?"

She picked up the hair ball and plucked one hair free, rubbing it between her fingertips. "It's real hair."

He stopped beside her and took the hair ball from her, his fingers brushing hers and sending little shocks of electricity up her arm.

"Didn't the rangers find black hair on several of the victims?"

"Yeah." She studied the ball dubiously. "But the killer is male, not female. It can't be Betise."

"Until they match the DNA, no one can say for certain," Duncan said, his expression grim. "And there's always the possibility that Betise is working with the murderer."

"But where would she have gotten the hair?"

"In the heat of release," he said dryly, "few males are going to notice if a couple of hairs are plucked from their heads."

"Meaning we should steal a couple of hairs and get my sister to compare them?"

"Yes. And if they do match, then the rangers can come here with the proper paperwork and grab the rest of the hair as evidence."

She separated a couple of hairs, then carefully replaced the hair ball and went to find a plastic bag while Duncan continued his search through the rest of the drawers. She picked her way through the unpacked boxes sitting in the living room and found a bag in the kitchen—along with a whole heap of rubbish that was no doubt the source of the smell in the house. She made a hasty retreat back to the bedroom.

"Nothing else," he said after a few moments.

"That's not really surprising," she replied. "If she is

up to something, she wouldn't be stupid enough to leave evidence of it lying around."

"She left the hair there, so don't give her too much credit when it comes to intelligence." He sat on the edge of the bed and flicked through the tattered-looking organizer that had been sitting on the side table. "It looks like she knew the victims."

Neva frowned. "No, she didn't."

He glanced up at her, one eyebrow raised. "Their names and phone numbers are in here. And while the organizer *is* a year old, she mentions having lunch with the last victim."

She looked over his shoulder. The name was there in black and white. "She told me she didn't know any of them."

"Then she lied. I wonder why?"

"Maybe she didn't want the hassle of dealing with the rangers."

"Maybe." He leaned forward and brushed a kiss across her lips, his eyes bright with the same hunger that stirred her blood. "I think we'd better head over to her apartment and do a little more investigating. It looks as though she's moved the more personal stuff first, so we might just find something."

Going to Betise's place was the last thing she wanted to do, especially when his taste still lingered so enticingly on her mouth. Her wolf was definitely off the leash, and she suspected there was no going back to the way things had been before. She'd foolishly walked into the mansion, thinking she could control both the moon and her own responses. And now, in the space of a couple of days, just about everything had changed, and she wasn't sure whether to be happy about that or not.

She stepped away, allowing him to brush past. They walked into the back room and climbed out the window. Then Duncan slid his knife along the edge, knocking the catch back into place again.

"What about our footprints?" she asked, staring at the deep imprints they were leaving in the snow.

He grabbed the snow-laden lid off the nearby trash can and dumped the snow onto the telltale prints near the window. Then he kicked the bin over, scattering the rubbish around the base of the window, covering the rest of them. "Let's get back to the—"

He stopped. Across the night came the sound of a car engine drawing close. Neva met his gaze. "You don't think . . . ?"

"We can't take the chance that it's not. Shift shape and jump the fence."

She did, barely clearing it, her belly scraping across the rough top. Leaping from a standstill had never been one of her strengths. She was too small to get any great height. She landed lightly and padded along the fence line until she found a gap in the wood. Lights speared the darkness—twin beams of brightness that lit the alley and highlighted the rubbish hiding their prints. A red car cruised into sight, stopping close to the front porch. Betise climbed out, cursing softly and kicking away a soda bottle as she headed for the door.

Duncan stopped beside Neva, his silver coat blending with snow. *I'm surprised she's not already at the mansion. The dance has been going for a good two hours.*

Maybe she's not going to the dance.

Betise is an addict. I doubt she can stop.

She looked at him. He was as powerful in wolf form as he was in human, and his eyes glowed like black glass. *Are you an addict?*

Once, he admitted. *But no more.*

Why?

He shrugged. *I grew tired of the chase. Tired of much-used flesh.*

That's not a very nice way to put it.

His amusement spun around her. *But true.*

So you chased me because I was new to the dance?

Yes.

So I could have stood there fully clothed and you still would have come after me?

Yes.

Damn. Wish I'd known that.

I'm glad you didn't. It's not often I get to enjoy the sight of a nubile nymph playing in the fountain.

And it's not a sight you're likely to see again. That water was freezing. She glanced toward the house as Betise came back out. She appeared to be carrying something small, but from this angle, Neva couldn't see what it was.

I can't see it, either.

She glanced at him. *Maybe it's just something warmer to wear after the dance.*

Maybe, he commented. *But it might be worth following her, just to see what she's up to.*

What about searching her apartment?

We can't risk going there until we know she's going to be gone for a while.

She's likely to notice a car tailing her.

But not a pair of wolves. In this snow, she can't go very fast, so we should be able to keep up.

Maybe you can, she grumbled. *I've got shorter legs, remember?*

He grinned—and in wolf form, it was a fearsome sight. *Legs I wouldn't mind wrapped around me right now.*

That conjures some damn weird images when we're in wolf form.

I don't care what form you're in. You're beautiful either way.

She studied him a little warily. *Okay, what are you after? You're being entirely too nice all of a sudden.*

His amusement spun through her mind, as warm as sunshine. *I'm a wolf, and the moon is rising. What do you think I want?*

You can get that without being nice.

He gave the mental equivalent of a shrug. *Maybe you're just seeing the real me.*

Yeah, right. If the man was that nice, he wouldn't have the reputation he had.

People change, Neva. My reputation was earned a long time ago. His mental tones were flat, but the air burned with the flash of his anger.

But you've more than lived up to it with me, haven't you?

He didn't say anything, and the swirl of his emotions died. Had he been in human form, she very much suspected the shutters in his eyes would be up again.

Betise started her car and cruised off slowly. Duncan stepped back several paces. *Keep close.*

He leapt the fence, clearing it easily. She followed,

scraping her belly a second time. She'd be bruised in the morning, for sure. They loped after the car, keeping it in sight easily enough. Duncan had been right. Betise wasn't able to drive very fast with all the snow on the road.

The car headed east along Main Street until they'd reached the outer limits of Ripple Creek, then it turned south, onto Mayflower Street. It was a back road, rough and narrow, and the wash of warm light from the streetlights behind them quickly gave way to darkness. Houses were few and far between out here, and the silence was almost eerie. A shiver rippled across Neva's skin. Anyone coming out to this wild and lonely section of town at this time of night was surely up to no good.

From up ahead, mingling with the purr of the engine, came the bubbling rush of Hunter's River, the biggest of the two rivers that flowed through Ripple Creek. This road crossed it, then took a long loop back to Main Street. Where the hell was Betise going? And why?

Neva lolled out her tongue, trying to catch more air as she concentrated on running in the tire tracks, where the going was easier. Loping long distances was all well and good when you had long legs and were fit, but the longest distance she'd ever run was between the diner and home last year when she was late for a date. A date that hadn't been worth the effort of getting ready for, let alone running.

Which was basically the story of her dating life—at least until she'd decided to seduce Duncan. And while they weren't dating, they were certainly dancing. She had to wonder how she was ever going to find another man who could make her feel the way that Duncan had made her feel.

But what, exactly, *did* she feel? And did she really want to acknowledge those feelings, given the fact that he was leaving? Perhaps it was better not to know. Not to examine too closely. Otherwise, she might end up getting hurt.

The sound of bubbling water got stronger, and the car's bright lights picked out the old wooden bridge from the surrounding darkness. Betise slowed, easing the car onto the narrow bridge before stopping in the middle.

Stay here, behind the car, Duncan ordered. *I'm going forward a little to see what she's doing.*

Be careful. I don't like the feel of this.

Neither do I.

He padded forward, his silver coat blending with the snow, making him difficult to see. A second later there was a small splash, then the car began to creep forward again.

She's thrown something in the water, Neva guessed.

That she has. I'm going in to retrieve it. He hesitated. *You want to keep following her? We can't afford to lose her right now.*

Will you be all right? The water is freezing.

In wolf form I won't feel it as much. Go, before we lose her. Just make sure you keep out of sight.

Like she needed to be told. Biting back her annoyance, she loped over the bridge and continued to follow the tire tracks.

Betise made her way back to Main Street, turned left, then headed back to town. When she turned right onto Bunting Street, a sick sensation ran through

Neva. She had a horrible suspicion she knew where Betise was headed.

Her place.

She swore softly, though it came out little more than a rumble of sound. She leapt the nearest fence, taking a shortcut across her neighbors' backyards, and shifted shape as she ran for her back door.

She thrust it open, kicked off her shoes and shucked her coat, then slammed the door shut and raced for the stairs. Lights gleamed through the living room windows as a car pulled into her driveway. She raced up the stairs, stripping as she went, throwing off her clothes in the hallway before racing into the shower. Thrusting on the taps, she wasted a few precious seconds waiting for the water to warm up, then jumped in.

A second later the doorbell rang. She got out of the shower but left the water running, grabbed a towel, and padded down the stairs. "Who is it?" she called, dripping water everywhere as she tucked the towel around her breasts.

"Betise."

The older wolf's voice sounded slightly surprised, and a shiver traveled down Neva's spine. It was almost as if Betise hadn't expected her to be home—and that would only be the case if she'd suspected they'd been following her.

Neva opened the door. Betise's gaze slid down Neva's body, and her lips twitched as if in amusement. But it was an amusement at odds with the anger in her silvery-green eyes.

"Hope I'm not interrupting anything," Betise said, her voice warm but her eyes cold.

"Well, actually, you are. What can I do for you?"

"Is Duncan here?"

Neva clutched the door handle tightly. "Yes. Upstairs. Having a shower. Why?"

"It's personal. Perhaps I should wait?"

"I really don't think—"

"It's important that I speak to him. I'll wait in the kitchen, if you like, while you two finish your . . . showering." She hesitated. "Unless, of course, you think my presence might disturb your relationship with Duncan?"

Neva wondered what in hell was going on in Betise's mind. "Duncan and I don't have a relationship, so I have nothing to fear." *And certainly not from the likes of you.* Which was an extremely bitchy thought, but one that was certainly true. "But we could be a while. Why don't I get him to phone you once we're done?"

"This is urgent." Betise crossed her arms, the anger and suspicion deep in her silvery eyes. "Why don't you just go upstairs and tell him I'm here? I'm sure he'll come down to see me."

"Given the choice, I certainly wouldn't." Duncan's dry comment came from the top of the stairs. "What the hell do you want now, Betise?"

Neva's heart leapt in her chest, but she hid her relief as she looked over her shoulder. Duncan was standing at the top of the stairs, a towel wrapped around his hips, his skin as gleaming and wet as hers. The smile that touched his lips curled her toes, and though the shutters were up in his eyes, she could feel his amusement. And his anger—at Betise.

Betise all but glared at him. "I thought you might

like to know about an interesting conversation I over-heard at the Blue Nights."

Neva shared a glance with Duncan. *Has Betise really been at the Blue Nights? And if so, why there rather than the dance?*

It'll be easy enough to check, Duncan said. *The Blue Nights has lots of security cameras. I'll get Rai to review their tapes.*

And here I was thinking the "good friend" you mentioned was male. I really should have known better. Her mental tone sounded as catty as her words, but she just couldn't help it.

She's married.

That didn't stop you in Denver.

He didn't answer. He didn't need to, when his anger damn near sizzled her mind. His gaze went past her. "What did you overhear?"

Betise stepped inside. "One person, male, talking on a cell phone. About René."

He crossed his arms, his eyes little more than black slits. "Are you going to spit it all out, or do I have to come down and shake the rest of it out of you?"

The suppressed hostility in his voice left Neva in no doubt he'd do it. The sudden flash of uncertainty she got from Betise suggested she had no doubt, either—and yet that uncertainty was mixed with an animosity that almost matched Duncan's. What was going on? None of the emotions she was catching from Betise made any real sense. On the one hand, there was love and a deep belief in destiny. On the other, a far-reaching anger. And while she knew it was more than possible to feel both for the same person, there seemed to be something else here, as well. Something that left a bad taste in Neva's mouth.

"He was talking about going after your brother," Betise said coldly. "Tonight, while the dance is on."

Duncan didn't react in any noticeable way. Nor did he move. "Did you see this man?"

"No."

"Would you recognize his voice if you heard it again?"

Betise hesitated. "Probably."

"Did he say when or how?"

"No."

The phone rang shrilly. Neva jumped, then glanced up at Duncan.

"Answer it," he said, his voice clipped.

She did. "Neva Grant speaking."

"May I speak to Duncan, please?"

The voice was cultured and rich and reminded her very much of an older version of Duncan. She glanced up at him. "For you."

His gaze went to Betise for a second, then he walked down the stairs and took the phone from her hands. Neva rubbed her arms, but it didn't ease the goose bumps racing across her skin.

Duncan listened to the caller for several seconds, his expression never changing, then put the phone down. But his black eyes gleamed with fury as his gaze met hers. "That was my father. René's been shot."

Chapter Thirteen

DUNCAN TOOK A deep breath, trying to control the anger pounding through his veins. The need to protect the pack and all its members was a natural instinct—and something he'd failed to do.

Neva rested a hand on his arm, her fingers warm against his skin. He shook off her touch and spun around, ignoring the flash of her hurt as he stalked toward Betise.

Though her eyes widened slightly, the smell of her anticipation and desire spun through the air. He wrapped his fingers around her neck, resisting the urge to squeeze but still holding her none too gently.

"If I discover you have had anything to do with René being shot, I'll kill you."

Her expression seemed fear-filled, yet he could taste her emotions as clearly as he smelled her arousal, and fear played no part.

"This is the thanks I get for coming to warn you?"

"We both know you're up to something."

"I'm up to nothing more than trying to get promises fulfilled."

"I never made any promises to you, Betise, and I

very much doubt René did, either." He thrust her backward, sending her sprawling into the snow. She landed in an ungainly heap, flashing bare thighs and a thatch of golden hair. His gut turned. "Take your lies elsewhere from now on. We don't want you at the mansion anymore."

He slammed the door shut against the rush of her fury and turned around. Neva was staring at him, her arms crossed and her expression a mix of relief and worry.

"That might not have been the wisest move, especially if she is somehow involved in the killings."

"Right now, I don't particularly care." He had a suspicion that time was running out and that the killer had just upped the ante. He took the stairs two at a time and walked into the bedroom, crossing to the still-open window he'd climbed through earlier. He closed it, then grabbed his clothes and began dressing.

Neva stopped in the doorway. "You never mentioned how René is."

"That's because I don't really know."

"Then he's not dead?"

"No."

"You're going up there now?"

"Yes." His voice was slightly clipped, and the growing tide of her annoyance washed around him. He ignored it and pulled on his boots. Right now, he didn't have time to waste. He had to get back to the mansion to help his father. "Are you getting dressed, or are you going like that?"

"I thought you'd class this as pack business and not suitable for outsiders."

She was no longer an outsider, even if she'd yet to acknowledge him or her feelings. Even if she never did. "If Betise is somehow involved in these killings, I'd be a fool to leave you here alone—and especially after I've just tossed her out of the house."

"I can take care of myself."

"I'm sure your sister thought the same thing." He saw the glimmer of hurt in her green eyes and took a deep breath, releasing it slowly. "Just get dressed. I don't have the time to argue right now."

"Fine. Don't argue. But I'm not going."

"Listen—"

"No," she cut in. "If Betise is up to something, it's important we keep an eye on her."

"If she is involved, she's probably just raised the stakes. I don't want to risk you getting hurt."

She crossed her arms. "You have no say over what risks I do or don't take. You and I are sharing a moon dance, nothing more."

He met her gaze. Saw her uncertainty and her determination. Realized then that she still saw him as the man he had been rather than the man he now was. And that was something he could not combat—not with words, and not in such a short amount of time. "Are you sure of that?"

She hesitated. "Yes."

"Well, I'm not."

Her eyes widened a little. "What do you mean?"

"What I said." He picked his coat up off the floor and walked toward her. She didn't back away, but the uncertainty in her eyes grew. As did the scent of her arousal.

He stopped so close her peaked nipples brushed his

chest with every breath she took. Heat sparked the air between them, fierce enough to draw sweat from his skin and hers. The desire to take her, to bury himself in the warmth of her willing flesh and let the rest of the world take care of itself, burned fiercely. But duty and his pack had to take priority. For now.

"I don't like the thought of you going after Betise alone."

"I'll keep my distance."

"Make sure you do." He wrapped an arm around her small waist and crushed her against him. Kissed her hungrily, fiercely, claiming her mouth as completely as he'd claim her body later, when they had more time.

The sound of a car starting forced him to pull away. "You'd better hurry and get dressed," he said, "or she'll slip away. Keep in contact with me."

She nodded and spun away, her hips swaying enticingly as she walked into the bathroom. He took a deep breath and forced his feet toward the stairs. Light swept across the windows as Betise backed her car out of the driveway. He headed for the back door, ensuring it was locked before he stepped into the night's snow-filled darkness.

Then he shifted shape and ran for the mansion.

Neva padded through the white-cloaked darkness, following the red gleam of taillights. She'd half-expected Betise to head for the mansion despite Duncan's warning, but it was clear she was headed back to her mother's house. Which was a little surprising, especially given the heat of the moon. Addicts did whatever they needed to do to ensure the supply of their drug, didn't they? So why wasn't Betise out hunting a mate?

She pricked her ears as the sound of another engine rolled across the night. It came from behind her, but was headed her way. She leapt off the road and made for the trees, weaving her way through the trunks as the gleam of headlights flickered across the night.

Ahead, Betise turned into the driveway of her mom's house and stopped in front of the garage. Neva paused, her tongue lolling as she battled to catch her breath. If there was one thing she was going to do when this was all over, it was get into shape.

Betise climbed out of her car and glanced back toward the road. The roar of the engine drew closer, then lights swept across the stand of trees where Neva hid. She didn't move, hoping the shadows and the surrounding pines would hide her golden coat.

The lights swept past, then a truck pulled into the driveway and stopped behind Betise's car. A chill ran through Neva. A blue truck. Just like the one that had hit her.

Maybe her accident wasn't an accident after all.

Iyona climbed out and spoke to her daughter. Though the night was quiet, Neva was too far away to hear what they were saying. And she didn't dare move, just in case either woman spotted her.

After a fierce, somewhat animated conversation, Betise and her mother headed inside. Lights shone in the kitchen and a few seconds later gleamed from the windows at the far end of the house.

Neva retreated through the trees and back onto the road, following the tire tracks down the driveway so she didn't leave any paw prints. When she reached the truck's tailgate, she hesitated, flicking her ears forward. There was a lot of movement inside the house. Hurried movement. Frowning, she crawled under the truck and out the other side. There she shifted shape, and in human form followed the footprints up the stairs.

When she reached the window, she stopped, flattening her back against the wall before peering carefully in. Through the gap in the curtains she could see Iyona throwing things into cardboard boxes. Neva raised her eyebrows. Were they leaving? And if so, why?

She watched a moment longer, then ducked past the window and jumped off the veranda. She pulled her clothes back into place, then walked the length of the house, keeping to the shadows so her footprints wouldn't be so noticeable. The house was on a slope, so by the time she reached the room Betise was in, the window was higher than she stood and she couldn't see in. But if the sound of things being thrown around was anything to go by, Betise was either having an almighty temper tantrum or, like Iyona, was packing. Neva leaned back against the wall and waited. After a few minutes, Iyona appeared, marching toward the truck with a large box.

Neva shifted shape again and hunkered down, the snow cold against her belly. Iyona dumped the box in the truck, then went back inside. Several more minutes passed, then Betise came out, backpacks slung over either shoulder and bags in both hands. The lights went off, then Iyona reappeared, carrying another box.

"You got everything?" Iyona's voice was sharp with anger and perhaps a little contempt.

"Yep. Rang the rangers, too, just to let them know we'll be away for a few days." Betise's smirk was easy to see, even from where Neva lay. "They said they'd come by and check the house for us."

Iyona snorted. "That's kind of them."

"I thought so, too."

Iyona dumped the box in the back of the truck, then paused, glancing toward her daughter. "You sure you want to do this?"

"They owe you. And he owes me."

Iyona nodded and climbed into the truck. Betise followed suit, and the truck backed quickly out of the driveway. Neva took a deep breath, then bounded across the snow-covered lawn and began following them again.

The mansion was ablaze with lights by the time Duncan got there. There was a ranger stationed at the main gate, and the guards his father had hired were manning the other two. Duncan backtracked and slipped in through one of the tunnels, making his way through damp and rarely used passageways to the medical rooms.

He shifted shape as he neared the entrance and hit the switch. The door swung silently open, and Duncan stepped through.

Martin jumped and spun around. "You damn near frightened the life out of me," he grumbled, turning back to the sink to wash his hands. "You'd think those doors would have the decency to squeak and give an old man some warning."

"Is René okay?" Duncan left the door open, just in case he had to make a fast retreat. He couldn't smell anyone else close except the doc and his brother, but that didn't mean the rangers weren't nearby. Or even outside the door.

"He's lucky. The bullet hit him low in the shoulder, and the wound looked a lot worse than it was. I wouldn't be surprised if the killer thought he'd scored a true hit."

"Does he have to go to the hospital?"

Martin nodded. "I'm not set up to deal with that sort of surgery anymore. I've patched him up the best I could and stanched the bleeding, but that's about all I can do."

"Can I talk to him?"

"Quickly. We called for an ambulance ten minutes ago, so it should be here any minute."

"Where are the rangers?"

"Down in the main ballroom, interviewing folks and taking samples from pack members." Martin shook his head. "The damn fools even insisted on getting a sample from me."

Duncan raised his eyebrows. "Were they already here when René was shot?"

Martin nodded. "Lucky, too. With the snow still falling, they might not have found the footprints and tire tracks otherwise."

Both were evidence that could be used in court, but was the attack on René linked to the attacks on the women? That's what they had to discover—and fast, he suspected.

"You'll let me know if the rangers come back?"

"The clinic door is locked, and these old bones don't move all that fast."

Duncan smiled and headed into the next room. René was lying on the bed closest to the wall, stripped to the waist, and he had a huge swathe of bandages around his shoulder and left arm.

"I think I'll sit out the moon dances for the rest of this cycle," René said without opening his eyes.

"At least he didn't hit your vitals."

René snorted. "I guess there is that to be thankful for."

Duncan stopped at the end of the bed and crossed his arms. "So what were you doing when it happened?"

René opened his eyes, a smile twitching his lips. "What do you think I was doing?"

"And your mate?"

"Frightened, but okay." He grimaced. "I doubt she'll ever dance with me again, though. Reckons I'm dangerous to be around."

"You're dangerous to be around even when you're not getting shot."

"True." Amusement touched his mouth but quickly fled. "I never heard them approach. Never smelled them."

"Which probably means they had a long-range rifle. Where were you when it happened?"

"In the summerhouse."

"Where, exactly?"

"Sitting on the seat, my back to the outside fence, with a wet and willing wolf snugly on my lap."

The shooter had to have been in the trees beyond

the wall. If he'd been in one of the trees close to the summerhouse, René would surely have heard him. Or, at the very least, smelled him. "Martin told me they found tracks."

"Apparently. I was pretty out of it for a while, so I can't really tell you much of what went on after I was shot."

"Then tell me what was going on between you and Betise."

Contempt was evident in René's dark gaze. "That bitch is nothing but trouble!"

"She claims you made promises you've failed to live up to."

His brother snorted. "The only promise I've failed to keep was the threat to knock her out if she didn't stop harassing me."

"So you've done nothing more than dance with her?"

"Three times. Which was two times too many, I've since discovered."

Duncan frowned. "What do you mean?"

"The woman's certifiable. After the second dance she was talking like we had a future together. By the third, she was acting territorial and talking about having kids."

"You never gave her reason to believe you might have cared for her?"

René snorted. "Care for her? Good grief, have you caught her rancid scent?"

"So why go back a second and third time?"

"Because my brains lie in my little head, not my big one." He shrugged. "She was there, she was willing, and I've never been particular."

None of them were, and one way or another, it had gotten them all into trouble. "Was last night the last time you danced with her?"

"Yes. And that's when I told her she was delusional." He hesitated and frowned. "You know, she said something weird."

That didn't surprise him. Betise had been saying a lot of weird things lately. "What did she say?"

"She said the Sinclairs owed her mother, and by the end of this moon phase she intended to take what was promised."

Duncan frowned. What did they owe Iyona? She'd already told him she'd never been to any of the dances here. "Is that all?"

"All I heard. I must admit, I tuned out before I walked away."

Someone rapped against the outside door. "Coming, coming," Martin called, then stuck his head through the doorway. "If you don't want to be seen, then you'd better leave."

Duncan nodded and glanced at his brother. "I'll make sure Zeke provides protection while you're in the hospital."

René raised his eyebrows. "You really think that's necessary?"

"Until we know what's really going on, yes." Duncan spun on his heel and headed back for the tunnel. After ensuring the door was closed, he made his way toward his father's rooms. Zeke wasn't there, but that wasn't surprising. As head of the pack, he'd need to be present while the rangers were interviewing and taking samples.

Duncan picked up the phone and quickly dialed Lance.

"Wilton residence." His friend's cheery tones came through loud and clear.

"Lance, Duncan."

"Hey! I was just about to call you."

"You found something?"

"Oh yeah. I discovered who else was in that little raiding party over at the Bitterroot Reservation. Would you be surprised if I said one of the others had moved into Ripple Creek just over a month ago?"

"With what has been going on, no."

"Well, if everything I've dug up is true, this woman has a pretty big ax to grind. Seems that when she was barely a pup, she was promised to Tray Sinclair in a deal that was meant to strengthen business and blood ties between the silver and golden packs over there."

Arranged marriages had gone out with the Dark Ages, mainly because so few of them worked. It was extremely rare for such a couple to be soul mates, and for most wolves, commitment to anyone other than their true mate was almost impossible.

"When Tray turned eighteen," Lance continued, "he decides he can't stand the woman and reneges. To say she didn't take the rejection kindly is an understatement."

In many respects, she had every reason to be angry. But burning down the mansion and killing innocents went beyond anyone's idea of fair retribution. "So she led the raiding party to the mansion?"

"Along with half a dozen drunken buddies, yes."

"Did she get jail time?"

"Oh yeah. They threw the book at her. Got out after ten years on good behavior, and apparently is a very nasty piece of work."

"She got a name?" Not that he really needed to ask; he had a damn good idea who the woman was.

"She's known as Iyona Myna. She got married about a year after getting out of jail, but the marriage was abusive and she ended up back inside again. After that, I think she traveled around a bit, then finally settled with some relatives down south—until they kicked her out a month ago. I believe she has a daughter from a previous relationship who's also living in Ripple Creek at the moment."

"Betise."

"That's the one."

Duncan rubbed his hand across his jaw. He now had a possible suspect—two, actually. Except for one thing. The wolf attacking the women was silver.

"Don't suppose you know what coat color she was?"

"No. But she's from the golden pack, so you'd presume gold."

Logic would dictate as much, but nothing in this case was going the way logic said it should. "Any idea who Betise's father is?"

"A couple of the gossip magazines suggested Iyona was pregnant when Tray rejected her. They also suggested Tray wasn't the father. I haven't found anything to confirm this yet."

The timing was about right for Betise to be that child. "I don't suppose you found any interviews with Tray?"

"He died the night of the fire."

So Iyona had gotten her revenge, even if she had killed twelve others in the process. "Let me know if you find anything else."

"You bet."

Duncan hung up and leaned back in the chair. If Betise was indeed Tray Sinclair's daughter, then her comments about the Sinclairs owing both her and her mother made a little more sense. But if she was after some form of blood recognition or compensation, why not go through a DNA test to prove paternity? What she was doing now—trying to hook a Sinclair through marriage—was surely going the long way around. And while none of Zeke's get were related to the Bitterroot Sinclairs, there were others in the pack who were. Moons, if Betise wasn't careful, she could very well end up mating with a half brother—though he suspected it wouldn't really bother her.

He glanced at the time and wondered how Neva was doing. Was she keeping her distance like she'd promised? He frowned and rose, walking to the window. The snow was still falling, the night's chill evident through the glass. He hoped she wasn't out in it. Hoped she was warm and snug in bed.

He closed his eyes and reached for her, but there was nothing in the mental lines beyond a buzzing warmth. Wherever she was, she was too far away to hear him. Worry snaked through him, and he half-wished he'd followed the desire to demand she stay put in the house and not run after Betise.

The door behind him opened and Zeke stepped in. "I thought you might be here," his father said. "Martin handed those samples he took from Betise over to my friend in forensics. I suggest you mention them to our head ranger when you talk to her."

"I will." Even though the mere fact that they'd taken samples wasn't likely to impress Savannah.

"You talked to René?" Zeke asked.

"Yes. And I just spoke to Lance." Duncan closed the curtains, then turned around and leaned back. The chill of the glass was still evident through the thick material. "Betise's mother—Iyona—was apparently promised as a child to Tray Sinclair. She and Tray had a huge argument several days before the night of promising and Tray refused to be bound to her."

Zeke frowned. "Detrek didn't mention anything about Tray and Betise's mother when I talked to him about it."

"So he didn't mention the fact that Iyona had been one of the people behind the burning, and that she had, in fact, spent ten years in prison for it?"

"No." Zeke paused. "Did Lance question anyone? Maybe find out what the argument was about?"

"No, but Betise *is* about the right age to have been fathered by Tray."

Zeke snorted. "*That* is highly unlikely."

Duncan frowned at the certainty in his father's voice. "Why?"

"Because Tray was sterile. It was something they'd discovered only a few weeks before the fire." He hesitated, "Detrek told me that in confidence, so please don't mention it to anyone.

"You'd have to hazard a guess that's probably what they argued about." That and the impossible pregnancy.

"Probably."

Zeke moved across to the bar and poured himself a drink, then raised the bottle in query. Duncan shook his head.

"I suspect Iyona or her bastard is probably responsible for the attack on René, but what about the murders?" Zeke met his gaze. "Do you think they're related?"

He shrugged. "That depends on whether the rangers are right in believing it's a man."

Zeke grunted. "I might talk to my source again. See if there's any actual evidence pointing to it being a male. Might be easier than trying to talk to the rangers." He paused. "Is it true that Savannah has been in intensive care, and that someone attempted to attack her in the hospital?"

"Yeah. And you're right; the rangers are not going to tell us anything. Savannah won't even give me the time of day right now." And not just because she suspected the Sinclairs of being murderers, but because of how he'd treated Neva.

Zeke studied him. "You do realize she and Savannah are twins, don't you?"

"Yes, but what has that got to do with anything?"

"Possibly everything. The golden tribe share an extremely powerful psychic connection. It's very possible your Neva experienced her sister's attack and saw what her sister saw."

Your Neva. The words seemed to echo through Duncan, and he had to curb a smile, because in reality, there was no reason to smile. She was his nothing until she looked deep into her heart and acknowledged what existed between them. And right now, thanks to his initial treatment of her, she was too scared to even try.

"I hadn't thought of that," he admitted. "I'll talk to her when I see her again."

Zeke took a drink, then said, "If your connection with her is strong enough, you might be able to touch her mind and share her memories."

"That takes trust."

Zeke's half-smile was sympathetic. "Many fences to mend, huh?"

"Maybe a lifetime's worth." But there was no bitterness in his voice. With the benefit of hindsight, he did regret his actions. And yet he knew, given the same circumstances, the same information, and the chance to do it all again, he'd probably make the same mistakes.

"So what do you intend to do?"

He knew his father was talking about Neva rather than the murders. He shrugged and moved away from the chill of the windows. "I really don't know. I'm committed for at least another two months in Eagle. I can't walk out on Dave without giving him time to find and train a replacement, and I need to find myself another job."

"You have the ski lodge your mother left you. You could always return and manage that. And I've heard that they're thinking about setting up a search-and-rescue team here in Ripple Creek."

He nodded. He'd heard the same from Dave. "I'll worry about it when we have our current problem solved. I'll head over to the hospital and attempt to talk to our head ranger, then I'll see if Neva remembers anything. I'll let you know if I get anywhere."

"I gather Neva didn't warn you about the rangers' raid tonight?"

"No." Nor was he surprised. Her allegiance lay with her sister, not with him. Maybe one day that would change, but not today, that was for sure.

Zeke took a long drink, then said, "I don't know why Savannah's so damn convinced it's one of us."

"Because they found black hairs on several victims. It wasn't a human who killed those women. It was a wolf, and we're the only pack with black hair." Although that didn't mean the black hair couldn't be human, even if the DNA results had come back negative on those humans tested by the rangers.

"And silver coats. If the murderer was in wolf form when he attacked, how could the rangers find black hair?"

"And why didn't they find prints? And why were there no scents to track?" Duncan shrugged. "Who knows? Maybe they changed shape to gloat."

"The bastard behind this is certainly sick enough to do that."

"That they are." Then he frowned. Why had he said *they* rather than *he* or *she*? "Are you arranging a guard for René at the hospital?"

"Tye, Kane, and I will be taking it in shifts. Right now, we don't dare trust anyone else. Just in case."

Duncan nodded. "I don't think you'll have to do it for long. I have a feeling this thing will be over within the next day or so."

"I hope you're right. And I hope we can avoid any more killings."

"Amen to that," Duncan said and headed back to the tunnels.

Neva lost the truck halfway down Main Street. By that stage, her legs were aching, her lungs felt as if they were on fire, and the snow she'd gulped down hadn't done a thing to ease the dryness in her throat.

She padded along the street, following the truck's tire tracks and hoping the snow didn't decide to fall any heavier, because then she'd certainly lose them for good.

The Blue Nights came into view, an oasis of warmth and energy in the cold night. Music pumped, beating through her blood like fire, and she momentarily wished she was inside, dancing and laughing with everyone else.

But not alone.

She sighed. *Admit it, that damn man has gotten under your skin.* And had she felt this deep an attraction to anyone else but Duncan Sinclair, she would not be dithering about her feelings. But she couldn't change years of conditioning, and he was everything she'd been taught to avoid. Not to mention the way he'd treated her.

And while she should, undoubtedly, be doing as Ari had advised—screwing that beautiful man's brains out and letting the future take care of itself—she just wasn't built that way.

Yes, her wolf might be free, but her wolf loved Ripple Creek, loved working at the diner, and—as much as she'd toyed with the idea—really had no hankering to explore the wider world. Her sister was the wild child in the family, not her. And Savannah was probably a more suitable match for Duncan than she'd ever be.

So why did the thought of him leaving tear at her so?

She didn't know.

She didn't want to know.

Coward, an inner voice whispered.

But better a coward than holding out her heart to a man who'd long ago vowed to remain a lone wolf.

The tire tracks led her to the far edge of town, then veered left onto Heather Creek Road. Neva paused, trying to catch her breath as she listened to the sounds of the night. Beyond the pounding music and happy laughter coming from the Blue Nights, there was little noise. If the truck was moving anywhere nearby, she couldn't hear it.

She shook off the snow that had settled on her coat and continued on. She'd head down the road another mile or so, but if the tracks went on after that, she was going home. The night was too cold, and her legs were too tired to go much farther. Besides, Heather Creek Road eventually made it all the way down to Dillon, and there was no way in hell she was traveling that distance. Not on foot, anyway.

The glow of lights from Main Street faded, and the darkness and the snow seemed to close in. Unease slithered through her. She didn't know this area all that well, but knew there were very few people living out this way. A few ski lodges, a house or two, but that was it. If she got into trouble, she'd find no help close by.

The thought made her pause. Through the silence, she heard the sound of an engine—one that seemed to be stationary rather than moving. Unease prickled down her spine, raising the hairs along her backbone. The urge to run away was so great she half-turned. Only the knowledge that more people might die if she didn't keep going made her press forward.

Lights glimmered ahead. Red taillights, gleaming in the night like a mad wolf's eyes.

She shivered and padded forward more cautiously. It was a blue truck ahead. Iyona's truck. Halted in the middle of the road, lights on, engine running. Neva stopped and sniffed the air. She could smell oil and gas fumes from the exhaust but couldn't pick up Betise's sharp scent, or Iyona's strange, sourly acidic aroma. There was no sound apart from the idling engine.

And there was no way in hell she was going any closer. It looked like a trap, and right now the safest thing she could do was hightail it out of there. She could always come back later—in the safety of the car, and with Duncan by her side.

She retreated, but she'd barely gone three steps when the night blurred and she suddenly found herself under the snarling weight of a silver wolf.

Chapter Fourteen

DUNCAN'S FOOTSTEPS ECHOED as he walked down the hospital corridor toward Savannah's room. The young officer stationed at her door eyed him warily, his hair gleaming carrot red under the harsh lights and his hand drifting toward the gun at his side.

Obviously a ranger who was new to Ripple Creek, otherwise the youngster would have known who *he* was. Duncan held up his hands and stopped. "Duncan Sinclair. I wish to talk to Savannah, if that's possible."

The ranger leaned around the doorway to speak to her. Duncan shook his head. The fool was obviously *very* new, because turning your back like that was *not* a good idea. Savannah must have said something along those lines, because when the young ranger looked back, his face was almost as red as his hair. "You can go in."

Duncan held back his smile. "Thanks."

The carrot-topped ranger nodded, his hand still resting on his gun and a watchful look in his blue eyes as Duncan walked into the room. Savannah was sitting up in bed, still wearing bandages on the worst of her wounds, but her eyes, at least, were uncovered. Overall she looked a whole lot healthier than she had yesterday.

"What can I do for you, Mr. Sinclair?" Her voice held none of the warmth so evident in Neva's.

He dragged a chair up to her bed and sat down. "I believe we might be able to help each other out."

A smile touched her lips. "Oh, yeah? Have you come to confess?"

"Are you interested in hearing what I have to say, or are we going to dwell on a past I can do nothing about?"

She studied him for a moment. Her eyes, unlike Neva's, were about as expressive as a brick wall.

"You hurt my sister," she said in that same flat, no-nonsense tone, "and I'll bust your balls from here to kingdom come."

He smiled faintly. "Fair enough."

"Then talk."

He did. She said nothing, listening intently, nodding every now and again. When he'd finished, she said, "There's one problem with your theory that Iyona, Betise, or both might be involved with these murders—"

"The black hairs found at the murder scene?"

"And how did you know about those? Neva?"

"Yes."

"Then she trusts you."

With evidence, but certainly nothing else. Yet. "She targeted me at the mansion because not even *you* think I'm the murderer."

"That doesn't mean the rest of your pack isn't involved. Betise or Iyona might be working with one of them."

He reached into his jacket pocket and pulled out the plastic bag he'd fished out of the river earlier. "Try matching this with those hairs you found." And he placed it into her hands.

She glanced at it, distaste flitting across her features. "A hair ball?"

"A *black* hair ball. We were following Betise earlier and saw her throw it into Hunter's River. I fished it out."

"We? You and Neva?"

"Yep. So you've got a believable witness as well as me."

"A hair ball doesn't make her the murderer. It's a silver wolf attacking these women, not a golden."

"But both Betise and Iyona have a better motive than anyone else. My pack aren't saints, but none of us are behind these murders. I guarantee it."

"Well, a guarantee like that is certainly going to go a *long* way in a court of law." But she said it with a smile, and he took no offense.

"Has anyone seen Betise's coat color?" he asked. "If she *is* the child of one of the Bitterroot Sinclairs, she might very well be silver."

"Possibly." Savannah's voice was noncommittal. "I'll have this checked out along with the samples we took tonight. Hopefully, we'll get an answer."

"We have something else you might be interested in, too. Martin took skin and blood samples from under Betise's nails the night she was attacked. They're currently being analyzed at the forensics lab."

"Any samples not taken by us under controlled conditions won't be accepted as evidence in court."

"Perhaps not. But it may provide a link to the women who were killed. Once you have that link, you can concentrate on collecting evidence that is rock solid."

"Maybe." Her tone was, again, noncommittal.

He hesitated, then asked, "Can you remember anything of your own attack?"

"No, it's all still a blur."

"Have you asked Neva?"

She was silent for a long moment, then swore softly. "I didn't even think of it."

At least he wasn't the only one. He rose and put the chair back. "She was there with you in spirit."

"She's the reason I'm alive," Savannah said softly. "The only reason. The wolf was silver. That's all I remember."

"But it may not be all Neva remembers."

"No." Savannah paused. "Are you intending to ask her yourself?"

"Yes."

"Then I have only one thing to tell you. Don't try taking the law into your own hands, Sinclair. Not in my town. If you find anything, bring it to me to deal with."

"Right." After he'd found whoever was behind this and given him—or her—a beating or two.

"I mean it, or the threat I made earlier will apply."

He didn't reply. Didn't get the chance to. Neva's fear slammed into his mind and, hot on its heels, her pain. The force of both, one on top of the other, hurled him back against the wall and left him gasping.

"Neva!" Savannah's cry spun through the air and his mind, filled with fear for her sister.

He shook his head, trying to free himself from the haze of Neva's pain and terror to reach for her mentally, but she was too consumed by whatever was happening to her to hear him.

He pushed away from the wall and staggered to the door. He had to find her—and fast. The young officer had rushed in at Savannah's cry and was near her bed. There were quick footsteps coming toward the room, then nurses came through the doorway. He pushed past them and thundered down the hall.

You heard? Savannah's surprised thought cut through his shields and arrowed into his mind.

Yes.

Oh, Moons . . . does she know?

No. Nor will she, until she is ready to acknowledge it for herself.

Can you find her? I can't get any sense from her; I have no idea where she is.

I can find her. He didn't need to feel her thoughts for that. All he had to do was follow his heart.

Do you need help?

No. Because if anyone had hurt her, he'd kill them. And he didn't need rangers as witnesses.

Run swiftly.

He didn't answer. Simply obeyed.

It was Savannah's attack all over again, and for one second Neva froze. All she could smell was the other wolf's putrid breath, and all she could hear was the rumble of its growl. All she could feel was the drip of saliva against her face as the gleaming white teeth slashed through the air, searching for her throat. She twisted desperately, and the teeth tore into her foreleg instead. Pain ripped through her, burning away the fear.

Savannah had defeated this wolf—but only because she'd siphoned Neva's abilities at the last moment. But there would be no desperate last moment here. As she'd told Duncan, she was far from defenseless.

She reached for the fear singing through her veins and flung it back at the other wolf, smashing through her foe's shields and driving it deep into the other's mind. A mind that was crazy with the moon's heat. Crazy with hate. For her.

The wolf was female. Not male.

Betise? Was she silver?

The mad, yellow eyes went wide, then the silver wolf cowered away, whimpering and shivering. Neva scrambled upright onto her paws and ran. With every step, blood flew through the air, glistening with black fire as it spattered across the pristine snow.

Air stirred, arrowing toward her. Another wolf, coming from the right. Out of the corner of her eye she saw the blur of gold rising high as the wolf sprang. She slammed past this second wolf's shields, filling her mind with the terror and hatred she was still feeling from the first wolf. The golden bitch dropped, trembling and whimpering with fright. Neva kept on running, though her lungs burned and the warmth of blood pulsing down her leg felt like a tide.

Lights beckoned brightly through the darkness

ahead. She ran onto Main Street but didn't stop, too fearful that if she did, those wolves would catch her. She couldn't hear them behind her, but that didn't mean they weren't. Warmth and music pulsed through the night, but she didn't head for the Blue Nights, even though it would be safe. There was only one place she wanted to be right now—and he was close. She could feel him in her mind. With her heart.

Neva? Savannah's thought was as sharp as glass. *Are you okay?*

Fine, she lied, not wanting to panic her sister any more than she already had. *I'll come and talk to you soon.*

She saw Duncan a second later—a sleek silver shadow exploding out of the snow-filled night. She shifted shape as he did, and all but fell into the warmth of his arms.

Trembling, shivering, she wrapped her arms around him and held on tight. Breathed deep the spicy, foresty smell of him, letting the sense of warmth and security and strength he exuded infuse her. Calm her.

The arms that held her so protectively were taut, and his heart was a rumble of rapid thunder in the ear she pressed hard against his chest. His anger was a cloud of red that burned her mind and stung the night, but behind it was fear. For her. And the knowledge made her heart do a weird little dance.

She didn't know how long they stood there like that, holding each other in the middle of Main Street as the snow fell around them. She didn't really care, because she'd never felt so safe in her life. When he eventually pulled away, he caught her chin, directing her gaze to his.

"Was it Betise and Iyona?"

She nodded. "I doubt that it could have been anyone else, if only—"

"Tell me about it later," he cut in. "Right now, you need to get to the emergency room." He bent, swinging her up into his arms.

"I don't—"

"No arguments." His voice was almost savage. "That arm needs stitches."

She glanced down. The sleeve of her coat was ripped to shreds, and blood covered her arm and fingers. "It's not as bad as it looks."

"Maybe. But who knows what you can catch from the bite of a bitch like Betise?"

A smile played across her lips. "A rather nasty thing to say." Though as nasty comments went, she was thinking far worse.

"Right now, I'm feeling particularly nasty." He glanced at her. Though his black eyes were as unreadable as ever, something in his expression made her tremble. "You're mine, if only for the rest of this moon phase. No one attacks anything of mine and gets away with it."

His words seemed to echo through her, doing strange things to her heart. Moons, it would be so easy to believe he cared. But that was something she dared not do, because it would be all too easy to fall.

If she hadn't fallen already.

No. It was the moon and the power of the man himself. Nothing more. She couldn't fall for a man like Duncan. He was everything she'd *never* wanted.

He strode through the night, not saying anything, just holding her with a tenderness that suggested she was precious cargo. Tears prickled her eyes. She wouldn't think that. Couldn't think that. It wasn't safe.

"Safe isn't always what it's cracked up to be," he said softly, obviously replying to her thoughts. "Safe can be horribly lonely."

Which she'd discovered over the years, so why was she holding on to it so tightly? She didn't know, and that scared her almost as much as exploring what she might feel for him. She let her gaze rake the face she knew would haunt her dreams forever. "How could a relationship between us ever work?" Especially given her father's edict? "You don't want to come back to Ripple Creek, and I don't really want to leave. I want a family. You want nothing more than a good time."

"All relationships must compromise to survive."

"But not all relationships are worth the effort. It's just the moon that binds us, nothing more. I can't help what I feel."

"You haven't explored what you feel." He paused as the doors to the hospital swished open. "But let's discuss this when we're alone."

"There's nothing to discuss." And there would be no later. Not for them.

Because of who he was. Because of who she was, and the way she'd been brought up. She was willing to bend the shackles of her parents' beliefs and rules, but she didn't want to break them completely. She was a wolf, and family was everything. She couldn't walk away from her parents—not forever—and if she wanted Duncan in her life, that's what she would have to do. Her father had made it clear he would not forgive a continuing dalliance with someone like Duncan.

If it came down to a choice, there really was none. To keep her family in her life, she had to stick to her original plan and walk away from him. No matter what she might feel.

No matter how much it hurt to do that.

Duncan paced the confines of the waiting room. He itched to be a part of the posse Savannah was arranging to go after Betise and Iyona, but his first priority was Neva and her safety. Though once he had her tucked securely away, he was going after those two bitches. No matter how forcefully Savannah ordered him away.

And yet even as he paced, he knew the anger that was burning him was not so much the need for revenge, but rather annoyance at Neva's continuing insistence that this was nothing more than a moon dance. Because of who he was. Because of what he'd done in the past and the way he'd treated her this week.

But most important, because of her parents.

His mother had once told him that fate had a way of catching up with you and making you pay. He'd thought that jail time had been his punishment, but this was far worse. He'd once been sure there was never going to be anyone out there for him. To actually find her, and hold her, and yet be faced with the knowledge that she might never admit what clearly existed between them, was surely a punishment that far outweighed any of his past crimes.

But as he'd told Savannah, the past was something he could do nothing about, beyond regret it. It had shaped him, had helped make him what he was today, but it wasn't *who* he was today. Surely time would make Neva see that. If she'd give him time. And right now he doubted she would.

Footsteps echoed down the hall. He looked up and saw a nurse wheeling Neva toward him. Her face was pale and she looked tired, but her smile made his blood surge.

"The doctor says I have to take it easy with my arm for the next day or so." Her green eyes twinkled mischievously. "So it looks like you're going to have to do all the work tonight."

He fell into step beside the wheelchair as they headed toward the exit. "I was under the impression I was doing all the work anyway."

A slight blush crept through her cheeks and she cast a sideways glance at the nurse, who was grinning with delight. But if Neva was at all worried about what the nurse might be thinking, her next words belied it.

"And who approached whom to start with?"

"Ah yes," he said softly, his gaze meeting hers. "An amazing experience I shall never forget."

The bloom of heat in her cheeks grew, but so did her smile. "Well, there you go. Having done all the hard work to begin with, I deserve to sit back and enjoy myself for a while."

"Then I shall endeavor to see that you do." He swung her out of the wheelchair and into his arms, kissing her briefly but passionately before glancing at the nurse. "Thanks."

Still smiling, the nurse nodded and retreated back inside. He glanced down at Neva. "Ready?"

"That all depends on what I'm supposed to be ready for."

Her voice was low and sexy as hell, and heat shot to his groin. She smelled so good, so damn desirable, it was all he could do not to take her right there and then.

He forced his feet to move down the pavement. "To go home, witch."

"If that's all you're offering, then I guess so."

He couldn't help smiling. In a couple of days she'd gone from a hesitant lover to an all-too-willing participant. She was amazing. Totally amazing. "Let's get out of the snow first."

"I've never done it in the snow," she said thoughtfully. She was running her fingers up and down his arms, a gentle caress that burned deep. And made it damn hard to walk.

"It's cold."

"But romantic."

Her breath was warm and sweet against his neck, and the smell of her arousal stirred his senses and made him hunger. Half a block had never seemed so far away. "Hypothermia is never romantic."

She raised an eyebrow, eyes glimmering with green fire in the darkness. "You only get hypothermia if you're out in the cold a long time."

"I plan for it to be a long time."

"With the moon rising high and the urgency I feel beating through your skin? Doubtful." She paused and looked around. "This is not the way to my house."

"No, it's the way to mine." Luckily, the lodge was down the other end of the street from the hospital; otherwise, he'd be calling a cab. She might want to make love in the snow, but right now she was beginning to shiver.

She frowned. "I don't want to go to the mansion."

"Good, because we're not going there."

Her surprise rippled around him. "You own a house here in Ripple Creek?"

"Sort of."

"What's 'sort of' supposed to mean?"

"That I own it, but it's not a house."

She gave him a long look that was filled with annoyance. "Then what is it?"

"It's Snowflake Lodge. My mother left it to me when she died." And he'd already called ahead to ensure that one of the cabins was open and ready for them.

"Really? I thought the Harpers owned it."

"They manage it on my behalf, but I doubt Betise and Iyona would think to look there, as it's one of the smaller lodges and definitely mid-range."

"And the Sinclairs are well-known for their luxurious tastes."

"Exactly. You can stay there until I get this all sorted out."

Fear touched her eyes, and the warm caress of her fingers against his skin stopped. "You keep saying *I* rather than *we*. You're going after them, aren't you?"

"Yes. They have to be stopped."

"Savannah and the rangers will stop them."

"I intend to be there as a backup." Not that he distrusted the abilities of Savannah's team. He just suspected Betise and Iyona would not be so easily caught. Not if they'd been planning this for a long time.

He walked down the lodge's driveway, past the main lobby entrance and through the terraced gardens. The cabin they'd been assigned was at the rear of the property and extremely private.

"You're leaving once they're caught, aren't you?"

He hesitated. "For a while."

"So this could be our last night?"

He didn't answer. Didn't dare, lest he blurt out exactly what he was feeling. She wouldn't believe it. Not until she'd reached deep inside and discovered the truth for herself.

He placed her gently on her feet, then opened the door and had a quick look inside to ensure all was ready. The room was warm, lit by the golden light of the fire burning in the huge stone fireplace. Two sofas and a couple of well-padded chairs corralled the fire, and on the other side of the room there was a TV and a bar. The bedrooms and bathroom were upstairs. It wasn't much, but it was comfortable.

"After you, my lady," he said, turning around.

Only to discover she'd stripped. For one brief second, he allowed himself the pleasure of simply looking at her, letting his gaze travel down the long length of her neck, taking in her small but perfectly formed breasts, watching their peaks harden with desire. Her breathing was quick and sharp, every intake seeming to shudder through her entire body. Her desire stung the air—a rich scent that called to the wildness in him and made him harder than he'd ever thought possible.

But the full moon was too close, and if he started

loving her, he might not want to stop. And she was injured.

"Neva—"

"No." She stepped into his arms, her words hot and breathy against his lips. "Just dance with me. Right here, right now."

He took a deep breath and puffed it out. "It's better that we don't—"

"Don't what?" she murmured saucily, her fingers cool against his chest as she slipped her hands under his sweater.

He pulled her hands firmly away. "You need to rest."

"I need to dance." Her gaze searched his, eyes gleaming in the darkness. "Are you going to take me up on my offer, or shall I find someone who will?"

Even a saint would be unable to resist such an invitation—and he was a long way from sainthood. He crushed her close, his mouth finding hers almost savagely. She wrapped her arms around his neck, holding him tight, matching his urgency. Desire shimmered between them, but even a heat so fierce was not enough to stop her shivering. He picked her up and carried her inside, kicking the door shut before making his way to the sofa nearest the fire. Once he'd set her on her feet again, he stepped back and quickly stripped. The musky scent of her desire grew stronger, fueling the need already raging through his veins. But rather than pulling her close and claiming her as he ached to do, he reached out, running his hand down her neck. She trembled, her pulse galloping beneath his fingertips.

"I don't want to dance," he said softly.

Her gaze swept down his body, and a smile teased her kiss-swollen lips. "Well, certain parts of your body are belying that statement."

"That's not what I mean. I want to make love to you."

Confusion flickered through her bright eyes. "They're the same thing."

"No, dancing is for pleasure. Making love is something more." And he ached to show her what he dared not say.

She ran her tongue across her lips, and he had to resist the sudden urge to follow that moist trail with his mouth.

"In what way?"

Though her voice was calm, panic gleamed in her eyes. She understood all too well. He let his hand drift past her throat. Her already puckered nipples seemed to become harder, as if straining for his touch. "If you wish to discover the answer, you have to play the game."

He brushed his fingers across the top of her breasts, circling but not touching the dark centers. She took a deep, shuddery breath. "What game?"

"Let's pretend we are lovers. Let's pretend it's the night of the full moon, and we are about to promise our souls to each other."

She studied him for several heartbeats, her expression a mix of confusion and alarm. "Why?"

"Because I've never had a true lover, just dancers."

She hesitated. "I'm not sure this is a game I can play."

"Why not?" He gently plucked one nipple.

Goose bumps rippled across her skin and her pupils

dilated, almost swallowing the leaf green of her irises. "Because I don't see the point of it."

He shifted his touch to her other breast, this time rolling the firm nub between his fingertips. "It's not the night of promising, Neva. No harm can come from pretending."

"Can you be sure? The magic might lie in the ritual itself rather than the night."

"Have you ever heard of the ritual being performed on any other night but the one of the full moon?"

"No, but—"

"No buts. Just yes or no."

Neva took another deep breath. His gentle touch shuddered through every fiber of her being, and though she wanted him with a fierceness that was almost painful, she feared to pretend what lay between them was anything more than just a dance. Because such pretense might lead to an examination of the feelings she'd managed to avoid up until now. "What if I don't want to answer at all?"

"Then you go to bed and rest as the doctor ordered."

"That's sexual blackmail."

"No, that's honesty. This one time, I want more than just a dance."

She closed her eyes. It was a risk. She knew in her heart it was a risk because no one truly knew if the magic of promising was confined to just one night. And because, deep down, she knew that her heart was already on the line and this might tip it over the edge and down the hill toward heartbreak.

But could she let him walk away tomorrow or the

day after without knowing what it might be like to be truly loved by this man?

He raised a hand, cupping her cheek. It felt like he was branding her skin for eternity. "Your answer?"

"No, I've never heard of the ritual being successful on any other night. Yes, let's pretend."

He smiled, his dark eyes filled with a heat that caused a meltdown deep inside her. He caught her hand and tugged her onto the rug near the hearth. The thick fur pressed against her toes, and the warmth of the flames caressed her skin, but they seemed oddly cool compared to the fire burning inside and out.

He pressed her fingers against his chest. The heat of his body and his warm, woody scent washed across her senses, stirring her in ways she'd never thought possible. And the wild beat of his heart under her fingertips only fueled her desire to greater heights.

"Does my lady know what night it is?"

His voice was little more than a stroke of sound, yet it seemed to sing through every part of her. She took a deep breath and released it slowly. His question was the start of the ritual. If she replied, if the magic *could* be raised on nights other than the one before the full moon, she could bind herself for eternity to a man who did not love her. Because once begun, there was no retreat. Not unless the participants were familiar with the paths of magic.

But if she didn't reply, if the magic *couldn't* be raised on any other night, she'd miss the chance to know what it might be like to be the woman he loved enough to commit to.

Let's pretend, he'd said. *Nothing more.* She could

pretend she loved him. Pretend that he loved her. Even if it broke her heart.

"It is the night before the full moon. The night of promises." She briefly closed her eyes against the sudden sting of tears. Deep down, part of her wished that this was real. That the words were real. That he truly did love her.

He stepped closer. Her breasts were pressed against his warm bare chest, and the heat of his erection scorched her stomach. "Or the night of destiny."

The air seemed to stir around them—or was it merely his breath stroking her mouth with warmth?

"You are my heart, my soul." And she knew even as she said the words that she shouldn't have started this. She couldn't pretend, because she did care—as much as she'd tried *not* to admit it.

"I can't do this," she added. "Let's just dance."

But he didn't hear her. Or maybe he chose not to hear her. "Kneel with me."

"We can't do this." Because she didn't want to pretend when part of her ached so fiercely for it to be real.

His eyes were black fires of determination that burned through her soul. "Kneel with me," he repeated and tugged her down in front of him.

"Duncan—"

He stopped her with a kiss that was both ferocious and passionate. One that left her mind reeling and her body aching.

"Dance with me," he said, voice so husky, so damn sexy, chills ran across her skin. "This night and the rest of our nights, for as long as the divine light shines in the evening skies. For as long as we live beneath it."

The air seemed to thrum, to burn, at his words. Magic, or her imagination?

"No," she choked, trying to pull away.

His touch slid past her hip to cup her rear, holding her in place, his grip gentle but firm. "Pretend," he whispered, brushing a kiss across her lips. "That's all it is."

But this was more than just pretend. Something was happening. Surely he could feel it. Surely the tingle in the air wasn't just her imagination . . .

He caught her chin, raising her gaze to his. His eyes were ebony pools she wanted to lose herself in forever.

"I feel nothing more than desire. Want nothing more than to love you as you should be loved. Pretend with me."

She closed her eyes and shifted her stance. "Under her light, I offer you my body."

Desire and something else—something more ethereal—shimmered between them, warming the night. Warming her. His rigid heat slid deep inside, until it felt as if he was claiming every inch of her. He began to rock. It felt so good, so right, a moan escaped her lips.

"Under the divine light of the moon," he said, "I offer you my heart."

It felt like her own heart was pulling tight, ready to shatter. "Under her light, I offer you mine."

The sting in the air was becoming stronger. Sweat skated across her skin. *Pretend,* she told herself fiercely. *Nothing more.*

His grip on her rear grew stronger, holding her steady as the tempo of his thrusts increased. "Under the divine light, I offer you my soul."

Deep down the tremors were beginning, spreading through her body like a wave. She gripped his shoulders, digging her nails into his flesh, fighting the sensations rippling through her, fearing the burning in the air. Fearing the fact she could not stop the words flowing from her lips.

"By her light, I offer you mine."

He was thrusting deep and hard. The world seemed to be spinning, and every fiber of her being was tingling with magic. Burning with the need for release.

"Then let our souls become one as our bodies have become one."

"Let the moon bless and rejoice in this union," she somehow gasped.

"Do you accept the gift of my seed?" he growled. "Do you accept the promises of the night and the moon?"

"Yes," she cried. "Yes."

He went rigid against her, the force of his release tearing her name from his throat. Heat seemed to explode around them, through them, and her climax came in a rush of power that stole her breath, stole all thought, and swept her into a world that was sheer, unadulterated bliss.

For a long moment, neither of them moved. Then she rested her forehead on his chest, desperately trying to catch her breath, desperately hoping the ritual hadn't worked. But the air still hummed, her skin still tingled, and he was still so very hard inside her.

After a while, he lifted her chin, his lips seeking hers, his kiss a lingering taste of passion.

"What the moon has joined, let no wolf break." He brushed sweaty strands of hair from her forehead, then kissed her again. Sweetly. Gently. But it wasn't his kiss that sent goose bumps racing across her skin. It was the caring in his dark eyes. The gentle, almost loving smile touching his lips.

"May the moon bless this union and grant us life," she whispered.

Energy seemed to flow through every pore of her being. For one moment, it felt as if the moon itself was blessing her. Blessing them. She fought the sting of more tears and closed her eyes. Thankfully, the moon *couldn't* bless this union with life. Not when Duncan had been given the fertility-control injection.

"By the moon's divine light, let us now celebrate this union." Though the words were the last in the ritual, they were also what she wanted. All she wanted.

All they did, through the remainder of the long night. By the end of which she truly knew what it felt like to be loved by a man like Duncan.

But did she dare believe it?

A distant ringing stirred Duncan from slumber, but it was a sound that stopped almost the moment he woke. He swore softly and looked around. The morning's light peeked past the bedroom curtains, indicating dawn had come and gone. He hadn't meant to sleep so long. He hadn't meant to love Neva so long. He hadn't meant to do a lot of things.

But he regretted none of them. Least of all binding Neva to him heart and soul.

He smiled and splayed his fingers across her belly, pressing her close against him. She was his, and there was nothing on this Earth that could separate them now.

And while it was supposed to have been nothing more than pretense, the minute he'd said the first words of the ritual and felt the stirrings of magic in the air, he'd known what was happening. And there was no way in hell he'd been about to stop—or let her stop. Neva was his, and the ceremony ensured that. From this point on, she could no more turn to another wolf than he could. It wasn't playing fair, it wasn't giving her the choice, but in all honesty, he didn't care. He'd spent more than half his life looking for his soul mate, and now that he'd found her, he wasn't about to let her go. He wasn't about to sit back and watch her walk into the arms of what her family might consider a "more suitable" mate.

Because he very much suspected that was what she might do. Family was everything to a wolf, and to Neva more than most. The break with her parents was killing her. And while he was responsible for that, he had no intention of walking away to mend the rift.

The ringing started again, soft but insistent. It seemed to be coming from downstairs . . . his cell phone, he realized. It was still in the pants he'd discarded in the living room. Neva stirred, and he brushed a kiss across her shoulder.

"Sleep," he said, using the power of the moon binding to make it an order. She'd probably fry his brains when she woke and realized he was still using that hold on her, but right now he didn't care. She needed the rest.

She murmured something that sounded suspiciously like a curse, then drifted back to sleep. He kissed her again, this time on her cheek, then climbed out of bed and padded downstairs, finding his pants and pulling out the phone. "Hello?"

"There's been a fire at the hospital."

His father's voice was flat, devoid of any emotion, and Duncan's gut began to churn. "René?"

"Is missing. Kane was found unconscious but alive in one of the stairwells. Looks like he'd been trying to stop the kidnappers."

"He's okay?"

"Nothing more than a bruised ego and a mighty bump on the back of the head."

"I gather it was Betise and Iyona?"

"Yes. Betise let him chase her into the stairwell where Iyona jumped him."

Duncan took a deep breath and released it slowly. "What about Savannah and the other patients?" Neva would want to know her sister was okay, even though she would surely have known if something bad *had* happened. The link between the two of them was strong.

"They're fine. The fire was in the basement, set merely as a distraction."

"You're heading up a hunting party?"

"Tye's on his way to join me and Kane. Savannah's given permission for us to be included in the official party."

Probably because she knew they'd form a hunting

party of their own if she didn't. "Do you intend to join them?"

"Yes. If only because if I find those two alone, I might be tempted to kill them. The Sinclair name has taken enough of a beating these past few weeks. We don't need to add murder to our crimes."

Duncan glanced around for his sweater. "I'll be there in five minutes."

"We're meeting over at the rangers' office."

"I'll be there."

He hung up and quickly dressed, then bounded up the stairs. He knelt by the bed, kissing Neva's lips gently, feeling the stirrings of passion in the sleepiness of her response.

"Sleep well, my love. I'll be back soon." He brushed the hair from her eyes, kissed her nose, then left.

The phone rang again as he was walking toward Main Street. He pressed the receiver and said, "Don't tell me, the location's changed."

"It certainly has."

It wasn't his father on the phone. It was Betise. His knuckles went white with the force of his grip. "How did you get this number?"

"How do you think? You really must teach your brother to shield better."

"If you've hurt him, bitch, you're both dead."

Betise tsked. "Such language."

"Just tell me what you want."

"My mother is waiting at my apartment for you. I'm not sure where you are, but you have two minutes to get there and into the truck. We hear, see, or smell the rangers anywhere nearby, and René is a dead man."

"This is not going to achieve anything."

"Promises were made. Tonight they will be fulfilled."

The bitch was definitely crazy. He hit the END button, then dialed his father's number as he ran. "Betise just called me," he said, the minute his father answered. "She wants me in front of her apartment, alone, within two minutes."

Zeke swore. Duncan didn't give his father the chance to say anything else. "Follow the truck's tracks," he said, "and don't get near enough for them to see or smell you, or René's dead."

He hung up, sped around the corner, and saw not one waiting truck but two. Out of the corner of his eye, he caught movement, and something sharp plunged into his arm. He swore and swung around, fists flying. Betise laughed and danced out of the way. He glanced down. A dart was buried hilt deep in his forearm.

"Do you really think I'd trust you to sit quietly like a good little wolf while we take you to René?" she taunted. "I may be 'well-used flesh,' Duncan, but I'm not stupid."

He lunged for her, but it felt like he was moving through glue, and his feet were extraordinarily heavy. Betise laughed, capering just beyond his reach. The dart must have been drugged. He cursed her and lunged again, but suddenly found himself falling face-first onto the pavement. Then the darkness rushed in, accompanied by harsh, almost maniacal laughter.

Chapter Fifteen

NEVA WOKE TO the nagging sensation that something was wrong. Frowning, she lay still in bed, listening to the silence haunting the cabin. Duncan wasn't there. His smell was little more than a lingering tease on the air, and there was no sound of footsteps or breathing. Maybe he'd joined the hunt for Betise and Iyona.

She glanced toward the window. The light filtering past the curtains was soft, almost muted, as if the day had come and gone, and dusk was almost over. Surely she couldn't have slept that long.

Neva? Savannah's thought was abrupt, and the feeling of wrongness increased.

What's happened? Neva swung out of bed, shivering a little as the cool air caressed her skin, and padded downstairs to find her clothes.

Plenty. Savannah's mind voice was grim. *There was a fire at the hospital, which we've since discovered was little more than a cover. René Sinclair has been snatched. Then Duncan got a phone call ordering him to meet Iyona in front of Betise's apartment if he wanted to see his brother alive again.*

He wouldn't have gone to such a meeting alone. Surely he wasn't that stupid.

He was given little choice, and little time. But he did call his father. By the time we got there, the trucks were gone. We followed the tracks, but the snow came down again and we lost them.

Neva cursed the unseasonably late onslaught of snow, though no doubt the skiers still lingering in Ripple Creek were rejoicing. *I'm coming to the hospital.*

I'm not there.

What? Savannah—

I'm fine. I'm being careful. But I'm a ranger, and I'll be damned if I'm gonna lie on my back while these bitches run around killing and kidnapping people.

Neva moved across to the window and looked out. It was no longer snowing, and the moon was rich and yellow and full as it began its ascent in the darkening sky. She stared at it for a moment, remembering Betise's words. Remembering her conviction, her certainty, that she and Duncan were soul mates. *She's going to perform the promising ritual.*

What?

Betise believes she's Duncan's soul mate. She grabbed her coat, swept a set of keys off the coffee table, and ran for the door.

Impossible, when you— Savannah's thought cut off abruptly.

It's the night of promising, Savannah. The magic can be raised whether it's your soul mate or not. God, how she wished their pretense last night had been real. While she might then have bound herself to a man who did not love her, she'd rather that than see

Duncan fettered to a murdering fiend like Betise. *Have you searched down Heather Creek Road?*

We did last night, after they'd attacked you, but we found nothing. And the truck tracks didn't head that way tonight.

Well, that's where they are. Why she was certain, she couldn't say. And if she was wrong, Duncan would pay.

Where are you?

Just coming out of Snowflake Lodge.

I'll meet you on Main. Be there in five minutes.

Savannah was there in two, and she didn't come alone. There was a convoy of four trucks in all. Neva climbed into the first one, relieved to see Ronan at the wheel. Her gaze swung left to meet Savannah's. The main bandage had been removed from her sister's face, but there were still dressings on her right cheek and above her left eye. "I'm a little surprised to see you in the backseat rather than the driver's."

Her sister's eyes twinkled brightly in the shadows. "I may be stubborn, but I'm not a fool." Her voice was dry. "Besides, I can't see well enough to drive just yet."

"Mind you," Ronan commented, a smile touching his gray eyes as he glanced at Neva, "it took the threat of a revolt for her to lose that foolhardiness she claims *not* to have."

"Why am I not surprised?" Neva slammed the door shut and buckled up her seat belt as Ronan took off. Lights swept through the rear window, briefly setting Ronan's russet hair aflame as the trucks behind fell into line.

"Probably because doing stupid things runs in our family," Savannah replied.

Neva met her sister's gaze. "That it does." Things like deciding to seduce the most dangerous man in the Sinclair pack, or pretending to perform the promising ritual. One had led her heart into danger, and the other had forced her to confront what she'd been trying to ignore—the fact that in a mere couple of days she'd fallen in love with Duncan.

She pulled her gaze from Savannah's and stared out the window. "It doesn't matter," she said softly.

It does if you love him.

I love Mom and Dad, too. I won't give up my family for the sake of a man. No matter what I feel for him.

Savannah didn't say anything. There was nothing she *could* say, because they both knew the truth of the words.

Ronan turned the truck onto Heather Creek Road, and they quickly left the lights of Ripple Creek behind them. Under the cold light of the rising moon, the land became a vast expanse of black and silver. It was stark and oddly beautiful, but also eerie.

Neva stared out the window, her gaze roaming the lustrous landscape without really seeing any of it. They were closing in. She wasn't sure how she knew, but the sensation was similar to what she shared with her sister. It was as if somehow Duncan had become a part of her, as if he was reaching out to her not only psychically but physically. She could feel him not only in her mind, but on her body. Almost as if he were caressing her, trailing his fingers across her skin, sending little tingles of electricity through every nerve ending. She was attuned to him. Totally attuned. She briefly closed her eyes, too afraid to confront the reason for why that might be. Because confronting it wouldn't change the facts, and would never change her parents' opinion. It wouldn't change her refusal to walk away from them completely.

She bit her lip, her gaze moving past the trees and spying a flicker of gold in the darkness. "Stop," she said quickly and was out the door before Ronan even touched the brake.

"Neva, wait," Savannah cried.

She stopped on the verge of the road, and waited for her sister. The night was cold and still, the snow beyond the road powdery light, glittering brightly under the moon's harsh light. The nearby trees cast deep shadows, and the smell of pine and balsam was rich in the air. She sniffed deeply. But behind those two scents was another—a warm, woody aroma that sent the blood pounding through her veins. Duncan was here somewhere. And so, surely, were Betise and Iyona, even though she couldn't smell them.

The other trucks pulled to a halt behind them, and men poured out. Savannah stopped beside her, sniffing the air lightly. "I can't smell them."

"Duncan's here. Betise will be, too."

Savannah looked past her, and Neva followed the direction of her gaze. Zeke Sinclair was walking toward them, his stride long and powerful, his angelic face expressionless, his dark eyes shuttered. For one moment, he looked so much like Duncan that her heart ached. Behind him were two shadows just as potent, though they hid their anger less skillfully. Tye and Kane.

Zeke stopped in front of Neva. The sense of his power, the sheer force of his masculinity, swept over her, and yet didn't stir her. She glanced at her sister and saw that Savannah was similarly unmoved. Which was a good thing, but odd, given the night and the moon.

"Where?" His voice was sharp. Abrupt.

Neva pointed to where she'd seen the brief flicker of light and mentally passed the image and the information on to Savannah. "About half a mile in." How she'd managed to see the light from such a distance she didn't know. Nor did she care. Not if it freed Duncan.

Zeke looked to Savannah. "How do you want to do this?"

"Neva suspects Betise will try to perform the ritual of promising. If that's the case, they'll more than likely be in a clearing. We need to get René free first, then we'll surround the clearing and get Duncan out." She hesitated, her green eyes narrowing. "No accidents, Zeke. I want these women alive."

Zeke raised his hands. "We have no weapons."

"A wolf doesn't need a weapon to kill."

There was nothing warm in Zeke's sudden smile. "I will protect my sons, Ranger, no matter what your rules say."

"You can protect all you want. Just don't kill."

Zeke's gaze flickered to Neva, studying her so intently she shifted uncomfortably. After a moment, his smile became warmer. "Perhaps I won't need to. There are other emotions, and other players, here tonight."

Heat touched Neva's cheeks. She had a horrible

feeling this man saw far more than normal men—and in her case, that he saw the feelings she was trying hard to ignore. She pulled her gaze from his and glanced at her sister. "You want me to lead?"

"You take Ronan and the Sinclairs and head around to the right. The rest of us will head left."

As Neva nodded, she glanced at the sky. The moon was bright, and magic was beginning to stir the night. If they didn't hurry, they'd be too late.

She shifted shape and lunged forward through the soft snow.

It was the cold that woke Duncan. It surrounded him, filled him. He frowned but didn't move, allowing awareness to surface fully as he listened to the night. Someone breathed close by—someone whose scent was all too familiar, and relief surged. René.

He cracked open an eye. They were in a small cave. Warm shadows danced across the walls, flickering shapes that indicated a fire was close. Naked, his brother leaned against the opposite wall, his eyes closed, though he wasn't asleep. The tension riding René's bruised and cut shoulders told Duncan that much. René's hands and feet were tied with chains that gleamed silver in the night, and the bandages over the gunshot wound were bloody—an indication that the wound had opened again.

Anger surged through Duncan, but he thrust it back. Right now, anger wouldn't be of use to either of them. He glanced down at himself. He also was naked, though he couldn't have been undressed for long, because he could still feel his fingers and toes.

Hypothermia was a ways off yet. But he had a fair idea why they were both naked, and what Betise intended to do. Tonight was the night of promises, and that mad bitch was undoubtedly going to try to raise the magic.

Worse, though, was the fact that he, too, was in chains, and if the warmth against his skin was anything to go by, those chains didn't just look silver, they *were* silver. Which meant neither of them could shift shape until the chains were off, as silver was the one metal immune to magic of all kinds. He moved his arms, trying to find some give in the looped chains and work them loose.

I wish you luck, René said. *Because I certainly haven't had any.*

But the two women must have been less careful about tying him, because the chains weren't as tight as they had been.

Are you all right?

Yes. Though I have to say the moon dance is not much fun when you're just a body and not a willing participant.

It could be worse, Brother. And probably *would* get worse, unless he could find a way out for both of them. He very much doubted that René had been taken just as a hostage. There were two women and two of them, and this was all about revenge. Revenge for past wrongs. Revenge for promises never made.

And what better revenge was there than to bind yourself to a man who hated you?

There is nothing worse than being forced to dance with Iyona, trust me, René said grimly. *But what I don't get is, why murder those women? If this is all they wanted, why not just wait for the full moon and kidnap me?*

Duncan smiled grimly. *Because Betise is even more fixated with me than she is with you. I think the murders were merely a way of drawing me back home.*

A shadow loomed across the wall, shifting from wolf to human shape. He craned his neck to the left and watched Betise enter. Like them, she was naked. Oddly enough, her body was covered with a white powder, and he couldn't smell her. He couldn't smell Iyona, either, though she was undoubtedly just as close.

Betise's gaze met his, green eyes glowing like ice in the darkness. "The time has come to keep your promises, Duncan."

"Tell me first why you killed those women." Not that it really mattered now. He just needed to buy more time. Time to loosen the chains some more. Time for his father and brothers to track them down.

"If I killed the competition and gave the dance a bad name, my chances of catching a Sinclair mate increased." She shrugged. "And it had the bonus of bringing you back home. We figured it might."

So his guess had been right. "Then why make it look like they were raped?"

"To confuse the rangers. Worked like a charm, too, didn't it? They were so convinced it was one of you Sinclairs they didn't even bother looking for other culprits."

"And why attack yourself?"

"Neva told me her sister was waking, and that she couldn't remember what had happened. But I couldn't take the chance that she would." She shrugged again.

"I was hoping it would throw everyone off, but it didn't. You suspected me, didn't you?"

"Yes." Though not of the killings. Not at first.

She nodded. "I smelled you in the house, you know."

"Is that why you got rid of the hair ball?" Surprise flitted across her face, and he smiled coldly. "I fished it out of the river, Betise. Savannah has it."

"You lie."

"It doesn't matter if he's lying." Iyona stepped out of the shadows, a rifle in her steady hands. A rifle aimed straight at René. "The time of promising has come."

"I made no promises to Betise. I never will."

"You will if you want your brother to live to his time of promising."

His gaze flicked to hers. Where Betise's gaze was crazy, Iyona's was hard. Intent.

"This will gain you nothing."

"You're a Sinclair, and the Sinclairs owe me."

"My pack had nothing to do with what happened to you."

"You're all Sinclairs. I don't care which pack pays me what I am owed."

"And what the hell are you owed, Iyona?"

"A name. A child. A comfortable life."

The woman might not look mad, but she was every bit as insane as her daughter. "Neither René nor I can give you a child. That's taken care of every moon dance."

Betise snorted. "You taking bets on that?"

He stared at her, a sick sensation in his gut. "What are you saying?"

Betise's smile was contemptuous. "I substituted a box of injections with another harmless drug. The good doctor keeps meticulous records, and I knew René was being done early. But if I'd known for sure you were coming back, I would have swapped yours, as well."

Relief slithered through him. At least he didn't have to worry about Neva being pregnant. They might have performed the moon ceremony and, for all intents and purposes, be married, but right now, they did not need a child. Not when they were still very much strangers and she was still wary, both of him and of her own feelings.

"The clinic is locked. How could you possibly get in?"

Betise arched an eyebrow. "Through the tunnels, of course." She glanced at René, a cold smile on her lips. "You really should work on your shield, you know. Your mind is such an easy read when you're dancing."

René didn't even bother opening his eyes as he said, "I will never give you a child."

"My dear boy, you probably already have," Iyona commented dryly. "And not only Betise, but me and your other half dozen partners as well."

"I wouldn't bet on it." René's voice was cold. Harsh. "Martin is not the fool you think him to be. He saw the box had been tampered with and got rid of it."

Betise stared at him. "You're lying."

René opened his eyes and looked at her. His dark gaze was as hard as the rocks behind him. "Am I?"

Are you? Duncan asked.

No. That part of their idiotic plan, at least, will fail.
Betise studied them both for a second, her eyes gleaming moon bright in the night. "Get up, both of you."

If they were ever going to escape, it had to be now, when the two women were overly confident and right before the ceremony was performed. While he could not get caught by the promising ritual, René could. And he knew René would say the words, and link himself forever with a bitch like Iyona, if it meant saving his brother's life. He glanced at René's set face. *You fit enough to fight?*

Just say when, Brother, and I'm there.

Good. Duncan pushed back against the wall and struggled to his feet. "The promising ritual won't work, Betise."

"If you don't say the right words, René is a dead man."

"Better a dead man than being bound to dead-smelling flesh," René commented as he struggled upright.

"Dead flesh that you will be bound to for eternity," Iyona snarled.

"Over my lifeless body."

"Or your brother's." The sound of the safety clicking off seemed to echo ominously in the cavern. "We're not overly fussy about which one we kill. All we want is a child so we can claim our share of the Sinclair fortune."

Duncan couldn't help the harsh laugh that escaped his lips. "Do you really think our father will acknowledge any child you bear?"

"Blood is blood, and everyone knows Zeke is an

old-fashioned wolf. He'll support the get of his sons."
She stepped to one side. "Now move, both of you."

Duncan shuffled forward until he'd moved up
alongside his brother. *Not yet,* he said, as they walked
clumsily forward. The chains around their legs
clinked softly, the bell-like sound covering the noise
Duncan made as he slid the loosened chain from his
arms and caught them in his hand.

In that same moment, awareness surged through
his mind. Neva was close. He couldn't smell her, but
he could feel her—in his heart, with his soul.

Neva?

*Here. So is Savannah, as well as your father and
brothers.*

How far away?

Not far. Why?

Hurry. He didn't tell her why. Didn't have the time,
because they were too close to the two women. If they
shuffled forward any farther, Betise would see that his
hands were no longer tied. Tension emanated from
René, telling Duncan he was ready to move.

Dive low, he said and swung the chain, lashing it
around Iyona's face and neck as René hit her low and
hard, sending her sprawling backward. Her scream
was a high-pitched sound of pain and fury that got
lost in the sound of a gunshot.

René grunted, but Duncan had no time to see if his
brother had been hurt, because a snarling fury hit him
hard and sent him sprawling backward.

Teeth tore into his shoulder and arm. He hissed and
thrust his hands between them, grabbing Betise by the
throat and forcing her back, away from his neck. Saliva dripped from her huge jaws, splashing across his

chest as she snarled and snapped and twisted, her strength almost as great as his own. Her nails tore into his bare stomach and slashed his side as she scrambled to gain purchase. Her eyes gleamed with malevolent fire, and he had no doubt that she intended to kill him. Not because she hated him, but because she loved him. Because he wouldn't—couldn't—love her.

He thrust her back with all his force and lunged sideways. The rush of howling air told him she was closing in again. His nails scraped the cold dirt floor as he wrapped his fingers around a rock. With a grunt of effort, he swung around, smashing it across Betise's snarling snout, beating her away. Her growl became a yelp of pain as she leapt out of his reach. He let go of the rock and reached desperately for the chains around his feet. He had to work them free so he could move, could change. Claws scrambled against dirt and stone behind him, then air rushed over him. He threw himself sideways, punching upward at the silver form that flew overhead. His fist hit hard, but she didn't seem to feel it, twisting in midair so that she landed facing him. Then with one bound, she was on him again.

He thrust his hand out, his fingers digging into her thick neck, his whole arm trembling with the effort of keeping her snarling, snapping canines away from his throat.

Warmth flooded across his skin, and a golden haze of energy covered her form as she shifted shape once again. He bucked, trying to get her off him, but she screamed—a sound so high-pitched it hurt his ears. Then her knee found his groin. Pain flooded him—an all-consuming red haze—and suddenly it was all he could do to even breathe. Energy rolled across his skin again, then she was on him in wolf form, tearing into his shoulders and chest.

Somehow he forced his arms between them and pushed her back. Her teeth sank deep into his forearm—a sharp pain that battled the deep ache in his groin. He swore and thrust two straightened fingers deep into her throat. She coughed but didn't release him, worrying at his flesh like a dog with a bone.

He swore again and punched her across the ears. She shook her head, sending saliva and blood flying, but still didn't let go. She just kept tearing and gnawing at his arm.

Then, from out of the night, came a flash of gold that hit Betise broadside and sent her flying. The two wolves tumbled beyond his line of sight, their growls mixing with the sound of snapping teeth and tearing flesh. He swore and sat up, hurriedly undoing the chains from his legs before surging to his feet.

He swung around and saw the two wolves, silver and gold, at the back of the cavern. Neva was on the bottom, but her teeth were deep into Betise's throat, and blood gleamed on Betise's silver fur.

He shifted shape and arrowed toward them, hitting Betise and sending her rolling off Neva, who scrambled to her feet and spat out a large chunk of hair and flesh.

Are you all right? Her mind voice was rich with concern and caring.

Yes. Just seeing her made everything seem all right, though he knew it wasn't.

You're bleeding. She licked his wounds tentatively,

then a rumble rose up her throat and she nudged him sideways, taking the full impact of Betise's lunge.

He swore as he hit the ground, though it came out little more than a harsh growl. He rolled to his feet again and saw the two wolves tearing at each other near the cavern's entrance. He felt the sharp caress of electricity in the air—a sensation that built and built until every hair on his coat stood on end. It was similar but far stronger than the force he'd felt building in the kitchen the night Neva had slammed deep into his mind and assaulted him with her fear and pain.

Shield. Neva's warning blasted him, and he thrust up his shields immediately.

A heartbeat later, the force in the air seemed to explode, and Betise was torn from Neva's body and flung out the cavern entrance.

He shifted shape and walked toward Neva as the changing haze rolled across her. He stopped beside her and slid his fingers into hers. They were trembling, and as wet with blood as his own.

Betise lay ten feet away. She'd regained human form and was half-curled up in fetal position, her bloody body shaking, her gray-green eyes wide and staring.

"I fried her mind," Neva said, her voice flat and emotionless.

He didn't say anything, just wrapped an arm around her and pulled her close. She rested her cheek against his chest and, though she made no sound, warm tears slid down his skin.

Over the top of her head, he saw a russet-haired ranger holding a gun on Iyona as Savannah cuffed her. He watched his father and brothers kneel beside

René's still form. Felt the surge of relief as his father looked up and nodded. His brother was okay.

"It's over," he said softly.

"Yes, it is."

He closed his eyes at the starkness in her voice. And knew that, for now, it was.

Neva winced as the needle slid into her forearm.

"Sorry," the doctor said, much too cheerfully, "but I can't do much about it. Tetanus shots are never pleasant, no matter how careful we are."

She nodded vaguely, her attention more on what was going on in the other room than what the doctor was doing to her arm. They'd been at the rangers' office for over an hour now. Because of the fire at the hospital, the emergency doctors had come to them, looking after her, Duncan, Iyona, and Betise. Only René had gone on to the emergency room.

She hadn't seen Duncan since they'd come here, and she desperately needed to see him, to talk to him. Needed to make him understand why she'd come to the decision she had. Savannah was probably talking to him, as she couldn't see her sister, either. But Betise and Iyona were visible—the older wolf cursing and fighting every order, the younger wolf catatonic, not responding to anyone or anything. A living, breathing zombie.

Neva closed her eyes, not wanting to see what she'd done. And yet part of her didn't regret it. Betise had killed without remorse, and would have killed her and Duncan and anyone else who got in the way of her mad scheme.

"Don't go lifting anything heavy for the next couple days," the doctor said. "And if there's any sign of soreness or infection, go straight to the emergency room."

She nodded then slipped off the table and walked into the other room. That's when she saw her parents. She stopped and met her father's gaze for a moment, and saw the relief and worry haunting the green of his eyes. Her mother started toward her, tears on her face and one hand outstretched. But Neva spun away, not ready or willing to talk to either of them just yet, and walked down the passage to Savannah's office. Her sister was there. So was Duncan.

Savannah rose and walked around her desk. "I'll leave you two alone." She placed her hand on Neva's good arm and squeezed it lightly. Then she walked out and closed the door behind her.

Duncan rose from the visitor's chair. Neva let her gaze travel up the long, lean length of him, etching it into her memory. His left arm was in a sling, and there were scratches across his beautiful face.

He didn't step any closer, just reached out, cupping her cheek with his palm, letting his thumb brush warmth across her trembling lips. She briefly closed her eyes, breathing in the scent of him, battling the tears that suddenly threatened her control.

"You haven't changed your mind?" he asked softly.

"No." It came out little more than a tortured whisper.

He stepped closer, his dark eyes holding hers, shimmering with deep determination. With love. "I won't give up on us, you know that, don't you?"

"Yes." The word seemed to stick somewhere in her

throat. She swallowed, but it didn't ease the burning in her throat. Didn't ease the burning in her chest. "I have no choice, Duncan, not with my father's ultimatum. I can't walk away from my family."

"Nor do I expect you to. But I intend to come back to Ripple Creek, and I intend to make your father see that we are meant to be."

"My father will never accept you."

"I won't give up," he repeated, his breath warm against her lips. "You are mine, Neva. And you always will be."

He kissed her. Softly. Sweetly. Then he turned and walked out the door.

Her heart felt like it had shattered. Pain unlike anything she'd ever felt before welled, and she raised a hand to her mouth to hold back the sobs. To hold back the need to cry out his name as the echo of his footsteps grew softer, until all that was left were the caress of his scent on the air and the taste of him on her lips.

A sob escaped. She closed her eyes and slumped back against the desk. Tears slid down her cheeks, and she swiped at them impatiently. She wouldn't cry here. Wouldn't cry in front of her parents. Heartbreak could wait until she was alone.

And alone was what she'd be for the rest of her life.

She bit her lip and pushed away from the desk. Savannah was standing next to their parents, and all three were standing near the exit. As much as she didn't want to talk to anyone right now, she had no choice but to approach her family.

The relief so evident in her father's expression had Neva clenching her fists.

"It is for the best," he said gruffly. "You deserve far better than a man with a past like his."

"Father, you have no idea what you're talking about," Savannah said, voice sharp and impatient. "Why don't you just get over—"

Neva touched her sister's arm, stopping her from saying anything else, and met her father's gaze squarely. "Did you marry your soul mate?"

He frowned. "You know I did."

"And don't you wish both Savannah and me the same happiness?"

"Yes, of course, but—"

"There are no buts, Father. And you've made me choose between my family and my soul mate."

And with that, she pushed past them and walked out the door.

Chapter Sixteen

"I'M REALLY TEMPTED to give the old bastard a piece of my mind," Ari said as she plopped down in the booth seat opposite Neva. "I mean, how dare he spout words of tolerance to the council when he's not even practicing it in his own backyard?"

Neva smiled as she swished the straw through the froth of her strawberry shake. "He'll fire you again."

Ari airily waved the comment away. "He's fired me three times this week already. We both know he can't afford to lose me. You and I are the only ones crazy enough to work for peanuts."

That was certainly true. She sipped her drink and glanced out the diner's window. Nearly two months had passed since Duncan had left. Spring had truly come to Ripple Creek, but the warmth hadn't touched her heart. And wouldn't. Not until he came back into her life.

And that couldn't happen soon enough. She blinked back the sting of tears and tried not to think about him. Tried not to think about the long nights of dreaming about his touch and waking to nothing more than loneliness and despair.

But at least not seeing or talking to him for so long had convinced her of two things. The first being the fact that she loved him, heart and soul, and wanted him in her life no matter what the cost. And, second, that she was the biggest goddamn coward on Earth for letting him walk away from her that night. They should have confronted her parents together. She should have given *them* the ultimatum to accept their relationship if they wanted to be a part of her and Duncan's future.

But even when her heart had been breaking, part of her had still refused to believe love could happen so fast. Nor had she believed the ritual they'd performed was real—not until the next full moon, when the moon's heat did little more than make her ache for his caress. They were one, now and forever, committed to each other heart and soul.

And if her parents couldn't accept that, too bad. She had come to the point where she was more than willing to walk away—except when it came to Savannah.

A hand slid across Neva's, and her gaze jumped to her friend's.

"Your father is a fool," Ari said softly, "but I'm beginning to think you're a bigger one. If you love this man so much, go after him, babe. Your parents will come to their senses once they see how happy you are together."

Neva's smile was slightly bitter. "It's not quite as simple as that."

"Crap." Ari leaned back in the seat and crossed her arms. "Do you love him?"

"Yes."

"And does he love you?"

"Yes."

"Then what else is there to worry about? Go get your man, and to hell with your parents."

"My father swore an oath to the moon that I'd be evicted from the pack should I continue my relationship with Duncan."

Ari stared at her for a moment, then cursed softly. She knew, as Neva knew, that such an oath was binding to *all* members of the family. If she walked away to be with Duncan, she'd never be able to talk to her sister again. And that was something she wasn't willing to lose.

"Moons," Ari commented. "What a mess."

"That it is." And she didn't see a way out of it. Not without putting Savannah in the middle.

I'll never be in the middle of it. The strength of Savannah's mind voice told Neva she was close to the diner. *Because I'm on your side, completely and utterly. You finally ready to do something about this whole situation?*

More than ready, Neva replied with a smile. With her twin by her side, all things were possible.

The bell above the door chimed as the door opened. Savannah walked in, dragging their mother in behind her. If the look on Nancy's face was anything to go by, she definitely wasn't here by choice. Neva glanced at the clock. No wonder. She was missing her weekly facial.

Nancy's scathing glance took them in, then swung back to Savannah. "What the hell are you doing?"

"What I should have done a month ago." The scar above her sister's left eye looked as angry as her expression. She thrust their mother into the booth next to Ari. "You move, Mom, and I swear to the moon, I'll shoot you."

With that, she spun and marched toward the kitchen. Ari chuckled softly, a sound she quickly smothered as Nancy glared at her.

"This is your doing, isn't it?"

Ari's eyes were dancing with mirth as she held up her hands. "Nothing to do with me, honest. But you know, I'm damn glad someone is doing something. You and the boss seemed content to sit back and watch your daughter die of a broken heart."

"Ari—" Neva warned.

"You're fired," her mother said at the top of her voice.

"Yeah, right." Ari sniffed and crossed her arms.

Nancy slid out of the booth and pointed an imperious finger at the door. "Leave now."

Ari glanced at Neva, a smile playing around her lips. "Call me. And good luck."

"Thanks. I'll probably need it."

Neva crossed her arms and watched her mother slide back into the booth, but she didn't bother saying anything. Even though she'd been back working at the diner for the last month, she'd barely exchanged a civil word with either of her parents since the night she'd let Duncan walk away. She saw no reason to change that until Savannah came back with their father.

Her mother obviously had no such inhibitions. "If you've ended up hurt, you have no one to blame but yourself."

"You're right," she bit back. "Because I let him

walk away from me rather than having the courage to confront Father's edict with him by my side."

Her mother blinked. "Have you lost all the sense we bred into you? Why on earth would you think someone like Duncan Sinclair would ever make a suitable mate?"

"I don't know. Maybe the fact that we're soul mates?"

"Men like him don't have soul mates. They have lovers, and plenty of them. It's the sex that has you hooked, Neva, nothing more."

"If this is just sex, then I can sure as hell understand why the dance is so popular." Though her voice was flat, she had to thrust her hands under the table to hide the angry trembling. How dare they not trust her enough to know her own heart?

"Don't be crude," her mother replied stiffly. "A man with a past like his is not the sort of man we want—"

"And what of *your* past, Mother? Or has that been conveniently forgotten?"

Her mother's face went white. "What are you talking about?" But the fear in her widening eyes suggested she knew exactly what Neva was talking about. And it also meant it was true.

"Dad doesn't know, does he?" Neva said, suddenly understanding.

"I don't know *what*?"

Her father's voice was sharp as he stopped in front of the booth and glared at the two of them. Savannah stood behind him, arms crossed and expression severe. Neva had a feeling she intended to stand there like that until this whole mess was sorted out.

"About mother's double standard," Neva replied. "About how it's all right for her to be given a second chance, but not Duncan."

"It all happened a long time ago," Nancy said, her face white, lips trembling. "I was only a teenager."

"So? Duncan wasn't much older. And nothing he has ever done has led to anyone's death."

"What are you talking about?"

She met her father's stony glare and let the anger finally boil over. "We're talking about double standards. You stood up in front of the council yesterday and supported the Sinclairs' right to the moon dance, stating that no harm had ever come from it in all the years of it being here in Ripple Creek, and that people had the right to take part in the dance if they wished. Yet in private you say the dance is little more than a festival of whores, and you won't let your family participate."

"Decent people do not—"

"Decent people do, and have. Half of Ripple Creek was up there the night I was there, and I'll wager many of them are on the damn council."

"That's beside the point—"

"That's *exactly* the point. You've always told me you should treat people as you find them, not as other people make them out to be."

"Duncan Sinclair has a past longer than my arm, and he's not likely to change now." Her father's voice was a mix of patience and anger. "Sinclairs don't believe in commitment, Neva. Look at Zeke. A century under his belt and still dancing with every female that comes within range."

Neva crossed her arms, her fists clenched against

her sides. "If we follow that theory, both Savannah and I should be drunken louts who run around burning houses and killing innocents."

Her mother's gasp filled the shocked silence. "How dare you—"

Neva thrust to her feet and leaned across the table. "'How dare you'? How can you look at Duncan's past and judge him unworthy when you have done far worse?"

Her father's hand came down on her shoulder. "You will not talk to your mother like that—"

Neva shook off his touch and swung around to face him. "And how dare you make me choose between the man I love and the family I love?"

"I knew his mother," Levon said softly. "She was a good friend. I know the pain she went through watching the man she loved dance with others, time and time again. It killed her, Neva. I'm only trying to save you from that."

"I'm old enough to choose my own destiny."

"But not old enough to understand the heartbreak to come. He will never commit to you."

She glanced at Savannah, saw her sister's slight nod. Knew that her twin would walk when she walked. "That's where you're wrong, Father. Duncan has already committed. We performed the promising ceremony the night before he was kidnapped."

His face went as white as her mother's. "Impossible! The magic can't be raised except on the night of promising."

"Well, apparently it can, because we did it."

"But . . . why didn't you tell us?"

"I told you we were soul mates, and it didn't seem

to make one goddamn bit of difference. Why would I think telling you we were promised would?"

"But . . . you can't. Not to him."

She sighed. "You know, I'm sick of arguing. I'm sick of trying to make you see. I've chosen my path. It's up to you to choose yours."

"And choose wisely," Savannah intoned, "because I'll walk out that door with my sister, and I won't be back until you both come to your senses."

"This is stupid—"

"No, Father, this is the last straw. I don't want to live my life without Duncan in it, and if you can't accept that, then too bad."

She glanced at Savannah, and as one they walked out of the diner and down the street to the rangers' office. Neva took a deep breath and puffed it out slowly. "Well, that went better than I thought."

Savannah grinned. "But there were no fisticuffs. Where's the fun in that?"

Neva laughed and gave her sister a hug. "Thank you."

"No probs. Now, stop worrying about our folks and go get that sexy man of yours. Either drag him home, or shag him senseless where he is so *I* can get a decent night's sleep."

Neva kissed her cheek. "That sounds like a plan to me." And it was exactly what she intended to do.

Duncan leaned a shoulder against the windowsill and stared at the slowly rising moon. It was hard to believe that exactly two months ago he'd met Neva.

Hard to believe he hadn't seen or heard from her for almost the same amount of time.

And while he hadn't really expected her to call, part of him had hoped that she might. Not that it mattered. In five days, he was going home to Ripple Creek, whether or not he got the job as head of the rescue team being set up over there. And he fully intended to claim what was his and make her parents see he was more than just his past.

Footsteps echoed in the hall beyond his office. He glanced over his shoulder and watched Dave Richards, the man in charge of the Eagle County search-and-rescue team, walk in.

"You want the good news, the bad news, or the 'not again' news?" Dave asked.

"I'm guessing the 'not again' news would be another hiker getting lost." There certainly had been a rash of them lately. The latest influx of tourists didn't seem able to read a map and often panicked when darkness set in.

"You guessed that right." Dave handed him a piece of paper with the woman's details and last known position. "At least this one had a cell phone with her. She's up near Paddy's Hut from the sound of it. I told her to stay put until you arrived."

"Let's hope she does." The last one they'd rescued decided to keep on walking and had almost walked off a damn cliff. "What's the bad news?"

"My spies over in Ripple Creek tell me you were passed over for the search-and-rescue post."

"I'm not entirely surprised." He might have had the experience, but his reputation was shot to hell in Ripple Creek, and Levon was a strong voice on the council. He wouldn't willingly approve any action that would bring Duncan back home. "The good news?"

"Is that the head ranger caught wind of the decision and confronted the council. Apparently she told them that if they refused to pick the best man for the job, she'd hand in her resignation. When the rest of her team stood up with her, the council backed down."

Duncan smiled. He'd have to remember to thank Savannah when he next saw her. "When will it be official?"

"I'm told they'll be calling tomorrow."

"Good." At least he had a decent job to go back to when he went home. While he might own Snowflake Lodge, he had no intention of kicking the Harpers out to manage it himself. They were doing a far better job than he ever could.

He pushed away from the window and grabbed his coat off the hook. "I'll give you a call when I locate our errant hiker."

"Do that," Dave said. "And good luck."

Duncan nodded and grabbed his gear on the way out. The night air was crisp and the sky above so full of stars it almost looked silver. He let his gaze drift toward the moon, still hanging low in the evening sky. Two full moons without Neva were two too many, but at least the promising ritual had ensured that neither of them suffered moon fever while they were apart. And yet he ached for her tonight. Ached with an intensity that cut through every part of him.

He shouldered the pack and headed up the mountain. Trees crowded in closer the higher he went, the various pines still hiding drifts of snow under their green skirts. He was almost at Paddy's Hut when awareness surged, followed closely by a joy greater than anything he'd ever known.

Neva was here.

He walked on, not rushing, even though his whole body trembled with the need to grab her and hold her and love her. Through the trees ahead, flames flickered and danced. He smiled. His lost hiker had made herself at home.

He came into the clearing and shucked off the pack, tossing it toward the hut's door as he walked on. Neva was standing in front of the fire, her back to him as she stared out over the valley below. The warmth of the flames caressed her golden skin so that she almost appeared to gleam like precious metal in the darkness.

She didn't turn around or acknowledge his presence in any way, and yet he knew she was as aware of him as he was of her.

He stopped near the fire and took off his jacket. There was a sleeping bag at her feet, and a bottle of champagne and two glasses off to one side.

"I owe you an apology," she said softly.

"For what?" He pulled off his boots, then stripped off his jeans.

"For not having the courage to ask you to stay two months ago."

"We were only together for four days. Confusion and doubt is understandable, I think." His shorts joined the pile of clothes. The night air caressed his skin but failed to cool the fever burning through him.

"You didn't doubt."

"But I have spent the last ten years of my life looking for my soul mate. You were looking for nothing more than your sister's attacker."

"We found her."

"Together." He stopped behind her, not touching her, but so close that every breath held the warm citrus scent of her. So close that the heat radiating off her skin burned across his. "What of your parents?"

"That I don't know."

He ran a finger down the long line of her neck and across one shoulder. He felt her skin tremble under his touch, as her desire burned the air. "I'm sorry."

"Don't be. I have Savannah on my side and she won't obey any edict my father gives. That's all that matters for now. Time will change their minds. And if it doesn't . . ." She shrugged.

He let his touch slide down to her waist and across her stomach, pressing her back against him. She felt so good, so right, and all he wanted to do was turn her around and kiss her and make love to her. But there were still things that had to be said. A sigh escaped her lips. It was a sound he felt like echoing.

"Did you tell them we were soul mates?"

"I told them that I loved you. I told them that I didn't want to live without you. I told them that we performed the promising ritual."

"Ah." He brushed a kiss across her neck. She tasted warm and tangy, and far better than he remembered. Far better than she had in any of his dreams. "When did you realize the pretense was real?"

"Not until much later. How about you?"

"From the moment I spoke the first words. And I

wasn't about to stop—or let you stop. I told you, you're mine, and I don't intend to share. Not ever."

"Good." She turned and wrapped her arms around his neck, her green eyes shining wickedly despite her stern expression. "Because neither do I."

He raised a hand to her cheek, brushing his thumb across her ripe lips. "So where does that leave us?"

She raised an eyebrow. "Long term?"

"Long term." Because he knew exactly what they'd be doing short term.

She considered him for a minute, her smile growing and love so evident in her bright eyes that it reflected through every fiber of his being. "I'm thinking at least six children."

He feigned shock. "Six? Good grief, woman, do you want me working night and day to support you all?"

She rolled her eyes. "Oh, okay, then. Four."

"A nice even number," he agreed, sliding his fingers down to her rear. "We'll have to buy a bigger house, though. Yours isn't big enough to house us all."

"You don't want to return to the mansion?"

"You wouldn't be comfortable living there."

"No," she agreed, "I wouldn't. But only because I don't think it's the best environment to bring up a pack of kids."

He cupped her rear and lifted her until he was able to slide deep inside. She felt so good, so wet and warm and ready, that he groaned. God, how he'd missed her. "A pack of kids? I thought we agreed on four?"

"Oh, yeah. So we did."

Her grin was pure cheek as she wrapped her legs around him and pushed him deeper. He groaned, his whole body trembling with the effort to remain still. Which she certainly wasn't.

"You do realize twins run in my family?" she continued, rocking her body gently against his.

"You do realize if you keep doing what you're doing, in a matter of moments I'm not going to be able to concentrate on anything you're saying?"

"You want me to stop?"

"Not really."

"Good, because I wasn't intending to."

"Wicked wench."

"It's the company I keep." Her eyes twinkled at him. "Such a bad, bad man."

"I never thought you'd be the type to fall for a bad man."

"Neither did I. But I have. Hook, line, and sinker. There's no hope left for me now."

"None at all," he agreed. "Because that bad man intends to keep teaching you wicked things for the rest of his life."

"That sounds like a plan."

He smiled and kissed her nose. "So, we've discussed long-term goals. What about the short term?"

"Well, for the first hour or so, I plan to be ravished senseless, then I think we should drink some of that champagne and celebrate being together."

"Forever and ever," he murmured. "Now shut up and kiss me."

She did. And he couldn't think of a better way to start the rest of their lives together.

If you enjoyed Neva's story in *Beneath a Rising Moon*,
be sure not to miss Savannah's tale in:

BENEATH A DARKENING MOON

by

Keri Arthur

A Ripple Creek Werewolf book

Here is a special preview:

SAVANNAH GRANT CLIMBED out of the truck and
took a deep breath of the crisp, fall air. Though it had
snowed last night, the sky this morning was rich and
blue, and the sun was surprisingly warm.

The aspen trees surrounding the small clearing
glowed a rich, vibrant gold that contrasted sharply
with the blue of the sky and the white of the snow-
covered peaks looming high above. Leaves littered
the ground beneath her feet, but the snow that had
covered them earlier had melted. Now the sunlight
gleamed through the drops of water that remained,
making them glow like tiny diamonds.

But this tranquil setting hid a darker heart.

She slammed the door shut and turned as a second
truck came to a halt in the clearing. Three men
climbed out—two deputy rangers and a brown-haired
teen who looked positively green around the gills.

The teenager's gaze skirted the clearing, resting momentarily on the barely visible trail that disappeared
through the aspens. Then he gulped and looked at
Savannah. His blue eyes were wide and frightened—a

sure sign that, for once in his short life, Matt wasn't crying wolf. "I don't have to go back up there, do I?"

"No." She tried to give the kid a reassuring smile, but it probably looked as fake as it felt. But then, it wasn't every day that two human tourists were murdered within a week of each other inside the confines of the Ripple Creek werewolf reservation.

And it certainly wasn't every day that these murders replicated those that had happened long ago and in a very different place.

A shiver ran down her spine. Not from the cold, though here in the mountains it was chilly despite the sun's heat. Clairvoyance wasn't something she'd laid claim to, but she'd had premonitions in the past that had certainly come true, and that was what she was feeling now. These murders would not stop with the current two—and the past she'd tried so hard to forget was about to be resurrected.

She rubbed her arms and stepped away from the truck. "Ike, do you want to stay here with Matt?"

"But—"

"Ike," she warned, in no mood to take any of the young deputy's crap today. "Either you do as I say, or you head back down the mountain."

"How the hell am I going to learn anything—"

"You could always sit at a desk and do paperwork," she cut in. "Your choice."

Sullen didn't even begin to describe his expression as he nodded. Guilt slithered through her, but she shoved it away and glanced across at Ronan. "Ready?"

The russet-haired deputy nodded and hitched the

small backpack onto his shoulder. She spun and walked across the clearing. Sunlight filtering through the golden leaves dappled the faint path, but quickly gave way to deeper shadows as they moved into the pines.

"You were a bit hard on the kid, weren't you?" Ronan said, his deep voice seeming to resonate through the silence. "I know he can be annoying, but he truly *is* eager to learn."

She blew out a breath. "I know. It's just that—"

"You're dreaming again, aren't you?"

She looked over her shoulder. Ronan's gray eyes gleamed almost silver in the shadows, full of concern. But then, they'd known each other a very long time. Ronan was not only one of her few close friends, but her very first lover. And even though it went against her policy of not mixing business and pleasure, they still shared a moon dance when one of them was feeling lonely.

"What makes you think that?"

His smile echoed through his eyes. "The only time you're so short tempered is when you're feeling the heat of the moon or have been dreaming. Considering we shared a few rather energetic nights last weekend, I figured it was the latter."

She grinned. "Have you made the bed yet?"

"Yeah. Otherwise Conor would be curious."

She nodded. The cabin they used for their retreats had been in Ronan's family for years, but these days it was only occupied in spring, when the fishing was good. It was the perfect sanctuary the rest of the year, except that Conor, Ronan's younger brother, was one of those wolves who had a nose for intrigue and always seemed to be three steps behind them. While he didn't appear to know about their sometime affair, neither of them wanted him to find out—if only because the kid was a blabbermouth. Besides, their illicit meetings not only went against her own rules, but council rules as well.

The council, she thought grimly, definitely needed to pull their heads out of their asses. Not so much because of the no-fraternizing-with-co-workers rule, but for all the other rules they were trying to institute—like a ten o'clock curfew for anyone under eighteen. This was the twenty-first century, for God's sake, not the Middle Ages. It was rules like that that had driven *her* out of both her home *and* Ripple Creek when she was barely seventeen.

Of course, her views on the matter, though often aired, weren't taken into consideration, despite the fact her dad was the head of the council. He also happened to be the main force behind all the saving-yourself-for-marriage bullshit currently going on, despite the hassle and heartache such beliefs had caused Neva, Savannah's twin, just over a year ago.

"What are the dreams about this time?" Ronan asked.

She brushed a tree branch aside, waiting until he'd passed before letting it go. "Same old, same old. Death, destruction, and mayhem."

Only this time, it wasn't in the past, but the present. And that scared her, because the man behind those murders was supposedly dead.

So how could they be happening again, here in Ripple Creek, in the exact same way? The press had never released all the details, so it couldn't be a copycat. Yet the murder—or at least, the first murder—was *exactly* the same. Right down to the mutilation of the victim's genitals.

A shiver ran down her spine. Fear, she acknowledged. Fear of what was coming. *Who* was coming.

She frowned at the thought but, at that moment, death touched the air. She stopped, sniffing the faint breeze and tasting the scents entwined within it.

"A new death," Ronan said, stopping close enough that she could feel his body heat. "The blood is still fresh."

She nodded. "The hint of sage and musk suggests the victim is male."

"Same as the first one."

She glanced over her shoulder and met his gaze. The grim certainty reflected in his eyes echoed through her. They had themselves a serial killer—and with autumn giving way to winter and drawing in the cross-country skiing crowd, soon there would be far too many potential victims in Ripple Creek.

"Let's get up there before the scavengers do."

She followed the ever-thickening scent of death through the trees. The path became steeper, rockier, as the tree line began to recede. The clumps of snow became drifts, and the chill in the air was more noticeable. Yet, despite that, sweat trickled down her spine. The past she'd fled was merging with the present, and all she could see in the future was disaster.

She swiped at the moisture dribbling down her forehead and tried to get a grip on her imagination. It was *just* a murderer—just a crazy person. The past *wasn't* coming back to haunt her. It was a weird coincidence, nothing more.

Maybe, that deep-down voice said. *And maybe not.*

"There're the egg-shaped boulders Matt mentioned," Ronan said, pointing to the rocks off to the left-hand side of the trail.

She nodded and made her way toward them. Beyond the stones, death waited.

Like the first victim, this man had his arms and legs stretched wide, his penis and scrotum sliced away, his heart removed, and his left hand offering a one-finger salute. For a moment she closed her eyes, fighting not only the sickness that churned in the pit of her stomach, but also the memories that came crowding back.

Yet even without those memories, it was doubtful that scenes like this would ever become easy, she thought, as her gaze swept around the stone circle that surrounded the mutilated body. She might have spent the last nine years as a ranger, but death was not something she'd encountered often. Which was why finding someone so brutally and methodically slaughtered still had the power to shock her.

"We have ourselves a nut-job," Ronan said, as he came to a halt beside her.

"That we have." The question was, did this nut-job re-create past events by chance or by design? "You want to secure the area and take some preliminary photos? I'll call headquarters, and get them to send in the coroner."

"The doc's not going to be happy," Ronan commented, as he swung the pack off his shoulder and pulled out the crime scene tape. "It's barely eight in the morning, and Wednesday is his day off."

"Obviously no one told our murderer that," she snapped, then met his sharp glance with a wave of her hand. "I know, I know. I'm going to have to stop being so bitchy."

"Or go see someone about those dreams."

She nodded and dragged her cell phone from her pocket. Then she stepped out of his way and made her call. Kelly, who was both their administrative assistant and communications officer, answered on the second ring.

"Ripple Creek Ranger's Office."

"Kel, can you ask Doc Carson to head on up to Pike's Clearing at the top of Red Mountain Road? Ike will be waiting for him."

"Will do. You've a visitor, by the way."

"Who?"

"An investigator from the Interspecies Investigation Squad. He wouldn't give me his name."

Savannah swore under her breath. The IIS were an offshoot of the FBI, and by law they had to be notified whenever a human was killed on werewolf land. But she hadn't expected them to come running so quickly. The men and women of the IIS had the reputation of riding roughshod over local law enforcement and had, in the past, caused a lot of bad feelings between the community and its police officers. She certainly didn't want that happening here in Ripple Creek.

"Tell him I'm coming in." At least that would give Ronan, Ike, and the doc time to do a preliminary examination of the scene and the body before the IIS charged in and took over. She glanced at her watch. "I'll be there in twenty."

"I'll tell him. I'll even offer him decent coffee."

Which, in Kel speak, meant the man in question

was not only single but gorgeous. She smiled slightly, half-wondering if, just this once, they should use Kel as a distraction. Hell, there were few men of *any* species that didn't take a second, third, and fourth look when Kel walked by, so it might just give them a chance to do their job without IIS inference. But the way their luck had been running of late, the investigator would probably end up preferring dark-haired men rather than voluptuous blondes—and none of her deputies fit the bill.

She hung up and met Ronan's gaze. "The IIS are here."

He swore, long and loud.

"Yeah," she said. "Exactly. I'm heading back down. I'll get Ike to meet Carson, and he'll have to assist you here."

Ronan nodded. "He's damn good with the cameras, so he can take over that job."

"Just keep an eye on him. With the IIS involved, we can't afford any of his exuberant mistakes."

Ronan nodded and began taking photos of the body and the ceremonial ring of small stones surrounding it. She cast one more look at the victim, her gaze resting momentarily on the severed genital area, noting once again the lack of blood in the dirt beneath the body. Then she shivered and turned around, making her way back down the hill.

If history was repeating itself, she just had to hope that *everything* about that time wasn't about to make an appearance. Because there were some parts of her life that she had no desire to revisit in any way, shape, or form.

"Ike," she called, once she'd reached the clearing,

"I want you to go down to the main road and wait for Doc Carson, then bring him up here and take him to Ronan. You'll be helping Ronan after that."

The young deputy's eyes lit up. "Really?"

"Really." God, was she ever that enthusiastic? Probably not. By the time she'd applied for the deputy position, she'd truly seen the darker side of human *and* wolf nature. She'd known all too well the damage some people could do to others—physical *or* emotional.

"Matt, do you want a ride back into town with me?"

The teenager nodded and climbed into her truck. She glanced back at Ike. "Do what Ronan tells you to—nothing more, nothing less."

Ike grinned and gave her a thumbs-up, his carrot-bright hair glowing like a beacon in the morning sun. Savannah shook her head, climbed into her truck, and headed back to town. By the time she'd dropped Matt off and talked briefly to his parents, thirty-five minutes had come and gone.

Kel looked up as Savannah opened the front door of their little section of city hall, her expression a mix of amusement and annoyance. "Our dear IIS officer is not impressed with tardiness. Or so he's said every five minutes for the last fifteen minutes."

"One of those, huh?"

"Yeah. All looks and no charm." Kel placed a mug on the counter, and the rich aroma of cinnamon coffee wafted up. "Here, take this. You're going to need it."

Savannah picked up the steaming mug. "What excuse did you give him?"

"I didn't. He's not my boss and he certainly wasn't polite, so he didn't deserve an update."

She couldn't help a grin. "So what coffee did *he* get?"

"Machine blend only."

Meaning he'd really pissed her off. "Could you take all my calls while I deal with him?"

"Will do."

"Thanks, Kel."

Savannah sipped the sweet, aromatic liquid, fortifying herself as she walked around the counter and down the long hall to her office. The door was shut and the blinds shuttered, affording her no glimpse of this paragon who'd managed to annoy their usually jovial administration assistant.

She grasped the handle with her free hand and pushed the door open. "Sorry to keep you wait—"

The rest of her words died as the man inside turned around.

Shock and something else—something she couldn't quite define—rippled through her. The man standing so calmly in the middle of her office was the one man she'd hoped never to see again.

For too many minutes, all she could do was stare. This man had haunted her dreams for nigh on ten years, yet except for the crow's feet near his eyes, his too-handsome features showed no real sign of aging. He was a big man, just over six feet tall, his build lean but powerful, like a sprinter. His hair was dark brown, but the mahogany highlights she'd so adored now contrasted with the flecks of silver that gleamed in the sunlight streaming in through the window behind him. Once upon a time, his hair had been long and tied back carelessly in a ponytail—a ponytail she always used to undo, just so she could run her fingers through its gloriously silken length. Now it was short, barely even brushing the shoulders of his starched blue shirt.

Her gaze finally, inevitably, locked with his. For several heartbeats she couldn't think, was barely able to breathe. The navy blue of his eyes all but consumed her.

Heat prickled across her skin and ignited a familiar ache deep inside her. She knew she had to move, had to do something other than simply stand here. Yet, she couldn't tear herself away from the power of that gaze. From the memories she saw deep within it.

A slight smile touched the lips that were still as sensual as she remembered. Then his gaze rolled languidly down her body—a touch that wasn't a touch, and yet one that sent energy singing across every fiber of her being. Her nipples hardened, pressing almost painfully against her shirt, and the deep-down ache grew stronger.

His gaze completed its erotic journey and rose to meet hers again, lingering a little on the scar that marred the left side of her face. But it wasn't the heat in his look that made her tremble. It was the sudden flash of anger.

As if *he* had anything to be angry about.

"Well," he said. "Fancy finding you here."

His voice was husky, deep—and conjured memories of whispered endearments and long, sweaty nights of lovemaking. And even after all the time that had separated them, his voice still had the power to undo her. Maybe because she still heard it in her dreams—dreams in which he'd spun his web of desire and deceit around her as easily as he had in real life.

And it was *those* memories, as well as the anger that was now so visible in the depths of his eyes, that got her moving.

"What are you doing here, Cade?"

The smile that touched his lips never warmed the icy, dark-blue depths of his eyes. "You reported a murder. I'm here to investigate."

She sat down at her desk and waved him to one of the visitor's chairs. He sat down, his movements still full of power and grace.

"I mean, why are you really here?" She drank more coffee, grateful for the flush of warmth it spread through her otherwise chilled system.

He raised a dark eyebrow. "As I said, I'm here to investigate the murder of a human on this reservation."

"And did you happen to tell your superiors that you were once involved with the chief ranger of said reservation?"

"Why should I?" His gaze met hers, and all she could see—all she could feel—was his cold, cold anger. The warm caring that had once attracted her to this man had long gone—if indeed it had actually existed. "You were nothing more than a means to an end, Vannah. A pleasant way to pass the time as I tried to catch a killer."

Though she'd long known the truth, his words still hurt. After all, she'd once cared deeply for this man. Probably too deeply. To discover it was all nothing more than lies had cut to the quick. Yet his lies were not the worst of his actions. Far from it.

She leaned back in her chair and feigned a calm she didn't feel. "My name is Savannah. Kindly use it."

"*Savannah*," he mocked. "Such a sweet name."

"So was the girl you knew as Vannah. You sure as hell cured her of that."

Something flashed in his eyes. Not anger, because that was there already, but something deeper, darker. "The girl I knew as Vannah put on a damn good show, but time sure proved otherwise."

"Time?" She gave an unladylike snort. "We knew each other less than a month."

But it had been time enough to think she was in love. Time enough to prove how bad a judge her heart could be.

"Sometimes a month is all it takes to prove how very wrong first impressions can be."

"How very true," she said dryly. "So why don't we just drop the Happy Trails memory hour and get down to business?"

"Suits me."

He crossed his legs, drawing her eye down the powerful line of his thigh and shin to the garish blue and red of his boots. A smile touched her lips. It seemed even the starched blue correctness of the IIS couldn't break his love of cowboy boots.

"Tell me about the murder."

Her gaze came back to his. "Everything is in the report, which I've no doubt you've read."

"But I want your impressions."

"Really?" Bitterness crept into her voice. "And why would you want the opinion of a no good—what was the term you used that night? 'Whore'? 'Strumpet'?"

His face closed over. "I thought we were keeping this to business."

So they were. But it was harder than she'd thought it would be, especially when the warm mix of sage and tangerine that always accompanied him touched the air, stirring her hormones as much as it did memories of the nights she'd spent in his arms, drinking in that same scent.

"There's been a second murder," she said, the annoyance in her voice aimed more at herself than him. God, anyone would think she was still that dizzy teenager, not the wiser woman she'd become. "Same MO."

He sat up a little straighter. "Why didn't you mention this straightaway?"

"It could have something to do with seeing the one person I never wanted to see again."

Again that darkness flared in his eyes. "Tell me about the second murder."

"As far as we can tell, it's exactly the same as the first one. My people are up there now, locking down the scene and taking preliminary photos."

"Who discovered the body?"

"A local teenager out for an early-morning run."

"You've taken his statement?"

Anger flickered through her. What in moons did he think she was, an amateur? "Hell no," she drawled. "Was I supposed to?"

"Sarcasm is not what either of us needs right now." His gaze bored into hers. "If you can't handle me being here on this case, then step aside and let someone else take it."

She didn't bother answering. As the IIS officer for this region, he had no choice about being here—and as head ranger, neither did she. But he was right about one thing—she had to get a grip on herself. "The coroner should be up there by now. You've got a team following?"

He nodded. "Two people. They should be here this afternoon. We will, of course, take over the investigation, though we'd appreciate your department's help in dealing with the townsfolk."

And he was going to need it, because the citizens of Ripple Creek didn't cotton to the sort of superior attitude he was currently displaying. She took a drink of coffee and asked, "How far behind are they?"

"They'll be here in a few hours."

"Are you going to wait for them, or do you want to head up to the crime scene now?"

"I'd like to get up there before the scene gets too contaminated."

That flicker of anger became a roar. "*My* people are well trained and damn good at their jobs!"

"But they aren't trained for this sort of investigation, which is why the IIS is always called in."

The IIS being called in had nothing to do with skill—or the lack thereof—but was simply a means of pacifying the humans who always seemed to think that the murder of one of their own on a werewolf reservation was the first sign of a planned uprising. Humans—or some of them, at least—seemed to live in permanent fear of wolves. Why, she had no idea—especially when humans had all but wiped out the werewolf population in America. Hell, of the twenty reservations that had been originally granted, only eleven existed now. And two of those were in jeopardy from the encroaching human population. Resettlement was currently being discussed, but she knew from her old man that *this* time the wolves were going to give the government the legal fight of its life.

But she didn't bother saying anything, because voicing her opinion wouldn't matter a damn. Cade Jones was here, and that was that.

She gulped down the rest of her coffee and rose. "I'll take you out there now."

"Good. And on the way, you can give me your opinion about these killings."

She bit back the instinctive urge to throw another bitchy comment at him. And as she walked past him, she tried to ignore the warm scent of tangerine in her nostrils. But it wasn't so easy to ignore his familiar presence at her back, or the way his heat seemed to caress her skin, burning her like the summer sun.

It had been that way the first time she'd met him—a rush of heat, and a fever that had become fiercer the longer she'd stayed in his presence. No wolf since had ever elicited that sort of reaction, and she was damn glad of that fact. These days, she was quite content to spend her time in Ronan's arms, secure in the knowledge that the sex was good, that she was safe, and that he would never do anything to hurt her.

Kel turned around at the sound of their footsteps, and her gaze went from Savannah to Cade and back again. Though her expression was perfectly pleasant, Savannah was hard-pressed not to smile. Cade had a lot of ground to make up if he expected anything more than the most basic assistance from Kel. And considering that the smooth operation of this ranger station greatly depended on the efficiency of its admin assistant, Cade was in deep trouble.

Unless, of course, he brought his own admin assistant—which, considering the sort of money being thrown at the IIS these days, was highly likely.

"Kel, I'm taking Mr. Jones up to Pike's Clearing. If anything urgent comes up, call Steve in to handle it." She glanced over her shoulder. "Have you booked rooms for yourself and your people?"

The deep blue of his eyes seemed to bore right through her. "Not yet."

She repressed a shiver and glanced back at Kel. "And arrange two rooms at one of the local lodges."

A smile touched Kel's lips. "Right away."

Savannah knew that look, and suspected that luxury accommodations—or at least, as close as they got to it here in Ripple Creek—were not in the cards for Cade and his people. "In town," she added, just to ensure they didn't end up in some godforsaken corner on the outskirts.

A pout touched Kel's lips, and Savannah smiled and led the way out the door. At least Cade couldn't berate her about the accommodations—but she very much suspected that he'd have a lot of other things to discuss. Most of them in the past, and most of them things she'd much rather forget.

But if he thought she was still that meek, mild teenager, he had another thing coming. And if he wanted a fight, he'd get one.

Because after ten years of dreaming about those events, she was more than ready for it.